To Staci Hart - A new, old friend

Also by
Kerrigan Byrne

The DUKE
with the
DRAGON
Tattoo

KERRIGAN BYRNE

St. Martin's Paperbacks

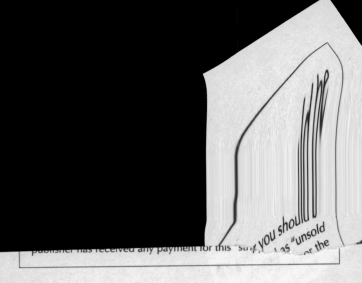

This is a work of fiction. All of the characters, organizations, and events portrayed in this novel are either products of the author's imagination or are used fictitiously.

THE DUKE WITH THE DRAGON TATTOO

Copyright © 2018 by Kerrigan Byrne.
Excerpt from *The Highwayman* copyright © 2015 by Kerrigan Byrne.
Excerpt from *The Hunter* copyright © 2016 by Kerrigan Byrne.
Excerpt from *The Highlander* copyright © 2016 by Kerrigan Byrne.
Excerpt from *The Duke* copyright © 2017 by Kerrigan Byrne.
Excerpt from *The Scot Beds His Wife* copyright © 2017 by Kerrigan Byrne.

For information address St. Martin's Press, 175 Fifth Avenue, New York, NY 10010.

ISBN: 978-1-250-12256-8

Our books may be purchased in bulk for promotional, educational, or business use. Please contact your local bookseller or the Macmillan Corporate and Premium Sales Department at 1-800-221-7945, ext. 5442, or by e-mail at MacmillanSpecialMarkets@macmillan.com.

Printed in the United States of America

St. Martin's Paperbacks edition / September 2018

St. Martin's Paperbacks are published by St. Martin's Press, 175 Fifth Avenue, New York, NY 10010.

10   9   8   7   6   5   4   3   2   1

And his eyes have all the seeming, of a demon's that is dreaming.

—*The Raven,* Edgar Allan Poe

The DUKE with the DRAGON TATTOO

*P*ROLOGUE

"I'm going to hurt you," Walters warned in a cockney in-flection graveled by pipe tobacco and East End coal smoke. He could have passed for a much older man if one never marked the almost infantile features supported by a neck the width of a mooring post.

"I rather find I like the pain." Even as he said it, the boy wondered if he'd ever mean it. In Newgate Prison, if one did not make friends with his pain, it became nothing but a constant tormentor. There was no escaping it, so the boy and his mates had learned to invite it in, study its effects, and then mete it out with vicious efficiency.

The boy was almost a man. Indeed, at the age of eigh-teen, he was a leader of men. Walters, likely the largest brute of his acquaintance, did his bidding without ques-tion. Everyone did. Some because they liked and respected him. Others because they owed him. More yet, because they feared him.

Well, if he was being honest, they *all* feared him.

Because he was an agent of pain.

"Just get on with it, will you?" he ordered.

Walters's meaty fingers wrapped around the sharpened quill, which he proceeded to dip into the ink.

Such delicate motions, the boy thought, for such a large and unwieldy man. This precision of movement probably made Walters the best forger in the empire.

Or had, before his incarceration.

In prison, Walters became an artist of a different kind. A man had to do what he could to stay busy behind these gray stone walls. To stay sharp. Either to stave off madness, or monsters.

For every kind of torment lurked in the shadows of this place.

"Where'd you say you got this again?" Walters gestured toward the dingy leather scrap upon which intriguing lines forked in black ink, weighted by the ancient sigil etched into obsidian.

"From the first blighter I killed," the boy lied. "A pirate."

A man was as good as his reputation. As true in prison as it was on the outside. The boy had never been one to let the truth get in the way of a good story, especially if it made him appear more dangerous.

Truth was, he'd filched the map and sigil on the day he'd been arrested, from a kindly but impoverished Danish historian who'd boarded with his mother.

That had also been the day they'd pulled Caroline Morley's corpse out of the Thames.

Swallowing emotion he'd considered as dead as the beautiful golden-haired girl, he found the first sting of the quill a distracting relief as it broke the thin skin on the underside of his forearm.

An easier pain to bear than that of Caroline's death.

The boy made calculations in his head as Walters

worked. Plans. Contingency plans. Failsafe plans. Infinite estimations.

What if he pulled this off? The Blackheart Brothers could rule the empire by the time they turned twenty.

Controlling the excitement palpitating in his chest, he did his best to keep the quivers in his belly under control. The last month inside this hell on earth would be nothing less than excruciating. Like the tattoo, the moments of pressure before the skin broke caused the most discomfort.

He just wanted it over with. He wanted to breathe in the night air again. To enjoy food free of maggots. And drink water that didn't taste of piss and smell of rotten eggs. He dreamt of a bed of fresh straw but would settle for a blanket against the cold.

Just one soft thing. One kind word. One beautiful sight.

In his years at Newgate, he'd forgotten such pleasures existed.

Except in his dreams. He'd always had such vivid dreams.

"Tell me again what this pirate said," Walters encouraged, rubbing away wells of blood from the boy's flesh with a tattered cloth. "Talking will help keep you still and pass the time."

The boy nodded, recalling that the historian, Johan Sandergaard, had enthralled him and his mother with the story over dinner one night. The usually sedate man's glacial blue eyes flashed with the fires of conquest he'd inherited from his ancestors.

"Legend has it that approximately fifty years after Christ was killed, Claudius, the first Roman to successfully invade Britannia, wrote in his personal journals that he found something here so astonishing it would make him wealthier than any emperor had ever been. Because of the wars with the vicious native tribe, the Trinovantes, he was unable to bring whatever it was back with him. Desperate to claim it, he sealed it up, and left it guarded by the Sigil of the Scythian Dragon, the banner of the Roman Cavalry. And do you know what dragons protect?"

"Everyone knows that dragons protect treasure." Walters dipped the quill once more, wiping the trails of blood down the boy's forearm. The repetitive abrasion over the fresh wounds inflamed the skin. Resisting the urge to grind his teeth to nubs, the boy bared his teeth in the semblance of a smile.

"*Exactly,*" he validated through a jaw that wouldn't unbind. "Claudius was poisoned before he could ever return to Britannia, and the only clue he left was this sigil."

Both men gazed down at the seal. The figure of a serpentine dragon with four claws and a tongue snaking between fearsome teeth snarled beneath the etching of two words. *NIGRAE AQUAE.*

The boy had hoped when his blood brother, Dougan, had taught him to read, that he'd finally be able to make out what the words meant, but no such luck. They certainly weren't English.

"So, wot's the sigil got to do with the map?" Walters prodded, as he finished the forked lines in their exactitude, and began to etch the sigil into the boy's raw skin.

"Nine hundred years later, King of the Danes Sweyn Forkbeard invaded Britain. Only one bridge stood over the terrain, and three heroic Anglo-Saxon warriors held that bridge with but a few of the village men, fending off all two thousand marauders. It is said they protected a secret wealth, a buried magic treasure that lent them indefinable strength and stamina.

"Thus defeated, the Danes took sanctuary on a small island, where they found a cave protected by a dragon. *This* dragon. Inside the cave was treasure too large to be conducted back to Denmark by a fleet of ships carrying *two thousand men,* can you imagine?"

"Indeed, I cannot." Walters's bulbous, bald head swung back and forth on something too short and thick to truly be considered a neck as he etched the words beneath the crease of the boy's elbow.

Impassioned and a little drunk on pain, the boy barely felt the meticulous punctures anymore. "Invigorated by his find, King Sweyn attacked Maldon, and was paid off by King Æthelred the Unready to leave Britain. King Sweyn was never able to retrieve the treasure and it remains in that spot to this very day. The one marked by the dragon on this map."

"'Ow do you know that?" Walters queried.

"Because Sweyn left this map with his daughter, but she hated and distrusted her father, and never came to look for it. So, it sat in a royal library in Denmark until recently."

"I don't know . . . these don't look like any roads 'round here, and I've been all over." Walters skeptically gestured to the strange branching lines.

"I don't think they are roads," the boy speculated. "The Vikings were seafarers, sailors, so it makes sense that their maps did not depict roads, but rivers."

Walters froze, studying his work with new eyes. "Well . . . buggar me both ways."

"Exactly."

"So you're going to 'unt this treasure when you're released in a month?"

"I'm not going to stop hunting this treasure until I find it," the boy vowed.

By the time Walters finished, the boy's nerves were as frayed as a tired gallows rope, but the tattoo was some of the finest work he'd ever seen.

Packing his implements into a loose stone crevasse in the floor, Walters asked, "Are you going to tell Dougan?"

"Of course I'm going to tell him, just as soon as we are able to switch cells again." The boy moved to the far wall, to Dougan's pallet, and slid a stone free of its place in the wall. Reaching in, he pulled out some contraband, and then removed one more stone behind that. *There* lay the hideaway no one thought to look for after discovering the initial alcove. "I'm leaving this map and sigil for *him*. For you, and Murdoch, and Tallow. But Dougan has three years left on his sentence, so I'll be searching while he's still incarcerated. Maybe I'll have found it by the time you're all out. I'll send word, of course. I'll come back for you all."

"Sure you will."

The boy looked up sharply, ready to deliver a reprimand for the disrespect he heard in Walter's tone. But the hint of melancholy etched into the craggy lines prominently displayed on the forger's filthy face turned any words to ash in his mouth.

Walters had lived long enough to doubt every man's word. He regarded the boy with pity, but no scorn. With kindness, but no faith.

"I'll. Come. Back."

Walters turned away. "You'll want to wrap that before we start work on the rails in the morning. Don't want it going putrid."

He'd show Walters, the boy thought. He'd blow the walls of this place wide open. He wouldn't leave his family behind.

Swallowing his frustration, the boy carefully replaced the stones over the map, placed the contraband in front of it, and then secured the outer stone.

He'd tell Dougan where to find it in the morning.

Walters blew out the candle he'd worked by, and stowed it somewhere the guards wouldn't think to look for it.

Stretching his long body out on the pallet, the boy laced his fingers over his empty stomach and contemplated the darkness. He counted moments by the throb of his new tattoo. The acrid scent of candle smoke was a welcome temporary balm over the ever-present wreak of dank humanity clinging to these ancient walls.

Once they released him from this place, the boy decided he'd find Cutter. He'd take his oldest friend on this adventure with him. For, as Dougan had become his brother in Newgate, Cutter had always been his brother on the streets.

It was Cutter's crime for which the boy paid, and he did it gladly. He owed him after what happened to Cutter's twin sister.

Caroline . . . sweet Caroline. Gone forever . . .

He couldn't say why the scuffle of the boot broke his drowsy ruminations. The night guards made rounds every hour. Maybe he heard a few boots too many. Or the twinge of violent anticipation raced like a specter through the still, humid night.

One developed a sense for danger in this place. Especially one so young as he. Unlike in the wild, predators outnumbered the prey in here, and would tear each other apart to make a meal of him.

In the early days . . . they had.

In the days before Dougan and Argent. Before the Blackheart Brothers.

The ominous creak of the cell door brought him to his feet, the knife he'd fashioned from obsidian he'd found in the tunnels at the ready.

Lanterns blinded him in the windowless room. He slashed out at the men spilling into his cell, his power and speed wrought by days of backbreaking work digging railways beneath the city. He cut something. Someone. The warm rush of blood slicked over his hand.

Fuck. Now his knife would be difficult to wield.

His vision cleared in time to see the back of Walters's head connect with the stones, leaving so much blood and some of his skull behind when he fell.

Five guards cornered the boy in a room hardly big enough for two grown men to stretch across.

"Dougan Mackenzie?" The sergeant sneered, close enough that the boy could count the flecks of tobacco in his teeth.

"No! I'm not Dougan Mackenzie. I'm Dor—"

"Your father sends his regards."

The boy blocked the first blow with his fresh tattoo, the pain turning him feral. He didn't see the cudgel arcing toward his temple until it was too late. Nor the boot that snapped his ankle, dropping him to the ground.

Now he counted time with impacts. With the snaps of bones and spurts of blood.

The boy's last thought was that Walters had been right to doubt him.

He'd never hunt for his treasure. He'd never return for his friends.

For no one could come back from the dead.

CHAPTER ONE

If Lorelai Weatherstoke hadn't been appreciating the storm out the carriage window, she'd have missed the naked corpse beneath the ancient ash tree.

"*Father, look!*" She seized Lord Southbourne's thin wrist, but a barrage of visual stimuli overwhelmed her, paralyzing her tongue.

In all her fourteen years, she'd never seen a naked man, let alone a deceased one.

He lay facedown, strong arms reached over his head as though he'd been trying to swim through the shallow grass lining the road. Ghastly dark bruises covered what little flesh was visible beneath the blood. He was all mounds and cords, his long body different from hers in every way a person could be.

Her heart squeezed, and she fought to find her voice as the carriage trundled past. The poor man must be cold, she worried, then castigated herself for such an absurd thought.

The dead became one with the cold. She'd learned that by kissing her mother's forehead before they closed her casket forever.

"What is it, duck?" Her father may have been an earl, but the Weatherstokes were gentry of reduced circumstances, and didn't spend enough time in London to escape the Essex accent.

Lorelai had not missed the dialect while at school in Mayfair, and it had been the first thing she'd rid herself of in favor of a more proper London inflection. In this case, however, it was Lord Southbourne's words, more than his accent, that caused her to flinch.

As cruel as the girls could be at Braithwaite's Boarding School, none of their taunts had made her feel quite so hollow as the one her own family bestowed upon her.

Duck.

"I-it's a man," she stammered. "A corp—" Oh no, had he just *moved,* or had she imagined it? Squinting through the downpour, she pressed her face to the window in time to see battered knuckles clenching the grass, and straining arms pulling the heavy body forward.

"Stop," she wheezed, overtaken by tremors. "Stop the carriage!"

"What's bunched your garters, then?" Sneering across from her, Mortimer, her elder brother, brushed aside the drapes at his window. "Blimey! There's a bleedin' corpse by the road." Three powerful strikes on the roof of the coach prompted the driver to stop.

"He's alive!" Lorelai exclaimed, pawing at the door handle. "I swear he moved. We have to help him."

"I thought that fancy, expensive school was supposed to make you less of an idiot, Duck." Mortimer's heavy brows barely separated on a good day and met to create one thick line when he adopted the expression of disdainful scorn he reserved solely for her. "What's a cripple like you going to do in the mud?"

"We should probably drive through to Brentwood," Lord Southbourne suggested diplomatically. "We can send back an ambulance to fetch him."

"He'll need an undertaker by then," Lorelai pleaded. "We must save him, mustn't we?"

"I've never seen so much blood." It was morbid fascination rather than pity darkening her brother's eyes. "I'm going out there."

"I'm coming with you."

A cruel hand smacked Lorelai out of the way, and shoved her back against the faded brocade velvet of her seat. "You'll stay with Father. I'll take the driver."

As usual, Lord Robert Weatherstoke said and did nothing to contradict his only son as Mortimer leaped from the coach and slammed the door behind him.

Lorelai barely blamed her passive father anymore. Mortimer was so much larger than him these days, and ever so much crueler.

She had to adjust her throbbing leg to see the men making their way through the gray of the early-evening deluge. Just enough remained of daylight to delineate color variations.

The unfortunate man was a large smudge of gore against the verdant spring ground cover. Upon Mortimer and the driver's approach, he curled in upon himself not unlike a salted snail. Only he had no shell to protect his beaten body.

Lorelai swallowed profusely in a vain attempt to keep her heart from escaping through her throat as the man was hoisted aloft, each arm yoked like an ox's burden behind a proffered neck. Even though Mortimer was the tallest man she knew, the stranger's feet dragged in the mud. His head lolled below his shoulders, so she couldn't get a good look at his face to ascertain his level of consciousness.

Other parts of him, though, she couldn't seem to drag her eyes away from.

She did her best not to look between his legs, and mostly succeeded. At a time like this, modesty hardly mattered, but she figured the poor soul deserved whatever dignity she could allow him.

That is to say, she only peeked twice before wrenching her eyes upward.

The muscles winging from his back beneath where his arms spread were ugly shades of darkness painted by trauma. The ripples of his ribs were purple on his left side, and red on the other. Blunt bruises interrupted the symmetrical ridges of his stomach, as though he'd been kicked or struck repeatedly. As they dragged him closer, what she'd feared had been blood became something infinitely worse.

It was as though his flesh had been chewed away, but by something with no teeth. The plentiful meat of his shoulder and chest, his torso, hips, and down his thigh were grotesquely visible.

Burns, maybe?

"Good God, how is he still alive?" The awe in her father's voice reminded her of his presence as they scurried to open the carriage door and help drag the man inside. It took the four of them to manage it.

"He won't be unless we hurry." The driver tucked the man's long, long legs inside, resting his knees against the seat. "I fear he won't last the few miles to Brentwood."

Ripping her cloak off, Lorelai spread it over the shuddering body on the floor. "We must do what we can," she insisted. "Is there a doctor in Brentwood?"

"Aye, and a good one."

"Please take us there without delay."

"O'course, miss." He secured the door and leaped into his seat, whipping the team of fresh horses into a gallop.

As they lurched forward, the most pitiful sound she'd ever heard burst from the injured man's lips, which flaked with white. His big arm flailed from beneath the cloak to protect his face, in a gesture that tore Lorelai's heart out of her chest.

The burn scored the sinew of his neck and up his jaw to his cheekbone.

Pangs of sympathy slashed at her own skin, and drew her muscles taut with strain. Lorelai blinked a sheen of tears away, and cleared emotion out of her tight throat with a husky sound she'd made to soothe many a wounded animal on the Black Water Estuary.

His breaths became shallower, his skin paler beneath the bruises.

He was dying.

Without thinking, she slid a hand out of her glove, and gently pressed her palm to his, allowing her fingers to wrap around his hand one by one.

"Don't go," she urged. "Stay here. With me."

His rough, filthy hand gripped her with such strength, the pain of it stole her breath. His face turned toward her, though his eyes remained closed.

Still, it heartened her, this evidence of awareness. Perhaps, on some level, she could comfort him.

"You're going to be all right," she crooned.

"Don't lie to the poor bastard." Mortimer's lip curled in disgust. "He's no goose with a defective wing, or a three-legged cat, like the strays you're always harboring. Like as not he's too broken to be put back together with a bandage, a meal, and one of your warbling songs. He's going to *die,* Lorelai."

"You don't know that," she said more sharply than she'd intended, and received a sharp slap for her lapse in wariness.

"And you don't know what I'll do to you if you speak to me in that tone again."

Most girls would look to their fathers for protection, but Lorelai had learned long ago that protection was something upon which she could never rely.

Her cheek stinging, Lorelai lowered her eyes. Mortimer would take it as a sign of submission, but she only did it to hide her anger. She'd learned by now to take care around him in times of high stress, or excitement. It had been her folly to forget . . . because she knew *exactly* what he was capable of. The pinch of her patient's strong grip was nothing next to what she'd experienced at the hands of her brother on any given month.

Ignoring the aching throb in her foot, Lorelai dismissed Mortimer, leaning down instead to stroke a dripping lock of midnight hair away from an eye so swollen, he'd not have been able to open it were he awake.

Across from her, Mortimer leaned in, as well, ostensibly studying the man on the floor with equal parts intrigue and disgust. "Wonder what happened to the sod. I haven't seen a beating like this in all my years."

Lorelai schooled a level expression from her face at the reference to his many perceived years. He was all of twenty, and the only violence he witnessed outside of sport, he perpetrated himself.

"Brigands, you suspect?" Sir Robert fretted from beside her, checking the gathering darkness for villains.

"Entirely possible," Mortimer said flippantly. "Or maybe he is one. We are disturbingly close to Gallows Corner."

"Mortimer," their father wheezed. "Tell me you haven't pulled a criminal into my coach. What would people say?"

The Weatherstoke crest bore the motto *Fortunam maris,* "fortune from the sea," but if anyone had asked Lorelai what it was, she'd have replied, *Quid dicam homines?* "What would people say?"

It had been her father's favorite invocation—and his greatest fear—for as long as she could remember.

Lorelai opened her mouth to protest, but her brother beat her to it, a speculative glint turning his eyes the color of royal sapphires. "If I'd hazard a guess, it would be that this assault was personal. A fellow doesn't go to the trouble to inflict this sort of damage lest his aim is retribution or death. Perhaps he's a gentleman with gambling debts run afoul of a syndicate. Or, maybe a few locals caught him deflowering their sister . . . though they left those parts intact, didn't they, Duck?" His sly expression told Lorelai that he'd caught her looking where she ought not to.

Blushing painfully, she could no longer bring herself to meet Mortimer's cruel eyes. They were the only trait Lorelai shared with her brother. Her father called them the Weatherstoke jewels. She actively hated looking in the mirror and seeing Mortimer's eyes staring back at her.

Instead, she inspected the filthy nails of the hand engulfing her own. The poor man's entire palm was one big callus against hers. The skin on his knuckles, tough as an old shoe, had broken open with devastating impact.

Whatever had happened to him, he'd fought back.

"He's no gentleman," she observed. "Too many calluses. A local farmhand, perhaps, or a stable master?" It didn't strain the imagination to envision these hands gripping the rope of an erstwhile stallion. Large, magnificent beasts pitting their strength one against the other.

"More like stable boy," Mortimer snorted. "I'd wager my inheritance he's younger than me."

"How can you tell?" With his features beyond recognition, Lorelai was at a loss as to the man's age. No gray streaked his midnight hair, nor did lines bracket his swollen lips, so she knew he couldn't be old, but beyond that . . .

"He's not possessed of enough body hair for a man long grown."

"But he's so big," she reasoned. "And his chest appears to have been badly burned, the hair might have singed right off."

"I'm not referring to his chest, you dull-wit, but to his coc—"

"Mortimer, *please*."

Lorelai winced. It was as close to a reprimand as her father ever ventured. Mortimer must have been very wicked, indeed. It was just her luck that he did so on perhaps the first occasion Lorelai had actually wanted her brother to finish a sentence.

A rut in the road jostled them with such force at their frantic pace, Lorelai nearly landed on the injured man. His chest heaved a scream into his throat, but it only escaped as a piteous, gurgling groan.

"I'm sorry. I'm so sorry," she whimpered. Dropping to her knees, she hovered above him, the fingers of her free hand fluttering over his quaking form, looking for a place to land that wouldn't cause him pain.

She could find none. He was one massive wound.

A tear splashed from her eye and disappeared into the crease between his fingers.

"Duck, perhaps it's best you take your seat." Her father's jowly voice reminded her of steam wheezing from a tea-kettle before it's gathered enough strength to whistle. "It isn't seemly for a girl of your standing to be thus prostrated on the floor."

With a sigh, she did her best to get her good foot beneath her, reaching for the plush golden velvet of the seat to push herself back into it.

An insistent tug on her arm tested the limits of her shoulder socket, forcing her to catch herself once more.

"Lorelai, I said sit," Lord Southbourne blustered.

"I can't," she gasped incredulously. "He won't let me go."

"What's this, then?" Mortimer wiped some of the mud away from the straining cords of the man's forearm, uncovering an even darker smudge beneath. As he cleared it, a picture began to take shape, the artful angles and curves both intriguing and sinister until mottled, injured skin ruptured the rendering. "Was it a bird of some kind? A serpent?"

"No." Lorelai shook her head, studying the confusion of shapes intently. "It's a dragon."

CHAPTER TWO

He inhaled agony, and exhaled anguish.

Just as he'd done for an eternity, at least.

Swallowing the constant hysteria and confusion evoked by the waves of discomfort and pain upon waking, he lay in the absolute darkness behind the bandages on his eyes and began his list. A pitiful list he frantically added to with stubborn determination.

What he knew: he'd been born a man in a mass grave. His midwives were named fire and torment, delivering him into an unfamiliar world. His siblings had been ravens, feasting on the dead.

The fire had been lye, a chemical poured on the corpses to help them disintegrate faster.

The torment had been everything else.

He suffered from amnesia. The word meant nothing to him. But disembodied voices repeated it with increasing astonishment.

The damage to his head had been such that they'd wrapped all but his mouth. Constant headaches plagued him, and a particular pain in his temple throbbed ceaselessly.

He lived in England, but knew not where.

He'd broken five parts of himself: a left ankle, two ribs, a collarbone, and his nose.

Something in his eye had ruptured, turning it red and swollen.

He'd sat up yesterday, and could lift his previously dislocated shoulder a little higher than before, though it remained secured to his chest by a sling.

His burns had stopped oozing, then scabbed, and were beginning to scar.

Though he could not see, his ears worked just fine.

Thus concluded the sum total of what he knew about himself.

For weeks now, he'd slept among strangers.

An attentive doctor: Dr. Holcomb. A man more concerned about efficiency than kindness, with a rough voice and a gentle touch. Holcomb had supplied most of the information on his list whether the good doctor had meant to or not.

A doddering old fool: Lord Robert Weatherstoke, the Earl of Southbourne. Anxious. Dejected. Weak. Constantly shifting and fiddling with something that made hollow, tiny clicks. A watch? His footsteps shuffled like sandpaper against the floor, and his voice often shook when he spoke in whispers.

A man he wanted to kill: Lord Mortimer Weatherstoke, the Viscount Munthorpe. Someone who communicated in jibes and sarcasm. Every observation curious and morbid. Every reply an insult. His footsteps fell like hammers, and jangled nerves already taut with pain. A furious temperature rose on the rare occasions Mortimer visited. And the heart pumped with hatred, lips twisting into a snarl.

Then . . . there was *her.*

The girl he kept waking up for.

Dr. Holcomb called her my lady. The other two called her Duck.

When he could do something about it . . . they wouldn't call her that anymore.

Lips parting on a constricted breath summoned at the thought of her, he rested the hand unencumbered by a sling against his heart.

He desired to know her name more desperately than he desired his own.

A flushing sensation conjured a troubling heat into his cheeks.

Her beatific voice had brought him back from the beckoning abyss above which he'd floated those first feverish days.

Don't go, she'd murmured. *Stay here. With me.*

And so he had.

He'd lived only because she bade him to.

Whenever death seduced him with an end to the agony, he waited to hear the soft timbre of her admonishments just one more time. And once more after that. The slide of her fingers against his palm somehow banked the terror of an empty past. It suddenly didn't matter who he'd been. Or what would become of him.

He measured time in the increments between her visits.

When he'd been reassembled, bathed, stitched, or simply had a bandage changed, she'd been there. Touching him. Crooning reassurances and praising his progress. Promising recovery.

She sang to him sometimes, her voice high and sweet and . . . unencumbered by talent or pitch of any kind. Christ, she really was terrible. But every time she finished, he promised the devil his soul for one more song.

What did heaven and earth even mean if not for her?

Not a single thing.

She was his prayer in the night. His song in the dark. His past and present.

His future.

And he hadn't even laid eyes on her yet.

It wouldn't matter what she looked like. His heart had already decided to beat for her.

Ears pricking as he heard the sound of her uneven gait coming down the hall, he fought to control his breath against a belt of eagerness tightening across his ribs.

He gulped as the door whispered open on well-oiled hinges. Her footsteps mirrored the thumps of his heart. *Ka-thunk. Ka-thunk. Ka-thunk.*

She set something on the stand to his right, then the slight depression of the mattress told him she'd perched on his bedside. It took everything within him not to roll into her. To wrap himself around her.

His hand on his chest curled into a fist. He quivered, knowing she would touch him, but not knowing when.

Those moments between her appearance and her caress were the most agonizing of all.

He'd never spoken to her. Never reached for her. Not only because his wounded body wouldn't allow it, but because he was fair certain his hands would sully her perfection, somehow. He imagined they were filthy. Tainted by the kind of shame one couldn't wash off. Whenever he opened his mouth to speak, a dread of her repulsion, of her retreat, wrapped their icy fingers around his throat. Choking him into silence.

If he stayed very still . . . she wouldn't leave. If he said nothing, he'd not offend her.

If he didn't breathe, maybe she'd touch him.

To his everlasting astonishment . . . it worked.

Like an answered prayer, her fingers closed over his wrist and lifted his good hand to clasp between her two smaller ones.

"Exciting news," she sang in the enthusiastic whisper of someone with an incredible secret. "Dr. Holcomb is taking the bandages off your head today."

It took a full minute for her words to permeate his slack-jawed amazement. Not because of the chance that he might see again. Or breathe through his nose. But because she'd hugged his hand to her chest.

Just below her throat.

Lace rasped against his knuckles, and a row of tiny buttons indented the meat below his thumb.

She dropped her cheek against his fingers and he *felt* her smile.

Lord love a goat, he could die a happy man. He'd caused one of her smiles.

Dr. Holcomb entered with sure, confident strides. "I say, old boy, do you think you can sit up again?"

He'd answered Dr. Holcomb before. Verbally. When they were alone. But he'd never before had to form words with "my lady's" bosoms grazing his forearm.

He must have nodded, because Holcomb's strong arms slid between his shoulders and the pillow. It took the three of them, but they wrestled him into a sitting position once more.

The darkness spun, and the world tilted.

She didn't let go. Her hold on his hand anchored him to the world. And eventually, the dizziness abated and the ringing in his ears, vibrating like a plucked wire, dimmed and died.

"Are you ready?" Holcomb asked.

He swallowed and nodded.

The snick of the scissors echoed inside his head rather

than against it. He held his breath as the pressure of the wrap released, and the grip of her hands intensified. He didn't know which of them trembled. Maybe they both did.

The cotton patches unraveled from beneath his nose, then lifted from his eyes, which he immediately peeled open.

Sapphires danced in a blur of gold.

"Can you see me?" she whispered breathlessly.

He should answer her. He really should. But nothing seemed to obey him. No words could escape past the thickness in his throat.

"Close, if you please," Dr. Holcomb clipped.

He impatiently submitted his closed lids and tender nose to a warm wash with a cloth, then blinked them open the moment he could. His gaze starving for her.

"You *can* see me!" she exclaimed.

See her? He *absorbed* her. Devoured her. Committed every detail to his empty memory with inhuman precision. In fact, he could see nothing else. And never wanted to.

The downy curve of her beaming cheeks, dimpled with a delighted smile. The fullness of her expressive lips. The riot of untamed curls spilling like dark honey down her plain peach gown.

He was no poet, this he knew, because every word that came to mind was both crass and insufficient.

He had no frame of reference with which to compare her. No metaphors to pronounce. But he remembered that in the graveyard, he'd dragged himself beneath the statue of an angel. Soft-cheeked and solemn, with the striations of gray stone curls tumbling down to her hands pressed in prayer. Her head tilted to the side, as she gazed in grace, guarding the dearly departed.

The thought of that angel—of someone like her— missing him, loving him, assuming he was gone, fueled his ability to crawl, broken and burning, through the storm to the roadside.

But during these weeks in the dark, when he could think through the pain, he'd realized a few things. No one had come for him, though the old earl had sent word far and wide.

He'd awoken in a pauper's grave, one saved for the unloved and the unwanted.

Or worse. The condemned.

He had an enemy. One who'd beaten him to death. Or at least assumed they'd succeeded.

And now . . . he had an angel. One come to life. More beautifully rendered than any artist could compose. Hers was a face molded by a loving celestial hand.

She was young. *Quite* young.

Was he? He didn't think so. He felt as old as time.

Though they'd drawn the drapes and lit a single candle for the unveiling, the room may as well have been illuminated by the noonday sun. *She* glowed with some inner luminescence, a light both otherworldly and pure. Her wide lapis eyes glinted like jewels against fresh, gilded skin. She was too soft to be real, surely. Too divine to be mortal. Too golden to be made of the same clay as himself.

And he . . .

Oh, buggar me blind! he thought. *What do I look like?*

He needed . . . something. Something that wasn't on the dark wardrobe on the far wall, nor the bedside table, but—

There. Above the ivory washbasin to his right.

A mirror.

"It's . . . best you don't look just now." An impish nose wrinkled with worry as the rest of her features battled with composure when she correctly guessed the reason for his distress.

His shoulders gave out, curling in upon themselves. He wanted to pluck his own eyes out. He wanted her to look away. To let him go. His heart shriveled like a piece of wet rubbish thrown on the fire.

Because she'd confirmed his worst fears.

"I'm a monster," he groaned.

Was that his voice? As raspy and graveled as the pit he'd pulled himself from.

Fuck, how could those be the first words he spoke to her?

"Oh no!" She clasped his hand even tighter. "You mustn't think that! You're a miracle. An absolute *miracle.*"

Her eyes shone so earnestly, he couldn't bear to look at them.

"You don't have to lie." As he glanced up at Dr. Holcomb's impressive muttonchops, his stomach clenched around emptiness at the grim expression tightening the man's sharp features.

"Your nose didn't heal as straight as I'd hoped and there's more swelling than I like. But your more . . . superficial wounds shouldn't take too much longer to heal. Your ankle will take the longest, and you should stay off it until I relieve you of the plaster cast in a few weeks' time." The doctor bent to pick up the candle and hold it in front of both eyes, tracking their movements.

He wanted to shrink away from the man. The impulse powerful enough that he couldn't suppress a wince. His skin crawled and his blood sang with ferocity and . . . fear.

Holcomb pretended not to notice. "Though your eye remains red, it's reactive to light and movement. Can you see as well as before?"

The truth was, he had no idea.

"I . . . think I can see fine."

"All things considered, Miss Weatherstoke is correct. Your continuing recovery is nothing less than miraculous. To be honest, I didn't expect you to survive."

"You see?" she encouraged. "A miracle, not a monster. In order to be considered a monster, you must first do something monstrous."

He had.

The revelation hit his gut like a swallowed stone.

The evidence was in his violent, visceral reaction to everyone and everything.

Except her.

Scrambling around the aching emptiness in his brain for the barest hint of a past, he found nothing. He remembered *nothing*. Not his name. His age. His origin. Not even his own hair or eye color.

Yet certain powerful, primal information gave him a terrifying glimpse into his nature.

He knew things a monster would know. Noticed what a monster would notice.

He could kill. With that decorative letter opener, the pillow beneath his head, the pitcher of water broken into lethal shards. He could and would open an artery, or throat if necessary. He knew exactly how much damage he could inflict. How much time it would take. Where to exert the most force or pressure.

Pain was not only his oppressor, keeping him useless upon this bed. It was his tool.

His friend.

The only friend he could remember.

How was it he knew nothing, but could ascertain that?

The doctor's touch repulsed him, in every confusing and conceivable way. A strong man with cold eyes. Someone who wielded more power than he did.

For now.

This he could not abide. Why? *Why?*

He leveled a cautionary stare at the doctor as Holcomb measured the pulse at his throat.

Holcomb regarded him strangely, in turn, before standing. "I—think I'll go tell the earl the news." He paused in the doorway. "My Lady, would you like to accompany me?"

"I'll stay and make certain our patient keeps down a few sips of soup."

"Are you certain you should be alone with—"

"We'll be fine, Dr. Holcomb, thank you ever so much." Even her dismissal sounded like a compliment.

The doctor's eyes narrowed dubiously. "As you say."

Then they were alone.

Could she hear his heart pounding? Could she see how quickly his chest rose and fell? Did she feel anything but pity when she looked at him?

She released his hand, and reached for the bowl of soup at his bedside.

Bereft, he brought his empty hand back over his heart, which ached more than it beat.

"Hungry?" she asked brightly.

Unable to find words again, he shook his head. He couldn't think of eating. Not in front of her. She was a lady, refinement evident in her every graceful gesture. What if he did something embarrassing?

"It's very good." She lifted the spoon. "I've been feeding you every day while you've been here. This is a favorite of yours."

It was? He eyed the brown liquid dubiously, wondering just what floated beneath the surface.

"If I have some first, would that help?" She lifted a healthy spoonful of what appeared to be broth and soggy vegetables to her plump pink lips.

The inside of his own mouth dried as he alertly watched her savor the bite of stew. His hand dropped from his chest to cover his lap.

"Mmmmmm," she moaned with overwrought appreciation. "It's *extra* delicious today."

Disturbed by his body's reaction to her, he crossed his legs and covered the moan of pain the movement caused him.

"You must have some nourishment in order to heal." Her eyes became pools of concern. "Is there nothing that could entice you to eat? What would it take?"

"Your name . . ." The words escaped before he'd properly formed the thought.

She blinked rapidly, the bowl in her hand threatening to spill when she trembled. She turned peach rather than pink when she blushed. He stored that away for future reference.

"Lorelai. My name is Lady Lorelai Weatherstoke."

Lorelai. He couldn't bring himself to repeat it. The name was too lovely. Too lyrical. He needed to practice first. To test it by himself before addressing her.

"Are you a man of your word?" she asked.

His heart stalled. "What do you mean?" *Was* he a man of his word? He had an ominous feeling that he was not.

"You said you would eat."

"Oh . . . yes." That he could do. In fact, he realized then and there that he would never break a promise to Lorelai. He'd keep his word to her, or die trying.

She dipped the spoon, crafted a bite, and lifted it to his lips.

As he took it, she unconsciously mimed the action of eating, opening her mouth and then closing it to mirror him. Swallowing when he did as if to teach him how.

She transfixed him so utterly, he didn't even taste the food until the second bite.

She'd been telling the truth. It was very good. The soup consisted of dark, briny meat, sweet carrots, and was thickened with potatoes, herbs, and a luxurious taste he couldn't identify. Something told him he wasn't used to decent food.

His tongue lingered against the spoon. Pondering what he considered the illicit intimacy of sharing the utensil. Of tasting what she'd tasted. Of putting his mouth where hers had been.

Perhaps *she'd* been the secret ingredient all along.

"You're probably wondering what makes this broth so scrumptious," she guessed.

He blinked at her. She couldn't read minds, could she? He dismissed the ridiculous notion right away. If so, she'd have run screaming from the room already.

He found that in order to swallow, he couldn't look at her lips, her eyes, her hair, her throat, below her throat or . . . well, anywhere, really. He affixed his focus to the tiny bob dangling from her lobe. It danced and twinkled in the light of the lone candle, a diamond floating on a disk of iridescent blues and greens and pink. Crafted from a shell, maybe?

She reached out another bite to him, and a discoloration on her wrist snagged his attention. A faded bruise showed beneath the delicate lace of her sleeves. A purple tinge barely visible beneath an unsightly yellow. Had she hurt herself?

"It's salt," she revealed cryptically.

"It's what?" He forgot himself long enough for her to plunge the spoon into his mouth once again, forcing him to chew.

"Black Water salt is the *best* in the world, and the rarest. It's so difficult to render, that there isn't much of it, but we locals have our ways." She gifted him an impish wink and he nearly choked.

Lorelai. Her name had as many curls as the unruly flaxen hair spilling past her shoulders. Shorter wisps fringed about her face like a halo. How apropos. With such a lovely name, why would they . . . ?

"Why do they call you Duck?"

She paled, even in the golden light. "You don't know?"

He flushed along with her, wishing he could take it back. Or scoop out his own tongue with the spoon. Anything to avoid the shimmer of mortification in her eyes.

It had something to do with her uneven gait. He should have surmised that.

But he'd hoped it was an endearment rather than a taunt. A familial moniker given to a girl with a tendency to rescue motherless ducklings and the like. She'd told him about her little menagerie in one of his more lucid moments. And, for a blessed time, he'd not wanted to claw off his own flesh as he listened to her tales of silly animal antics.

He pondered the long sleeve of a shirt that didn't belong to him. Horrible scabs stretched along his arm, his torso, and down his waist. He could not see them, but the tangible tugs and aches on his flesh alerted him to their presence.

"My ankle was broken, too, a long time ago," she murmured. "The same one as yours, in fact. But mine didn't . . . heal in time." Lifting another spoonful of soup, she summoned a smile, punctuating the end of that topic.

Obediently, he ate.

The sound of heavy bootsteps interrupted the ensuing silence. Big, blond, and brawny, Mortimer Weatherstoke looked exactly like he'd imagined the bastard would. He surveyed the scene with the air of a princeling watching the slaughter of his supper. The novel carnage both revolting and fascinating.

"Dr. Holcomb said that the blighter had woken . . . Dear God." His ruddy, handsome face crumpled into a grimace. "How positively grotesque. It's worse than I thought, Duck."

"No it isn't!" she huffed at her brother. "No it isn't." She hastily turned back to reassure him. "Dr. Holcomb said you were fortunate it rained so mightily on the day the lye was poured on your . . . body." She whispered the word, as though it were a naughty one. "The water diluted its effect. You were again lucky that the burns didn't become infected. And now, once the scabs turn to scars, you'll recover fully. But . . . better you don't look until then, yes? Promise me?"

He opened his mouth to disagree and again found it full of the soup spoon before he could make a noise.

His impish angel was craftier than he'd given her credit for.

He glared at them both as he gnawed a particularly chewy piece of stew meat.

Mortimer rested a manicured hand on Lorelai's shoulder, and she winced as though she'd been stung by a wasp.

His heartbeat sped to a murderous pace. The bruise on her wrist . . . had been the shape of a finger. Of two fingers. And if she lifted her sleeve, he'd bet he could find others. The places where she'd been mishandled by the oafish lummox looming over them.

"You truly remember nothing?" Mortimer scratched his scalp through hair several shades lighter than his sister's. "Not your name. Not your parents. Not even where you live?"

Swallowing the stew, along with the madness that threatened each time he tried to ponder what he didn't remember, he shook his head.

"I've heard of this happening before . . ." Mortimer stroked the sparse beginnings of a mustache on his upper lip. It looked like a half-plucked baby chick. "To soldiers and the like. Are you a soldier?"

What a fucking imbecilic question.

"I. Don't. Know."

Their glares locked, and suddenly he knew his own eyes were black. Black with instant hatred.

Whereas Lorelai's honey-wheat hair was threaded through with streaks of dark gold, and her flawless skin bronzed by many hours spent in the sun, Mortimer was simply . . . yellow. Sallow, even. His hair, his ridiculous mustache, and his pale skin tinted an almost sickly color that was exacerbated by his mustard silk house coat.

He had an apelike quality about him. Arms too long for his stocky body. Posture curled with indolent apathy, though blessed with brute strength. A golden gorilla.

Barely fucking human.

"Here." Lorelai offered him another bite of soup, doing her best to dispel the tension gathering in the room. "Do you think you can finish?"

"Like rabbit, do you?" Mortimer asked.

"Rabbit?" An adorable wrinkle appeared between her brows. "Cook didn't get any at market, did you finally catch some in your snares?"

"No." Mortimer packed the single syllable to overflowing with cruel anticipation.

"Mortimer . . . what did you do?" Setting the half-empty bowl down with such haste, the contents sloshed onto the bedside table, Lorelai stood to question her brother.

A fear the boy didn't understand feathered across her features.

"Why go through the trouble of snaring rabbits, when there were perfectly good ones out back in the pens?" Mortimer obviously savored the devastation of his sister's features. Her abject shock melting to horror and then to heartbreak.

"No," she sobbed, clutching at her throat. "Mortimer, how *could* you?"

Her brother shrugged his shoulders. "Oh, come on, Duck. Rabbits are rabbits. What does it matter if I snare them in the fields or take them from the pens?"

"You *knew* they were mine, I saved them from starvation when they were just orphans. They had names, Mortimer! They were my friends!"

"And now they're your food," Mortimer said smugly.

"We . . . ate them." All color drained from her face, replaced with an alarming shade of puce. Lorelai clapped her hand over her mouth, convulsed once, twice, then lurched out of the room as fast as her limp would allow.

"Watching her run never ceases to amuse me," Mortimer chuckled.

Unable to reach for her from his useless spot on the bed, the boy watched her steady herself on the wall as she fled, eventually disappearing around a corner in a frenzy of curls and grief.

Bile crawled into his chest, flooding his mouth with stinging moisture. The sides of his jaw ached and his throat closed off with a lump of rage as hot as a brick of coal from the fire.

"What a little fool," Mortimer commiserated. "She'd

likely release those beasts into the fens, and they'd just end up in my snare anyhow. Or on a rack at the butcher's. Will we ever understand women?"

"You . . . did that on purpose." Eventually his throat released enough for him to rasp words around his rage. "To hurt her."

Blue eyes darkened to a granite gray. "Careful, cripple. Father says you can stay, but only because I wanted it."

"Why?" He'd meant the question in regard to Mortimer's cruelty to his sweet sister, but Mortimer mistook his meaning.

"I'm bored." Another shrug, as though he could barely punctuate his apathy with his shoulder. "And you're a mystery I'd like to solve."

The anger felt good, in a way. It poured through him like molten metal, molding him into an eventual weapon. It overtook the eternal throb in his broken ankle. The pounding in his head. The sharp stab of his ribs with every breath. It strengthened him.

It forged him.

Rage was something he knew how to wield. Just . . . not yet. Not until he was stronger.

Mortimer hadn't finished. "You should have seen yourself. When the burns bubbled, then burst. It was the most putrid thing. And Duck, she was always there, playing the little nurse to Dr. Holcomb. Bringing herbs in from the fens. Mixing you potions. I'm surprised she didn't poison you or cause you to shit yourself to death."

They both stared down the hallway where she'd retreated.

"Don't get attached," Mortimer scoffed. "You're just another wild animal to her. She'll release you back to whatever shit pile you crawled away from just as soon as you're able. She keeps none of her patients for long. Besides, a highborn cripple cannot show interest in a lowborn cripple. Though, watching you two travel anywhere would be hilarious in the extreme."

The heat in his veins instantly turned to ice. Hardening him in tense, torturous increments. His blood stilled, awaiting his next command. He'd expected an explosion of temper, an inferno of rage. But no. He sensed he'd felt this way before. Before he'd ended a life.

Lives.

Calm. Cold. Almost . . . anticipatory.

So, he thought serenely. *I am a monster, then.* And in this moment, he was glad of it.

"You fancy yourself dangerous, don't you?" Mortimer correctly assessed.

"I fancy nothing."

"Maybe you are. I went with Dr. Holcomb to that open grave, you know. Full of cholera victims from the East End that the queen paid mightily to be buried far away from the city. Those corpses mixed with a few of those who met their fates at Gallows Corner thrown in for good measure. Sometimes . . . before the graves are slated to be filled, a murder victim or two finds their way onto the pile."

Mortimer bent down, bringing his big, square face uncomfortably close. "Dr. Holcomb says you're too big and healthy to ever have suffered from cholera. You had bruises round your neck, but not ones caused by a rope. So, what are you? we wonder. A criminal or a victim?"

Likely both.

Mortimer chucked him on his injured arm. "Maybe we'll find out one day, which of us is more dangerous . . ." Straightening with a derisive snort, he turned on a boot heel, and walked away, hands clasped indolently behind him.

Chest heaving, he trembled in the light of the lone candle. Railing at his own helpless body.

Oh, Mortimer Weatherstoke was going to find out a *great* deal about him . . .

On the day he slaughtered Lorelai's brother for making her weep.

CHAPTER THREE

Lorelai's lantern trembled, turning midnight shadows into sinister wraiths as she crept through the hall, as best her foot would allow. Her heartbeats echoed off the walls of Southbourne Grove's east wing. Her breaths like rapid-fire pistol shots in the consuming silence. Loud enough for the ghosts to hear, surely.

When the horrible sounds had first roused her, she'd thought maybe Cyrus and Joan d'Arc were at it again. Howling and scuffling. The two hounds boasted only seven legs, three eyes, and one tail between them, but still they played like puppies. And sometimes their play turned serious.

They were not, however, nocturnal animals.

The raw, animalistic cries beckoned her to *his* room. She paused at the door, pressing her ear against the cool wood.

No animal she knew made a sound like that.

No man, either.

The torment expelled upon such a cry was almost

otherworldly in its macabre timbre. A whimper. A plea. And then a long lament, too hoarse to be a call, but lower than a scream.

Something about the noise caused her to hesitate with her fingertips on the door handle. What if he wasn't alone in there? Could someone be hurting him? It certainly sounded that way. Should she go for help?

What if Mortimer was disturbing him?

Urgently, she pressed the door open, hurling herself into his room.

Lorelai didn't know whether to be more relieved or distressed that his great body battled naught but the darkness.

And whatever demons haunted his dreams.

Dr. Holcomb had relieved him of his sling some two days past, and his long, powerful arms fought off invisible assailants with alarming desperation.

"You'll not have me," he growled. "Not tonight."

Who would not have him? Have him what?

She abandoned her lantern on a sideboard by the door, convinced it wasn't safe anywhere close to his flailing limbs. Venturing closer, she noted the damp sheets tangled about his lean, restless hips. His nightshirt lay crumpled on the floor, as though he'd rent it from his body for some imagined offense.

His face remained in the shadows, surging side to side on a neck corded with strain.

"Touch me with that and you'll regret it," he warned.

"Me?" she squeaked, lacing her hands together.

"I'll gut you with a dull blade and fuck your corpses, see if I don't!"

"Pardon?" she gasped.

His voice sounded younger than it did when he was awake. A note of terror thrummed beneath the bravado.

"Let me go," he threatened.

"Let me . . . go." This time, he begged.

Begged. And thrashed. Fighting a battle that became more and more evident he was about to lose in some horrific way.

Dear God. Let this be a nightmare and not . . . a memory.

She had to stop this. Somehow.

Fists as large as his became hammers. This she knew. But what other choice did she have but to approach?

She wasted precious seconds strategizing. Where did one touch a man in the throes of a violent nightmare to avoid injury? A skittish horse, you touched his withers. A snake, you held behind his skull. A rabbit, you turned upside down by both feet until the blood rushing to his head calmed him. A dog, you dug your fingers against his throat, like an alpha would with his teeth.

Then you stroked them, comforted them. Let them come to trust you.

But first, the animal must be subdued for the safety of all involved.

A good rule, with creatures great and small, was to avoid the face at all costs.

But a man? What sort of animal was he, really? She'd learned no tricks to calm such a violent soul but avoidance.

And that wouldn't do in this case.

A low groan decided it for her as she neared the bedside. His cheeks were wet with tears. His ebony hair matted with sweat.

Someone *was* hurting him. She couldn't bear it.

His knuckles narrowly missed her throat as she ducked around them, and tentatively splayed the fingers of one hand over his chest above his bandaged ribs. "Wake up," she admonished him, jostling him a little. "Come *back*."

Two monstrous hands shackled her arms like iron cuffs

as he gasped awake, his entire body seizing, convulsing. He wrenched her hands away from his skin.

Fearing he might snap her bones in two, she couldn't contain her own sob of pain as it cut through her.

To her astonishment, he didn't let go.

He stared up at her, his eyes two volcanic voids of unfocused wrath. His teeth were bared, sharp and menacing. His breaths sawed in and out of him, as though he'd run a league at full tilt.

This was not the man to whom she'd fed soup only two days prior.

This man . . . might just be a monster.

"It's me," she whimpered. "It's Lorelai."

As quickly as she'd been seized, she was released.

A low groan tore from him as he regarded his hands like they'd betrayed him. Like he would rip them from their wrists.

Ignoring her smarting arms, she ran tentative fingers over his fevered brow. It twitched with little shocks where they connected.

"It was just a dream," she crooned. "You're safe."

Though he said nothing, tears leaked from the corners of his eyes in an endless river, running down his temple and joining the beads of sweat glistening at his hairline.

His breath hitched and gasped. Deep grooves appeared between his brows, and his entire visage tightened.

"You are in pain," she realized aloud. Had he reinjured something? The bandages about his ribs were secure, as were the ones over his shoulder, neck, and right torso covering his rapidly healing burns. *Oh no.* Should she call the doctor? Did she dare check beneath the blanket twisted around his lean hips and tangled about his legs?

"What can I do?" she asked frantically.

He'd not wept the entire, agonizing time they'd treated him. Not once.

If he did so now, he must be in absolute anguish.

"Where does it hurt the most?"

Black eyes rimmed in red searched her face, as though he might find answers to a question he didn't know how to ask. The air shifted as threads of trust weaved through the space between them, adding a soft color to their tapestry.

Silently, cautiously, he took her hand, and placed it over his heart.

His skin was warmer than she'd expected. Harder. His pulse kicked beneath her palm, the rhythm unsteady and frenzied, still waging the battle he'd carefully schooled out of his expression.

He was as stoic as ever, except for the moisture still gathering his sooty lashes into wet spikes.

She understood then.

His body, strong, young, and virile, healed with incredible alacrity. But what remedy was there for a lonely and broken heart?

She could think of none.

His eyes fluttered closed, forcing more tears from between the lids. She had the sense that he hid whatever . . . *whoever* would stare out from the darkness at her. His hands were clenched tightly, burrowing into the sheets. Shadows played across his jaw as he worked it to the side, battling to regain control of himself.

Instinct whispered that she must walk the line between compassion and pity most carefully here.

Struck by impulsive sentiment, she lifted her hand, bent over him, and pressed her lips to his chest, just above his heart.

He tensed. Froze. Not so much as drawing a breath until she pulled away.

"I'll heal that too," she promised. If it was the last thing she did, she'd figure out how to stitch his broken heart back together.

His eyes snapped open, regarding her as if she'd taken his soul just then, or maybe returned it to him.

Nervously, she licked her lips. They tasted of soap and salt and . . . him.

The air shifted again, dangerously this time, becoming heavy with the promise of something she couldn't identify and didn't understand.

Lorelai did her best to ignore it. "Someone was hurting you . . . in your dream . . . did you recognize who it was?"

He shook his head. "Men . . . they were . . ." His breath sped again, his features twisting with revulsion.

"They were what?"

He shuddered. "Never mind what."

"Is there anything I can do?" Driven to touch him again, she bent to place a hand back on his chest. The cold night air prickled dangerously through her thin nightshift, reminding her of the untied ribbons hanging loose at the collar.

His tears had dried quite suddenly. His sweat had turned to salt. And the way he looked at her now . . .

Lorelai swallowed, thinking how she had always considered black a cold color, until this very moment.

Banked obsidian fire danced in the meager light of her lantern.

"Go." The word seemed to strangle him as he plucked her hands away from him by her wrists, giving them back to her roughly.

"Pardon?" She hugged her hands to her body.

"Never visit me at night. *Never again.*"

She didn't understand. Wasn't she helping him? Hadn't she saved him from the assailants who hurt him in his sleep?

"What if you have another nightmare?" she contended. "I can't just let you—"

"Leave me to it. Let it take me." A feral, primitive warning lurked beneath the bleakness in his eyes.

"But I—"

"You can't control them!" he snarled. "And I can't control my—" His hands lifted toward her, then plunged into his hair, grabbing great handfuls of it. For some reason she couldn't look at the parts still covered by the sheets. She feared him like this, because he feared himself. But . . . she ached for him, too. Ached in ways she didn't yet comprehend.

"Just get out. *Please*."

The plaintive note in his plea brooked no argument. Warned her away as surely as the hiss of a cornered cat.

Perplexed, dejected, Lorelai limped to the sideboard as slowly as she could, waiting for him to call her back. To change his mind and realize he needed her company after all.

When he didn't, she lifted her lantern and shut the door behind her. Wishing with everything she had that she could forget the bewitching taste of him lingering on her lips.

A week later, Lorelai peeked around the door, and found his dark lashes fanned against his pale cheek, trembling with a dream.

A good dream this time, she hoped.

She trembled, too, but not from any of the emotions evoked on the night of which neither of them had spoken.

Today, only excitement quivered through her.

They'd become careful friends while gentle rains had

kept everyone inside over the last several days, and she'd gathered that along with pain, he was also plagued by boredom. She'd check on him after the evening meal, and when she often found him awake, she'd distract him from dark moods with a hand or two of cards. Écarté, upon occasion, or whist. She'd taught him cribbage and chess, at which he'd never best her. Though . . . there were times she wondered if he didn't let her win. With such clever intellect glittering behind his somber, dark eyes, it seemed incongruous that he didn't best her, even when she made what she knew to be devastating mistakes.

She had the sense he did more than tolerate her company. Perhaps he even enjoyed it. However, a distance often crept into his gaze or, conversely, an intensity would tighten his words to a clip and his motions into sharp blades of strain.

What torture it must be to rely upon the kindness of strangers.

To be a stranger, even unto yourself.

Waving a few indulgent servants in stocking feet into the room, she silently directed them to set their wares here and there, a tiptoed dance they performed to perfection. Even the contents of the boxes made little to no noise as they were carefully jostled into place.

Indulging in a giddy smile at her impending success, she gestured her thanks to her cohorts. Signals which were readily returned. Then she shut the door behind them with nary a click . . . and turned to the sight of two unblinking, coal-black eyes affixed on her.

Lorelai did her best not to allow her disappointment to show.

Could her patient have not stayed asleep for just a few more minutes? Then everything would have been perfect.

Her belly clenched alarmingly low, as it often did when

he looked at her like that, and her hold on the burden in her hands dangerously tilted as her smile died.

Even as she berated herself for being foolish and fanciful, she always interpreted his stare as appreciative, somehow. As though she'd rescued him from something dreadful, even if it was just a nap.

She'd been silly to hope to surprise him, she supposed with a disenchanted sigh.

Other than the night—*that* night—it became evident that the mere sound of breath stirring the air brought his long, slumbering body to life, tensing his muscles with an ever-ready vigilance. A vigilance not generally observed in human creatures, but saved for those who slept with an ear to the ground.

Those who needed to eat, or to avoid being eaten.

This tendency of his tugged at her heart, for she'd the feeling a man developed these senses through a life lived in feral environs. One where survival was a constant battle.

She approached him as she did other wild, uncertain creatures: slowly, steadily, hand outstretched.

Bending his elbows and planting his hands flat on the mattress, he pushed himself into a sitting position with almost no difficulty, never taking his eyes away from her.

His strength had returned with alarming speed.

Today Dr. Holcomb had unwrapped his ribs.

She tried not to note that his sleep shirt had been left unbuttoned. Nor mark the flex and swell of his smooth chest as he lifted his own bulk. As with every attempt at propriety where he was concerned . . .

She only *mostly* succeeded.

The bruises on his torso had healed, as had the broken ribs beneath. And yet he never seemed to breathe easier. Not in her presence, in any case.

It occurred to her that she'd stood there staring for an inordinately rude amount of time.

He didn't prompt her to say anything. Nor did he move to cover himself or regain modesty. Something about the way he watched her . . . or perhaps the way he sat, straight-backed and broad-shouldered, conveyed a certain awareness she hadn't previously noted.

His chin dipped, black gaze dropping to his bare torso as though discovering his own topography. The sinewy swells of his chest. The deep valley between them. The neat, symmetrical bunches of muscle at his stomach. Four ripples, she counted before they disappeared beneath the blanket.

She knew there were more. She'd seen it all in the carriage.

Swallowing around a dry tongue, she wrenched her notice back to his eyes. This time, when the coals of his irises met hers, they glowed with something as dangerous as invitation. Something as genuine as admiration.

Did he *want* her to look at him? Did he want her to like what she saw?

Because she did. And . . . she did.

Clearing her throat, she hobbled forward, painfully aware of her limp. "I decided today is your birthday." She injected as much sunshine into her voice as she could, to make up for the dreariness of the sickroom.

Two satirically arched ebony brows knit over deep-set eyes. "Why? Why today?"

She liked his voice this way. Rumbled with sleep and disuse, yet smooth with caution. His reaction encouraged her, as well. Not because it was especially reassuring, but because he'd had a reaction at all. Usually, his features remained carefully, *infuriatingly* impassive.

Some of her eagerness returning, she lifted the offering judiciously balanced in both hands. "Mostly because Cook made a cake today, and the icing is *especially* good."

Claiming her perch on his bedside, she took her time pressing the side of the fork through the different layers of the decadent dessert. First buttercream frosting the color of a speckled robin's egg. Then the moist dense cake, yellow starch and sugar held together by lard and butter. The center delighted the palette with a layer of chilled raspberry preserves, only to reverse the order on the way down. Yellow cake. More frosting.

Balancing the fork over the plate so as not to spill crumbs on him, she slid the confection toward his awaiting lips. Oh, she couldn't wait for him to taste it. Could only imagine the joy on his—

Gently, but decisively, the plate and fork were plucked from her hands. "I can feed myself."

"Oh." Ridiculous emotion stung the back of her nose. "Right. Of course you can." She smiled through the threatening tears, as was her habit, though her lashes lowered to hide her reaction.

Why did this dismay her so? she wondered as she studied the edge of the blanket, and the dusky flesh of his ribs above it.

It wasn't as though she desired him to remain an invalid.

She just wanted him to . . . *remain*. Here. With her.

Dr. Holcomb had reported that he'd limped around a bit on the cast, and was able to put weight on his ankle. In a few days, they'd cut the cast off.

What if . . . what if he didn't need her anymore? What if he left Southbourne Grove in search of his missing past?

The prick of tears became a burn.

"It *is* very good." He lowered his head to his shoulder,

as though to bring it into her line of sight, rather than require her to lift her gaze.

Glancing up, she found his jaw flexing and working. Movements made when the fare needn't be chewed, merely rolled and processed by an enterprising and appreciative tongue.

She swallowed when he did, her mouth watering as though she'd taken the bite.

"I can't ever *remember* having better." His next bite was not so dainty as the one she'd cut for him. Indeed, it was almost half the slice of cake. As he savored it, his eyes crinkled a bit at the edges. Not a smile, but a resemblance of amusement.

Belatedly, she realized he'd just attempted a joke at his own missing memory's expense.

A giggle escaped her. Then another.

Before preparing his next bite, he asked, "If you decided today is my birthday, did you also decide how old I am turning?"

Heartened, she rushed to answer him. "Mortimer thinks you cannot be as old as he, and he's twenty."

At the mention of her brother, the sparkle in his eye turned into a glint. "What do *you* think?"

Lorelai blinked. No one had ever asked her that before. A little spark of delight warmed her from behind her ribs. He asked because he wanted to know; she could see the patient curiosity blinking out at her.

His age took up a great deal of her idle speculation. Studying him now, she made her best assessment of him.

Whoever created him had not only been particularly detailed, but disproportionately punitive to the rest of mankind. His features were nothing less than aggressively masculine. Sharp. Broad. With deep lines and hard planes. And yet . . . if one looked closely, there was a sense of the sensual his sculptor must have tried hard to conceal. His upper lip, for example, was little more than a thin slash, but not so with the one beneath. His crooked nose was patrician enough for Caesar himself to have looked down from as he wrested power from all the world, and resided between rather barbaric cheekbones. His jaw was nothing less than belligerent. Not so square as Mortimer's but neither was it diminutive.

It was the sort of jaw that, when painted, rendered the subject a villain rather than a hero. A cleft split the middle of his chin. Dimpled and webbed by pink, healing burns scarred his jaw from his left ear, and down his neck to the deep lines created by his collarbone before disappearing into his sleeve.

His jaw, she realized, strong as it was, had required very little shaving in the weeks he'd been at Southbourne Grove. And, as she'd previously tested with her own fingertips . . . with her lips . . . his chest remained smooth. Hairless.

Men had hair, didn't they?

So he was maybe not yet a man . . . but most certainly not a boy.

His head had been all but shorn a month past. Now, thick layers of ebony tousled every which way, untamed by a comb or pomade.

It suited him, though.

Everything suited him.

Blushing, she remembered that he had a bit of dark hair protecting his . . . his . . . Well, never mind what it was called. But Mortimer had intimated that he was of the opinion there wasn't enough of it for a man grown.

Her gaze wandered lower. *She* certainly wouldn't know about such things, and it wasn't as though she could just *ask*—

"Lorelai?" Her name was more a plea than a question.

Golly, had she said anything aloud?

He'd stopped eating. Frozen in a thin-eyed calculation of his own.

She cleared her throat with a distinctly unladylike sound. "I—I know you must be older than me, as you have the voice of a *man*, and most of the *boys* my age have similar voices to mine."

"What is your age?" he asked alertly.

"Fourteen."

He made a sound in his throat, though whether affirmative or negative, she could hardly tell.

"Let us say that you are seventeen today. Younger than twenty, but still almost grown." He'd a very young—very vigorous—body, but the soul who peered out of those eyes had seen everything one would wish to in a lifetime.

And then perhaps a little more.

"That would put three years between us." He said this as if it were significant.

"Is that a good number of years? Or bad?" she couldn't help but ask.

"I couldn't say." He took a distracted bite, then asked, "What is the date? I'd like to know, should I live to see my next birthday."

She grinned. "It's August second, for future reference."

That noise again. Like the disinterested groan of a wolfhound. A thinking sound, perhaps?

"Do you . . . like your birthday?" she fretted. "We could always change it."

His eyes melted from hard sable to soft pitch. "It's my favorite day so far."

Pleased and discomfited by the gravity in his words, she groped for something to occupy her racing thoughts.

"I brought presents. Well, *sort of* presents. You won't

be able to *keep* them, but since you haven't been able to meet my friends . . ." Reaching for the covers to the pens she'd had conducted to his bedside, she pulled them away, like a magician unveiling his grand reveal. "I thought I'd bring them to you."

He surveyed her "friends" with the appropriate expression of curiosity and enjoyment. Enough to delight her into congratulating herself on such a capital idea.

From their respective pens peered three sleepy foxes, two turtles, a bunny, a ferret, and a snake.

"You . . . saved them all?" he murmured.

"I did, yes," she said, grimacing at the excess pride in her voice. She couldn't say why, exactly, but she very much wanted him to be pleased with her. Impressed, perhaps. "Oh! And the best one I brought just for you." Bustling to the wooden box at the foot of the bed, covered to protect a nest, she hoisted it next to him and lifted the lid. "Happy birth—"

He said words she'd never known to be curses until that moment, as he retreated across the vast bed.

Shocked, utterly stymied, she stared down into the disinterested eye of the young roosting rook with a broken wing in complete amazement. "You . . . you don't like it?" She knew it to be an obviously senseless question the moment it escaped on a quivering gasp, but astonishment had apparently stolen her wits.

"Like it?" he panted from several spans away. "Why the fuck would I—" Disgust had pilfered what little color resided in his cheeks, but once he looked into her swimming eyes, he clamped his jaw against whatever else he'd been about to say.

A hot tear slid down her cheek. She wished she could drown herself in it, somehow, so powerful was her mortification.

His panic seemed to intensify as he held out a hand. "Don't . . . don't cry."

"I'm *not*." She sucked in a shaky gasp, petrified into place by indecision and self-contempt as her breaths turned into hiccups.

"Please." He groaned. "I—can't bear it if you—" Decisive determination hardened his features, and he only spared the nest three sideways glances of unease as he inched back toward her.

"I—gave you a birthday—and—and then I—*ruined* it!" she sobbed.

"Lorelai." Big hands dragged her off her feet and onto the bed, until she was cradled against his chest. A warm body with not one soft place to be found, folded around her like a shelter from the storm of her sorrow.

She collapsed into his strength, abandoning her own. Never had she been held like this. Never had anyone taken the burden of her weight, nor the weight of her pain, and acted as a bulwark against it. If only she could stop crying long enough to marvel at the miracle.

Callused fingers snagged at her cheeks as tears disappeared the moment they fell.

"Lorelai. *Please.* Do not weep. I'm sorry." The desperation in his voice quelled her sadness, enough to give her the strength to fight the next wave of sobs. His breath was a sweet-scented breeze across her face as he pulled her closer. His voice broke often with uncharacteristic youth as he scrambled to explain. "When I woke in that grave . . . Ravens . . . they were *picking* at the bodies of the dead. Tearing things off them. Out of them. You understand? One came after me . . ."

Holy *God*. Lorelai hid her face against his chest as a fresh wave of tears crashed against her. She'd gifted him a nightmare. How could she be so thoughtless?

"Lorelai." The backs of his knuckles lifted her chin, forcing her to look at him. "Sweetest Lorelai." It was as though he could not stop saying her name. His own eyes melted. Misted. His rigid features impossibly tender. "I know you. You had a reason, didn't you? For bringing me this . . ." His dimpled chin gestured to the crate teetering dangerously next to them.

"It's *so* inane."

"Tell me," he soothed, his fingers brushing at damp curls trying to stick to the tears on her cheeks.

Snuffling her embarrassment, she peered over to the crate. "I thought the raven's feathers look like your eyes. Black upon first glance, but when you inspect them more closely, there are a great many colors, indeed." She leaned up a little. Not enough to leave his embrace, but to show him what she meant. "Sort of—sort of iridescent, aren't they? Extraordinary, really. Every time I looked at him, I thought of you. I thought—they were lovely."

She stared at the raven, currently running his long beak across the back of his feathers with improbable bends of his neck, impervious to her outburst of emotion.

The silence stretched out for a moment too long before one arm released her, and reached for the box.

"I suppose . . . *this* one isn't so terrible." He stroked a feather with the very tip of a square finger, palpably suppressing a flinch when the bird noticed.

Both man and creature didn't move for endless silent moments.

Her every fiber attuned to his, Lorelai sensed him relax in unfurling increments, turning to warm muscle again instead of cold steel. She'd never been so comfortable. Never felt so safe.

"Good God, what's it doing?"

The bird had rested its beak atop his wrist, inspecting them both with tiny, rapid jerks of his head.

"I think he likes you," she ventured. Perhaps if she educated him about the birds, he'd understand them better. Perhaps he'd even forgive them for mistaking him for a corpse. He'd been in a grave, after all. They could hardly be blamed. "Ravens are really such clever birds. Someone once told me they have a rather intricate language, not just all cackles and caws. They like puzzles, and play." She brushed her hand over the bird's uninjured wing, enjoying the inky sheen illuminated by the candlelight. "They fall in love."

"How do you know?" His whisper caressed her ear, and she shivered.

"For their whole life, they have one mate. One other to whom, no matter where the wind takes them, they never fail to return. I always considered them rather beautiful, romantic birds . . . That is, of course, unless they're eating people."

She felt him smile against her hair.

"It's why I'm so anxious for Atilla to heal," she babbled on. "What if he has someone waiting for him? Someone he's desperate to return to? What if she's afraid he won't come for her?" The very idea fragmented her.

After a pensive moment he said, "You named him Atilla?"

"Oh yes." She brightened, "And the snake is Hannibal. The turtles over there are Genghis and Kublai. The foxes are Vlad the Impaler, Ivan the Terrible, and Catherine the Great—it was Alexander the Great at first, but then for obvious reasons I had to change the name, and naturally I found a supplemental 'Great.'"

"Naturally."

She allowed her head to rest against his shoulder, lulled

by the rhythm of his inhalations. She didn't allow herself to consider what would happen should she be caught in such a posture, in such proximity to a man in his state of undress. It seemed that through nursing him, a sense of intimacy and familiarity she'd not considered until now had bloomed between them.

She wanted him close. Craved it with a ferocity her young mind didn't understand. She wanted his skin next to hers. Reveled in the scent and sight and warmth of him.

For warmth wasn't something she experienced enough of.

Furthermore, no one much cared about her pets. She had to protect them from Mortimer just as attentively as she did from each other and the elements. Her father's apathy toward her beasts was legendary, to say the least. And though she suspected they were too kind to say so, she had the idea that the servants found them more of a nuisance than a pleasure.

"What did you name the weasel?" he queried.

"It's a ferret, and his name is Brutus. Oh, and the little rabbit over there is Napoleon Bonaparte. We . . . We ate Josephine, Lucien, and Pauline. Now he's all alone." She swallowed grief that should not be so fresh.

He cradled her gently, but she didn't miss that his hand curled into a fist.

"Such fierce names you've given them." She glowed because it sounded like he approved. "Do you have particularly violent turtles?"

Lorelai had the sense they were both wondering how he could remember all these historical figures when he could not recall his own past.

"I've given them epic legacies to live up to. To be fierce, to be a conqueror or a warrior, one must first recover one's strength. I feel it might help them get better. A name is important, you know. It has power. A turtle named after a great Kahn would just feel silly if he died without a fight."

"Let's give me a name," he suggested. "William after the Conqueror? Julius, after the Caesar. Or Antony? Not Octavian or Augustus, I'll not have it. David, maybe? The one who defeated Goliath. David sounds close to something . . ."

"Oh, I named you ages ago," she informed him merrily. The veins in his arm she'd been mentally tracing momentarily distracted her from remembering that she'd planned to keep that fact from him.

He stilled. "What . . . did you name me?"

"Ash."

He snorted. "Because I'm more cinder than flesh?"

"*Because* I found you under an ancient, enormous ash tree, obviously."

"Ash," he repeated. "Not exactly a king's name, nor a warrior's."

"It's better than all that," she rushed to explain, distressed by the disenchantment in his voice. "Our housekeeper, Maeve, says her family is descended from Druids. According to her, the Tree of Life is an ash tree, and it holds the whole of the earth and the sky together. It heals the sick, protects the innocent, and endows immortality to the worthy. So . . . as legacies go, I'd say I granted you a right whopper."

"That you did." The look he slanted down at her brimmed with something so tender, her throat ached in response. "Ash it is, then. Until I recover my family name."

"You could be Ash Weatherstoke," she offered, knowing it was terrible of her to hope he never belonged to any family but hers. "Father doesn't mind. He says it looks good to society when a genteel family takes in a poor relation. A distant cousin, perhaps?"

The tenderness evaporated, his lips pressing into a tight crease. "I don't like the idea of being a poor relation. Someone not good enough for . . ." He broke off, glancing away from her. "Not if I'm to someday . . ."

She certainly wished he'd finish those sentences. She'd never wished anything so mightily.

"I did not mean to offend you." *Again,* she amended silently. Lud, but it was a blessing animals couldn't understand her. Or she'd probably drive them all off with her constant meddling. "I suggested we make you part of the family. It was Father who came up with the poor-relation bit."

"I do not want anyone to mock me. To think me less . . ."

"No one would dare." Of this she was certain. A man with such strength and height, such unusual musculature, wouldn't be ready fodder for the jackanapes. "Besides, it's not so bad really."

At his look, she hurried to explain.

"The thing about being mocked or laughed at is . . . you forget to fear it after a while. It's just something that happens."

"By Mortimer, you mean?" He said the name as though it tasted of tar.

"Mortimer, yes. And just about everyone else."

"Because of . . . your ankle?"

She nodded, suddenly very shy.

His palm gently landed on her knee, gathering the ruffles in his hand until the hem of the sky-blue skirt revealed her white-stockinged feet.

Lorelai could only stand shoes for so long, and almost never wore them in the house.

They both gazed at her slim ankle, forever turned inward at a grotesque angle.

"Were you born with it like that?"

"It happened when I was six." The gentle curiosity in his voice prompted her to answer questions she'd always avoided.

"What happened?"

"My ankle was broken, like yours."

"Like mine?" he puzzled. "But . . . Dr. Holcomb said by the end of the year my ankle would be like it was before. I can almost walk on it now. Why not yours?"

Wounded with a familiar shame. Struck dumb with unrequited fury, she simply shrugged.

"Lorelai?" A dark suspicion turned her name into an accusation. "*How* was your ankle broken?"

"I'm not supposed to say." She pulled away from him, but the muscles of his arms bunched, tightening around her.

"Mortimer." His one harsh word contained all the knowledge she wasn't supposed to impart. All the darkness contained by a moonless night. All the wrath of the devil, himself.

"I broke his wooden sword with my boot . . ." She wished her voice were not so small. That she could summon the acceptance she'd counterfeited for more than half her life. "So, he broke my leg with his boot."

Ash became very still. Unnaturally so. Only his chest lifting with the increasing intakes of breath.

"Does it hurt?" he asked tightly after a long while.

"Sometimes," she admitted.

"What did the doctor say?"

"I never saw a doctor. Father didn't want anyone to know." Suddenly frightened, she pulled away from him to implore. "You won't say anything, will you? Won't let on that I told you."

She'd expected fury on his face. Darkness.

But his cool expression reminded her of the serene, mirrorlike fens on a windless day. Almost pleasant. His demeanor unyielding, determined, but eerily calm. "I won't say a word." He petted her curls solicitously, the specter of a smile toying with his rigid mouth. "But it won't happen again."

Struck by the odd note in his voice, she straightened. "What do you mean?"

Glancing down, he peered into the rook's crate with a new appreciation. "Tell me more about our friend, here," he cajoled, daring to smooth the feathers at the tame bird's throat.

"But Ash . . ."

"It's my birthday," he reminded her. "Let's not think on the past . . . or the future. I want to hear all about Attila the Rook, and your collection of conquerors."

Easily diverted by her passion for her animals, Lorelai launched into an animated retelling of the day she'd found Attila flapping in a terrible circle, his wing somehow caught beneath a rock.

She didn't notice that Ash only half listened. That he stared at her exposed ankle with glittering obsidian eyes.

He hid his murderous thoughts for hours as they played with fleet-footed, mischievous fox pups, and fed grapes to appreciative turtles that trundled around on the mattress in no great hurry.

She'd never guessed that Ash was certain, memory or no memory, that this was the best birthday he'd ever had, by far. That he understood she fixed broken creatures because no one cared enough to fix her.

And yet, despite her impediment, she had built a life of enchantment.

A life Ash knew would be vastly improved if it had one less brother in it.

CHAPTER FOUR

The perfect opportunity to rid the world of Mortimer Weatherstoke presented itself several weeks later.

"Are you *certain* I can't accompany you into Heybridge today?" Lorelai asked, her azure eyes brimming with hope.

Ash looked at his feet, concentrating mightily on picking his way back through the verdant marshes toward Southbourne Grove. In truth, he simply hadn't the constitution to meet the hope, and subsequent disappointment, in Lorelai's expression.

He ran his hands over a clump of tall grasses, snatching at one and using it as an idle switch against an occasional cloud of gnats. "The trip will be dull as dishwater," he lied. "Sir Robert has secured me an apprenticeship, and I'll retrieve a suit at the tailor just in time to meet with dry old men all day. You'd be unspeakably bored."

As much as Ash despised denying her anything, he couldn't allow her to be privy to his nefarious intentions.

"I'm never bored when I'm with you," she said earnestly, threading her slim fingers through his, and grasping his bicep with her other hand. They often walked like this, her grip letting him support some of her weight. "And I should very much like to see you in a suit, I think."

His fingers engulfed her hand, perfectly cradled in the grooves between her knuckles. He did his best not to cling to her as an emotion shimmered through him, one he was beginning to identify.

One he fiercely hoped she'd one day return.

He hated the idea of wearing a suit less than he had before, if the sight of him in it would please her. Since he'd risen from his sickbed, his wardrobe had consisted of Mortimer's cast-off white shirtsleeves, some ready-made trousers, and dusty old vests. Not that he minded. Clothes were simply a means by which to cover his scars.

Ash found it a chore to match his long stride to her stilted one, even as the mud gave way to the vast grounds of the manor home, but he'd rather crawl on his hands and knees than cause her discomfiture over her impediment. How she made this trek through the treacherous marshes alone so often, he'd never know.

For a few months now, he'd become her official packhorse, carting crates and animals back and forth to the estuary. The journey had been difficult on his ankle, at first, but surging across soggy, unsteady ground seemed to strengthen him quickly. Besides, Lorelai knew all the paths through the wetlands, showing him just where to step to avoid a bog or a hidden pond beneath the cover of reeds.

This was her sanctuary, belonging as much to her as it did the wildlife here.

At dawn, they'd made the journey to free Hannibal the snake back into the reeds, his missing tail having healed over to a round nub sufficient for slithering about.

Lorelai had barely shed any tears this time, but they'd

stood for a silent while, watching the impossibly green fens dappled by ponds give way to the sea. The water stretched out until the curve of the earth met the low-hanging clouds on the horizon. Clouds that seemed to be crawling over each other in a race to reach the shore.

Now they had to hurry back to Southbourne in time for him to disembark.

"It's not fair that Mortimer can accompany you, but *I* cannot," she complained.

"Mortimer is your father's representative to the foundry owners." Ash lifted a nonchalant shoulder, as though he accepted that to be the way of things.

"Father is so old-fashioned, don't you think? Refusing to be seen with the working class is antiquated at best. He's only an earl, after all, and became one because his ancestors were industrious men, too rich for the crown to ignore." She rested her head against his arm as they walked along. "The older he gets, the more it seems he makes excuses not to leave the house. Especially since Mortimer hit him."

"Let's not speak of your brother just now." Ash squeezed her hand. That would all be taken care of soon. "It was kind of your father to secure me a position. He seemed to think that in a few years' time I could help Mr. Thatcher run the foundry or Mr. Robbins run the salt mines . . . There's a chance for me to make a good fortune there." He blithely changed the subject, and noted the moment she took the bait.

"Father knows how clever you are. And if you are to be a Weatherstoke, then it's important to him that you're respected in the community."

It was important to Ash, too. If he rid them of Mortimer's grip of terror, and spent the next few years working his way up the foundry ranks, perhaps he could save enough to approach Lorelai's father with a proposal . . .

Lorelai turned his arm so his palm faced up, idly tracing the strange lines branching from one of the tattooed dragon wings on his forearm. Often when they went to the fens, he rolled his shirtsleeves to the elbow, encouraging her perpetual fondness for tracing his tattoo.

Her touch was a balm he'd never be able to quantify. All he knew was that her fingers were magic, and they quieted everything within him that threatened to become monstrous.

"What a mystery you are," she murmured, not stopping her physical discovery when the scars interrupted the dragon with webs and welts of damaged flesh. Instead, she ran the pads of her fingertips gently over them in rhythmic, soothing gestures.

The sensation of her fingertips was different where the lye had burned him. Much like being stroked by a ghost, or a memory. Not quite as physically tangible, but just as powerful.

Perhaps more so.

"I know we don't often speak of it, but do you ever wonder what meaning this dragon had for you?"

"A bit," he answered cryptically. The only ideas he could come up with were not palatable. An army regiment? A gang, perhaps, or a guild of thieves or criminals. The missing words perplexed him the most. Above the dragon, the letters *R-A-E,* and below the dragon *U-A-E* finished words mostly eaten away by the lye.

Attempting to make sense of it threatened to drive him mad, and so, like everything else, he left the tattoo in the past, where it belonged.

"Don't you wonder what sort of work you did before . . . Before I found you, I mean?"

"Often," he answered, though he honestly spent more time pondering what enemy might have beaten him to death than what he'd done for wages.

"You might have worked underground," she posited. "You're too pale to have seen much sun, but your . . . physique suggests a great deal of physical labor."

"Does that offend you?"

"Decidedly not. You're perfect." She pressed her hand to peach-tinged cheeks, hiding a shy smile. "I mean—I think your strength helped to see you through your ordeal. And for that, I am most grateful."

He allowed her compliment to warm him, but didn't dare comment on it. "As am I. For a moment there, I feared that I'd *never* rise from that bed."

"As I always say, a lot can happen between now and never."

"Indeed." He counted on it.

A briny mist crept in from the bay just as they found their way back onto the expansive lawns at Southbourne Grove. It impeded their view of the stately white columns of the manor.

Unexpectedly, Lorelai stopped, tugging him around until he faced her. A troubled wrinkle creased her sun-kissed brow, and rather than smooth it away, as Ash yearned to do, he tucked a few wisps of curls behind her ear. The unruly tendrils sprang right back to frame her temple.

"Ash, what if you don't like it at the foundry or in the mines? Do you think you'll—go, now that you're able?"

"Go?" He puzzled. "Where would I go?"

"If you can walk, that means you can run. And if you

can do that . . . then . . . then you can leave whenever you like. Escape Mortimer."

"I run from no one." Least of all Mortimer Weatherstoke. "My home is here." *With you*, he added silently.

She rushed on, as though she hadn't heard the ardent finality of his words. "Suppose you want to look for your past? For your family?"

"I don't know. I have a feeling there's nothing in my past worth finding. Perhaps I'd only uncover a reason for you to not . . ." He swallowed, unable to lend voice to a fear that had been eating at him for a while now.

"To not what?" She stepped into the circle of his arms, running her hands across the muscles of his back and resting her cheek against his chest.

Ash had become accustomed to her abrupt gestures of affection. As innocent as they were socially inappropriate, he'd come to crave them. In fact, hers was the only touch that didn't repel him.

"To not hold me . . . in your esteem, that is." He enfolded her in the shelter of his arms, resting his chin on her crown. "I have the distinct feeling that whoever I might have been, was not anyone worth knowing."

"You are worth knowing *now*. You're worth everything."

Ash did his best not to crush her to him. To keep his hold gentle, reverent. This could be heaven, this place in the mist. Clouds were tossed about them in playful swirls by errant winds. Perhaps time did not exist in this enchanted moment. Nor did any of the thousand reasons he *should not* love her. But he did.

He loved her enough to kill for her.

"I'll miss you." She blinked up at him, her eyes azure orbs of affection. Her pretty lips pursed in a pensive frown.

His every muscle seemed to melt against her, their embrace warming from innocent to . . . something else.

"Lorelai. Have you ever been kissed?"

Her expression slid from pensive to perplexed. "No. Have you?"

". . . I don't know." He didn't care to know.

She winced. "Of course. Of course you don't know. What a stupid question. I'm incessantly ridiculous—"

He banished her tirade with the pressure of his lips against hers.

His mouth lingered rather than demanded. Brushed and tasted. Savored. He dared not use his tongue, or his teeth, or any other part of him that hungered for her.

He held in his arms the girl he loved. And thus was the cause for his caution.

Lorelai was just that.

A girl.

He was no longer a boy. The feelings he had, the desires. The hunger. The heat. They belonged to a man, a man who would slake them with a *woman*.

Not a girl.

She clutched at him, her artless sigh giving him breath. Her response both shy and lush. The promise of something more.

This could not be that. This was only a kiss of creation. A promise of something blooming between them. The overture to a symphony of longing he'd compose over time.

I love you. The confession danced behind his lips, and so they remained pressed to hers. This he could not say, not until his evil deed was done. Not until her grief for her brother, such as it was, had finally passed.

Ash would be a good man for her. After this one sin, he'd spend the rest of his life in repentant worship of her. She'd be his savior. His goddess. His life.

And if hell awaited him after death for what he was about to do . . .

So be it. He'd have lived a lifetime in the heaven of her love.

The earth beneath them trembled with approaching hoofbeats, driving them apart.

She held unsteady fingers to her parted lips, staring at him with eyes brightened by revelations and the whisper of something less angelic than usual.

More carnal.

I love you. The words would not leave his mind, nor his mouth.

Suddenly her expression shifted, an inexplicable anxiety concealing the innocent awe. "Don't go," she whispered.

"I must," he panted, struggling to regain control of his breath.

"But you'll come back, won't you?"

"I told you I would." Impassioned, he clutched at her arm. "Lorelai. There are only two indisputable facts in this world: One, that the sun will set in the west. And two, that I'll come for you. Always."

"I just have this feeling—"

Mortimer broke through the mists, nearly knocking them both over on his steed before he reined to a stop. Clenched in his fists were the reins of the nag upon which Ash would ride to Heybridge.

Apparently pleased to ruin their moment, Mortimer sneered at his sister. "You'll be releasing two pets today, Duck."

"You'll both be back tomorrow," she said, as though comforting herself.

"Let's get a move on," Mortimer urged. "I'd hate to miss *this* appointment."

Ash caught the reins Mortimer hurled at him, enjoying the displeasure his reflexes caused the man who seemed to suck the air out of any space he occupied, even here in the open, replacing it with derision and dread.

Not anymore. Not after today.

Reluctantly, Ash released her arm and mounted, his mind set to his task with grim determination.

"Take care," Lorelai called. "Be safe."

When Ash looked back at her, she pressed a kiss to her fingertips and released it into the breeze toward him.

"I'll come back," he reassured her.

I love you.

Had he known it might be the last time he'd see her, he would have said the words.

CHAPTER FIVE

Twenty Years Later

If Lorelai had thought to have pockets sewn into her wedding dress, she'd have weighted them with stones and let the Black Water River wash her corpse out to sea.

She gazed out her bedroom window feeling a growing kinship with the river. The disappearing sun turned the glassy, still waters a bittersweet coral. How tranquil it seemed. How serene. And yet, she understood the churning currents beneath. The murky, treacherous depths which swept many an unwilling soul into the Channel.

Take me, she begged. Anything to escape today.

All those people. All those eyes on her, the shy spinster cripple of Southbourne Grove, limping down the aisle to wed an old man with the face of a warthog, and a disposition to match.

An old man who'd come up in the world, desperate to solidify his place in society with a noble marriage to an ancient, titled family. Desperate enough to wed someone on the wrong side of thirty with a serious physical hindrance.

Everyone in the county had quickly sent their RSVP and, it seemed, more people would attend the wedding than could fit in their modest vicarage. Not because they cared, or wished her well, but because they hoped for a spectacle.

They would come because Mortimer's penchant for ruining parties bordered on the legendary. He'd gambled away both his home and his sister to a wealthy machinist whose parents had been pig farmers. What else could possibly go wrong?

Plenty. She cringed.

Their father had hoped age would calm Mortimer's cruel spirit. But the years only served to amplify it.

For Sir Robert, death had been a mercy.

Lorelai might have done something desperate long ago, were it not for the woman kneeling behind her, pins in her mouth, taking in the seams of her wedding dress at the last possible moment.

"You've lost an alarming amount of weight, dear," Veronica Weatherstoke, her sister-in-law, said, clucking her tongue sympathetically. "I believe I heard Mr. Gooch mention a certain aversion to slight-framed women."

"So he did." Their eyes met in silent commiseration until the delicate bones of Veronica's lovely features were blurred by offending moisture.

Lord, she hadn't cried since . . . Well, for decades. "Do you know what the worst of it is?"

"What's that, darling?"

"I'm going to be Mrs. Sylvester Gooch. *Gooch!*" she wailed, right before a hysterical bubble of laughter burst from her chest. How strange that her despair could be so hilarious. That a giggle could make a substitution for a sob. "As if my life couldn't get more pathetic and pitiful."

Veronica's cheeks dimpled with the suggestion of a smile, though a desolate sadness likewise lurked in the emerald of her eyes. "I imagine, were Mr. Gooch a kind man, the surname wouldn't matter *so* much."

"I should say not," Lorelai agreed.

Tamerlane, Lorelai's one-eared black cat, brushed against her skirts. Heedless of his tendency to leave tufts of long hair against just about any fabric, she picked him up to stroke his neck.

"When Mortimer came to court me . . . I thought the Countess Southbourne the handsomest-sounding title one could desire," Veronica recalled. "And now . . ."

Now Veronica Weatherstoke, her brother's young bride, once thought the loveliest woman in the county, had the solemn, wary eyes of a war refugee.

Lorelai took her dear sister's hand, and they clung to each other for a while. "Perhaps if Mr. Gooch is pleased with me, he'll allow you and Mortimer back to Southbourne Grove after a time."

"I shall miss you." Veronica's own tears brightened her gaze from emerald to jade. She pressed her gloves to her eyelids, not allowing the tears to fall. Lorelai suspected she didn't want smudges in the powder she applied to hide the still-healing bruise on her cheek.

Veronica's wealth of carefully arranged dark curls danced in the sunlight streaming in through the tall windows of her chamber. The grand manse had been her home for four years, and now she'd be forced to leave it, penniless and ashamed.

"Southend-On-Sea is not so very far away, and since our husbands' business interests are now aligned, I'm certain we shall see much of each other." Lorelai ascertained instantly her attempt at cheering the younger woman was an utter failure.

"Mortimer made it clear that I cannot visit until I conceive an heir." Veronica put a hand to her empty womb.

"Mortimer can suck rotten eggs," Lorelai spat, causing Tamerlane to change his mind about being held, and leap out of her arms, his tail held high with distaste.

Veronica *had* conceived a child and had lost it because of Mortimer's heavy fists less than a year ago.

Still pale with grief, Veronica never dared smile, but her porcelain cheek dimpled on the rare occasion she was pleased. "At least you'll get to stay with your animals. The estuary can remain your sanctuary."

"I only hope my new husband allows me to keep all of them."

"Do your best to give him a son," Veronica advised. "Perhaps an heir will entice him toward indulgence."

The thought of lying beneath her corpulent fiancé, who smelled of machine engines and bacon grease, was enough to incite a fit of vapors. Allowing him to touch her. *There.* To put his troutlike lips on her. A shudder oozed down her spine, fanning spikes of revulsion to lift goosepimples on her skin.

"Lorelai," Veronica ventured cautiously. "Have you ever . . . that is . . . has anyone ever discussed . . . your wedding night with you? What to expect? What to do?"

As much as she adored Veronica, Lorelai very much did not desire to have a woman eight years her junior explain marital relations to her. As if today could be any more demeaning.

"I've not doctored so many creatures for so long without obtaining a basic understanding of mammalian mating habits." Lorelai did her best to keep her mortification from coloring her voice. "I don't suppose a man of Mr. Gooch's age and . . . dimensions can manage such a physical undertaking well or often. It shan't last long, I'm sure."

Veronica turned away, but not quickly enough to hide her disconsolate expression. "If you're lucky, it won't. But surely you've more experience than the observation of beasts."

"I *have* been kissed," she huffed. *Once*.

"And was it a pleasant kiss?"

"It was like a dream. But better." *Twenty years.* Twenty years and she could still taste his warmth. Could still conjure the fullness of his lower lip, the intensity beneath his restraint. The sweeps and drags of his smooth mouth against hers. The utter, heartbreaking need.

He'd been a dark creature with fathomless eyes. A specter of some other time. Some other fantasy. A loss too devastating to be evoked.

Especially today.

Ash.

That hope had died a thousand painful deaths. And she'd cried enough tears to overflow the marshes before she'd accepted the soul-crushing truth.

He'd remembered who he was. And whatever he'd left in his past had been enough to make him forget the promise he'd made to her.

There are only two indisputable facts in this world. One, that the sun will set in the west. And two, that I'll come for you. Always.

"I'm glad you've had one pleasant kiss," Veronica was saying. "Perhaps you can remember it tonight whilst . . . you know. Also, there are . . . things you can do . . . to help hurry along—"

"Lady Southbourne, Lady Lorelai, the carriage is come to fetch you to the church."

Steeling herself, Lorelai turned to the footman. "Thank you—er—" *Strange.* She didn't at all recognize him, and she considered herself familiar with everyone employed at Southbourne Grove. Had Mr. Gooch already begun installing his own staff? The nerve of the man, really! And who was this footman, anyhow, who could step so lightly they'd not mark his entrance? "I'm sorry, remind me of your name."

"Moncrieff, my lady." He glanced from Veronica to her, and back to Veronica again.

Not someone Mortimer would hire, certainly. Her brother wasn't fond of men taller or more handsome than he. With hair rich and lambent as brandy tied into a queue, Moncrieff possessed the depraved sort of good looks one would attribute to a libertine like Casanova or Byron rather than your workaday footman.

"Thank you, Moncrieff, we'll be down presently." Lorelai dismissed him.

He executed a flawless bow, turned on his heel, and marched out.

"Moncrieff." Veronica blinked rapidly, as one might after glancing directly at the sun. "I'm sure I would have— that I've never—is he new?"

"Apparently." Taking one last glance at herself, Lorelai decided she looked perfect for a second-rate wedding day. Her dress, a simple gold affair, set off the sun-stained metallic highlights in her hair. Her maid had arranged it into an intricate coiffure of braids, leaving long darker curls to tumble down her back. Generally, her round cheeks and high color hid her age, but Veronica was right, her recent weight loss painted every one of her thirty-and-four years onto her terse features. She appeared as limp and listless as she felt.

"You look like a goddess." Veronica affixed the Southbourne sapphire tiara to her hair, arranging the attached veil with deft puffs and pulls.

"I look like a gibbon," Lorelai groused.

Usually, a maid or seamstress would make any last-minute adjustments to the clothing, but Veronica had both a talent and zeal for fashion.

"Do you want your cane?"

Lorelai shook her head. "Not today." With her luck, she'd rest her cane on her dress and rip it on the way down the aisle, or something equally mortifying.

They hurried—as fast as Lorelai hurried anywhere—to the carriage.

Mortimer had decided Veronica was all she required in the way of bridesmaids. The countess wrestled with the dress while Moncrieff was kind enough to lift the veil off Southbourne Grove's circular drive.

The carriage must have belonged to Mr. Gooch, as it was larger and grander than any Mortimer owned by at least half.

Clouds hung over the bay, inching toward the mouth of the Black Water River, pregnant with the promise of rain. A few ships moored in the distance bobbed in the choppy waves. Sloops, sailboats, and a rather large, dark ship with curiously few masts. A steam-belching stranger to these familiar shores. Though, she supposed, Maldon and Heybridge attracted more and more industrial commerce these days and, unfortunately, men like her husband-to-be.

Her ankle ached in weather like this, and she favored it as she made her way down the steps to the coach. A tall, ebony-clad coachman, with a collar turned up to ward off the increasing wind, held a team of four restless black steeds in check.

An appropriate color, in Lorelai's assessment, as it felt as though she were being conducted to her own funeral, rather than her wedding.

Tucked into the carriage with Veronica, Lorelai fought a suffocating sense of surrealistic dread the entire way.

Every moment this day progressed promised to be more horrifying than the last.

It would begin with a promenade down a long aisle, conducted by a brother who would think nothing of tripping her if only for the sake of his sick amusement. At the end of such a potentially disastrous walk stood a fiancé she'd only met but once, on the day he'd won her and Southbourne Grove in a poker game, and come to inspect his prize like one would a brood mare.

He seemed more impressed with the estate than his bride.

Sylvester Gooch. A beady-eyed, sour-faced glutton with prominent jowls who seemed to snore even when awake.

The soiree after the wedding would be nothing less than a chore, accepting disingenuous felicitations, watching others dance when she could not, and doing her best not to obsessively dread what came next.

The wedding night. God, how was she going to endure it?

She must. Or she and Veronica—to say nothing of Mortimer—would be out on the street. The ancient Weatherstoke name ruined beyond repair.

And worse, her animals would be without a home, and the meager staff she'd hired to keep them, unemployed.

Too many souls, both human and otherwise, depended on her for their survival.

And, once again, Mortimer had crippled her—hobbled her, more like—forcing her to suffer for his own heinous iniquities.

Devil take him, she railed to the incoming clouds. *Take him back to hell where he belongs.*

As though to answer her invocation, a burst of sudden thunder broke over the mouth of the river, gathering a parliament of angry clouds to the east.

"Frightful weather," Veronica mumbled, fussing with

the peacock feather in her lovely headdress. "I hope the footman and coachmen don't catch a chill should they become drenched."

"Perhaps we should order them to keep going right past the chapel," Lorelai suggested wryly. "Challenge them to outrun the storm."

"Tempting," Veronica sighed.

The coach trundled to a stop, fascinating a parcel of latecomers still filing into the church.

Lorelai held her breath as Mortimer forced his way through a small crowd rudely gathered at the open doors of the gray stone cathedral, his mottled skin matching the wine velvet of his vest.

"He doesn't look pleased," Veronica fretted, a sheen of sweat gathering on her brow despite the plummeting temperatures.

Lorelai forced herself not to remark upon the colossal proportion of her sister-in-law's understatement as the Earl of Southbourne stalked toward her. His hair had thinned, and his waist had thickened over the years, but he was still the same bulky, manipulative sadist she'd been raised to fear.

If she disembarked the carriage by the time he reached them, the people milling about would take note of their arrival, and an audience would at least decrease the likeliness of an unpleasant interaction of a physical nature.

Apparently, Veronica had been of the same mind, as she leaped for the latch before Moncrieff had even appeared from his perch to help them down.

Ungainly teal skirts barely seemed to hinder Veronica at all, as she daintily hopped down without the use of the steps, and turned to assist Lorelai. "Quickly, now," she urged.

Lorelai gathered up the length of her veil in a billowing

ivory armful, and reached out to take Veronica's hand. Her landing was decidedly less graceful, and the gathering wind threatened to rip her veil from her grasp.

The ground beneath her slippers seemed to tremble as the driver's heavy boots landed beside her.

Startled, both ladies gaped at his broad back as he advanced. The wind whipped his black leather coat around his long legs as he strolled toward the cathedral as blithely as an invited guest.

Just what did he think he was doing?

Mortimer jabbed an accusatory finger at her, condemnation seething from him like an inquisitor to a witch. "Did you do something to scare him off?"

Lorelai flinched. "W-what?"

"God, you're as bloody useless as a lame mare! Your fiancé," he thundered. "You couldn't even entice that tub of guts to show up to his own wedding, you—"

"It's my fault Mr. Gooch isn't here, I'm afraid," the coachman said casually.

With one nimble motion, he reached into his coat, produced a long, bejeweled dagger, and shoved it beneath Mortimer's chin.

He didn't stop pushing until the point embedded in Mortimer's brain.

Lorelai watched her brother die horribly. Slowly.

And quietly.

His hateful tongue skewered through right on the yard of the cathedral as his knees buckled and he fell to the earth.

A strangled sound emanated from Veronica, and she and Lorelai clutched at each other, shrinking back toward the carriage.

There must have been a commotion. A ripple of awareness as the attendees inside became cognizant of the turmoil out on the grounds. Sobs. Screams.

Lorelai marked none of it.

A weighty fatigue settled upon her and black spots danced in her periphery. The world swayed. Or did she? *No. Not now.* She couldn't faint. She couldn't leave poor Veronica alone to face whatever came next.

Because the coachman turned to address them both. He removed the cowl that had hidden his features and turned down his collar.

A black cloud of horror smothered her. Black, like his eyes. Like his hair. Like the grief that had swallowed her when he hadn't returned all those years ago.

Like the churning storm that framed him now, summoned by whatever ancient, malevolent God had unleashed him upon this earth.

She couldn't say his name. Because this devil before her surely was not Ash. He was taller. Wider. Darker in *every* way possible.

He'd just . . . *murdered* her brother. Without sentiment, explanation, or ceremony of any kind.

And now he simply regarded her with the same sort of triumphant expectation one would after a particularly well played bout of croquet.

"Captain." Moncrieff blocked her from flinging herself at him, whether to assault him or embrace him, she hadn't yet decided. "I do believe it's time we quit this affair."

"I do believe you're right."

He stalked back toward the carriage in long, primal strides. *His carriage*, Lorelai realized numbly.

For that's what she was. Numb. She couldn't feel her feet beneath her or her hands at the ends of her wrists. Not until he moved closer.

Lightning forked across a once-calm sky, but that wasn't what lifted every hair on her body.

It was the way he moved. Upright, like a man, but with the feral tread of an animal. Every motion maintained by absolute control and primal intent.

No pleasure brightened the pitiless voids of his eyes. No tender hunger. Nor bitter wrath. Not even a murderous fury to warrant such an act of violence.

And yet there had been no true violence in the deed.

Just a smooth, unhurried pressure. Utter, lethal precision . . . and a man's life ended. It had been as if he'd performed the act a thousand times. A million, maybe.

This couldn't be. Lorelai's mind hurried to reject the specter of a beloved ghost thought long dead.

Thrusting a hyperventilating Veronica behind her, she did what she could to stumble out of his way.

If only she could run. But, she realized, even an able-bodied person wouldn't easily evade such a man.

She'd thought him tall, but had been mistaken.

He'd been tall twenty years ago. Now, he was tremendous.

"Get in the carriage." The wind stole notes of his low, cool command, but Lorelai read every word on his lips.

Veronica scrambled inside.

A thousand, *thousand* refusals, questions, and emotions swirled in a maelstrom of hysteria inside of her head.

What escaped was, "Why?" The word was both all-encompassing, and completely insubstantial, but her rapidly closing throat couldn't force out one more word.

"I came for you," he answered dispassionately.

"*Why?*" she gasped again, hoping she could hear his answer over the hammering of her heart.

Coffee-dark eyes speared her with an arctic indifference she'd not known existed until this moment. "Does the sun still set in the west?"

The question stole her ability to breathe. She'd been hoping that despite the brutal features, despite the blue-black of his hair, and the unmistakable scars, she'd still been gaping at an interloper.

Mutely, she nodded.

"Then get in the carriage, Lorelai."

Something about his order broke the stricken chains of traumatic astonishment. "The sun has set in the west every day for twenty years." The words tumbled out before she could think better of it. Before she could call them back.

If she'd thought his eyes black before, she'd been wrong. They'd been dark, surely, but now they were little more than desolate, abysmal mirrors in which she could divine her own dire fate.

"You do not want me to *put* you into the carriage," he informed her pleasantly. "I still have your brother's blood on my hands."

Was he threatening her? Or showing her an unimaginably macabre form of courtesy?

He held out his gloves, demonstrating that he was in no way being figurative.

Swallowing the acid crawling up her throat, Lorelai complied, allowing Veronica's clutching hands to pull her in.

Lorelai had expected him to lock them in and mount the driver's seat in order to race away from the growing pandemonium.

Instead, he climbed in behind her, settling his bulk across from them.

"Who—who are you?" Veronica whimpered. "What do you want?"

He leaned forward, dark and sinister as death himself, and bowed his head in a strangely cultured mockery of tradition. "Allow me to properly present myself, Lady Southbourne. In the Orient, they call me the Black Dragon. In Africa, I am known as the Sea Panther. A warlord along the Persian coast once granted me the title the Djinn of Darkness. I have many names, and even more titles, but first I am captain of the *Devil's Dirge,* more commonly known in this part of the world simply as . . . the Rook."

CHAPTER SIX

"They'll come looking for us, won't they?" Veronica reasoned as she and Lorelai clutched at each other in the captain's quarters of the selfsame dark steamship she'd admired not an hour prior. "I mean, we *were* abducted from your wedding after he stabbed . . . after Mortimer . . ." She swallowed as a visible shudder ran through her. "Several people witnessed the murder and would have contacted the authorities by now. Probably the whole British Navy is after us. The Rook has been a quarry of theirs for ages. They'll rescue us and hang him for a pirate. And we can go home."

Lorelai knew Veronica meant well. She did nothing without the best of intentions, but the desperate words tripping on Veronica's shallow breaths did more to keep herself calm than anything.

"They'll be looking for us, but I don't think anyone can identify our captor by sight," Lorelai said gravely. "He wore that cowl and large coat, if you remember, and no one has had much of a chance to recognize him. He's not known to leave witnesses . . . alive."

"He seemed to know *you*." Veronica narrowed a questioning glance in her direction.

"Yes," Lorelai murmured through lips blanched entirely numb. "But he wasn't the Rook when I knew him." *When I loved him* . . . she finished silently.

Veronica's mind tended to work quickly, especially in times of crisis. During her tenure as the Countess Southbourne, she'd learned to deftly manage danger, as well as establish and implement evasion and problem-solving techniques learned through painstaking trial and error.

Lorelai fancied she could see the gears of her sister-in-law's mind whirring like a timepiece wound too tightly. Veronica had yet to cease trembling, though she hadn't shed a tear for her dead husband.

And why should she?

The ship lurched, chugged, and shuddered with a fantastic effort as they gathered strength and speed. Crystal tinkled from the shades of several hanging electric lamps, and exotic tassels swayed from the canopy of the monstrous bed upon which they huddled. A book slid off the table by the widest porthole, startling them both.

The ship had only two masts, and they'd not been unfurled when they'd boarded. But even a steamship was rarely so nimble as this one.

"You can swim, can't you?" Veronica asked. "If we hurry, we might be able to fit through these windows before they come back. Without the weight of our skirts, there's a chance we could make it to the estuary in time." Standing, she used the furniture to steady herself as she stumbled for the surprisingly wide window.

"We're too far out. We'd never make it, especially not

in a storm like this." Lorelai's arms itched where rain still dried on her skin. Her torn, soiled gloves had disappeared, though she couldn't remember where she'd discarded them now. Funny, that she'd worry about such trifles at a time like this. She'd rather think of anything, she supposed, than the dangerous pirate who'd come for her. Distantly, she wondered if this was all a dream. A nightmare caused by extreme prewedding anxiety. Would she wake back at Southbourne and be forced to relive the tedium and terror of her wedding day all over again?

This time, without murder.

Without Ash.

If he'd come for her . . . did she want to wake?

She dug her nails against her palm, wincing when the pain lanced her. No, she was fully conscious.

But unconvinced that the man who'd kidnapped her was the boy she'd loved.

Veronica grappled with the porthole latch. "I think I'd rather drown than endure what awaits us on this pirate ship." Hysteria edged out the reason in her voice. "How can you be so calm?"

Calm? Is that what she was? *Calm.* She supposed her inability to move must seem tranquil, but in truth Lorelai attributed her behavior to terrified paralysis more than anything.

Shock. Astonishment. Distress. Any similar word she summoned to describe her current state seemed woefully inadequate to the task. Traumatized, perhaps?

Ash? The Rook? *How?*

Reality had just collided with a nightmare, and she and Veronica were the reluctant debris left in the aftermath.

"Dash it, Lorelai, *help* me open this!" Veronica cried. "We've heard the stories of the Rook, read the news articles. You *witnessed* what that man did to Mortimer. The

Rook has a crew of men with rocks for hearts and *he's* the deadliest of the lot."

"Which is why it would behoove you both to behave." The air in the room cooled several degrees, and even the storm shadows deepened as the Rook ducked into the cabin. It was as though he brought the darkness with him. He wore it about his wide shoulders like a regal mantle tailored for the devil, himself.

Suddenly very aware that she sat upon his bed, Lorelai stood, her hand searching for Veronica, who instantly returned to her side. She wasn't sure why, but it seemed easier to address the most infamous and lethal pirate in centuries—one who wore the features of her first love—whilst clinging to her only friend in the world.

His cool, detached manner stung more than it should as he assessed her with distressing thoroughness.

Veronica probably assumed she tightened her grip out of a similar terror, but in reality, she did it to stay the impulse to smooth her bedraggled hair or fiddle with the veil that hung damp and limp from her crown.

She probably looked a fright, drenched and pale and wind-tossed.

Why should that matter? she admonished herself.

Because those eyes, those dark, empty eyes had once looked at her as though she were the most rare and beautiful treasure on this earth.

And now . . . now . . . nothing.

As the ship left the bay, the sea became as tumultuous as her own emotions, making it extra difficult to keep her feet beneath her.

The Rook advanced upon her with the unhurried but absolute concentration of a shark drawn to blood. He emoted no appetite, no aggression, no anticipation.

But he *was* hungry. Lorelai didn't understand how she

knew it. She just did. Like the conditioned responses of any prey animal, she sensed his need with the tiny hairs prickling on the back of her neck. Or by the twitches and shivers of ever-ready muscles, urging her to run.

She hadn't run in more than twenty-five years. Not that there was any hope for escape on a pirate ship.

Black trousers pulled tight against his thighs as he progressed, molding to legs much longer and thicker than she remembered. Brilliant, colorful, unidentifiable shapes of innumerable tattoos pressed against the white of his shirt as muscles he'd not yet built in his youth shifted when he reached for her.

As a boy, his body hinted at strength, now he rippled with it. He might have once been dangerous, now . . . danger seemed too mild a word. The peril she sensed in his presence defied description.

"How fortuitous that you're already wearing a wedding dress," he said without inflection.

Lorelai shrank away from him, but of course he didn't allow it as he firmly disentangled her from Veronica's clutching hands.

"Don't you touch her," Veronica cried.

"Do keep in mind, Lady Southbourne, the last person who presumed to command me now rests at the bottom of the ocean," he replied. "And I say rest, because, in the end, his death was a mercy."

Veronica paled, and for a moment, Lorelai thought she might swoon.

"There's no need to threaten Lady Southbourne." She kept her voice even, unchallenging, a tone she'd adopted and perfected during thirty years living with a volatile man. "I won't make any trouble. You know that. Just tell us what you're after."

The stare he leveled at her hinted at displeasure, but

Lorelai had the sense an incalculable fury seethed beneath the air of indifference. "Do not speak to me as you spoke to your brother, Lorelai. I am not a man to be handled."

"I wasn't trying to—"

Dark brows lowered in calculating evaluation, his stubborn jaw tilting slightly to one side in an achingly familiar gesture. "Do not lie to me. If you are afraid, show it. If you are in pain, tell me. I might not know, otherwise."

The moisture deserted her mouth. How did even the most innocuous sentences become sinister when uttered by him?

She attempted to accommodate him.

"I am afraid that you'll do Veronica harm," she admitted calmly.

His granite jaw relaxed slightly along with his grip on her arm. "Are you . . . not afraid I'll do you harm?"

Well . . . she was now.

"I tell you, Captain, I don't understand you one bit." Moncrieff was also tall enough to have to duck beneath the arch of the cabin door. He punched his long arms into a lush, expensive emerald-green velvet jacket with a black silk collar. "Correct me if I'm wrong, but don't we expend a great deal of our time and effort doing our best to *avoid* government institutions?"

"As a general rule, you are not wrong," the Rook casually acquiesced.

"Marriage would make the second government institution you've entered into willingly in as many months. To be honest, I'd rather take a stab at Newgate than nuptials. Easier to escape, if you catch my meaning." He aimed a mischievous wink at Veronica, as though she were in on some elaborate joke.

Veronica blinked once. Twice. Peering at him as though he spoke a language she'd never before encountered.

It might have been the rough heat of the hand shackling Lorelai's arm that impeded her wits, but a stunned realization interrupted her brewing temper at Moncrieff's unseemly remark in front of a traumatized recent widow.

Nuptials? Wedding? What had the Rook said when he entered? She'd been so busy cataloguing the differences between *her Ash* and the pirate who stood before her that the words hadn't truly registered.

How fortuitous that you're already wearing a wedding dress.

Her heartbeats stumbled and collided into one another, her nerves singing with dread and alarm.

Oh heavens. He didn't mean to—

"What in God's name are you wearing? Green velvet?" The Rook's crooked, aristocratic nose wrinkled with distaste. Oddly enough, it was the most demonstrative he'd been during this entire ordeal.

"You don't like it?" Moncrieff threw his arms wide and puffed out an already thickly muscled chest. "Bought it off a merchant in the Turkish bazaar. Said the color was unparalleled but he couldn't sell it on account of it being 'too fucking hot for velvet,' if you'll pardon his French, my lady." In any other situation, the flirtatious smile he bestowed upon Veronica would have been heart-stopping on features as handsome as his. "I wore it for the occasion because I thought it matched your eyes."

Lorelai's jaw slackened. How could someone flirt at a time like this?

Veronica looked away from him in disgust, but the color did seem to return to her cheeks. A great deal of it, in fact.

"Couldn't find a Bible." Unfazed, Moncrieff reached

behind him, retrieving a book he'd tucked into the waist-band of his trousers. "But I did, however, confiscate a copy of Hornbrook's *Encyclopedia of Admiralty and Maritime Law* from Montez's bunk, and I figured that would have to do."

An elegantly built man would not have been able to lay the heavy volume open with one hand as Moncrieff did. But from what Lorelai had encountered of the crew on the *Devil's Dirge,* the Rook wasn't in the habit of employing elegant men. Moncrieff's unceasingly sophisticated accent and affable demeanor was in such direct contradiction to his barbaric stature, it confounded her in the extreme.

A couple of expensive rings glittered in the lanternlight as Moncrieff ran a finger down a page. "Thou shalt not covet, fornicate, commit adultery, steal, murder, and so forth. Basically, the same stuff as the Holy Book with a bit of nautical language thrown in. To my way of thinking, we ignore just about as many laws in this book as the other one. Though it does beg the question, whom do you fear more, God or the British Royal Navy?"

"Neither," the Rook clipped. "Let's get this over with."

"Get *what* over with?" Lorelai demanded. Even before she'd said it, a part of her understood exactly what was about to happen. It just seemed so ludicrous. So impossible, she convinced herself she must be interpreting the situation incorrectly.

"Just so." The book snapped shut with such a crack, both women jumped, and Moncrieff adopted a mock-solemn demeanor, ruined by the ever-present twinkle of mischief in his eyes.

Panic seized Lorelai, enough that she had to fight little spots of darkness in her periphery. She reached for a chair tucked beneath a table that seemed to be bolted down. The

Rook's throne, she realized. A dark velvet so deeply blue, it might have been purple in brilliant light. Heavy wood arms with intricate braiding matched the tall, ornate post to which she now clung.

"You can't be serious," she cried. "Ash, *stop* this. Tell me what's going on!"

Slowly, deliberately, he bent until his brutal visage was a breath away from hers. From this close, she could trace every line of the fine web of scars on his jaw and neck, could discern how the lantern reflected a glossy sheen off the long-healed lye burns. She could see that the sun could not paint the old wound with as much color as it did the rest of him.

He smelled of wind and salt.

"Call me Ash again, and you will not like the consequences. For he does not exist anymore."

Her broken exhalation crashed against features cast from stone, and Lorelai could have sworn his nostrils flared on an inhale.

No. This creature of ice and darkness was not Ash. Gone was his protective vigilance. His appreciative silence. And his almost uncertain but reverent adoration. In its place towered a being of undisputed power, claimed by means of inhumane pillage and ruthless discipline.

"Then . . . Who *are* you?" she whispered, her heart in her throat.

He straightened to his towering height, a wry expression creating a crease next to his hard mouth. "I still have no idea," he answered cryptically. "So, what does it matter?"

Lorelai watched the familiar divot in his chin as he nodded to Moncrieff.

She scanned his face with the eyes of her once-fourteen-year-old self who had loved him. So many of his features were the same. Lush hair so black, it gleamed blue in the light. Twenty years had threaded a touch of silver into the roots by his ears and the evening stubble on his jaw. The skin in the creases branching from his eyes was the same shade of pale he'd been as a boy. The sardonic wrinkle between his dark brows remained identical to Ash's. The top lip drawn forever tight, balanced by the fullness of the one beneath was unmistakable.

Those lips had kissed her once. She'd yearned for them across the void of time between that moment and this one.

Now she feared them. Feared him.

Grief swamped her, threatening to buckle her knees. Somehow, she'd known he'd be this striking as a grown man. She'd just assumed he lived his forgotten life elsewhere. That he was happy.

Because why else wouldn't he come for her?

It wasn't until Moncrieff theatrically cleared his throat that she realized what the Rook's nod to him had signified.

Moncrieff opened the book to a random page and pretended to read. "Captain, did you literally *take* this woman for the purposes of being your wife? For profit and desire, for plunder and pleasure, in seasickness and health for as long as you are inclined to have her?"

"I did." The Rook didn't look at her. "She is mine."

"That's it then. By the powers vested in me by, well, *you* . . . I pronounce you pirate captain and wife. Felicitations to you both. You may kiss the bride."

"You may *not* kiss me!" Lorelai protested, though she belatedly noted he made no move to do so. "And I am *not* your bride." Whirling on Moncrieff, she demanded, "Aren't you going to ask me if *I* take *him*? Because I categorically do not."

Moncrieff laughed as though she'd said something

hilarious. "The entire world has tried to take the captain, woman, what makes you think you can?"

"This is a ship, where my word is law," the Rook reminded her. "You are not required to say 'I do,' only to do as I say."

"But—but this wedding isn't legitimate," she sputtered. "No country on earth would acknowledge it. You simply cannot marry a woman against her will!"

One dark brow climbed toward his hairline. "Are you saying it was your *will* to wed Sylvester Gooch?"

"Well, of course not, but—"

"Then your argument is null."

A flash of lightning gilded Moncrieff's queue with threads of bronze as he nodded sagely. "Women have been marrying against their will for untold centuries. In fact, marriage is usually the *worst* thing to happen to a woman in one way or another, and yet so many insist on spending their days pursuing a husband like a bloodhound does an escaped convict. Why do you suppose that is?"

"Moncrieff," the Rook clipped.

"Yes, Captain."

"Go get drunk. That's an order."

"With *pleasure*." He gave them both a halfhearted, two-fingered salute and did an about-face.

They all silently awaited the thunder to finish as though it were a loud and impertinent guest.

"And take Countess Southbourne to her quarters," the Rook amended.

"Lorelai?" Veronica's voice wavered, as Moncrieff's body blocked the women's access to each other.

"I could get *her* drunk," he offered.

"Don't you dare touch me. *Oof!*" Veronica lunged away from the man with such violence, she unwittingly threw herself on the bed.

"Come without a fuss and I won't have cause to."

Rolling to the side of the bed, Veronica placed the post between her and the towering pirate. "I won't leave you alone, Lorelai. Not with him."

"We could *both* stay," Moncrieff suggested with a lascivious waggle of his brows. "Why should the bride be the only one to bed a pirate tonight? If you should like to participate in what comes next . . ."

Veronica blanched.

"Best put her in a cabin with a small porthole," the Rook suggested with bland indifference. "We wouldn't want her doing anything . . . irrational. She's more valuable to me alive."

In one deft move, Moncrieff had Veronica's arms anchored to her sides as he picked up the struggling countess as though she were as limp as a sack of grain. "I know just the one," he said after blowing the peacock feather of her headdress away from his mouth with a distasteful grimace.

"Lorelai!" The helpless terror in Veronica's voice called her to action, and Lorelai lunged toward her reaching hand. An iron grip on her shoulder held her back.

Turning to the Rook, she clutched his shirt, searching his face for some semblance of humanity. "Please let her go. She'll keep your identity secret if I ask her to, I know she will. If it's me you're after, you don't need her."

Her hopes fell as she found him as cold and remote as ever.

"What's that charming saying about secrets? Two can keep them if one is dead."

Moncrieff shut the door behind them with an ominous sound; Veronica's protestations still tugged at Lorelai's heart.

"You . . . you didn't just threaten to . . . to *kill* her?" A shrill note climbed in tandem with her panic. "Is she safe with that lunatic?" She took a halting step toward the door.

The hand on her arm tightened just short of painfully. "You have my word . . . Veronica Weatherstoke will remain unmolested, so long as you comply."

"God! Why must you be so violent?" The moment the frustrated words left her lips, she regretted them.

She wondered if the bleakness had lurked beneath his sinister façade this entire time, or if she'd conjured it with her words.

"Violence has kept me alive these twenty years. It's all I know. All I remember. In fact, the second I walk out of this room, I'm going to war."

"Then go," she spat. "And the devil take you."

"He might do. Someday." He pried her white fingers from his throne and drew her toward him. He was a man aware of his power, physical and otherwise, and could wield or temper it with astounding control. "But tonight, I'm allowed *this*."

When his gaze dropped to her lips, Lorelai panicked.

Oh God.

After a wedding, came a wedding night, and the Rook was about to claim his.

CHAPTER SEVEN

How long had she dreamed of this? How many times had she imagined Ash galloping toward her on his white steed, whisking her off the moors, and the two of them disappearing together into the mist? In her fantasies, they'd married. He'd kissed her gently, tenderly, with as much reverence as he had the day they'd parted.

The day he'd disappeared.

How could she have known that his fervent promise to come for her, all those years ago, had really been a threat?

When the Rook's fingers brushed her neck beneath her veil, Lorelai trembled, but she held straight and still as a mooring post as he explored the delicate skin of her nape. His fingers threaded in her hair, tangling into the ruined coiffure until he cupped the back of her head.

"What a-are you doing?"

"You always wore your hair loose when we were young." He extracted pins as he discovered them.

"I—I am no longer young," she stammered. "Convention dictates that I wear it up." Dear God, how could she be arguing about her *hair* at a time like this? "I cannot simply—"

"Convention holds no place here," he interrupted, brushing her hair over her shoulder, so it spilled down her bodice. "You may do as you like."

"Then I'd *like* to leave. I'd *like* to go home."

A sharp breath escaped him. Not a chuckle, but perhaps a sign of amusement.

"Allow me to rephrase." His head dropped until his lips grazed her shoulder exposed by the wide neckline of the gilded gown. Chills speared her, thrilling up from some deep and forgotten place with such force her belly clenched, before they exploded onto her skin in a wash of tiny shivers. "You may do as *I* like."

The Rook eased her closer, and Lorelai remained so paralyzed, she couldn't even find the wits to resist. His full lower lip curled slightly into his mouth, emerging with a sheen of moisture, then parting in preparation—

No.

Lorelai rejected the notion of this pirate ruining what she considered her loveliest memory. Should he kiss her now, it would be nothing like what she shared with Ash once upon a time.

What if it was terrible?

Or worse, what if she *liked* it? What if he made her want it? What if this new demonic incarnation of Ash stirred in her the same awakenings she'd experienced as a girl in his arms?

Because, Lord help her, the Rook was possessed of a dark charisma she'd never before encountered, and it was wreaking havoc with her senses already.

Ducking her chin against her chest, she turned her tiara into a weapon.

A less dexterous man would have taken a Weatherstoke sapphire right to the eye.

Before she could process what was happening, he spun her to face the bed.

He stood behind her now, one arm clamped around her, just above her breasts, as he relieved her of her tiara and veil and tossed it to the ground, heedless of the glittering precious heirlooms.

She barely noted the tug as the bulk of her awareness was completely focused on the bed in front of her. A decadent, cavernous thing, the canopy strung with enough vibrant silk to shame Salome. The coverlet belonged in a sultan's harem, stitched with a riot of silver thread into sensual patterns across a vivid blend of fabrics.

She couldn't have conjured a more dissimilar wedding bower to the one she'd expected to endure this night.

They stood like that for several silent, heaving breaths as the storm raged outside, tossing the boat this way and that. His powerful legs stabilized them both. His thighs flexed against the curve of her rump in a disquieting dance with the unstable ground beneath them.

Rather than bother with a bustle, Lorelai had favored gathers and ruffles for a train, and she regretted that now, as every swell and sinew of his well-hewn body pressed against her back with naught but a fabric barrier.

The short but heavy breaths pressing his chest against her contradicted his inscrutability.

"Where are you taking us?" she ventured, frantically trying to distract them both from the bed looming right before them.

"Wherever I desire." His arm kept her prisoner against his unyielding bulk, as the questing fingers of his free hand continued to delve into her hair. He whispered something against her skin, but her heart beat too loudly in her ears for her to correctly perceive it. Questing lips trailed over her skin. He paused at heart-stopping intervals to drag in deep lungfuls of air as though he could store her essence inside of him.

"After everything . . ." He released a harsh breath. "After *twenty years*. You are *mine*."

A note in his voice froze Lorelai in place. Not with fear, but something adjacent to it. For the first time, humanity seeped into his timbre, and along with it some terrible mélange of bleak rage and awestruck anticipation. It was as though he were as astonished as she to have found themselves here.

So many questions stung like vicious wasps behind her lips, but she was too much a coward to give them breath. Ash would have patiently answered each one. But the Rook?

Who knew the depravity of which he was capable?

A hoarse gasp of shock escaped her as he roughly bent her over the bed, imprisoning her with his hips as he unlaced her gown with rough tugs against her ribs.

It was the thickening shape of his sex against her backside that finally galvanized Lorelai from panic into action. She clawed her way up the counterpane, kicking out at him from behind with her ineffectual leg and scrambling across the bed. It was an undignified retreat, to be sure, but an effective one.

Lorelai thrashed and struggled against her unwieldy skirts, but finally gained her feet by way of a clumsy roll. Now she stood against the terror of the high seas with only a bed between them. Blinking rapidly, she found him staring across at her with a possessive savagery she'd not expected from a face that had thus far been so carefully expressionless.

And yet he made no move to follow her.

"I'm *not* yours," she declared, rather courageously, in her opinion. She'd meant to say more, to talk sense into this barbarian, but a tightness in her chest stole her capacity for breath, and thereby, words. Her vision began to blur, distorting his brutal visage and clarifying the motes of dust sparkling in the dim silver light of the storm, aided by a few flickering lanterns.

Lorelai had never known true fear before. She'd lived her life under the thumb of a cruel and intemperate bully. But the trepidation and anxiety she'd considered a part of her every interaction with Mortimer ill prepared her for this pure, mortal terror.

She'd thought she understood what helpless was.

She'd had no idea.

A detached part of her marveled at it. At *him*. This man crafted of lethal strength and absolute Cimmerian ferocity. She had held him so long ago while *he* trembled in pain and fear as a boy. She'd brushed that inky hair away from those austere eyes and coaxed reluctant smiles from his hard mouth.

In this moment, no one would believe such a thing possible. Were her memories a lie? Had he never touched her with gentle deference? Had he always been this callous, violent beast?

Where are you, Ash?

For he was not here. Not with her in this room. Not inside the sinister villain who wielded his muscle and sinew to devastating effect.

Lorelai's chest burned and her heart hurled itself against its cage. Finally, her body forced her to expel a breath she hadn't realized she'd kept trapped in her lungs.

The movement drew his gaze to her bosom.

Glancing down, Lorelai found that her loosened bodice had drifted to her waist. Her corset pinched her breasts high enough that the shameful pink crescents of her areolas crested above the contraption, the abundant flesh quivering in time to the trembles of her body. If she'd been wearing her own cotton camisole, it would have shielded her flesh from his view. But Veronica's gauzy French chemise, so iridescent it barely deserved the name, shimmered like gossamer hummingbird's wings, revealing more than it concealed.

With an indecorous squeak, she yanked her bodice up to her shoulders, clutching it to her décolletage.

A flash of lightning turned his eyes into silver embers, glinting every bit as hard and hot as tempered steel. "Come here, Lorelai," he ordered. Was his voice less steady than before? Or had she imagined it thus?

"I am *not* your wife," she hissed. "You may not simply order me about like one of your crew. Just because I'm here against my will doesn't mean I belong to you."

His head made a serpentine motion on his neck. "That is where you're mistaken, Lorelai." He spoke through his teeth, reaching for a post of the bed as he carefully navigated around it.

"I—I won't like it," she threatened, taking an infinitesimal step backward.

Would he make a liar of her?

He advanced to the foot of the bed, and only one corner separated her from her fate. And then he stood before her once again, a dark tower of saturnine grace. A man who moved with such finesse, she'd not marked his footfalls. It seemed his shadow reached her before he did, and now here he was, close enough to share breath.

"I can promise your screams will be of pleasure, not of pain."

Lorelai found herself once again unable to move as his words evoked a quiver somewhere south of her belly. She became mesmerized by something both foreign and familiar in his dark eyes. He didn't blink. Never once did he break eye contact as both human and nature's laws dictated he should.

"Is there no kindness left in you?" A muted whimper escaped her as hot tears burned her temples. "Do I mean so little to you?"

"So little?" He spirited away a mystified expression as quickly as it appeared, replacing it with his maddening inscrutability. "I survived . . ." He paused. Blinked. Then seemed to change his mind. "I crossed *horizons* for you, Lorelai." He reached out to trace her jaw, her cheekbones, her trembling lips. Pausing at the river of moisture at her temple, he swiped at a tear, rubbing it between his thumb and finger and examining it like one would a foreign substance. "I've been watching you for several months, you know."

"Several . . . *months*?" She gasped, her mind swimming with implications she couldn't reconcile.

"I came for you the moment I made my way back to England."

Back to England? Where had he gone? Where had he been for twenty years? Why hadn't he come for her the moment he touched down on British soil?

"I spied you in the estuary," he continued. "Teaching a fucking orphaned otter how to swim. And I decided that I'd give you as many days as possible without me. It's the only *kindness* I can afford you, I'm afraid. I waited to inflict myself on you for as long as I could." The fingers he rubbed together now curled into a fist. "But I would *not* see you married to another man. So now . . . here we are. And there is nothing to be done for it."

"You speak as though it's out of your hands," she marveled.

"It is. It always has been." He might have sounded apologetic, which was both terrifying and ludicrous. "I was born the moment I heard your voice commanding me to live. And you have been mine ever since. You're right, Lorelai, there's nothing to be done for that."

"Then perhaps I should have left you to rot beneath that ash tree." She'd meant to lash out at him. To hurt him. To drive him away, somehow, until she could contain this rapidly disintegrating situation.

"Perhaps that might have been best for us both." He toyed with a loathed wispy curl at her temple, one of several which would neither grow nor be tamed, and forever framed her face.

Then his palms traced their way down her neck to her shoulders. They were even rougher than she remembered, the calluses like sandpaper against the tender skin. In a feline gesture, he brought his cheek to rest against hers, the stubble rasping against her jaw, as he seemed to savor her fragrance like one would an expensive wine before taking a sip.

His dark head lowered further to the hollow of her throat, dragging his lips across it. His warm breath made way for the heat of his tongue, and something damp and disloyal rushed between her legs.

Desire flared, and panic surged alongside it, surpassing the sensation with a dizzying rush of terror. She could not allow herself to submit. Not to him. Not like this. Not until she could find Ash behind the dead-eyed predator.

Lorelai's knee connected with hard flesh before she'd even made the conscious decision to fight. She rushed around him as a breathless sound escaped his throat followed by hoarse, horrid curses.

She hoped to put the table between them, if only to buy her some time.

She hadn't thought this through, had she? Where would she go on an unfamiliar ship? What awaited her on the other side of that door?

The boat pitched sharply, and her left foot met the ground with more force than she could take. She gave a cry of pain as her weak ankle gave out, and she sprawled forward, biting her lip hard enough to draw blood upon impact with the ground.

The tears didn't flow because of fear or pain anymore, but out of sheer, helpless frustration. She looked like a fool, prostrate on the floor. Despite her intensifying antipathy for the Rook, she didn't want Ash—if any part of him was left—to see her humiliated like this.

Maybe he'd be angry enough to kill her before she had to lift her head. Then she wouldn't have to face her own mortification.

He was on her in an instant, turning her, lifting her, cradling her to his chest. Much like he'd done so long ago. Lorelai's tears became as torrential as the storm. She did her best not to remember the last time she'd cried against him. The last time she'd made herself a fool in front of him. It had been over a raven.

A rook.

Silently, he conducted her back to the bed, limping only slightly. He sat her on the counterpane, rumpled by her struggles. This time, she didn't fight him, not even when he reached into a trouser pocket.

"Get it over with," she sobbed, crossing her arms over her corset in a feeble attempt to regain her modesty. "I'd rather die than live as your wife."

His hand froze, halfway out of his pocket. "You think I'm going to . . . *kill* you?"

"And why shouldn't I? You *murdered* Mortimer," she said woodenly. "In a churchyard, no less. In the late afternoon in front of God and everyone. You didn't even . . . hesitate or—"

"In my experience, hesitation is the number one cause of death." He flicked out a handkerchief and presented it to her, as though to prove a point.

To say she was surprised didn't cover half of it. She'd only just kneed him in his . . . manly bits. Wasn't he livid? Why was he not punishing her in some dastardly, piratey manner?

"Why do you weep over *him*?" He didn't sound angry, only confounded, but Lorelai didn't fail to note that he wouldn't say Mortimer's name. "He broke your fucking leg. He fed your pets to you. Life with him these past twenty years could hardly have been palatable."

He didn't know the half of it.

"Tell me you've not become so touched as to keenly mourn *his* loss."

The disgust in his words sparked a temper she'd long considered dormant. "It is *Ash*'s loss I mourn," she spat, delicately wiping at her nose. "For he is gone, and a stranger has taken his place. Ash would *never* have done something so monstrous. Even to Mortimer."

"You are both right and wrong about that," he responded wryly. He seemed about to say something, and then changed his mind. Regarding her with more curiosity than regret. "You once said that to become a monster you must first do something monstrous. And as a youth at Southbourne, Ash thought he might have done monstrous things in the boyhood he didn't remember. But I'm convinced that until the day we were parted, Ash only had dirt on his hands."

Lorelai puzzled over his use of the name in the third person as the Rook held his large, callused hands out to her, as though to demonstrate their filthiness.

"Now there is blood. Enough blood to stain this Channel a red no less than biblical. But that is not why it was so easy to kill your brother." His hands curled to fists. "Mark me, Lorelai, had you not been watching I would not have been kind enough to grant him such a painless death."

She closed her eyes against the sight of the blade skewered through Mortimer's open mouth. "His death did not seem so painless."

He gripped her chin, forcing her to look at his savage features. His other palm feathered over her hair with a confounding gentleness. "That is because you do not know enough of pain."

"Are you about to teach me?" She'd meant it as a challenge, but it escaped as a whisper. "Is that what this is? This so-called wedding night? Am I to suffer for Mortimer's sins? Do you want to stain yourself with the blood of two innocent people in one day?"

"Blood . . . innocent . . . ?" He released her, brows drawing together as though her words had confounded him.

She leveled him a speaking glare. "Virgins usually bleed, do they not?"

His eyes dipped to her lap, then closed for the space of one cavernous, never-ending exhale.

"You are still . . . innocent." He drew the word out on a hiss. "After all this time?" His fingers curled into talons before abruptly letting go.

He was at the door before Lorelai could form a reply.

Bracing one hand against the door frame, he clung to the handle as if at any moment someone might drag him away. The curious dark shapes of the tattoos beneath the thin white of his shirt rose and fell with three heaves of his shoulders. Feathers maybe? He turned the latch.

Paused. "You cannot be so blind as to think Mortimer was innocent."

Lorelai wiped at her tears with trembling hands. "For all his atrocities, he was not a murderer. No one deserves to die like that."

"He *was* a murderer." The Rook didn't look at her, but the creases of his fists turned white. "And he deserves to die seven thousand deaths."

Stunned, Lorelai almost dropped the edges of her bodice. Seven thousand was a very specific number. "What are you saying? Why seven thousand?"

"It doesn't matter."

She flinched as he wrenched the door open. "Your enterprising knee has saved you from a wedding night." He'd still yet to look at her, and for some untold reason, Lorelai was glad. "Get some sleep, Lorelai, but suffer no illusions. I'll not be denied. I *will* have you."

"Never," she vowed as he closed her in and locked the door behind him.

In an unprecedented moment of weakness, the Rook pressed his forehead against the barrier of wood and steel separating them. On a harsh breath, he repeated the same word he'd whispered at the end of every infernal day for twenty long years.

"Always."

CHAPTER EIGHT

"Fucking *hell*," the Rook muttered as he braced his legs against the bow and ripped his shirt open, allowing vicious nails of rain to drive themselves into his flushed, over-heated skin.

It hurt.

Everything hurt. The icy water against his flesh. His muscles stressed to their limit by herculean restraint. His cock, where Lorelai's resourceful knee had struck. The disused muscle palpitating against his ribs like a wild beast, hoping to splinter the iron darkness locking it away.

Never matter. He welcomed the pain. Pain was the closest thing he had to a friend.

Hell. He'd had a great deal of time to consider the venue. To contemplate its walls. Its origins. Its meaning. Twenty years, in fact.

To him, hell was taking a drink with Mortimer Weatherstoke at an inn in Heybridge and waking up twelve hours later out to sea on a merchant ship, leagues away from the only person who'd ever meant anything to him. Hell was years upon years of working on a deck like this one, in just such a storm, the seawater stinging the open whip wounds on his back. It was sleeping in so many chains, in holds stinking of filth and despair, starving, freezing, and dreaming of his precious few months in paradise.

Of Lorelai.

His very own paradise lost.

Hell was the vast, merciless oceans spread between himself and her. The hoary horizon had been his perdition for so many years until, one night, he'd had enough. What had Milton said in *Paradise Lost*? "Better to reign in Hell, than to serve in Heaven."

But to reign in hell, one must become the very Devil.

And so he had.

Because he thought he'd explored every corner of hell, that he understood its every torment.

God, what a fool he'd been.

For tonight, he'd found a fresh depth of the abyss.

Hell. True hell . . . had been standing at the door to his cabin, the memory of her warmth still fresh in his hands. The scent of her branded in his nostrils. Knowing that her lush, soft body was there for the taking . . .

And walking away.

Hell was looking into her beloved visage made only comelier by time, and finding the gaunt shadows of misery etched there. It was the denial on her lips. The refusal in her eyes.

Hell was becoming a devil for the sole purpose of claiming his very own angel.

Christ, the irony. The pure fucking tragedy of it all.

For an angel she still was, even so far as to have maintained her virginal purity. After all this time.

He'd made a fatal mistake. One he never could have

prepared himself for. He'd assumed that enough of his humanity had been beaten out of him by torture, tragedy, and treasure-hunting that he could claim her while remaining unaffected by her protestations.

But time did strange and dreadful things to memory, and he'd underestimated what her touch would do to him after all this time. He'd forgotten about her power over him. The girl whose voice could raise the dead.

He pressed a hand to the tattoo over his heart, willing the organ beneath to still as a familiar hatred welled within, smothering all softer sentiments.

He'd had a plan, goddammit. One he'd painstakingly shaped since making his way back to England. And, once again, Mortimer *fucking* Weatherstoke had bungled everything. By forcing Lorelai to marry, he'd likewise forced the Rook's hand.

As he'd stated, he'd left Lorelai in peace at Southbourne Grove because the Rook had ascertained through the spies he'd installed there that since the earl had married Veronica, he'd all but forgotten his sister existed.

A tragedy for the Countess Southbourne, to be sure, but it bought him the time to craft his revenge to correlate with his reclamation of Lorelai.

In order to claim any kind of life with Lorelai, he'd wanted to retrieve his memory.

His identity.

In the twenty years it'd taken to make his way back to her, he'd lost himself. Again. Not just his memory this time, but his humanity, as well. And he'd gained quite a few things along the way. Not just unimaginable wealth and infamy, but innumerable enemies, and a crew of men who would also make powerful adversaries should he not fulfill his duty to them.

To beat a metaphor to death, if he were the king of hell,

they were his demons. Demons with an insatiable appetite for blood, women, and above all . . . wealth.

So, he'd devised a plot in which he might satisfy all involved.

The Claudius Cache.

If he could find the fabled treasure, not only could the Rook and the crew of the *Devil's Dirge* retire, but the answer to the gigantic question mark in his past might be buried alongside it. Even if he found nothing regarding his lost childhood, he'd have mercifully granted Lorelai time without him.

Because the devil in him was a dark and needful thing. Selfish. Lustful. Oh, so lustful. He'd known that once he'd gotten his hands on Lorelai . . . he might lose all control. He might take if she didn't offer.

Tonight, he'd come so close . . .

It'd been so long since he'd even had a temper to lose. He'd learned that the most useful fury was a patient one. And that was why he hadn't ripped Mortimer Weatherstoke apart the moment he'd had the chance.

No. He'd had a *plan*. One that would have fed the devil's own sense of justice. One that fit the crimes Mortimer had perpetrated.

But the second word had reached him that Lorelai had been gambled away, that Sylvester Gooch had kissed her and was preparing to claim her. . . .

The plan fucking altered as swiftly as the ocean winds. That is to say in the course of a single day, he wrenched his ship around the island, made quick work of Gooch and Weatherstoke, and did the one thing he could think of that would irrevocably tie Lorelai to him until death did they part.

Perhaps . . . in hindsight . . . he might have been a *touch* hasty.

But for twenty years he'd been a man obsessed. A man *possessed* of a woman whom he could no sooner let go of than he could abandon his own appendages. She was a part of him. Perhaps the only part of him that mattered anymore.

And now she was his, for better or for worse.

So why did he feel worse instead of better?

Because, as he'd predicted, she wasn't particularly keen to attach herself to the devil.

To the Rook.

She wanted Ash.

A pity, he thought. Because, just like her brother, her beloved Ash had been murdered.

More than once.

And now *his* black soul occupied the shell of the boy who'd loved her. The body of the man who'd lay claim to her. He was the devil who'd returned to fulfill the promise of a ghost.

Because despite everything, the sun still set in the west.

CHAPTER NINE

Sebastian Moncrieff had sworn allegiance to the Rook four years ago chiefly out of sheer disbelief at finding a man who truly gave fewer dusty fucks than he did. About anything.

Or anyone.

Until now.

Sagging against the door frame of the galley, a fine cigar lodged in his teeth, Sebastian squinted against the spray of relentless droves of rain and frenzied white-capped storm surges breaking against the ship. The sea did its best to crawl onto the deck, and his captain stood with both legs planted against a widow-maker gale. One hand gripped the rigging, as the other was flung wide, daring the innumerable gods of the sea to strike with whatever they could. Fire. Lightning. A rogue wave.

Moncrieff saw this for exactly what it was.

A shower of ice to quench the flames in his blood. Or loins, as the case may be.

Sebastian had nearly taken one, himself, after a grapple

with a writhing, spitting countess left him as aroused as he was bedeviled.

However, he had orders to leave Veronica Weatherstoke untouched, and so he'd not seduced her, regardless of how badly he'd ached to do so.

If ever a woman was in dire need of a good . . . seducing, it was that one.

Thrusting the priggish countess from his thoughts with greater difficulty than he was comfortable with, Moncrieff considered his captain carefully. He'd taken a bride, but he'd obviously not *taken* her.

Why the fuck not?

Frowning, Moncrieff blew a perfect smoke ring into his whisky glass before drinking deeply. How many drinks did this make? Six? Seven? Didn't matter. He'd keep drinking until he'd puzzled this conundrum through. For what self-respecting pirate made decisions whilst sober?

None he'd want to know.

Inelegantly, he poured his seventh—eighth?—dram and decided to sip this one as he measured the only man he'd ever obeyed.

Together he and the Rook had turned apathy into an art form, and avarice into a religion.

For so long before his tenure on the *Devil's Dirge,* Sebastian had thought himself immune to fear. Until one glimpse of the quiet and ruthless brutality of which the pitiless Rook was capable taught him more about himself than did a lifetime spent in self-discovery.

Sebastian had realized he wasn't immune to fear, but addicted to it.

And no one frightened him like the Rook.

Did he not know better, he'd have thought the Rook some dark incarnation of Typhoon, the ancient god of chaos and the sea. The captain was possessed of a sense he'd never before encountered. Several, in fact. And before long, Sebastian had become convinced that the Rook was either a great friend or a mortal enemy of Death.

Because the demon had left him alone—left him alive—more times than *should* be humanly possible.

In time, Moncrieff's curiosity had become a grudging respect, and then—astonishingly—kinship. He was as close to the Rook as anyone dare get without his balls shriveling to the size of sun-ripened grapes. His general insouciance became the perfect counterpoint to the Rook's own brand of terrifying tranquility. They each had their parts to play. The Rook violently obtained things, and Moncrieff violently enjoyed those things. It went beyond treasure now. Titles. Power. Prestige. Land. They had so much. More than any one crew of ne'er-do-wells deserved.

But it was never enough.

Pirating for Sebastian was about pleasure. The rush of life-affirming exhilaration unparalleled by any other experience. The freedom of calling no man king, and no country home. Certainly, he followed the Rook's orders . . . usually. It was his ship, after all. But for all his brutality, the Rook was no tyrant. His crew consisted of men who were at one time or another hired to do some mercenary thing and liked either the work or the reward so much that they begged to stay.

Attrition caused from death by the Rook's own hand was astoundingly rare for a pirate ship. In the four years Moncrieff had known him, the Rook had only killed three of his crew. One, for turning state's evidence after his capture in Morocco. Another, for alerting the British forces of their cache beneath the catacombs of Inverthorne Keep. And what a fucking debacle that had been.

And, most notably, Jeremy Smyth, who'd snuck an eleven-year-old girl into his quarters.

An oily shudder oozed down Sebastian's spine at the memory, and he took a larger drink than he'd meant to. He'd never forget how the captain had reacted to that. He didn't punish Smyth so much as . . . dismantle him. Without a word, without the frenzy of rage, the captain had simply shoved the trembling child into Sebastian's hands, and gone to work on the man.

Not wanting the girl to see, Sebastian conducted the child back home with a bit of recompense, grateful Smyth hadn't had the chance to relieve her of any clothing. He'd returned to a ship so eerily silent, one could hear Samuel Barnaby muttering obscenities as he mopped up the blood.

What was left of Smyth had been displayed on the aft railing of the quarterdeck until the smell became untenable.

That was how the captain operated. Most often, no order need be given. No law need be written. The men just knew what was expected, and when they didn't, they stepped *very* lightly.

No one had quite discovered what drove the Rook. Greed? Perhaps. His own legend, maybe? Or blood. There was always plenty of blood. Though the crew often hazarded as to the captain's proclivities in careful whispers, it had never truly mattered before.

Until now. Until . . . her.

With no warning at all, they'd paused in the middle of the grandest treasure hunt since the Copper Shuttle had been uncovered, to kidnap a crippled spinster and murder an impoverished earl.

This behavior of the captain's was not only eccentric in the extreme, it was . . . troubling. And since the enigmatic Rook *never* explained himself, Sebastian and the rest of the crew were left scratching their heads, speculating as to what, if anything, Lorelai and Veronica Weatherstoke had to do with the Claudius Cache.

Lorelai had seemed to know him. She'd called him Ash.

Sweet Christ, did the Rook have . . . a name? A past? That didn't sound at all right.

It'd been easiest for the world—for Moncrieff, himself— to perceive the Rook as some sort of mythical character. Birthed by an ancient forgotten god in some ridiculously brutal way. A curse or a scourge of the seas dredged from beneath Poseidon's fingernail or Neptune's nut sac . . . or whatnot.

Could it be possible that he was . . . a mere mortal? That skill, cunning, strength, and sometimes blind bloody luck had seen him through all this fucking time?

When it seemed the storm had driven enough needles into the Rook's flesh, the captain drifted back toward the galley, navigating the sharply pitching deck with a curious hitch in his stride.

He accepted the towel Sebastian offered him and dragged it over his face before scrubbing at his hair. A small muscle tic appeared in his jaw, which was the equivalent of a temper tantrum for such a self-contained man.

"I'll never claim to be an expert on wedding nights, Captain, having only ever ruined a few, but I've operated under the impression they're not generally so abbreviated as yours."

"I'm in no mood." To describe the glare he received as threatening, was to call the Sahara dry or ocean wet.

Applicable, but not enough.

Sebastian suspected they were both stricken with a similar distemper. Driven to the same volatile, frustrated place by two appealing—yet unwilling—Weatherstoke ladies. "Very well, may I offer you some of this obscenely expensive Ravencroft Scotch? Top-shelf, worth every penny . . . or would be . . . had I actually paid for it. It'll warm you up enough to put your nipples away."

"No."

Moncrieff couldn't decide which of the two captains currently occupying his whisky-induced double vision was the right one, so he gaped at them both, his cigar nearly dropping from his slack jaw. "I've never known you to turn down a drink or five. What's gotten into you?"

Folding the towel, the Rook draped it over a basin, glancing in the direction of the captain's quarters. "If I drink, I might forget."

Sebastian snorted, dropping into a high-backed chair next to the galley fire. "I rather thought that was the point of drinking."

"I might forget all the reasons I left her alone. I . . . might go back."

"I see," Sebastian lied, kicking out the chair across from him for the captain. "Still a reluctant bride, then? Can't imagine why."

The Rook's silence spoke volumes, as did his posture when he lowered his impressive, dripping body into the chair.

Dangerous enough to warrant another drink.

"Since when have you ever allowed someone to deny you?" Sebastian challenged.

"She's different," his captain murmured.

"I know she's *bloody* different. We've never risked such an intricate shore excursion before for something so inconsequential as a *woman*. I mean—"

The Rook held up a hand to silence him, and something in the rigidity of the gesture lifted fine hairs all over his body. "It wasn't just for *her*, and you know it."

He knew nothing of the sort, but he wisely kept his own

counsel. Even *he,* who continually spat in the face of the fates, found it difficult to meet the Rook's sharp, eerie gaze. They'd barely rounded Cape Wrath in their cartographical search of Scotland's rivers. This little side venture put their whole fucking scheme in peril. But the Rook was right, capturing the captain's new bride hadn't been their only mission in Maldon. They'd also abducted a countess, murdered an earl, and the wealthy Mr. Gooch . . .

God's balls, but the navy would be on high alert.

"It's only that my curiosity is endlessly piqued," he ventured, crossing his ankle to his knee in a gesture of relaxed nonchalance. "We've never had a shortage of *young* and *willing* women. Why go so far as to wed one who is neither?"

The Rook stared, unblinking, into the fire. It took him so long to reply, Moncrieff began to wonder if he'd heard him.

"Did I ever tell you how I became a pirate?" The Rook rested his chin on templed fingers in a contemplative pose.

"No . . ." The odd reply both frustrated and intrigued Sebastian. The captain never revealed a bloody thing about himself. Sebastian *absolutely* wanted to know, almost as much as he wanted the damnably inscrutable man to answer his fucking question first.

"It all started with a mutiny aboard a ship I . . . worked on once."

"A mutiny, you say? Were you one of the mutinous? Or were you . . . mutinied upon? Mutinied . . . is that a word?" At his captain's level look, Sebastian gave a drunken nod. "You led the mutiny, of course."

Salt water still gathered in the Rook's lashes as he turned back to stare into the grate. Moncrieff had a suspicion the past danced inside those flames for the Rook.

He'd have given one of his eyes to see it.

"I'd been a slave for years. We were sold from Japan to a particularly cruel Argentinian shipping magnate. All we wanted was to get ashore. To go *home*. Before we could find land, we were overtaken by some meddling vessel of the French Compagnie Générale Transatlantique. The French captain claimed us as prisoners and pirates . . . as property . . ." He spat into the fire, which sizzled. "We'd . . . had enough of that. So, when reason didn't work, and threats were exhausted, we killed him . . ." Devilishly, the Rook's lips tilted as though reliving a cherished memory. "We killed them all, every last fighting man. Gods, how the sharks feasted. Suddenly, I found myself with a new ship, crates of Argentine gold, and more French roses than you can conceive of. Fertilized by the crewmen's own shit, can you imagine the stench?"

Sebastian could, and did, and drank some more.

"I should have turned around." The captain's whisper was almost lost to the din of the storm.

"Turned around?" Moncrieff puzzled aloud. "What do you mean?"

"We belatedly realized we had no idea where we were, and we'd slaughtered all the navigators." A wry sort of sardonic amusement glinted over his features. "Once we figured we were at the tip of the South American continent, we simply hugged the Chilean shoreline, trading with fishing villages. It wasn't until we picked up Montez in Peru that we discovered if we'd turned around and sailed north when we were still in the Atlantic, we might have made it back to England before . . ." The Rook exhaled a breath containing decades of regret.

"Before what?" Sebastian queried alertly.

"Before everything. So many of the crew at that point were Oriental. We struck a bargain to cross the Pacific, because I couldn't turn the boat around, myself. We were to dock at a central point from which most of the crew could disseminate to their respective nations with their share of the gold."

His hands curled, clawing through his hair in a shockingly affected gesture. "All we wanted was to go *home*," he repeated. "And someone always tried to stop us, to delay us, to capture or to kill us. The Japanese, the Chinese, Russians, Indians, Algerians, Spanish. The French, of course, as we had one of their ships. And *God,* the Prussians. What a brutal lot they are. It's why I fought so hard in the beginning, so fiercely, because the entire *world* stood between me and . . . and a promise I made very long ago.

"I could scarce believe how fucking crowded the oceans are. We were all of us so angry. So tired of being treated like animals, of having everything taken from us, that we began to take back. It seemed we were at war with every ship we came across, and I decided early on that I'd never start a war I didn't win."

"And so you haven't."

"But at what cost?"

Now there was a heavy question.

"They all asked for my name. Every man I recruited, assisted, or executed. They wanted someone to follow, or to curse, or to brag about capturing or killing. And so . . . I gave them one. And before I ever made it back to my own country, I'd become the Rook." He made a caustic sound. "No one even knows why."

"I always assumed it was because ravens are rather ghastly creatures. Harbingers of death and all that." Knowing his captain's affinity for chess, Sebastian posited, "I suppose it could be because rooks are considered more powerful than bishops or knights, let alone pawns. They can exert control in every square along his charted course."

A dark gaze darted at him, and then away. "I value your unique perspective, Moncrieff, I always have."

Grimacing, the first mate shifted uncomfortably in his chair. "Don't compliment me, I don't like it."

"Good, because I was about to tell you how incredibly wrong you are."

"I don't like that, either." He didn't like any of this. It unsettled him, made him believe that *this* storm was blowing in a transformation, one to be wary of. "The men are restless, Captain. They don't like women on the ship."

"They won't remain so for long."

To which "they" did he refer? The restless crew? Or the women on the ship? Figuring he'd exhausted the Rook's stores of good nature, along with the bottle of Scotch, he stood.

"We're sailing north, I see. Are we to resume our search of the rivers?"

The Rook gestured in the negative. "We're headed for the Isle of Mull."

Moncrieff's tongue froze on its quest for the last drop of butter-gold liquid from the bottle. "But . . . We've been there already. We've searched the western coast. None of the rivers—"

The Rook stood, the look in his eyes subtracting several years from Moncrieff's life span. "Are you questioning me, Bastian?"

Much like a chiding parent, the captain only used his name when displeased.

"I just . . . need something to tell the men."

"You tell them I gave them an order. That is all that ever needs telling."

Though the Rook's words irked him, he was not so drunk yet as to be suicidal. "Aye, Captain," he muttered as he turned toward the narrow hall to his cabin.

He left the Rook staring at his forearm, running nonsensical patterns on the half-ruined tattoo.

A ground-shaking revelation followed Moncrieff all the way back to his bunk, where no amount of Scotch could settle him.

The Rook was no god. No monster. No legend. He was . . . just a man. And a man had vices. Feelings.

Weaknesses.

All this time, had Lorelai Weatherstoke been the Rook's one weakness? Did she have in her small, elegant hand the one thing the whole world feared didn't exist?

The Rook's fabled heart.

If so, she'd just become the most dangerous woman in the world.

And the most valuable.

CHAPTER TEN

Pawing through the Rook's personal things was difficult with only one hand, but Lorelai had yet to find something to fasten her bodice closed and she couldn't reach her laces. She clutched at it as she pulled dressers and trunks open in search of something to wear.

Dawn threatened to break over a sea thick with soupy mist. Since Lorelai couldn't bring herself to sleep, she might as well do something other than cower and await *his* return.

She'd already wasted hours curled up on the counterpane for a sleepless, stormy night in a trembling heap contemplating all her captor had revealed. Which wasn't much, all told.

Ash. A pirate. *The* pirate. The Rook. A name more notorious and fearsome than those of piratical glory days of a century past such as Barbosa, Sir Francis Drake, Blackbeard, and Henry Morgan.

Combined.

Twenty years. He'd come for her after twenty years.

How? Why? And . . . *how*? The British Royal Navy was the most powerful in the world, and he'd managed to elude them like no other.

Was his continued presence in Britain known to the powers that be? Surely one of the Royal Fleet patrolling the Channel would spot him. He didn't fly a pirate flag, like they did in the stories. But even so. Remaining here seemed like an immense risk to take, even for someone so intrepid as he.

He'd claimed to have been observing her for several months . . .

Little butterflies erupted in her stomach at the thought. Several months could mean a year at least, if he was to be believed. She'd released the otter he'd spoken of, William Wallace, back into the wild the prior summer. The Rook had said he'd been there. Had spied upon her while she'd taught little Wallace how to swim. How to fish.

Hadn't she read in the papers somewhere the Rook had been recently captured in Scotland, had sent to Newgate Prison, and subsequently escaped?

She should have paid closer attention. But how could she have known?

Curled upon his cavernous bed, she'd filled a few ago-nizing hours wallowing in her memories of the past, in her anxiety for what came next. Eventually, her frayed nerves had tired of that. She had to do something, or she'd never be able to live with herself.

First order of business, she'd decided, was to find some-thing to keep herself warm.

Unsurprisingly, the Rook's neatly kept wardrobe and dressers held as many weapons as garments.

She unsheathed a thin but dangerously sharp dagger by a handle encrusted with gems. It looked like something an Arabian prince would wield.

Lorelai set the dagger close by, and renewed her search for a garment to cover her nakedness. Her fingers grazed a shirt thick as wool but soft rather than coarse. She lifted the plush fabric and tested its almost velveteen texture against her cheek. A briny scent combined with bay rum and frankincense enveloped her, evoking images of tropical climes and sun-sparkling seas.

Of places she'd never been, explored by a man she'd never thought to see again.

Glancing back at the door to confirm that she remained alone, Lorelai discarded her ruined wedding bodice, corset, and chemise, and donned the shirt. It fell past her thighs, and she had to struggle with foreign, intricate toggles rather than buttons to fasten it. The neckline was strange and wide, but the garment warmed her, instantly.

Upon searching further, she found a long cream sash and belted it about her waist, obscuring the dagger into the folds should she need to use it. Not that she knew how to correctly wield the thing, but one needed a weapon on a pirate ship, didn't one?

Lord, there was a thought she never imagined she'd have to consider.

She stumbled upon a pistol, as well, and a frantic search uncovered the bullets in another drawer. Having never shot a revolver, it took her a few precious moments to figure out how to correctly load it, but she managed.

She must look ridiculous in her ruffled ivory wedding skirts and a strange, masculine top, but that was the least of her worries.

Her sweet Ash had been transformed into the ruthless Rook. He'd made it clear to her that he intended to thoroughly consummate that laughable farce of a marriage just as soon as he recovered from the blow she'd dealt him.

Whether she consented or not. And she could only guess the fate that awaited poor Veronica.

Limping to the door, Lorelai considered her very slim options.

If she stayed in the captain's quarters, her fate was obvious. She'd be at his mercy.

And mercy seemed to be something the Rook had forsaken some twenty years hence.

With stealth, the mist, and a great deal of luck, she could find Veronica, and her clever sister-in-law might know where a vessel like this stored its lifeboats.

Veronica's father had been a wealthy shipping magnate, after all. She knew more about boats, navigation, and the sea than most men did.

Creeping to the door, Lorelai realized it wasn't the kind that could be locked from the outside. Which made sense. Why would the captain of a pirate ship ever hazard being locked in his own quarters?

Her fingers rested on the latch, and she paused.

What if he'd placed a guard at the door? The unscrupulous Moncrieff, perhaps. Or the Rook might have stood vigil, himself.

Shivering at the thought, Lorelai opened the little brass peephole in the door and pressed her eye to it. The short hall was full of shadows, but empty of pirates so far as she could tell.

Stepping back, she eased open the door and let the pistol precede her into the predawn gloom. She peeled her shoulders away from her ears when she found herself alone. Releasing a shaky breath as quietly as she could, she lifted her skirts and leaned on the rail, careful not to trip down the three wide steps into the narrow hall.

She'd been too terrified yesterday to marvel that the

Devil's Dirge boasted the accommodations of a luxurious steamship, but with decidedly rougher occupants. She'd stared at the glowing sconces all night, and had idly wondered how on earth electricity could be found on a ship. She'd never before heard of such extravagant possibilities.

As she dragged her lame foot upon lush red carpets, she wondered if this was what Pierre Aronnax felt whilst exploring the *Nautilus*. Flabbergasted, terrified, and more than a little impressed.

There was no time to dawdle, or explore, she reminded herself. She had to find Veronica.

Where had Moncrieff said he'd stash her? The blue room? That could be anywhere.

Dim electric lights reflected off the ambient mist stealing through the hall like a wary dream.

Lorelai searched what little her panicked memory had stored from her abduction. The captain's quarters from which she disembarked were located off the main deck below the open aft deck. The luxurious accommodations took up the entire rear of the ship on this level, which was why it had so many portholes and windows from which to enjoy the view. She stood at the end of a hall that had four doors, spaced evenly apart, two on the right and two on the left.

If her guess was correct, these were also accommodations for officers or important guests.

It would be folly to make much noise, as whomever the Rook chose as his officers had to be almost as unprincipled and ruthless as he.

As she crept up the hall, Lorelai found the last door on the right had been bolted, from the *outside*.

What were the chances that the Rook kept prisoners other than her and Veronica anywhere else but the ship's hold way below deck?

Truthfully, she had no way of knowing, but anyone she found that wasn't Veronica could become a potential ally. All to the good, in her estimation.

As silently as she could, she slid the bolt free and un-latched the door, revealing blue carpet that she took to be a fantastic sign.

Opening the door all the way, she called in a loud whisper, "Veronica?"

She almost dropped the pistol to devastating effect as the heavy candelabra Veronica swung stopped inches away from denting her temple.

"L-Lorelai?" They collapsed into each other's arms. The younger woman shook with the effort not to dissolve into sobs, still clutching the makeshift weapon. "I thought you were—that he—oh God! Your dress! Are you all right?"

Lorelai pulled back, pressing a finger to her lips. "I'm fine, darling. For now. Listen to me. We haven't much time. If we're to get out of this, our best chance is on a lifeboat. Do you remember seeing them? Do you know where they are or how to release them?"

Veronica was shaking her head, her pale features ghostly in the eerie mists. "This is a faster steamship than I've ever encountered," she whispered. "And we've been aboard for several hours. We could be anywhere by now." She paused, peering past Lorelai into the corridor. "Wait." She ventured forward, slipped into the hall and rounded the corner.

"What are you doing?" Lorelai caught up with her, and linked their arms so they could cling together.

"There are many kinds of fog." Veronica sagely pointed toward the open passage door to the deck completely con-cealed by thick wisps of mist. "*This* kind only gathers near land. *If* we get to the lifeboats and row far enough away from this ship and out of the clouds, we might have a chance."

Lorelai squeezed her, blessing all the gods she could think of for the clever woman and her merchant-class knowledge.

"It's better than being stuck here, I think."

Veronica nodded her agreement.

They crept to the door expecting an army of pirates to stop them at any time. The ship remained eerily quiet but for the constant sounds of the engine.

"The lifeboats are just beyond the galley, secured below the deck." Veronica pointed to their left. "We'll have to crawl down a ladder on the outside of the ship. Once we reach it, we'll have little time as the wheelhouse will most definitely be manned by a navigator and he'll likely see us if the mist dissipates even a little."

"Do you think we could incapacitate the navigator without killing him?" Lorelai pointed to the candelabra.

"If we're lucky." Veronica didn't look hopeful. "Let's just hope we remain concealed." They ducked below the windows of the galley and made their way along the deck, feeling for the rails of a ladder that would lower them to the lifeboats.

Veronica stopped so abruptly, Lorelai narrowly avoided bowling her over. Her hand reached back and gripped Lorelai's, leading it to the cold iron curve of a hang ladder.

"The lifeboats hang two decks above the water," Veronica breathed against her ear. "Since there's no one on deck to help, we'll need to release the ropes at exactly the same time for the boat to land and not dump us into the sea. Do you understand? We . . . we might be a bit injured in the fall."

Heart pounding, mouth dry, Lorelai nodded her understanding as she clung to her dearest friend. "It's the only way. You go first."

Veronica gathered her skirts and tucked them into her waist. Lorelai reached for her, readying to secure her so she could lift her leg up and over the high rail of the deck.

"Do you think you'll be able to climb down the ladder with your ankle?" Veronica asked. A worried frown pinched her brow.

In truth, Lorelai didn't know. "I'll have to," she decided.

"Oi! Don't move, you daft nanny." A familiar, grizzled voice broke through the mist back toward the overhang of the galley. "If you don't cooperate, I'll be forced to hobble you."

Lorelai's muscles seized, and Veronica's fingers became talons on her wrist.

A plaintive bleat both astounded and bemused Lorelai, but it became readily apparent the voice didn't address her or Veronica.

"If you kick me in the head, you stubborn old goat, I'll return the favor. Now give over!" The man's demands rose in decibel to the tune of his frustration.

"Barnaby?" Lorelai whispered. What was her game-keeper doing aboard the ship? And to whom did he speak? The poor old man was seventy, if he was a day. She'd hired him not quite a year ago to help her with her growing me-nagerie. He'd been guarded and gruff at first, as though he'd almost resented her for employing him, for having to take orders from a woman. But he'd stubbornly insisted he stay, and was a fair hand with the animals. Eventually, they'd found their stride, and lately, they'd become great friends. Lorelai's fondness for the old cantankerous sep-tuagenarian knew no bounds.

Lorelai drifted toward his voice, and Veronica jerked

her back toward the ladder. "What are you doing? We have to go."

"That's Barnaby." Lorelai tugged out of her grip. "They've taken him, too. We have to help him. He's so feeble, they might make him . . . walk the plank, or something equally frightful." *Did pirates still do that?* she wondered. "I'd never forgive myself."

Veronica cautiously surveyed the mist, now becoming thinner as the sun threatened the horizon. "Very well, but we haven't much time."

"Oi," Barnaby called again. "Whoever's lurking out there in this soup, come help me wrestle this stubborn bitch to the ground so's I can have at her tit—" His rheumy amber gaze widened as Lorelai broke through the mist frantically trundling toward him. Had she had any doubt the voice belonged to him, they'd have been crushed the moment she'd spied his ever-present red cap. Lorelai flattened him to her in a desperate hug.

"My lady, what the fu—er, what the devil you doing?" He gave her shoulders a few hesitant pats. "I—I didn't know you were about or I wouldn't have spoke like that . . . It inn't safe for you . . . for us . . . out here." He carefully extracted himself from her embrace, looking around with wild, worried eyes.

"Barnaby!" She gasped, clutching his thin shoulders. "I'm so sorry you were dragged into this. Did they take anyone else from the household?"

Rubbing a hand on his work trousers, he refused to meet her eyes. "Just me, m'lady. It be me job to look after the animals, inn't it?"

"The animals?" Lorelai breathed.

"Brought the motherless little mites with us so's they di'nt starve. Which meant Grace O'Malley had to come along, di'nt she? But beggared if she'll let me milk her on the ship, the slag."

Had the fog not been so thick, Lorelai'd have seen the makeshift pen behind the galley sooner. Inside, her milk goat, Grace O'Malley—ironically named for a fearsome Irish pirate—bleated her complaints at them from beneath perpetually angry brows. Next to her, the basket of eight kittens she'd only five days hence rescued from drowning in a burlap sack mewled at the familiar sight of her.

"Goodness," Lorelai marveled. "How'd you talk them into taking animals with you?"

"Funny story, that—" Barnaby shifted about diffidently, but was cut off when Veronica hissed for them to hurry from across the deck.

"Coming," Lorelai whispered back to her before she limped over to the pen and wrangled it open as quietly as she could. "We're going to escape on the lifeboat," she explained as she hefted the basket of kittens, to their noisy dismay. "Here." She shoved the pistol into Barnaby's hands, thinking he'd know how to use it better than she. "Take this for protection and follow me."

"Right behind you, m'lady." Barnaby gaped at the pistol for a moment, then held the pen door open for her and shuffled about in the fog. "I'll . . . just get old Grace, here, and meet you by the ladder in a tick."

"Good thinking, Barnaby. I'm glad I found you before we escaped. I'd never leave you behind." Lorelai kissed next to the tufts of silver hair at his temple, and plunged back into the mist using an outstretched hand as her eye until she found the railing and Veronica again.

"What's this?" Veronica's dark brows drew together as she peered into the basket.

"The kittens."

Veronica blinked twice. "The . . . the kittens? Your kittens? What on earth would pirates want with them?"

"I don't know," Lorelai rushed. "Maybe they wanted to eat them. Do you think you can climb into the lifeboat and I can somehow lower the basket down to you? Barnaby's bringing Grace O'Malley and hopefully a rope. Perhaps we can lever her weight—"

"Grace?" Panic flared brighter and brighter in Veronica's jade eyes. "Grace. The *goat*? Oh, Lorelai. We can't take them. There isn't time. We're going to have to leave them behind if we have any chance."

"I'm not leaving them behind!" Lorelai insisted. "These are heartless pirates, Veronica. They tear entire armadas apart without shedding a tear and then sleep like babies. What do you think they'll do to these helpless little things?" She held up the basket, forcing Veronica to face identically tiny aspects of three orange tabbies, a gray tabby, two calicos, one white, and a strange little silver, blue-eyed ball of fluff that didn't at all seem to belong in the sleek-coated orphan family. "These villains will probably drown them again, and that's if they're feeling merciful."

"They'll do no such thing." The Rook melted out of the mist like Hades emerging from a realm of ghosts to claim his most recent soul.

Lorelai froze, gaping at the sight of him.

He moved like a panther. Silent and predatory, with the languid ease of a beast at rest, comfortable in the knowledge that he was the creature to whom all in his vicinity showed deference.

He claimed first kill. He devoured the most desirable morsels. His very presence alerted the jackals to wait their turn.

If he was lord of the underworld, was she Persephone,

then? A prize to be claimed. An unwilling bride to be dragged down to the depths as his consort.

That certainly seemed to be his intent.

Veronica made a hopeless sound, and Lorelai instinctively stepped in front of her, wishing with all her might she'd not relinquished her pistol.

To her astonishment, Barnaby trudged alongside the Rook, his head down and his hands clasped behind his back like a scolded child.

Dash it all, where was the gun? Had the Rook wrested it from him?

Lorelai ached to go to the old man, to comfort him, but six feet plus of dark and deadly pirate stood in her way.

The Rook's lips tightened with a wry sort of amusement. "Why would old Barnaby here go through the trouble of milking a goat to feed motherless kittens if we simply planned on slaughtering them?" He gently but firmly pried Lorelai's hands from the basket, and handed the litter back to Barnaby, who reluctantly accepted it. "Everyone aboard a ship has a job to do, and Barnaby, here, is a surprisingly deft gamekeeper."

"You must let him go. He has nothing to do with this," Lorelai demanded. Well, she'd *meant* to demand. In reality, her words escaped as a half whisper, half question and landed somewhere in the vicinity of his chest. If she met his gaze, she might expire.

"You would presume to steal from me, and then order me about on my own ship?" Mirth shaded his smooth baritone.

Her limbs went cold. "Steal from you?"

"That's my flannel, is it not?"

"Flannel?" Lorelai had never before heard the word.

"My shirt. Though I'll admit it suits you much better."

She looked down, distressed to note two of the toggles

had come loose, and the nonexistent collar had begun to slip off one shoulder. She clutched it to her throat, finally gathering the courage to meet his sinister glare.

He assessed her with his own shark eyes as she searched his achingly familiar face. He looked so much the same, and yet she recognized none of Ash in him. And she searched. *God,* did she hunt for a glimmer of the boy she'd loved.

His jaw was stronger, wider than before. His skin shades darker, weathered by the sun and the wind. The hollows of his cheeks were deeper, as though the fullness of youth had been chiseled away by a cruel but masterful artist.

He still wore his clothing from last night, and his collar gaped open, just as hers had. Unlike the ink on his back, the tattoos covering his chest and winding up his neck had vivid hues. She thought she saw the stripes of a tiger's claw slashing up toward his throat.

Dashing away an unwelcome curiosity, she hurried to explain herself. "I had to cover myself with something. I selected the least expensive garments I could find."

"No you didn't. That sash is the rarest cashmere made from soft exotic beasts who may only be sheared once every three years. It's worth more than your entire wedding dress."

Veronica gasped, and ran her fingers over the sash as though to test his assertion.

"I—I didn't know," Lorelai protested. Even as the daughter of an earl, she'd never been afforded many expensive things, and the sash was a plain cream, unadorned by jewels, tassels, or intricate threads.

The dagger concealed within was most likely valuable as well, the hilt and sheath encrusted with enough gems to sustain a small village through the winter.

She glanced over toward Barnaby, pleading at him with

her eyes. Now was his chance. If he had the pistol, he could train it on the Rook and convince him to let them all go. If any of the crew showed up, it would be too late.

What if Barnaby shot the Rook?

The thought lanced a confounding fear and grief through her chest. She'd not overtly mourn a violent murderer. But to watch a man with Ash's beloved features die would crush her spirit into the dust.

What to do?

The Rook slid closer, lifting her chin, though her eyes darted anywhere they could to avoid his empty gaze. "You have more courage than you used to."

She really didn't. She'd always been timid. Afraid. She'd cowered beneath the heel of a tyrant her entire life and would rather freeze at night or starve at mealtimes than displease her own servants. A dive into the treacherous sea sounded far more comfortable than a verbal spar with anyone, let alone a pirate.

If she could dissolve into the very mist that surrounded them, she'd sell her soul to do so now.

"I—I didn't mean to steal from you. I'm sorry." Was she *really* apologizing to the man who'd murdered her brother, kidnapped her, her family, her favorite employee, *and* her kittens? "T-to be fair, you ruined my bodice," she reminded him hesitantly.

A few masculine chuckles erupted from the mist, and Lorelai's heart sank further as she realized they were surrounded.

Surrounded . . . by pirates.

The Rook's fingers tightened on her wobbling chin. "You should have stayed where I left you."

Veronica whimpered from behind her, and poor Barnaby's head dipped so low, he looked as though he wanted to disappear into the basket with the kittens.

Somehow, their fear emboldened Lorelai, and she rested a hand on the Rook's thick wrist, her resolve clicking into place. "What if I made you an offer?"

His gaze flicked to where her hand rested on his skin. "I'm listening."

"Let Veronica and dear Barnaby go, and . . . and I won't try to escape you again."

More laughter. That didn't bode well, at all.

His fingers stroked from her chin to her jaw, testing the downy skin there. Oddly, she salivated, and was forced to swallow as a wash of foreign awareness poured over her like warm honey.

"There is no escaping me, Lorelai." His silken voice deepened to a husky velvet. A threat of inevitable seduction. A promise of possession.

Lorelai's knees trembled, and she could have sworn the calm seas had become decidedly choppy beneath her.

Barnaby stepped forward, one hand out. "Don't you give a worry for me, m'lady. There inn't no need to—"

One look from the Rook silenced him, and he took a step back.

"Barnaby needs no saving," the Rook said. "He's been a loyal member of my crew for almost a decade, now."

The wash of warm awareness became a splash of cold betrayal as she gaped at her employee. "Barnaby?" He'd been a plant? A spy sent to inform on her to his ruthless captain? Tears pricked her eyes. She'd thought they were friends, that she'd saved him from the workhouse.

Was there no one on this earth she could trust?

"I needed someone loyal in your household," the Rook explained dispassionately. "And only *you* would hire a doddering old waif over an able-bodied or handsome young hand."

Barnaby's stooped old bones straightened, and he took

off his cap, suddenly losing ten years. "Forgive me, m'lady."

Pain and humiliation pricked and tore at her resolve, but still she fought for composure, "Veronica, then." Her voice was harder now. Colder. "She goes, and I'll stay."

Veronica clutched her arm. "Lorelai, no!"

The Rook snorted and released her, gesturing to the expanse of the ship they still could not quite see through the fog. "You are both in my custody. You're hardly in a position to make a bargain. This isn't a trade deal, it's me collecting what's mine."

"Veronica is not yours," Lorelai argued.

"But *you* are." His cold eyes blazed for a transient moment before he blinked it away. "She's just insurance."

Heaving a great breath, Lorelai stepped toward him, out of Veronica's grasp. "What will it take to secure her release?" she murmured. "What will I have to do?"

Dawn broke over them, then. Scalding the mists, but not completely dissipating them. Pillars of golden light graced the deck, spilling over the Rook as he regarded her. It gilded a cobalt hue in his midnight hair and glinted off the sable lust in his eyes.

After a protracted moment, he answered her. "I think you know."

CHAPTER ELEVEN

The hungry glint in his eye left no room for interpretation. He desired her submission. He was hungry for sex. Lorelai gulped as an explosion of butterflies erupted in her stomach.

"I'll do it," she said, then cleared the catch of fear out of her throat to proclaim, "I'll do anything you want."

"Lorelai, stop. You don't have to. Not for me." Veronica seized her, thrusting herself between Lorelai and the Rook. "She's innocent. Take me, instead. I am younger than she, and less fragile. I've been married, and I . . . I know how to please a man."

The glance of distaste the Rook flicked toward Veronica baffled Lorelai. Her sister-in-law was considered a great and mysterious beauty, and she accentuated her natural allure with a wardrobe fit for a queen, all designed and stitched by her own hand.

"I don't want you," the Rook bluntly informed Veronica.

"I'll take 'er!" a crewman with a heavy French accent offered from somewhere off to their left. A chorus of male guffaws spread across the deck like a wave.

Veronica spat at the Rook's feet. "What kind of monstrous brute forces himself onto a frightened, crippled woman after murdering her brother and her intended on her wedding day?"

He stepped forward, grim amusement deepening the brackets around his hard mouth. "This kind of monstrous brute."

Even in such an extraordinary situation, it occurred to Lorelai that she didn't at all appreciate being discussed as though she were not capable of making her own decisions. Her own sacrifices.

The Rook held his hand out. "Come with me, Lorelai."

Lorelai couldn't bring herself to release Veronica and reach for him. The woman next to her trembled, and a wild terror bled from her eyes.

"I gave you my word, Lady Southbourne will not be harmed." He motioned her forward. "If you behave, I'll let her go."

"We cannot trust his word," Veronica said.

Lorelai extracted herself from Veronica's clutches. "It'll be all right," she soothed in a voice that failed to even convince herself, let alone her terrified sister-in-law. "You had to . . . to lie with Mortimer. Nothing can be worse than that."

"A pirate could," Veronica wailed, gesturing wildly to the Rook. "Just look at him. He's enormous!"

Their audience found no end of amusement in her declaration.

"Just wait until she sees 'im without his trousers. She'll faint dead away," one chortled.

"Take 'em both, Captain. The pretty one could teach the other one what to do, and then you could show 'em a thing or two." Another's salacious suggestion was met with howls of encouragement.

Lorelai heated with abject mortification. As much as she was used to being the brunt of a joke, it still stung when they laughed.

The other one? Not the most hurtful moniker she'd been subjected to, granted, but still. Veronica was the pretty one. She . . . was the other one. Though, on a pirate ship, her status might, for once, be an advantage.

Except . . . the Rook didn't want the pretty one.

He wanted her.

"The next man who makes a sound loses his tongue." The Rook's soft threat had immediate effect. Silence landed like a heap of bricks. They might as well have been alone on deck.

Lorelai turned to Veronica and kissed her cheek. "I'll be all right. Every time we're broken, we get back up and limp along. Isn't that what we've always said?"

"Don't leave me alone." Tears streamed down Veronica's cheeks and she backed away to the railing, her wild eyes finding the hulking forms of surrounding pirates in the swiftly dissipating mists. "I'll jump into that ocean before allowing you to leverage yourself for me." She scooted onto the railing, readying to hurl herself backward into the sea.

"No!" Lorelai stumbled forward, but was caught around the waist and hauled back against the Rook's unyielding body.

Moncrieff surged out of the fog, and scooped Veronica off the rail at the exact, breathless moment she'd released herself to the whims of gravity. Once again, he ignored her screams and struggles as he carried her back toward the blue room with long, furious strides.

Lorelai panted with equal parts horror and relief. She'd almost lost her dearest friend in the terrible blink of an eye.

Thank God for Moncrieff's reflexes. She'd not have made it in time.

The Rook breathed a faint sound in her ear. "How noble you both are. It's almost inspiring."

"Someone has to be," she spat.

"On the contrary. The sea demands no such nobility, and neither do I. One of the many appealing aspects of being a pirate." Stooping down, he scooped her up with an arm behind her knees, and the other supporting her shoulder blades.

Pirates, apparently, were predisposed to carry their female captives.

It occurred to Lorelai to protest, but she immediately thought better of it.

"See that we're ready to disembark for Ben More at dusk," he ordered the faceless crew in the mists.

"Aye, Captain," came several calls.

"When the fog clears, you'll find we are near Tobermory on the Isle of Mull," he continued without looking back. "You'll all be happy to note a bevy of eager young ladies from the Siren's Song brothel preparing to board."

It astounded Lorelai that the crew saved their roars of delight until she and the Rook had taken their leave, still unwilling to disobey their captain's order for silence.

It seemed she was not the only woman who would be ravaged aboard the *Devil's Dirge* today.

They passed Moncrieff in the hall as he threw the bolt home on the blue room before pressing his back against the door. Veronica's fists knocked against her prison, her cries barely audible from within the sealed room.

"You think it's a good idea, Captain, to bring these ladies aboard *this* ship, with *these* men? If anyone but Barnaby had happened upon them trying to escape—"

"Why else do you assume I provided the whores?" The whisper of a smirk tugged at the Rook's lips. "The crew will be appeased."

Moncrieff considered this, then shrugged. "That's why you're the captain." He gave the Rook a two-fingered mock-salute, and sauntered off. "I suppose I'd better inspect our new cargo when they arrive . . . sample the goods."

Lorelai hung passively in the Rook's arms until they reached his lush quarters and he kicked the door closed. Delectable smells cloyed around her and she blinked over at a sumptuous repast laid out on the table she'd tripped on the night prior.

Another throne had been added to his, this one upholstered in green velvet.

How had he managed such a feast so quickly? She'd only just left this room not a quarter hour ago or so . . .

Of course. She squeezed her eyes shut, feeling foolish and small. He'd known the moment she'd left his quarters. He'd allowed her to get as far as she did in the mist, because he'd known someone would stop her.

Or that he would.

So, what now? Did he mean for them to dine together before or after he took her virginity?

Despite the tension she sensed in her captor's arms, the grim displeasure visible at the corner of his mouth, he set her down with care. He stabilized her with strong hands and didn't release her until she'd gained her balance.

The imprint of his fingers lingered on her arms long after he'd moved to a secretary desk and lifted the lid to riffle through a few papers contained inside.

"What makes you assume I'm going to break you?" He asked the question casually, not looking up from the document he'd lifted from the desk.

"What?" Had she misheard?

"You told Veronica, every time you're broken, you get back up and limp along."

She had said that, hadn't she? They'd said that to each other on multiple occasions.

"You truly believe that becoming my lover would break you?" He was looking at her now, expectant curiosity hanging quizzically on his formidable brow.

Lorelai couldn't form an answer. She felt very brittle. It wouldn't take much. And Veronica wasn't wrong about one thing, the Rook was enormous.

He could very, very easily crush a strong and sturdy man.

And she . . . she had proven herself to be someone easily broken.

He didn't have much patience for her silence, and slammed the lid of the secretary closed. "No matter." His voice sounded darker as he approached her, and Lorelai was only slightly aware that she instinctively moved to place a lounge chair and end table between them.

"You said you'd do anything to save your sister-in-law." His lids lowered to half-mast, wicked suggestion gleaming from their dark depths. "Are you a woman of your word? Will you truly do . . . anything?"

Lorelai gulped, and thought of Veronica. "I am." She'd meant to sound more certain. "I will."

Suddenly terrified, she squeezed her eyes shut and balled her fists at her sides, waiting for him to strike. Willing the instinct to fight or flee to abate. She'd just lie still. She'd close her eyes, and pretend her lover was Ash.

Just as she'd imagined more times than she cared to admit.

The Rook possessed Ash's demeanor, just not his soul.

"Here." His voice didn't sound much closer.

Lorelai peeked out of one eye, and then stared down in abject astonishment at the paper and quill he'd set before her on the side table.

The marriage certificate from last night. Somehow this frightened her more than the prospect of his ravishment had. "I—I thought you said you didn't need my signature."

"I don't need it. But I want it. And you said *anything*."

Her brows pinched together against a distinct feeling that she was Alice fallen down the rabbit hole. "I thought I was negotiating for . . . for sex."

"Oh well. Have it your way." He stepped around the chair and reached for her.

"No!" She snatched up the pen and held it out as though it would ward him off. "No, I'll sign." Bending over the table, she carefully scrawled her name with slow, methodical flourishes.

Thankfully, this seemed to appease him, and he sauntered to a screen beneath the far right window and folded it aside.

"What are you doing?" She instantly realized the question had been needless, as the screen revealed a deep copper washtub.

"I'm drawing a bath." He turned two curious knobs and steaming water flowed out of a curved copper faucet like magic.

"How?" she marveled. It was a silly question under the circumstances, but Lorelai had wondered several times at the unfamiliar technology he'd amassed for the *Devil's Dirge*.

The Rook understood her question immediately. "Prodigy inventors and enterprising engineers always need financial backing, and what better way to spend my ill-gotten gains than a few creature comforts?" He tested the water flowing from the spigot with a few clever fingers. "A Mr. Juengling in Germany installed water-heating barrels in my engine room. The same heat which produces steam can, at smaller, further intervals, also be used to boil for the kitchen and the bath. I understand none of the particulars but then I pay others for that."

Had Lorelai not been terrified for her virginity, she'd have marveled at the mechanism and asked a million questions. As it stood, she could only focus on the fact that he meant to get her naked and into that contraption. "A bath— it's really not necessary. It hasn't even been a day since last I bathed. And I washed hours ago in the basin."

"I'm not drawing it for *you*." He glanced back at her over his shoulder, and Lorelai caught her breath. Partly at the thought of being forced to watch this lean, masculine predator bathe. And partly because she glimpsed a part of the impish boy she'd once known in his wicked look.

"Ash?" she breathed.

The familiarity disappeared as he straightened to his full and terrible height, glowering onyx shards at her. "I told you not to call me that."

"Then who *are* you?" She gestured at him in frustration.

"I am none other than the Rook," he insisted.

"That is your *title*," she argued, holding up the paper she'd just signed with his part left curiously blank. "What is your name?"

"I still have no idea." He shrugged as though this had little consequence.

"Then how do people address you? What do they call you when they speak to you?"

"They call me the Rook, obviously. Lorelai, this is getting tedious."

Stymied, she made a sound of frustration in her throat.

"But one can't address another with a *the* before their name." She mimicked a benign conversation. "What do you think of these hors d'oeuvres, *the* Rook? When should we set sail, *the* Rook? Aren't you being ridiculous, *the* Rook? It's not only impractical, it's impossible."

It occurred to Lorelai that she was being rather insolent for a pirate captive, but her nerves stretched beyond the capacity for restraint.

Astonishingly, her captor didn't at all seem to mind. He touched his chin pensively. "You could shorten it to Rook, I suppose," he ceded. "There's no great need for a *the*."

"Is that what your friends do?"

"I don't have friends."

"Your crew then?" she pressed.

"They call me Captain."

"That certainly won't work for me."

"Address me as husband, then, and I will always answer." After a look that threatened to scorch the fine hairs from her body, he perched on the bed to rid himself of his boots.

"But . . . in the eyes of most countries, we are not truly married," she argued.

"You only just signed documents to the contrary," he reminded her without looking up from his buckles.

"They don't have *your* name on them!" She brandished the marriage contract in her hand as if they proved her point. "Why do you insist on being intolerable?"

"I've given you options," the Rook said reasonably. "You're just being stubborn. You weren't stubborn as a child. I remember you being quite agreeable."

"Well, we've both changed in twenty years, haven't we?"

He looked up at her then, conducting a thorough examination as though to test her theory. From her unruly hair, to her pilfered shirt, and down to the soles of her wedding slippers. The silence became thick, heavy, charged with whatever emotions didn't reach his dead, black eyes.

She knew what he saw. An old maid. A crippled spinster in her thirties who'd let loss paint her pale and gaunt, and allowed bitterness to etch wrinkles into her forehead.

Why, then, didn't he look away? Why did he not allow his disappointment to show? If he were not Ash, and she was no longer agreeable, why did he want her, still? What would their life together look like? Would he take her to sail the world with him, forever locked in his cabin for his own personal use? Would he install her somewhere like a kept woman, to visit when he felt the need?

And if he claimed not to be Ash, why carry out a promise a supposedly dead man made?

She could no longer stand the silence of torturous unanswered questions and opened her mouth to inform him thusly.

"You need a name," she blurted. Well . . . that wasn't what she'd expected to say, but it was true, nonetheless.

"Why?" He stood and approached her in his bare feet, his gait as quiet as a hunter stalking his prey.

"I need you to—I mean—you need to be a *person*. Not a title." When he drew close, she put her hand out, and it landed over his chest, over the shirt still rumpled because he'd slept in it.

Unless he'd not slept at all.

Though her strength was feeble next to his, he halted his advance as though her hand were a wall. He stood abnormally still but for the muscle twitching and tensing beneath her palm. The warmth of his body radiated through the fabric, heating her chilly fingers.

Lorelai stared at her white hand against his black shirt. She remembered touching him like this before. Over his clothing, enjoying the little intimacies of their budding young romance. The brush of his hand against hers. The way he'd tuck her hair behind her ear. The strength of his shoulders and arms as he provided her stability whilst crossing the treacherous estuary.

That kiss.

The long-ago kiss that launched their love from an innocent infatuation into another territory altogether. That kiss had promised this very thing. He'd sworn with his lips that he'd claim her one day.

That Ash would.

"Why can you not be my Ash?" she pleaded. "You said you liked the name. That you liked being him for me."

He stared at her a long time, retaining that unnatural stillness that unnerved her to no end. "The boy you—knew is dead," he informed her gravely.

But that made no sense. He stood right here. "Why?" she demanded. "Who killed him?"

His eyes burned with an onyx fire. "Mortimer Weatherstoke. Though Ash has died many times since the first."

"Mortimer?" Lorelai snatched her hand back as though she'd been burned. "What did he do to you?"

He said nothing, but his knuckles whitened as fingers curled into fists. It was the first sign of emotion Lorelai had observed since he'd taken her.

"What happened to you? To Ash?" she whispered. "Tell me."

"It doesn't matter," he rumbled. "The past has already been written. The blood is already dry. The only part left of Ash is the part who—"

"The part who what?"

"The part who . . . owns you." Had she imagined it, or had it seemed as though he'd been about to say something else?

"You don't own me." How cruel time could be, to turn the boy she'd loved into a man she loathed.

"Of course I do." He smothered his sentiment with a leer. "Haven't you ever heard it stated that possession is nine-tenths of the law?" Without the barricade of her hand, he crept forward, crowding her. "What if I *were* Ash? What would you say to me?"

Heart stalling and then sputtering back to life, Lorelai took a limping retreat backward. "Y-you only just said that you wouldn't answer to Ash. That he was dead."

He reached for the ever-present curls at her temple, and she flinched as he caressed them, and twirled them about his finger. "Indulge me," he purred in that voice as thick and sonorous as torn velvet. "Pretend we are not on a pirate ship. That I am not the Rook. Imagine I walked into your little estuary yesterday and called your name. And we now stand in the same place, in the same mist surrounding us the day we were parted. What would you say to Ash?" He leaned closer, his warm breath smelling of whisky and desire as his head dipped low. His mouth a threat hovering over hers. "What would you do to him, after all this time?"

Without forethought, her hand whipped up and slapped his cheek with such force, her palm stung with it. "You promised to come for me!" she cried. "I prayed for your return, and then I begged. I *pleaded* with God to protect you, to send you back to me. When he didn't, I mourned you. For *years* I mourned you like a beloved who'd died tragically. Mortimer told me you remembered who you were. I thought you'd gone back to your life. And as much as it pained me, I could have forgiven you for that. But you left me alone for twenty *sodding* years to become *this*?" She gestured at him in all his dark glory. "This heartless, violent, deviant man? If you are not Ash, then you are not he who promised to come for me! You are not who I wanted."

"Yet I am what you get." His eyes glittered dangerously as he straightened. "My condolences. But it doesn't change anything. You still belong to me, and you will from this day on. It'll be better if you just resign yourself to the in-evitability of it."

"Just how do you expect me to do that?" she demanded. "You would have me simply roll over for you? Swoon and submit gratefully to you? A stranger? To the most violent and deadly criminal the world has lately known?"

After a protracted moment, he said, "Well. Yes." He turned his back to her then, and walked to the sideboard, pouring himself a drink. "You would have done so for that fat slab of rotten blubber. Don't tell me you'd have rather been Mrs. Sylvester Gooch. That you'd prefer to spread your legs for that gibface mutton wank over me."

She flinched. "I was trying to save my family from ruin. Without my marrying Mr. Gooch, we'd have been homeless."

"I know." He knocked back his whisky.

It occurred to Lorelai that he might have been angry with her. That most men would have slapped her back, or worse. He might have attacked her with the sexual frenzy of the prior night, full of masculine indignation over her physical challenge.

But the Rook treated her outburst as though it were nothing. In fact, he didn't even flinch as her slap had col-lided with his face. Hard. He'd reacted to it like it had no more consequence than a fly landing on his cheek.

And yet, for a man who claimed to be so emotionless, Lorelai swore she glimpsed moments of the maelstrom churning beneath the smooth surface.

He went to the bath and adjusted the knobs so the water flow ceased before turning to regard her. "Why are you so thin?"

The question couldn't have surprised her more. "I have been too distraught of late to eat much," she answered honestly. Might she have seen a flicker of regret in his dark eyes before he hid them from her?

He motioned to the breakfast, cooling on the table. "Eat now."

"I'm not hungry." Her stomach made a rude noise, which she stubbornly refused to acknowledge.

He took a threatening step toward her. "I will feed you from my hand, if I must."

"You cannot just force me to do something every time I refuse you."

"Actually, I can. And I will. Now. *Eat.*" He gestured to the table. "Buttered croissants and apricot marmalade are your favorite."

She glowered at him. "How do you know that after all this time my tastes haven't changed?"

"Have they?"

". . . No," she admitted glumly.

He lifted a challenging eyebrow.

"Not in pastries anyhow," she amended.

His lip twitched in an almost charming semblance of a smile. "You eat. I'll bathe. How perfectly civilized we'll be."

"Oh yes," she mockingly agreed. "It'll be breakfast, a bath, and then a bit of rape before tea."

He cast her another one of his scalding looks. One that made her wonder if as much steam rose from her skin as did from his bath. Turning from her, he peeled his shirt off unnecessarily wide, smooth shoulders before announcing, "One cannot rape one's wife."

Lorelai really did desire to summon a rejoinder, but the salaciousness of his statement coupled with the sight of his skin struck her completely dumb.

She couldn't say why it pleased her to discover that she'd been right about the tattoo on his back. Fanned over mounds and mounds of sculpted muscle, a black-winged tattoo flexed and flowed with astounding artistry, leaving no expanse of flesh uncovered. If she were anything other than a practical—some would say cynical—woman of a certain age, she'd truly believe he could spread those dusky wings and take to the skies.

Her disobedient fingers itched to stroke the designs. To splay against the smooth flesh beneath and discover— Oh heavens! He'd dropped his trousers.

Gasping, Lorelai spun around, but not before she caught sight of his lean hips and a backside that had once not been so thick.

What else had changed in twenty years? She'd peeked where she ought not to have done when they were young. Did men change . . . intimately as well as they matured?

Stop it! she admonished herself. These treacherous thoughts didn't bear consideration. She must keep her wits about her, if she were ever to survive this ordeal.

"You couldn't be more wrong." She replaced her wicked thoughts with traumatic memories of Veronica's pleas echoing through their wing of Southbourne Manor as Mortimer violently forced himself upon her. Lorelai would tremble in her bed, helplessly weeping for her. And she'd often go to her after, helping the injured woman off the floor, or from wherever she'd been discarded, and into her nightgown.

Every time we're broken, we get back up and limp along.

"Wrong? About what?" he queried.

"A man can absolutely rape his wife. Legally or no, there is no mistaking the sound of the deed. The terror, the pain, and the . . ." She swallowed vehement emotion. "The irrevocability of it."

He met this with another of his infuriating silences. The sloshing sounds of displaced water drew insolent pictures in her mind of what she might find when she turned around.

Unwilling to do so, Lorelai drifted closer to the table and inspected the food laid out artfully upon it. She could have been at the sideboard of any royal, all told. Not only did she find croissants and apricot marmalade, but Devonshire cream, various tarts, thick slabs of crisped bacon, flat, round foreign cakes soaked through with melted butter. Next to these she found a syrupy amber liquid darker and less thick than honey. Little coils of steam rose from silver coffee and teapots.

Suddenly she felt faint with hunger.

She supposed that obstinately starving would serve no purpose at all. If she were to escape her fate, she'd need the strength a hearty breakfast and some strong coffee would allow her.

With her unsteady gait, she made her way around the table and daintily claimed the green chair, which placed the copper tub in her periphery. She stubbornly avoided looking at the dark head and wide shoulders above the rim as she slathered a croissant with a generous portion of marmalade and tucked into it with more relish than she allowed herself to display.

If she had to look away from her plate, she made a point of staring out of the windows, as more and more of the mist dissipated, unveiling an emerald sea.

"You know." His cavernous voice broke the silence, causing her to start and nearly choke on a splendid bite. "If you weren't so fixated on the physical aspect, you might bring yourself to consider that marriage to me could be the best thing that ever happened to you."

Though she'd promised herself not to look, he'd stunned her enough to evoke an openmouthed gape in his direction. He scrubbed his long, decorated arms with some sort of pumice stone lathered with soap. In complete contrast to his back, colorful tattoos wended their way across his chest, his shoulders, and stretched down the swells of his arms all the way to the wrists. Lather covered some of their particulars, and she snapped her eyes back down to her plate before she became completely transfixed by the shapes and forms.

"How could it possibly?" she marveled. "Other than your infamy, what do you have to offer me? I'd be the wife of one of the most wanted men in the world."

"Granted, but you'd be the wife of one of the wealthiest men in the world."

"Your wealth means nothing to me," she said tartly. "I'd rather starve than remain married to you."

"You say that because you have never starved."

Something about the way he stated this left no question that he had.

Her next bite tasted sour rather than sweet as an unwanted twinge of regret twisted in her stomach.

"I can offer more than money, you know." Casually, he lifted his arms to scrub at his hair.

Lorelai made a rude noise. "You have no past, no country, no family, no compassion. No kindness. You won't even claim a name. Just what do you have that could possibly entice me?"

"A kingdom." He gestured to the window where the panorama stretched endlessly now, until it disappeared around the curvature of the earth. "I rule the seas. I wield more power over innumerable leagues than your so-called empress could even begin to fathom."

"But you are ever at the mercy of those seas. Of the tides. No mere mortal can claim to control them," she argued, astonished by his arrogance.

He dunked his head beneath the water and rose again. Rivulets sluiced from his hair and chose distracting trails down the cords of his neck, the groves of his clavicles, and between the swells of his chest. To look at him, it was easy to forget that he was a mere mortal. That he'd not been crafted of clay and iron, fortified by volcanic stone, and tempered by unimaginable storms.

"The sea has no mercy. Upon that I can rely." He wiped a hand down his face, swiping away excess water, and Lorelai did her best not to notice that it still spiked in his dark lashes and gathered like gems on his skin in the invading sunlight.

"We are alike in that respect, the sea and I," he rumbled. "Mercy serves me no purpose. I have learned to become as devastating as any storm. I can count upon the tides. They ebb and flow by the will of the moon and stars. I can time my life to their pull." He studied her with such alert vigilance, she might as well have been crushed beneath a chemist's microscope. "It is people who are more difficult to predict. They are the indefinable variable."

Lorelai turned to the porthole window, their eye to the sea, and found that they'd somehow turned so an emerald coastline loomed in the distance. The Isle of Mull. The stronghold of the Blackheart of Ben More.

"Should my hoary kingdom not impress, I've plenty of

land holdings and the applicable titles to offer you," he continued. "For example, I'm the Duke of Castel Domenico in Italy. The Comte de Lyon et de Verdun in France, and—"

"You're a *duke*?" She nearly spurted coffee across the table.

"Well, a Continental one, but I believe it's still apropos to address me as Your Grace."

No, he had to be lying. "How . . . how did you . . . ?"

"Easily. I killed the previous one, but not before he named me his heir. Many Continental titles are not so entailed to primogeniture as English ones."

Lorelai had rarely been stunned so witless in her life. "You *killed* the . . ."

He held up a water-wrinkled finger. "To be fair, most of them tried to kill me first."

Most of them? "Does life mean so little you would discard it with such indifference?"

"Categorically."

"What *happened* to you?" she cried. "When did you decide to become *such* a villain?"

When were you on the Continent? she wanted to rail at him. *And why didn't you come for me then?*

His words from the prior night drifted back to her. *I waited to inflict myself on you for as long as I could . . . It's the only kindness I can afford you.* In this moment, she didn't know whether to be grateful, or angry.

Gods, but he sent her emotions scrambling in so many directions, she felt caught in the web of the most confounding, dangerous spider on earth.

His gaze became a dreadful void, swirling with a darkness so abysmally black, she feared that if she looked for too long, she'd find the depths of hell. "That is a story I do not wish to tell," he said in a voice as cold as the Arctic Sea. "And one you do not wish to hear."

She believed him. And yet . . . She did want to hear it. She wanted to know. To understand. But did she want to picture the sort of torments that could have torn Ash away from himself?

Categorically not.

"Come over here," he ordered. "I wish for you to wash my back."

"But I—I'm not done with my breakfast."

"Yes you are."

She meant to argue with him, but then she glanced down at her empty plate.

"Will you go back on your word?" His challenge landed harshly in the lush opulence of his quarters. "You promised me *anything.*"

So he kept reminding her.

Sighing, she slid her chair back and pushed to her feet. She approached him cautiously, as she did those wounded, wild animals, and his demeanor contained just as much lethal ferocity.

She'd wanted to run her fingers across his winged tattoos, hadn't she?

Here was her chance.

After rolling up her sleeves, she perched behind him on the tub, picked up a cloth and soap, and dawdled by creating more lather than necessary before she touched the cloth to his back.

Anxiety had leached the heat from her fingers, and the warmth of his water-heated skin immediately radiated through her, lancing up her arm. She'd been right, he was solid as stone and smooth as marble. The feel of him was as familiar as it was foreign. She'd washed him before, long ago. She'd run her fingers over these very same long, lovely muscles. Sometimes, her fingers found a ridge beneath the artwork. Scars, she realized. Wounds. Ones he'd covered with ink and time. He'd been scarred as a boy, but not like this. They were everywhere. Some of them shallow and wide, others long and deep.

Who had hurt him like this? Who would dare?

Mortimer?

"Heroes and villains . . ." he mused, a husky note was added to his already resonant voice. "Must men be defined thusly? There are none of either in the animal kingdom. There are only those who eat, and those who are eaten. The strong prey on the weak. There is an order to things. You adapt and survive . . . Or you die."

"Yes," Lorelai conceded. "But you are not a beast."

"Am I not?" His chin touched his glistening shoulder. "That may be the kindest thing anyone has said to me in ages."

"I meant you are human." She'd not meant to show him kindness. Had she?

"Some believe man to be a higher form of animal. The king of beasts."

"You certainly are a predator," she accused. "And I have become your unwilling prey."

"Think that if you like." His jaw hardened as he stared forward again. "I'm a conqueror. You are the conquered. To the victor go the spoils. You're the one who's lived among wild creatures your whole life, you should understand how this works. How many beasts apologize to their mates after taking them? What happens, Lorelai, when a powerful male creature wants a female? Does he woo her with flowers and poetry and pretty manners? Does she entice him with a dowry and a family name? No. The male fights off every other who would have her, he dominates them, kills them if he must. Then, he claims her. And she lets him, because he has proven himself the strongest. He can protect her and their offspring. It is the way of things in the wild, and so it is with us."

Lorelai's trembling fingers dropped the cloth, and it slowly disappeared beneath the opaque surface. She was glad he wasn't looking at her, that he couldn't see her chin wobbling. Or her thighs trembling. "It doesn't have to be thus," she ventured.

He twisted his torso to spear her with his frigid glare. "But it is. I was hoping you'd understand."

Her distress increased, and she loathed the tear that escaped her. "As a girl I thought . . . I *knew* . . . Ash would be the man I offered myself to when I came of age. I hate that, in the end, *you're* going to be the one who hurts me. Who treats me like Mortimer treated Veronica. I never thought in a million years you would cause me that kind of pain . . ."

"I won't!" he hissed vehemently. "Don't you fucking dare compare me to *him*." He slammed his lips shut, as though his outburst surprised even him. Frowning, he seemed to consider something for a long while. So long, in fact, her nerves stretched to the breaking point.

"What do you mean?" she prompted. "Are you saying you won't require me to . . . we won't consummate . . ." Lord, the heat of her blush could have immolated her right where she stood.

"Oh, we will," he vowed as the dawning of an idea swirled behind those dark, wicked eyes. "But what if I offer you a reprieve of sorts? A pirate's promise."

"Are pirates any good at keeping promises?" she breathed.

"I suppose we'll find out."

Why the change of heart? she wondered. "What are your terms?" What was his objective?

Her question seemed to encourage him. "*I* will not take *you*. Not by force. Not until you ask me to."

What? Considering the stance he'd taken since he returned for her, this didn't make any sense. "I don't understand."

"Don't you?" he challenged. "You were always a curious girl. I don't imagine that's changed. What if, instead of making you my offering, I offer *my* body for *your* use?"

Mouth suddenly dry, Lorelai stood. "What if I don't want it?"

Wings flexed as he stood and turned to her, revealing all of himself. His skin like molten gold shaped over the cold, tempered steel of his chest and decorated with brilliant color. The flare of his shoulders were molded into the fascinating mounds of his biceps before tapering down to sinewy forearms laced with thick veins.

Lorelai did her level best not to follow the obdurate ripple of muscles down his torso, arrowing right to the lean hips and his—

Eek. She slammed her eyes shut. That had definitely grown along with the rest of him in twenty years.

"Tell me you do not, and I'll tell you you're a liar."

Her lips parted to deny it, but not a word escaped.

"You may do what any other has died a torturous and painful death for even attempting."

"What is that?" She blinked up at him, resolutely watching his eyes and never drifting lower.

"Use me." He held his arms out, hands up like a pagan sacrificial offering. "Wield me, Lorelai. I am at your discretion. I am at your disposal. Whip me, bind me, torture me, degrade me. Any need you have, I will fulfill. Any curiosity you can conceive of, I will provide the answer."

The first smile she'd ever witnessed spread over his fiendishly sensual lips. It was the smile of a shark, all teeth and temptation. "Out there, I am captain and I am king. In this chamber, you rule me. You command me."

His eyes captured hers, and where she'd seen voids before she now saw nothing but opportunity. And something else. Something . . . she might have once called yearning.

"You own me."

CHAPTER TWELVE

He'd have done it all again, the Rook decided.

He'd have waded through twenty years of hell and oceans of blood to get to this moment. To see Lorelai's eyes glitter like the most precious gems in the Amsterdam markets. They sparkled with the cerulean agony of indecision.

Reality touched her with more beauty than his memory ever could. Even as tenaciously as he'd clutched at the memory of her visage, twenty years had dimmed certain details in his mind's eye. He'd remembered the unruly tendrils of gold at her temples, but not the matching flecks of gold in the azure of her irises. Likewise, the brilliance of her smile had benighted many of his dreams, but he'd forgotten that beloved dimple in her cheek. Just the one.

Time and melancholy had robbed some of the hope from her eyes, and the light from her smile. But none of her beauty.

If there was a better word for perfection, he would have used it.

The years, the sun, and the sea had been far unkinder to him.

Touch me. He didn't ask. He didn't beg.

Not out loud.

The Rook begged no one. He asked nothing. He commanded. He ordered. He decreed.

He used his cunning and ruthlessness to get what he wanted. He'd used it to get her here, into this room, in fact. He was the kind of man that ruined people. One way or another. And something had whispered to him that the moment he'd found his way back to Lorelai, he'd ruin her, too.

But for twenty long years she'd been the grit in his oyster. The one memory he could not be rid of. The obsession that had kept him alive. Had driven him to survive what so many had not.

He'd had his weak moments, of course, where he'd wondered if she was some halcyon specter of the past. Unreal and unattainable. He feared he'd find her a figment of perfection his defective mind had somehow enshrined as a mechanism for survival. His memory was faulty, after all. His brain seemed to work differently than others'. When men became impassioned, hot, and angry, he became cool, remote, and unfeeling.

He closely watched those around him, their hearts on fire with greed and lust and so many other human emotions. It made them reckless and illogical, but that fire also made them strong, tenacious, and brave.

Were he capable of envy, the Rook would have coveted that very human heat. But he realized early on his heart was made of other stuff. His internal workings emulated the complications of gears and cogs found in a watch. His was a clockwork heart. Where others' beat and burned, his only tick, tick, *ticked* away the hours, the minutes, the seconds that separated him from one other soul on this enormous globe.

Lorelai.

Every year he suffered, every chain he broke, every possession he took, and every man he killed, he'd done it in her name. Knowing all the while, she'd not want any of it. That she'd reject who he'd become the moment she laid eyes on him. It'd occurred to him she might even have moved on. Fallen for someone else, some gentle, pretty lord, and given him a brood of children.

Would he have taken her if that were the case? Stolen her from a happy life?

Probably.

He'd become a monster, after all, and monsters did monstrous things, despite the consequence to anyone else.

In fact, he could scarce believe that he'd found her just as he'd left her. Untouched by another. Unloved.

And unwilling.

Touch me. He silently yearned as she just stood there, paralyzed, doing her best not to glance below his navel where his sex jutted toward her, erect and throbbing, impatient to claim his mate.

He dimly realized part of the reason he'd finally come for her was because of this moment. This ultimatum.

This offering.

Here was the final threshold between man and monster. In his tenure as the Rook, he'd taken things from men and women who'd sobbed and pleaded for mercy and he'd felt . . . nothing. No scruples. No hesitation. No remorse.

They were weaker than he. And in this world, weakness was not rewarded. It was exploited. He'd known that even before he'd lost his memory. He'd understood it the moment he'd woken on that bed in the Weatherstoke mansion, broken and lost. His vulnerability had battered at him, taunted him. For no one protected the weak. No one rewarded the innocent. No one was kind to the maladroit.

If you wanted something, you took it, and then you fought to defend it, or someone would take it from you.

In every kingdom, either of man or animal, this was a fundamental truth.

Only one person had ever consistently contradicted that certainty.

Lorelai.

Kind, patient, tender Lorelai. Champion of the weak and wounded. She took beasts who should have suffered their fates with all the brutality nature could devise, and she healed them, taught them to thrive with their impediments.

She was what he desired above all else. He'd thought he could take her. Whether she wanted him or not. He'd told himself that he deserved her, that he was owed the one thing that had ever delighted him in twenty years. He'd given himself, and her, every reason why he should claim her as his right. Why he could. Why he *had*.

And yet . . . here she stood. Waifish and delicate, innocent and untouched.

Even by him.

Because here was the one threshold he could not seem to cross into his final damnation. The one thread that tied him to a flickering vestige of humanity. His one island in an endless ocean of unforgiveable depravities.

No matter how cold and cruel and inhumane he'd become . . . he physically could not bring himself to face a weeping Lorelai Weatherstoke. He could not stand to be the cause of those tears. He, who could burn all of London to the ground and not lose a blink of sleep over it, trembled at the sight of her distress. Quivered for one tick of his heart to be spent basking in her touch.

He simply could. Not. Hurt. Her. Even if it meant denying himself the one thing he'd lived for.

And so, the problem remained. How did he get what he wanted? What he deserved? How did he find the sanctuary he knew only existed in the circle of her arms? In the bliss of her caress. In the depths of her warm body.

He'd been up all night considering that very thing, until the answer had struck him with all the might of a rogue wave. Instead of forcing himself upon her, like the heartless fiend that he was, he could offer himself to her.

She could do the taking.

It was the perfect solution. All he wanted was her touch, in whatever form she could offer it. She'd only just proven that a sharp slap delivered by her palm was better than an intimate massage by any one of a thousand well-trained whores.

When he'd become the Rook, he'd vowed to slaughter anyone who'd ever dare raise a hand to him again.

And yet, when she'd done it, he'd wanted to purr. He'd wanted to growl, but not with his teeth. With his throat. With that bestial part of him who'd come to enjoy the blow. To crave the pain. For in the impact of lash against flesh, he did sometimes find his lost humanity.

Only to lose it when the pain subsided.

Would she hit him again? he wondered. And had to bite down on the inside of his cheek against an unbidden groan of anticipation.

"I—I don't understand." Her voice shook with a husky emotion he couldn't identify. Somewhere on the spectrum between terror and temptation. "You claim to possess me in one breath, and then proclaim that I own you in another. What . . . what am I supposed to do with that?"

You're supposed to heal me. Or hurt me. To save me. Or condemn me. To remind me that I'm human.

It was too much to ask of anyone, he knew that. And so he didn't. He truly expected none of that from her. He just wanted her to *fucking* . . .

"*Touch me,*" he said as evenly as he could through clenched teeth.

He stepped out of the tub and onto the plush rug beside it, but advanced no further, even when she retreated a step back.

"I—I'm not sure if I—or how to—"

"There is no right or wrong way of it," he pressed. "Just do what you want."

She did everything she could not to look at him, and why he found that charming, the Rook would never know. It was as though she desired to preserve his modesty, rather than hers.

Was there such a thing, he idly wondered, as a modest pirate?

"But . . . you're all wet," she protested.

That word, on *her* lips, nearly drove him mad.

Wet.

Yes. He was, indeed, wet. And if he had his way, she would be, too. But only in that sweet, hidden place.

And only for him.

He glanced down at his chilly, decorated body. "If you wish me dry, you may help." He gestured to a plush towel hanging from an ornate banister at her elbow.

Her delicate throat worked over a difficult swallow before she dragged the towel away from its perch and attempted a cautious approach.

She still wouldn't look at him, he noticed. For the most fleeting of seconds, her gaze would drift toward his body, land, and then dart away, like a hummingbird testing a flower.

Settling her hands—covered safely with the towel—on

his shoulders, she tentatively soaked up the bathwater with soft little drags.

He watched her as she did this. Delighting in her shyness. In her artless, gentle caresses. When one dried themselves, it was usually with firm, decisive strokes, but her touch barely deserved the designation.

It didn't matter. Nothing mattered. Lorelai was here. In his cabin. Touching him.

Sort of.

"W-where did you sleep?" she queried.

It was something she did, he remembered, when she was anxious. She tried to fill a fraught silence with polite conversation.

"I didn't, really. I stayed awake to watch the tempest." He obediently lifted his arms toward her as she pulled the towel down each one, revealing his colorful, permanent sleeves.

"Don't sea gales ever frighten you?" she asked, running the cloth down the ripples of his ribs.

"No."

She paused at his waist, unwilling to go further, and circled around to his back, drying his shoulders. "Why not?"

Because I tasted your lips on every rainstorm.

"Because fear is dangerous," he answered aloud. "Fear gets people killed."

She left that response alone. "What about my kittens?"

Something in his lust-clouded brain stalled. Kittens? Who could be thinking of fluffy, noisy little beasts at a time like this? "What about them?"

"Why go through the trouble of bringing them on the ship?"

Why, indeed? he wondered. "The crew can be superstitious. I figured, like the whores, the kittens would appease them. It's considered bad luck to have women on board at sea, you know. But quite good luck to have cats."

Her brow wrinkled. "But . . . if women are bad luck . . . why bring—er—other ladies onto the ship?"

"The bad luck doesn't apply if we are anchored."

"I see," she murmured, as though she didn't see at all. "Why are cats considered good luck on a ship?"

"It's been thus for as long as men have taken to the sea," he answered almost irritably. Was it her aim to torture him? To explore the sensitive columns of muscle beside his spine as they discussed maritime superstitions and accursed felines? "They kill mice and rats. Which was helpful in times of plague, I imagine."

"Oh . . ." His ears perked to a disenchanted tone in her voice. He realized, belatedly, that in this case the truth might better serve them both. He took a deep breath, willing himself to try. "Barnaby mentioned that the beasts in the menagerie would be all right without you for a time, but without constant care, the young kittens would die. Their deaths would have . . . distressed you."

"Oh." This time, her voice seemed a bit brighter, and he wished that she was not behind him so he could see her face. Had he pleased her?

Not that it mattered. It didn't. A delighted sort of warmth spread up his neck, taunting him for a liar.

"It has not been apparent that my distress is of great concern to you," she remarked dryly.

He scowled, his pulse elevating. "Were that the case, I'd have fucked you a dozen times by now. I'd have spent the night in here, instead of in the rain. I'd have pulled you into that bath with me and washed the sweat and leavings of our sex off of *and out of* you before supping on your slick flesh. So be careful of tossing about accusations, Lorelai, or I might decide to live up to them."

He clamped his lips shut, then. How distressing that she continued to goad him into speaking without careful estimation. A dangerous influence of hers, that.

The tickle of her short, shocked breaths against his back distracted him from his ire and spread chill bumps across his entire body.

She must have noticed, because she silently resumed her hesitant ministrations with the towel. When it dipped below his waistline, his hips, and he felt her fingers trail below his ass, he had to close his eyes against a wave of desire so exquisite, it threatened to buckle his knees.

She'd knelt down, drying his legs from the back and reaching around his thighs to be thorough.

He glanced back at her bent head, her eyes no doubt fixed firmly on the floor.

Clever girl. She'd avoided the sight of and all contact with his sex as best she could.

But she was on her knees. All he had to do was turn around and her mouth would be right there . . .

Something in his jaw cracked, along with his self-possession.

Without thinking, he bent down, grasped her arms, dragged her to her feet, and pressed his lips to hers. He wouldn't force her. He'd keep his word. But their first kiss had been enough to span the memory of two decades, and damned if he could live without tasting her again.

She made a sound, though whether shock, protest, or surrender he couldn't tell. It didn't matter.

He had, indeed, fancied that he'd tasted her lips on the rain, had savored the memory of her innocent kiss on the darkest nights of his life, and it had still been like trying to catch the warmth of the sun from its reflection on the cold moon.

A lovely, but pale comparison.

With a throaty growl, he locked her body against him with one arm. His other hand slipped past the collar of the shirt she wore until his fingers found the delicate nape of her neck. He spread his fingers up her scalp, threading them in the flaxen tangles of her unbound hair until her head rested in his palm.

How long had he waited? How many nights had he imagined this? Burned for it? When he'd been chained in the hull of a ship, whipped, stabbed, beaten, or starved, this was the future he'd clung to.

This was the moment he'd lived for.

He'd once been a tortured slave who had mutinied, looted, and gorged on the feasts of the wealthy exotic merchants who'd kept him like a ravenous hound.

And even that meal wasn't as splendid as this.

She tasted of simple joy. Of innocent pleasure. Of tea and honey and hope.

Her hands rested on his bare chest and, though her arms were tense, she didn't push him away.

He wanted to savor all of her. Every soft, delicate, hidden part. Behind her ears, the supple curve of her bare shoulder, the taut peaks of her breasts, her quivering belly.

His tongue slid past her lips, enticed by the wicked fantasy he'd conjured. He lapped and nibbled at her in a warm mimicry of what he thirsted for.

An intimate taste of her.

He yearned to feast on her desire, and then on the warm rush of her pleasure. A pleasure he wrought upon her before he finally claimed his own and lost himself inside her. His was an appetite crafted only for *this* woman, and he'd not be satisfied until he'd sampled every lush, pale or pink inch of her.

Driven by twenty years of pent-up need, he backed her

against the nearest wall, lifting her so her weight wouldn't rest on her ankle.

She might be slight, and delicate, but he had enough strength for them both. She never had to worry about that. He would bear the brunt of any cruelty. He'd shield her from pain. He'd fulfill her every whim.

All she'd have to do was endure him. Was that too much to ask?

Probably.

He swallowed her exhale of astonishment, fusing their mouths, their bodies. The blood danced in his veins when her arms slid around him. His frame went taut with triumph when she timidly kissed him back.

He folded over her. Into her. Curled around her as if she were the last bit of warmth in a world of ice and terror and deprivation. Even his joy became its own kind of torment. This was both everything and not enough. He needed to claim her. To crawl out of himself and to sink into her. He was like a pilgrim kneeling before a holy relic, desperate for a miracle. Praying for the touch of a deity. For the love of his goddess. Had he a soul, he'd have offered it to her.

But he didn't.

Not anymore.

All else he possessed was hers. His money. His body. What was left of his life.

Didn't she know that? How could he make her understand?

He would show her. Like this. He would drain every last gasp of carnal bliss from her lungs. He would worship her with his hands, with his mouth, until she begged him to stop. He'd deny himself his own fulfillment until she came to him. Until she was as desperate for him to be inside her as he was.

Reaching down, he parted her legs so he could get closer, cursing every single layer of her skirt, her undergarments, and even the air that took up the space between them. He drove his hips against the silk of her skirts, sex against sex, frustrated by the barrier, but aroused by her soft hiss of breath and the tremble he felt roll through her limbs.

The first of many, he vowed.

"Can you feel a whisper of what I can give you?" he asked, rolling against her again, knowing he abraded the sweet little nub with each flex of his hips.

"Y-yes . . . but I . . ." Her fingers became claws on his shoulders, as though she feared falling.

I'll not let you go. He kissed the corners of her mouth, her chin, and dragged his lips over the downy skin of her throat, stopping to nibble at the pulse he found leaping there. *I'll never let you go.*

"Are you wet for me?" he demanded in a harsh whisper.

It took her three tries to swallow. "I—I'm . . ." She lost her words when he bit at her earlobe.

"Let me make you slick and slippery," he urged.

"Make . . . what?"

"Let me make you writhe. And beg. And scream. I will exhaust you with ecstasy. You will come apart in my hands, beneath my mouth."

"Please, just . . ." She gasped on a shuddering breath. The words, combined with her slight squirming against his nude, aroused body threatened to drive him beyond all control.

His shirt, already enormous on her slight frame, had come lose in their clench, and his composure slipped in time with the collar as it drifted down her bare, pale shoulder. His lips followed the seam, exploring the softness of her skin on an expedition toward her breast. All he had to do was expose it, taste it—but in order to do that, he'd have to cease his soft thrusts against her core.

"Wait," she groaned, tugging at his hair. "I'm going to . . ."

Was she going to come already? He hadn't even started yet.

"I meant what I said," he crooned against her skin. "My body is yours, to use as you will. I will be a slave only to your desires. What do you want me to do?"

"Stop," she sobbed.

He froze, pulling away to gaze down at her, and saw the panic in her eyes. Her skin flushed from pink to pale in the course of a stunned breath, and a sheen of sweat bloomed at her hairline and over her lip.

"Lorelai?" He carefully lowered her to the ground, his arousal turning to alarm as she frantically pushed him away with feeble trembling limbs. "Lorelai, are you hurt?"

She shook her head, but her eyes clouded, her movements almost inebriated. "I'm sorry," she mumbled, reaching out for the edge of the tub, for something to stabilize herself upon.

"What's wrong?" he demanded, fighting the urge to shake her, to stun life back into her eyes.

"I'm sorry . . . Ash." Her eyes rolled back and every limb slackened. She felt as limp as a corpse when he caught her and lifted her into his arms.

He strode to the bed and laid her carefully upon it, all the while calling her name. He checked her breathing, which was shallow, but regular. He shook her, and tapped at her alarmingly pale cheeks, a bleak emotion welling inside of him, one he hadn't confronted in a handful of years.

Terror.

Because this was no mere maidenly faint. No matter what he tried, she wouldn't wake.

CHAPTER THIRTEEN

Veronica Weatherstoke pressed her ear to the wall. The muffled sounds of violence and distress in the next room remained unamplified.

A feminine cry of alarm had pulled her from her wretched state. She'd sat up on the bed, where she'd been heaped into a puddle of misery, at the first crash of what must have been glass. A second splintering crunch had drawn her to the wall decorated with surprisingly tasteful blue paint, and a collection of what appeared to be original and expensive art.

This turbine-propelled steamship was built better than any her family had crafted, and she'd noted the sturdy thickness of the walls, and the barrier it would make against unnecessary noise.

She couldn't hear footsteps or voices from the hallway. Nor could she make out the din of the sea just beyond the laughably small porthole windows lining the far wall.

The room was meant to be a gilded prison but, for some reason, sound could carry through this particular wall. But how? She ran her hand over the textured paint, tensing as a high-pitched pleading from the other side stoked her distress.

Not Lorelai, she realized with a shaky exhale. She would have recognized her sister's voice right away. She knew enough of the layout of this hall of the ship to understand Lorelai was being kept two quarters down at the end. Where she'd been carried by their black-haired, black-hearted captor.

Then who was next door? Another captive? Was one of the prostitutes the Rook mentioned being mistreated?

Men did not consider it an immorality to rape or beat a whore. Strange, they'd often similar standards for their wives.

A wife she was no longer. She had a pirate captain to thank for that, at least. Though, it seemed, she'd been delivered from one form of fearsome incarceration into another.

Whoever this man, this Rook, was to Lorelai, Veronica knew they were no safer on this ship than they'd been at Southbourne with Mortimer alive.

Less so, surely, as evidenced by the chaos being wrought in the very next room.

Veronica pulled her head back and examined the wall. If the sounds weren't coming through the barrier itself, then there must be a weakness in the structure somewhere.

She found it after only minutes of running her hands along the paint, all the while following the ceaseless clamor of chaos. An insignificant, circular perforation, no larger than her smallest fingernail, had been bored beneath the shadow of a bucolic painting with a disproportionately large frame.

The faint cries were most audible here.

Bending down, Veronica took a bracing breath against

the dread gathering in her chest before placing her eye directly at the fissure.

Squeaking, she popped back up again, leaping back from the sight.

Clapping one hand over her mouth, and another over her racing heart, she stood and blinked and breathed for an unaccountably long time.

Not only did the pirates keep their captives in this chamber, they spied on them, as well. This she knew, because the spyglass would have shrunken everything in the blue room for the examination of a watchful eye on the other side of the wall.

Conversely, it focused on and magnified only one place in the next bedroom for her view.

The desk.

The desk from which everything had been violently swept to the ground.

The desk on which a dark-haired woman writhed and squealed and pleaded as Moncrieff's head danced between her thighs.

Drawn by a macabre curiosity, Veronica returned to the spyglass, her breaths as loud as one of the band saws in her father's factories.

The sight was no less shocking the second time, even though she'd prepared herself for it.

The woman was positioned so Veronica could see down the length of her naked body. Her coiffed, dark head lolled from the edge of the desk, her chin pointing at the ceiling.

Veronica could assess her every expression, though upside down.

Her eyes squeezed shut and her powdered skin stretched tight in a grimace of torment, or was it enjoyment? Her mouth remained open, forming perfect, rhythmic *oh*s.

Veronica listened intently. What she initially interpreted as pleas could very well have been demands.

But . . . why?

Heartbeats became claps of thunder as Veronica looked between—what she could only assume was a prostitute's—quivering bare breasts, past her taut belly rippling with strain, to where Moncrieff's bronzed hair gleamed from between the V of the woman's open legs.

Veronica's own thighs clenched on an aching pulse. The sensation threaded down through her veins to land in the very place that so absorbed his lewd attentions.

She remembered the times her husband had demanded to use her mouth. How she'd hated it. Hated him. Resented the pleasure he found there. The pain and degradation he left behind.

Never once had the possibility occurred to her that a woman might use a *man's* mouth for pleasure.

That a woman might find pleasure at all.

The prostitute could be faking her bliss, she supposed. But why, then, would she hold such a craven look upon her face when he could not see it? The expression was so unnatural. So unpracticed. Almost madcap to an astonished voyeur.

Moncrieff pulled back, and the woman's eyes flew open. She lifted her dark head, and said something in a frustrated whine that Veronica could not quite catch.

His wicked laugh awakened something inside of Veronica she wished she could lull back to sleep. Something that felt like the empty ache of hunger, in her belly

No, not her belly. Lower.

She watched the play of muscle on his arms bunch and ripple as he gathered his untidy hair into a queue and secured it behind him. His smile was teasing, dazzling. His words were guttural and crass, this she knew.

What did he say to the harlot? What wicked things caused the woman to moan and part her legs in further, seemingly desperate, invitation? One of the nude lady's bejeweled hands lazily toyed with her own breast, and the other idly slid down her lithe body, finding their own way to her sex.

Veronica gasped at the luridness of it. The unabashed ignominy of them both. At the shameful response building in her own treacherous body.

He seemed to enjoy taunting the woman. In watching her as she stroked at herself. She, in turn, seemed to be attempting the same physical repartee. He encouraged her as his big hands stroked up her ankles, her calves, thrummed behind her knees, and smoothed their way across her splayed white thighs.

Her hips lifted off the table, and she made another desperate sound as his hands encircled her wrists and roughly pinned them to the desk beside her hips.

Veronica groaned in protest before she pressed a hand to her mouth. They were making too much noise to hear her, and the spyglass was simply too small to see through unless one was pressed to it.

Even so . . . it wouldn't do to get caught.

The woman spat lurid curses at him, wrapping strong thighs around his shoulders.

Grinning lazily, he settled those broad, bare shoulders back between her legs, and lowered his full mouth back toward her sex.

The inside of Veronica's own mouth dried, her chest stilled, all breath becoming a rote impossibility.

He hovered over the woman for longer than he ought, before his long, flat tongue slowly emerged and lapped at her softly. Once. Again. And yet once more.

The strength gave out of the prostitute's neck, and her

head collapsed back below the edge of the desk again, a relieved and triumphant smile spread on her face as her hips surged up, seeking his tongue. Demanding it.

He latched onto her, and in the space of a few breaths, the prostitute's gasps became pants, her pants became cries, and her cries became screams as she bucked beneath him, her hands freed to wildly grip and clutch at his hair.

Something warm and wet released from Veronica's own body as a persistent throb established in her sex and began to spread a foreign flush through her entire middle. She hadn't realized her other hand had settled over her corset until she noticed it slipping over her womb and down toward her skirt.

She hadn't known.

How could she *not* have known?

Those disgusting, straining distortions of Mortimer's features when his rutting reached its pounding, painful climax . . . the pleasure her mother told her only belonged to a man . . . could be had by a *woman*?

A sob of wonder escaped her, and she looked from the pretty prostitute's ecstatic expression back to the man who provided it.

He was staring at the spyglass as his jaw flexed and rolled with the unfathomable, magical motions of his tongue. His gaze glittered wicked speculations. But not at the woman upon whose body he dined.

At her.

Veronica jumped away, propelling herself to the far side of the room to lean against the wall beneath the open porthole. Her quivering legs refused to properly sustain her.

He hadn't seen her. He couldn't have done. Not from that distance, surely.

But he'd looked.

She sucked in moist, cool sea air and willed her boiling blood to cool, painfully aware of the slick sensation present each time her thighs rubbed together.

Not him. She guiltily shook her head. She didn't desire *him*. An unfeeling, hedonistic pirate with no blood, nobility, or conscience to speak of. Nothing could be more absurd.

It was merely the act that had fascinated her. The witnessing of it. The illicitness of it.

The unveiling of the truth.

A woman could claim pleasure, if a man was willing to give it.

Which posed another question What manner of man would pay a prostitute for her time in order to provide the lady *her* pleasure?

His behavior certainly made no sense.

And *why* had he looked at *her* room when another woman climaxed into his mouth?

Another slim, mahogany-haired woman.

With green eyes.

Oh, dear God, had he been spying on her through that glass all this time? Had he watched her sleep? Eat? Wash?

Her hands flew to her burning cheeks as different sounds drifted to her now.

Rhythmic, masculine ones.

Veronica blinked back toward the spyglass, invisible in the wall from this distance. Was he coupling with the woman now? Would the muscles in his neck and shoulders strain with his own pleasure? Would his eyes go dark with need? With danger. With violence.

Just as Mortimer's had.

She wanted to see. Wanted to know.

Should she look again? Perhaps this act wouldn't disgust

her if she witnessed it performed properly. Would the pirate's oddly hard, magnificent body bunch and cord as he found his—

The bolt to her door slammed aside seconds before the door, itself, crashed into the wall.

The Rook's black void of a gaze swept the dim room until he found her huddling in her corner. An icy chill instantly swept away the heat accumulated in Veronica's body. His was a gaze you hoped never found you.

Veronica dumbly tried to recover from the terrific and terrible sight of him in only hastily donned trousers and nothing else.

He reached her in four monstrous strides, and hauled her toward the door by her arm. "She won't wake up," he snarled.

"What?" Drat. Her blood didn't seem to reside in her head anymore.

"Lorelai—she fell. She won't wake up."

"She *fell*?" Fully present now, Veronica picked up her skirts and kept his frantic pace down the hallway, her breath already short and labored. "Did you push her? Or *strike* her?"

"I didn't fucking hurt her," he said from between clenched teeth. "She just—fainted."

Crossing the threshold, Veronica rushed to her dearest friend, carefully arranged on top of the counterpane, still in her wedding skirts and the pilfered flannel.

Lorelai's mussed, unbound curls spilled in a waterfall of gold down the side of the bed, as her lashes fluttered softly against cheeks bereft of color.

"Lorelai?" Veronica searched her face for swelling, or redness, for the early signs of a blow, and surprisingly found none. Lord knew they both had suffered plenty.

What if he'd hit her where it wouldn't leave a mark? Her stomach, maybe? Her back? Maybe she'd hit her head.

With gentle fingers, Veronica checked for bumps, again finding none.

"Is she still fucking breathing?" The Rook almost shoved her aside to press his ear to Lorelai's chest, which rose and fell with the gentle rhythm of a sleeping child. "I'll get the doctor."

"There's no need." Veronica sighed out a hitching breath of relief.

"What do you mean?" the Rook demanded, seizing at her wrists in a crushing grip. "What's happening to her? Has it happened before? What is to be done?"

It occurred to Veronica to be frightened, but an odd sense of wonder replaced her panic at a man's aggressive touch. The Rook, the terror of the high seas and their ruthless, devilish captor, was . . . worried.

She gaped at him. "I-it's just a faint, she does this sometimes."

"This is more than a fucking faint. I've knocked men to sleep with my bare fists who've come around faster. I tried smelling salts, ammonia, even loud noises and shaking her. It's been *minutes*."

"Sometimes a cold washcloth helps," she ventured. "Or some ice."

"Ice. I can get ice." He released her, and stalked to the door. "Ice will wake her? It'll bring her back?"

Veronica smoothed a hand over Lorelai's clammy forehead. "In time."

"How long?" he demanded.

She shrugged and shook her head, unable to venture a guess.

He took a threatening step toward her. "How. Long."

"Hours, maybe." Veronica stood her ground. "Once she was gone for an entire day. Thirteen hours in all." That had been a good day to leave, she remembered sourly. A good time to miss one of Mortimer's drunken rages.

The Rook stilled, his black gaze smoothing over every inch of Lorelai's prone form. His entire lean, predatory body rippled with tension and strain. "Gone?" he echoed.

"The doctors all said it's hysteria," she explained, taking Lorelai's limp, clammy hand in her own. "That it's how her body reacts to trauma."

"Trauma . . ." He swallowed heavily, losing some of his own high color.

"What did you do to her?" Veronica asked in a horrified whisper.

He said nothing.

A protective rage welled within her. Only hours ago, she'd been ready to take her own life on her best friend's behalf, and now, it seemed, she'd be willing to do it again. "Did you hurt her?" she demanded. "Did you . . . did you force yourself upon her?"

Had she been awakening the long-dormant lust within her body at the very same moment this monster had been thrusting his own upon poor Lorelai?

Dear Lord, she'd never forgive herself.

The Rook's features darkened from sinister to brutal. It was a look that would fill demons with dread, but Veronica was beyond that.

"It was only a kiss . . ." he muttered.

"Not to her, it wasn't," she snapped. "She's never even been truly kissed, you bloody fiend! Not since some sacred chaste encounter as a child. Now she's been forced to wed a pirate? You terrified her, you—you monstrous boor! I mean, just look at you!" She gestured rudely to his unclad body. The vibrant, menacing tattoos of things with teeth and tails. The vast breadth of his shoulders. The muscles built upon other muscles screaming of brutal labor, vast years of violence, and barely leashed ferocity.

Dear heavens, where did they build pirates these days? On Mount Olympus? Weren't they supposed to be a scurvy lot, unkempt and unwashed, with leathery skin and missing limbs?

Not that such casts of males would be preferable to these men. Especially when coerced weddings were concerned.

She realized they'd been glaring at each other for several seconds, and only then when he shocked her by breaking eye contact first.

Did she read regret on his features? Was a man like him capable of such human emotions as remorse?

"Stay with her," he ordered. "I don't want her alone when she wakes. I'll send my valet in to fetch my clothing. Make certain she is well by the time I get back."

"When will that be?"

He pierced her with a warning glare. "When I'm finished storming Ben More Castle."

"In the middle of the day? You can't be serious." She stepped forward before reason screamed at her to be less reckless with her life. "What if the Blackheart of Ben More overwhelms your forces and decides to take the ship? We'd be helpless."

Better the monster you know . . .

"You're helpless now," he snarled.

No they weren't. Somewhere in the Rook's dark soul, he fancied he cared for Lorelai. It's what had kept them both safe up until now. But what if the Rook could no longer protect them?

He answered the question he saw in her eyes. "A man like Dorian Blackwell is more vigilant at night. He is ready for his enemies to come at him in the dark because the dark is his domain. So, I will not strike when he is ready. When he is watching. I will raid when he is most relaxed. When he and his children are sitting down to supper. When his servants are busy and his men are full of food and sluggish with ale. And I will not relent until I get what I want."

"How . . . how do you know he won't see you coming?" she couldn't help but ask.

"No one ever sees me coming. Until it's too late." He said this almost gently as he returned to Lorelai's side and touched every inch of her face with his gaze, as though committing it to memory.

"What . . . what do you want from her?" Veronica wouldn't have dared ask, but for a ludicrous moment, he seemed almost . . . human. "What do you mean to gain from all of this?"

"That, Countess, is none of your concern." She'd expected the man to slam out as he left, but he only shut the door with a silent click behind him.

A quarter hour later a smallish Jamaican man by the odd name of Saxby tiptoed in, bringing with him afternoon tea, a pitcher of ice shards, and leaving with an outfit for his captain.

Where one kept ice on a pirate ship was beyond her.

Veronica ate a little, and nursed her tea in between bouts of ministering ice-cold cloths to Lorelai's forehead.

When the sun began to dip toward the west, the door opened and heavy footsteps fell behind her. Veronica didn't bother to look up. She didn't want to meet the Rook's cold stare again.

"If you hurry, I can help you escape."

Every part that made Veronica a female clenched at the sound of *that* voice. It took a moment longer than it should for the words to register.

She whirled to find Moncrieff filling the doorway. It should be illegal for a man to appear both an angel and a rogue at once, Veronica thought unkindly. Especially when she knew the deviancies of which he was capable. Not to mention the unwelcome, but not unpleasant, sensations he'd elicited within her.

He'd dressed in fawn trousers and a cream shirt. The afternoon sun gleamed off his hair, damp and lambent from a recent wash.

Had the prostitute bathed him? Why did the thought of that intimacy between a woman she didn't know, and a man she didn't wish to be acquainted with, turn the corners of her mouth down?

Also, why couldn't she bring herself to look at his mouth? Or, anywhere above his neck, really.

She knew why.

Did he?

Finally, the word *escape* permeated her mortification.

"You're letting us go?" She found that hard to believe. Could he be playing some sort of terrible game with her? "Y-you would do that to your captain?"

His hazel eyes turned gray with the threat of a storm. "I do this *for* my captain." He gestured to Lorelai, who still slumbered unnaturally deep. "Whoever this woman is to him, he forgets that he is the Rook around her. He becomes someone else."

"Who?"

Moncrieff scowled. "I don't know. And I don't want to know, not until we find the Claudius Cache."

CHAPTER FOURTEEN

In his tenure as the Rook, he'd only been outmaneuvered . . . well . . . never. He'd plotted a successful invasion at best, and a slightly protracted siege at worst.

In no scenario he could devise would Dorian Blackwell, the Blackheart of Ben More, be meeting an ambush with an invitation to open battle.

Yet there the bastard stood, yards away with twelve men to the Rook's ten, matching him pistol for pistol. Brute for murderous, bloodthirsty brute.

Almost.

Moncrieff had offered to take Barnaby and another rifleman to the other side of the isle to approach from behind, in case such an occasion should occur. They would offer long-range cover from the hills.

So, where were they?

From beneath his cowl, the Rook scanned the jagged peaks beyond which Ben More Keep settled in the distance, lording over a crystal cove. They were the castle's only weakness, these treacherous, mossy mountains. Even from the keep's tower, it was impossible for a lookout to see over the black stone knolls to the swath of beach where they'd moored the longboats. Just above the ridge closest to Ben More Peak, the charred stone skeleton of burned Jacobite ruin told of a century-old British invasion.

The Rook had brought his most fleet-footed men, and they should have been able to navigate the perilous mountain terrain and reach the ruins of the castle before needing to concern themselves with discovery.

When the Blackheart of Ben More and his men had melted from the shadows of the ruins upon the Rook's approach, his astonishment turned into anticipation.

Better a battle, mayhap, than an invasion. Castles had fortifications, hiding places, armories, and corners in which to be trapped. Out beneath the sky, beneath the sunset to the west and the threatening clouds above, he could take full measure of the men before him.

And calculate exactly how long it would take them to die.

With luck, Moncrieff and his riflemen were in position to provide cover. But when had luck ever been on his side? Never. Fate was an enemy with which he waged a constant war. He'd carved his own destiny out of the flesh of his enemies.

His men were trained more for naval combat, but they'd overwhelmed many an opponent on land. Today would be no different.

The Rook kept his pistol leveled on the raven-haired, black-eyed bastard standing in the exact same position as him. Several yards away, out in front of his men, who took a similar formation as the Rook's own crew.

He could have been looking in a mirror, but for the eye patch over his adversary's left eye.

The handicap would make Dorian Blackwell a weaker shot.

That shouldn't matter. It didn't usually. But . . . what if Blackwell's bullet found its mark this time? Death possessed a particular repugnance today, as the thought of leaving Lorelai unprotected on his ship produced a foreign thump against his ribs.

"Which one of you goes by the name of Frank Walters?" he called across the divide. His crew needed to know which man *not* to kill. Not until he gleaned the information he came for. "If you give him over, I'll grant the rest of you your lives."

No one moved. No one spoke. So, he cocked his weapon, aiming for Dorian Blackwell's infamously black heart.

A shimmer of electric sensation tensed the very organ neither of them claimed to possess. This paroxysm had long since ceased to astonish the Rook. Every time that name crossed his mind, a slight impression of recognition or revulsion came with it.

Dorian Blackwell.

To chase the emotion or the memory the name evoked was like searching for shadows on a moonless night. Impossible.

It haunted him, though. A specter of dread. The ghost of some long-forgotten pain.

Had they been enemies, once?

He'd gleaned that Dorian Blackwell and the prisoner known just as "Walters" had become acquainted in Newgate.

He'd also learned that his half-ruined dragon tattoo was undeniably Walters's work. Which meant Walters had answers. Not just about the Claudius Cache, but about his past, as well.

No one, not even *this* fearsome one-eyed blackguard, would stand in the way of that.

After a moment fraught with impending aggression, the Blackheart of Ben More took a step forward in the manner of a man after parlance rather than violence.

"I've spent the better part of an hour trying to imagine what would bring the notorious Rook to *my* island." His voice slithered through the space between them with a sinister, serpentine grace. "I thought, perhaps, the King of the Seas sought to usurp the King of the London Underworld. Tell me, Rook, have the vast oceans become too small for you? Do you seek to conquer the empire, as well?"

That voice. Something . . . something beneath the cultured British accent and the leashed menace. Smooth as silk, and yet it raked at his skin with the soul-flaying swipe of a jungle cat.

"I want nothing you can claim as your own. Not your stinking city or your lonely castle. I want Frank Walters. Give him to me, and I'll return to my ship. Our paths need not cross again."

Blackwell spoke as though their words traveled across a desk, rather than down the barrels of their guns and across a narrow valley with black peaks that could, at any moment, become their gravestones. He stood just barely too far off for the Rook to identify his exact expression, but he got the impression he'd bemused Blackwell. "Frank was once a master counterfeiter. The best, in fact. Are you here because you've taken exception to his previous work?"

"That's my business."

"He's one of my men," Blackwell stated. "His business *is* my business."

If Frank Walters held the secrets of his past, it wasn't

information the Rook wanted in the hands of a canny criminal like Dorian Blackwell.

"He's just one man." The Rook also took a step forward, closing the divide. "If you don't produce him, my crew will attack, including the sharpshooters I have in the hills. Is Frank Walters worth the loss of a dozen men, and your own life?"

Blackwell's notice darted to the hills, as well. His first show of uncertainty. "I'd rather no one die today," he stated rather blithely, considering. "It's something of an anniversary, you see, and you've interrupted some rather lengthy and amorous plans my wife and I have been anticipating."

The Rook tried not to be impressed. The sight of him and his men sent warlords, generals, and even kings scurrying underground. Not Dorian Blackwell. He barely seemed riled.

Which meant he either was very foolhardy.

Or he knew something the Rook did not.

"If you don't recognize Frank Walters on sight, then any one of these men could be him," Blackwell reasoned. "What is he worth to you dead?"

"If you don't produce him, I get silence either way. However, in one scenario, I'm granted the pleasure of killing you. A prospect which becomes more attractive with each passing moment." It wasn't that the Rook had ever learned to school emotion out of his voice, it was more that he'd never had much to convey.

Apathy had always been his ally.

So, he considered it alarming that he had to carefully relax his throat and unbind his jaw in order to maintain the same tone of disaffected nonchalance. "You have my terms. Give me Walters, and you'll return to your wife's embrace. Refuse, and I'll leave your corpses in this valley, as I return to mine."

"Will you, indeed?" A dark hint of whimsy in Blackwell's voice produced another breath-stealing palpation.

The Rook took a threatening step forward. "Speak your piece, or meet your fate," he snarled.

"You may have superior numbers, Captain, but I believe I have in my possession something altogether more valuable." One step closer brought the inexplicably familiar half-smile on his grim mouth into view.

A headache bloomed behind the Rook's right eye, which he summarily ignored. "What's that?" he asked from between clenched teeth.

"Collateral."

"In the form of?" *Information?* Had Walters already told Blackwell his secrets? Secrets even *he* was not privy to because of the iron wall in his mind separating him from his memories?

"Two lovely doves," Blackwell taunted. "One dark and morose, one sweet and fair with a broken wing. One of them, I gather, is your recent bride."

The Rook had experienced fear and fury before. He'd used it, cold and menacing, to kill so many. To wreak the vengeance that had garnered him international renown. But never, *never*, had he immolated with an inferno of rage this lethal. His blood burned inside of him, scorching through pathways to his muscles screaming for him to strike. To tear limbs from bodies. "I will murder your entire family. I will burn all you hold dear to the ground and smear your body with the ashes."

"Yes, yes, I know. As would I in your situation." The Blackheart of Ben More's eye shone with an infuriating victorious gleam. "She will remain quite safe so long as there is no violence."

"There is always violence," the Rook vowed.

"Not this time."

"You sealed your fate the moment you touched her."

"I didn't have to touch her," Blackwell scoffed. "The two washed up on my shore like attractive, exhausted driftwood. If I didn't know better, I'd say your wife had left you, though now I can see why. You're every inch the sinister, heartless pirate. I don't imagine that makes for a desirable spouse."

A pang permeated his rage. *Lorelai.* She'd awoken, and the countess had succeeded in spiriting her away this time.

She'd left him.

He'd frightened her, and she'd left him. Had run straight into the clutches of one of the most dangerous men alive.

"What are we waiting for, Captain?" Haxby hissed from behind him. "He's lying. Let's paint this valley with their blood and be done with it."

Any other day, he'd have given the order. He'd have ripped the Blackheart of Ben More's spine out through his throat.

But he couldn't. Not if Lorelai was in danger.

"How do I know you have her?"

"My wife remarked upon how shamefully one of them was attired. Flannel and muslin rarely flatter each other." He slid him a sly look. "Had she landed anywhere else, she'd have made quite the scandal . . ."

"Ye're wasting time, Blackwell." A stout, middle-aged Scotsman at Blackwell's left elbow was as eager for blood as Haxby. "Let's gut them before they get their land legs."

Blackwell held up a staying hand. "I'm a businessman first, and a warrior second. Tell me what you want with Walters, and perhaps we can still strike a bargain."

The Rook's skin burned everywhere. His skull, which had gone numb but for the ache in his head, pulsed with the accelerating rhythm of his heart.

One didn't earn a title like the Blackheart of Ben More by showing mercy. What would he do to Lorelai?

Suddenly Walters no longer mattered. The treasure. His past. The men behind him.

He lowered his gun. "You'll give her back?"

Blackwell nodded, pointing his own gun at the ground. "If you give me cause."

"Captain—" Haxby protested.

He held up his own fist, silencing all dissent.

"I need Walters to identify some of his work," he muttered. "A tattoo."

"That might be difficult," Blackwell admitted after a cautious hesitance. "He was injured in an attack in prison. His memory isn't what it once was."

"Neither is mine," the Rook said wryly.

"I was his cellmate. I watched most of his work. Perhaps I can be of assistance."

The Rook scanned the ever-ready faces of Blackwell's forces. Feeling the tension of his own crew slam into his back like the waves battering at the black cliffs below Ben More.

Moving slowly, as one does in the presence of so many primed pistols, he took a few steady steps forward, rolling his sleeve back from the underside of his scarred forearm. "It was— *I* was damaged twenty years ago. I don't remember what it means."

Dorian Blackwell gazed down at the webbed flesh of burns on his arms, becoming unnaturally still. "The dragon," he breathed. "The map."

The Rook's temperature spiked once again. "You know it?"

With lightning speed, Blackwell's pistol leveled right in between his eyes. His own chest heaved beneath his fine wool jacket. "Take. Off. Your. Cowl."

For the first time in years, the Rook followed another man's orders.

A raw sound erupted from Blackwell's throat. Then another. The first carried disbelief, and the second a tortured form of sorrow.

To see such a fearsome man tremble astonished the Rook into bewildered silence.

"You're . . . You're dead." Blackwell depressed the hammer on his pistol before it landed in the grass.

"Buggar me blind," groaned the Scotsman as he frantically pressed the arms of his cohorts down, pointing their pistols at the ground. "It's a ghost ship."

"What are you talking about?"

"Are you a ghost?" Dorian reached for him, but the Rook lunged first, grabbing Blackwell by the collar.

"You think you know me?" He brought his face close, ignoring the metallic clicks of weapons. "Did you think you'd killed me?"

"Yes." A strange and discomfiting moisture glittered in the Blackheart of Ben More's one good eye. His smooth voice was now hoarse with barely leashed emotion. "You've haunted me for twenty years. All this time I thought your death was my fault."

A band tightened around his chest. He looked at Dorian Blackwell differently now. The ebony hair. The marble-black eye. The height and breadth and scope of the man.

It was like looking into a mirror. Almost. Could they be . . . ?

"How is this possible?" the Scotsman marveled. "Dorian—?"

"They made us scrub your blood from the stones." Blackwell's hand curled over the Rook's wrist with a gentleness that bedeviled him. "So *much* blood. How could you have survived? I watched them take your body away. I'll never forget . . ."

His other hand gripped the Rook's shoulder with a ferocity he hadn't expected. "I avenged you, brother. *We* avenged you, Argent and me. We killed them all, Dorian. Every Newgate guard who put his hands on you. Know they died screaming."

"*Brother? Argent?*" The Rook pressed a hand to his temple as an ice pick slammed into his eye, nearly buckling his knees. The pain. His head. He couldn't . . .

The Blackheart of Ben More supported him with an anxious hand on his arm. "You . . . You don't remember? You don't know who I am?" Concern mingled with increasing alarm in his voice.

The Rook pushed him away, weaving as a wave of dizziness threatened his composure. "We've never fucking met," he growled. "What are you saying? What are we to each other? Are you or are you *not* Dorian Blackwell?"

"No." His one dark eye sparkled, welled, and a tear streaked down his cheekbone as torment etched into the brutal lines of his oddly familiar features.

"I am *not* Dorian Blackwell," he whispered. "You are."

CHAPTER FIFTEEN

The moment the Rook darkened the doorway to Ben More's magnificent library, Lorelai found it almost impossible to look at him for a myriad of reasons.

All of them ridiculous, she'd be the first to admit.

The last time she'd been in his company, his wide shoulders hadn't been straining the seams of a fitted black shirt and vest. He'd been wearing nothing at all. That frighteningly formidable body had been pressed to hers, offering pleasure in lithe, sinewy movements and guttural, sinful words.

Words, she found, were more powerful than she realized.

And offering . . . was a rather tame expression for what he'd done. If she could claim that he commanded her to *allow* him to give her pleasure, she would. But . . . didn't that sound preposterous?

His mouth, now drawn into a tight line of strain, had been hot and demanding against hers. Full, lush, and astoundingly wicked.

Not only did the memory of his mesmerizing kiss heat

her cheeks, but so did another, more bewildering sense of shame.

A shame fed by the daggers of accusation flung from his narrowed eyes, ripping through her composure.

It'd been more than a year since she'd surrendered her consciousness thus, and this time she'd been gone for hours.

She'd insulted him, obviously, by fainting in the middle of their kiss.

And then she'd left him.

Why did it feel in her heart that an escape from a pirate ship, from a coerced marriage, was somehow a betrayal? Why did the bleak austerity in his midnight eyes cause her own form of frantic sorrow?

Because he was her Ash. Despite everything. He was in there, locked away somewhere, somewhere beneath the tattoos and the brutal strength and the emptiness. He'd come for her. She just . . . she just needed to find him.

She thought she had for a moment when his lips touched hers. They were the same lips she'd remembered, filled with the same need. Only amplified a thousandfold. Oh God, she wished she could tell him, that she could convey somehow that she'd not lost consciousness out of terror, or pain, or lack of affection.

Quite the opposite.

His kiss had done something to her. Had unlocked a part of her that she'd not known existed. It was as though he'd breathed some part of his own animalistic lust into her, and the raw, primal desire had overwhelmed her so completely she'd just . . . collapsed.

Strange, that she'd not done so when Mortimer died. Or when the Rook had married her under a piratical threat. Historically, such stressors would have put her under for days.

It was just a kiss . . . and it was so much more than that.

She'd tasted Ash on the Rook's lips. She'd wanted a taste of more. Wanted him to do all of the things he'd offered to do. She'd wanted it with such a ferocity, and feared it with such a timidity, that the contradiction had seemed to tear her consciousness from her.

Lorelai's first instinct was to go to him. But, of course, that would not do. Not in a room filled to bursting with wealthy, and possibly dangerous, strangers. She laced her fingers together and crossed her ankles beneath her borrowed dress to keep from reaching for him.

At first, his gaze had consumed her from the top of her freshly washed curls, to the beribboned hem of her peach gown. As though making sure she wasn't some counterfeit sent to confound him.

More emotion played across his sinister features in the space of a few breaths than she'd identified in the entire time he'd been her captor. A desperate sort of relief warmed his gaze before a dreary disenchantment slackened his proud shoulders in the same instant it tensed his jaw.

It was a long time before he looked at her again.

I didn't leave you, she wanted to shout. *I woke up on a boat halfway to shore, and all I wanted to do was turn around.*

Which clearly proved she'd gone mad. Didn't it?

She yearned to smooth the wrinkles of strain from between his forehead. To press a calming kiss to the twitch above his left eyebrow. To shape her hand over the scars on his jaw.

He prowled into the room ahead of Blackwell, appearing every inch the self-possessed predator, stalking into the den of a rival wolf pack.

But Lorelai noted the whites of his knuckles. The roving eyes. The calculations of each exit, of every man and woman assembled. She saw the trickle of sweat break from his hairline and roll toward his neck.

Something had happened out there. It had to have been terrible to affect him like this.

Lady Farah Blackwell, Countess Northwalk, pressed her hand into Lorelai's, a silent, reassuring smile on her angelic face. The countess had let her borrow this gown, a confection that hadn't fit Farah since her second pregnancy, or so the lady had lamented as she'd gently burped her infant son in the nursery.

On Lorelai's other side, Veronica sat ramrod straight, reminding her of Ann Boleyn awaiting her death sentence from Henry the VIII.

When Moncrieff sauntered in behind Blackwell, Veronica tensed so abruptly, had she been an instrument, her strings would have snapped. She and the first mate stared at each other, not with distemper, but with a sense of silent warning.

Like distrustful comrades sharing a secret.

Troubled, Lorelai regarded her dearest friend. No matter what happened between herself and the Rook, she needed to get Veronica to safety, Lorelai decided. She owed her that much. Everything the woman had been through was the fault of her terrible family.

Herself, included.

In all their years as sisters, Lorelai had underestimated Veronica's bravery. Her capability. She was so very heroic, rescuing her from a man who'd begun to capture Lorelai in ways other than the physical.

It had almost worked, too, had they not been beset upon by Blackwell's men the moment they touched the beach, and conducted to Ben More to hold court with the reigning King of the London Underworld.

The man in question was followed by his valet, a stocky Scot named Murdoch. Blackwell's gaze found his wife instantly, and Farah greeted him from where the ladies sat on the long settee perpendicular to the fire.

A wrinkle appeared between Lady Farah's brows, as though she knew something was wrong the moment she met her villainous husband's eye. Her finger anxiously twisted a silver-blond curl, even when the Blackheart of Ben More offered his wife what was meant to be half of a reassuring smile.

Not for the first time, it struck Lorelai how much he resembled the Rook. Perhaps his nose was more patrician, and his mouth softer. His skin decidedly less swarthy and weathered. More marble than bronze. He'd spent his life beneath the eerie pallid lanterns of the London night, or the constant clouds of Ben More.

Not on the deck of a ship with no escape from the relentless sun.

Neither the Rook, Moncrieff, nor Blackwell or Murdoch claimed the two monstrous leather chairs across from where the ladies anxiously perched.

Blackwell instantly went to a hearth large enough to house a small village, bracing his arm on the mantel and staring into the roaring fire as though he could see the past in the flames with his one good eye.

Lorelai glanced from him to the Rook, who'd strategically positioned himself off to the left of the assemblage, at the edge of where firelight and shadow met and melded. From his vantage no man stood at his back, only a wall of books, and he had a view of both the north and west entrances to the room.

And everyone in it.

He'd belonged there. He'd lived his entire life half in shadow . . . the darkness threatening to claim him.

Come back, Lorelai thought. *Come into the light.*

His boots planted wide, his arms crossed over his chest, he stood like a sentinel.

Large and lethal and . . . lost.

As much as he claimed to no longer be Ash, he resembled the boy she'd loved in this moment. His passionless, emotionless demeanor now tightened and flexed with any number of expressions. And none of them pleasant.

Though he didn't move, torment and menace rolled off the mountains of his shoulders in palpable waves. Did anyone else feel it?

She ached for him. In every possible way. She ached for his pain. She ached for his attention. For his touch.

God help her, what did that mean?

Lunacy, surely. To feel for the man who'd not a few days ago murdered her brother. Who'd murdered countless more, by his own admission. The most wanted man in all the world.

And *he* wanted *her*.

Moncrieff stood at his shoulder, his handsome façade set somewhere between disbelief and discontent.

Farah broke the fraught silence. "I take it, husband, that since you have brought guests into our home, with our children, your . . . negotiations were successful." A thread of steel weaved into the soft tapestry of her voice.

Mortimer would have throttled his wife for speaking to him thusly.

Blackwell only released an eternal breath. "I've a story to tell," he murmured into the flames. "Everyone gathered needs to hear the telling of it."

Though Lady Farah had been unceasingly polite and kind, Lorelai hardly knew the woman, and the obvious affection between the silver-haired beauty and her unaccountably forbidding husband was the source of much consternation.

The so-called Blackheart of Ben More was the quintessential villain. He could have unfurled from the pages of one of a dozen penny dreadfuls, dark, sly, and disturbingly inscrutable.

And yet, he'd patiently cleaned baby sick from his lapel before gathering his garrison of mercenaries to defend his keep against a pirate siege.

On the opposite side of the coin, the cherubic countess seemed to calm or cheer anyone she met, Lorelai included. But she reigned as the undoubted queen at her husband's side. A lioness for which any number of men would lay down their lives.

"Let us make introductions, then." Farah stood, crossing to the pirates. "I'm Lady Farah Blackwell. And you are?"

"Moncrieff, my lady." He took her hand and pressed a kiss to the air above it, flashing that devastating smile.

"Moncrieff?" She tapped a finger to the divot in her chin. "I knew a Moncrieff family as a girl. Any relation to Thomas Moncrieff? The Earl of Crosthwaite?"

The fearsome pirate actually flinched. "My late father, I'm afraid."

"His firstborn went to fight in India; I was told he never returned," she marveled. "You *cannot* be Sebastian."

"In the flesh."

"The Erstwhile Earl!" she exclaimed. "Where have you been all this time?"

Lorelai looked to Veronica, who watched the exchange with perceptible interest.

"Everywhere and nowhere." Moncrieff shrugged, not bothering to hide his discomfiture. "I found I'm more suited for pirating than Parliament."

"Just so." Farrah laughed. "It's a pleasure to meet you."

"Likewise." He nodded, his eyes shifting about the room in a gesture more disconcerted than Lorelai had imagined him capable.

"And you are?" She turned to the Rook, but he didn't uncross his arms. Instead, his eyes darted over to her husband, who answered for him.

"Farah." Her name escaped as a raw sound from her husband's throat. "*That* is Dorian Blackwell."

She snatched her offered hand back to cover her mouth. "My God," she breathed. "You're not dead."

Lorelai's breath became trapped in her lungs as her throat closed around a multitude of emotions. He had a *name*. He had . . . another man's name?

"W-what is going on?" She lamented the tremor in her voice. The pity in Farah's eyes as she turned back to her. The malice with which Moncrieff regarded her.

She hated that *he* still refused to look her way. What did she call him in her mind now? The Rook? Dorian? Ash? Husband?

Did it matter?

He stared at the Blackheart of Ben More with a mixture of speculation and skepticism. The man who'd lived with his name for twenty long years. Would he take it back? Would there still be violence?

Farah returned to Lorelai, sinking into the place beside her as though she'd lost the starch in her knees.

"I was born Dougan Mackenzie, the unwanted bastard of the hated Laird Hamish Mackenzie," the man at the mantel revealed as firelight played across his stark, pallid features. "Farah and I were children in the same Highland orphanage where I killed a priest to protect her honor."

From beside her, Farah gave a watery sniff, and Lorelai

found her hand clutched in hers again, though she wasn't sure just who reached for whom.

"I was sent to Newgate Prison. Where I met him." Blackwell's savage features melted into something that looked like fond nostalgia. He looked over at the Rook, who'd yet to move a muscle but for the unsteady rise and fall of his chest. "Gods, how we hated each other at first. You threw a rock at me once, and we fought like devils. Beat each other bloody." His lip quirked as though visiting a fond memory. "I'm the reason your nose is crooked, though it seems to have become more so over time."

Lorelai glanced over, noting the slight imperfection of the bone just below the Rook's eyes. She'd thought that had been wrought from the damage he'd sustained the day she saved him.

"We became inseparable after that, and together we ruled Newgate Prison by the time we turned fifteen. I had the use of both eyes then, and you'd no scars or tattoos. They called us the Blackheart Brothers. Partly because of how we resemble each other, and partly because . . . of the merciless means we used to wrest power from those who wielded it before us. Against us."

The Rook opened his mouth, but it took him several moments of indecision to speak. Everyone waited. No one breathed. "The Blackheart Brothers," he echoed. "Then we . . . are not related . . . by blood?"

Lorelai wondered if anyone else caught the note of dejection beneath the monotone voice. It tore at her heart and produced an aching lump in her throat. He'd hoped he'd found family.

And those hopes had been dashed.

The man known as Blackwell pushed away from the mantel and turned to him. "There is plenty of blood between us. Enough to make us brothers. But to your lineage, I cannot speak."

"Why did you steal my name?" The question hung in the air like a sword.

It took several fraught moments for Blackwell to produce the answer, and when he did, it was with a voice roughened by a dangerous masculine sentiment. "One night, when we returned from digging the tube tunnels, you asked if we could switch cells so you could pay Walters for a tattoo." He shrugged. "We did this sometimes. Covered in dust as we were, it was nigh impossible to tell us apart, and the guards rarely bothered. We all looked the same to them. What I didn't know was that that night, my malevolent father had paid four Newgate guards to finally be rid of me. They invaded my cell in the middle of the night to beat Dougan Mackenzie to death . . . and as far as anyone ever knew, that's exactly what they did."

"And you never corrected them?" Lorelai spoke without thinking.

The regret in his gaze seemed genuine as he addressed her. "Dorian only had one more month to serve for his sentence as a thief. Dougan Mackenzie had years for his murder of a priest. As much as I mourned my brother, his death provided me a very singular opportunity for freedom. The only thing that mattered was finding Farah. I was safer if my evil father thought he'd succeeded in ridding the world of me. And so was she." He looked over at his wife, seeming to draw strength from her. "She was all I had left. She is all that matters."

Lorelai suddenly felt like an interloper, sitting as a barrier between two such bonded lovers.

A prickling on her neck drew her notice back to the man she'd named all those years ago. A man she'd known had been possessed of a name before she'd found him, but as a girl, she'd selfishly wished him not to remember it.

What about now? What did it mean for him?

For them?

"Ye really doona remember us?" Murdoch asked the Rook from where he stood behind the settee.

The pirate summarily ignored the Scotsman as he locked eyes with Lorelai. His nostrils flared, and his arms surged in time with his hastening breaths. The rest of him remained still, his features hard as stone, as though one tap with a hammer and chisel would shatter him.

His name had been Dorian. Dorian Blackwell.

And she hated it.

As unfair as she knew she was being, that's not who he was to *her*.

Yet, Ash—her Ash—was dead.

Hadn't the Rook said it a thousand times by now?

She couldn't imagine all the emotions he must be battling. All the questions building upon themselves ready to erupt like a volcano. She could see it in the set of his bones. In his restless breath.

Suddenly she just yearned to be home. Back in his little room tucked near the attic stairs at Southbourne Grove. The bed swallowing their innocent idle hours. Back when her touch had soothed him, and his had made her feel safe.

How unbearable it was, to look into the face of the man you once loved, and to be told by his own lips that he's nothing but a ghost. To recognize him sometimes, looking out through achingly familiar eyes, only to lose him in the void of darkness.

"Who else knows of this?" The hesitant beat of silence greeted the Rook's question. He'd startled them all. "I'm acquainted with your half brothers, the Demon Highlander and the Earl of Thorne. They mentioned you were related, though they didn't refer to you as Dougan Mackenzie."

"My natural-born brothers and I keep each other's sins and secrets, and we all have many." The Blackheart of Ben More took a tentative step toward the shadows in which the Rook still stood. "If I'm honest, in my heart you were more my brother than they ever were. We protected each other, you and I. Fought and bled and ruled together. I never had that with them. I've never truly been a Mackenzie." His brows rose with a dawning idea. "There were others to whom you were close as Dorian. Christopher Argent, a boy born in captivity to a criminal mother. He resides in London with his wife. And Murdoch here, along with his man, Gregory Tallow. And Walters . . . though his wife took him on holiday, if you'd believe it. Some brigands in my employ will remember you. They've been loyal since Newgate. If you need any more proof of your identity—"

"It won't matter." The Rook finally pinched the bridge of his nose, squeezing his eyes shut as though in a great deal of pain. "I won't remember *them*," he said tightly.

"Considering what those guards did to you . . . I'm not at all surprised." Blackwell—at least, Lorelai still considered him to be Blackwell—strode to the opposite library wall and selected an ancient volume. *The Histories of Roman Invasions of Britannia*. He split the spine open almost reverently.

Murdoch snorted. "I hardly think this is the time for a lesson in ancient hist—"

One look from his master silenced the valet.

"As I said, the guards made us clean the carnage from the cell the day after the attack. You and I had a place in that cell where we hid things. A stone behind a stone. When I checked it . . . I found this."

Blackwell lowered his long frame into one of the chairs, and laid the open book on the coffee table.

This time, it was Moncrieff who made a choked sound of utter disbelief. Seized with excitement, he expelled a victorious laugh and clapped his stunned captain on the shoulder. "Captain. Can you believe our bloody luck?" He put his hand on his forehead, as though checking his own temperature. "I'll be goddamned."

Unfolded in the carved-out pages of the tome was a thin, rusted sigil. The figure of a serpentine dragon, with four claws and a tongue snaking between fearsome teeth, snarled beneath the etching of two words. NIGRAE AQUAE.

"Your tattoo." Lorelai gasped.

The Rook collapsed into the other chair, wrenching up his sleeve. Only the dragon's head and front claws crawled from beneath the web of scars surrounded by additional tattoos. The first time Lorelai had seen this, it had been the only ink on his body.

The letters remained the same, if somewhat faded with time. RAE. UAE.

The NI and the AQ had been burned away by the lye along with half of the dragon's body.

"What about the lines behind it?" Lorelai asked, reaching across the table to trace the ink breaking from the dragon like the branches of a dead tree. "Did you ever figure out what they are?"

He gazed down at the tip of her finger as it stroked across the tattoo, his eyes closing for the softest of moments, as though savoring her touch. "Yes," he finally answered. "It's a map."

"It's *this* map." Blackwell untucked an ancient leather scrap from a separate fold in the book and stretched it flat.

Lorelai reeled, stunned so profoundly, she couldn't find words.

"This is the Scythian Dragon," Blackwell said. "The night you were . . . attacked, you had Walters ink *this* to your body." He grinned up at the Rook, and Lorelai could see how they must have been as boys. Their dark heads together dreaming of treasure and adventure. "Are you still looking for the Claudius Cache?"

"Captain." A note of warning lanced through Moncrieff's usual good humor.

"There's no use denying it." The Rook flexed his forearm, and the veins beneath his skin rolled over the taut muscles beneath his scars. "Once I figured out what the Scythian Dragon meant, my crew and I began searching Britain, but it's not easy working from half a map with no marker."

"*Nigrae Aquae.*" Veronica finally broke her silence, leaning in with the rest of them. "It's Latin."

"For what?" Murdoch asked.

"Black Water," Veronica and Moncrieff revealed in tandem, blinking at each other in surprise.

The Rook's eyes burned into Lorelai's with an onyx fire. "As in . . ."

"The Black Water River," she confirmed. "I'd recognize these waterways anywhere now that I can see the whole of them. They're part of the river's tributaries."

"And this?" Moncrieff pointed to the small, hastily drawn dragon on the leather map.

"That is a very small island to the left of the mouth of the river. Tersea Island. You can see it from the shore, but the coast is naught but rocks and cliffs, it's nigh impossible to land on." She sat back, her entire frame quivering with equal parts excitement and alarm. "But if you can figure out how . . . I think . . . I think that's where you'll find your treasure."

"All that time you spent on the Black Water, Captain, we could never make sense of it." Moncrieff bent his knees to inspect the rudimentary drawings of the waterways. "Even though you couldn't remember, you must have known it in your bones, that the treasure you'd sought your whole life was hidden there."

"Yes. I knew it in my bones."

Lorelai didn't look up from the map, but a strange ache lodged at the base of her throat at his words. He'd come for her, to fulfill a vow he'd made as a boy. But . . . what took him so long?

And what did they do now? What if he found his treasure? The one that'd meant so much to him, he'd left her at Southbourne Grove for how many years to chase it. He'd mentioned suffering and servitude, but the Rook had been in the papers for the better part of five years. The sun had risen one thousand eight hundred and twenty-five times, at least, since she'd first heard of his exploits as the Captain of the *Devil's Dirge*.

In an age where a fast steamship could cross the Atlantic to America in six days and circumnavigate the globe in a matter of weeks . . . why hadn't he come for her?

And why come for her now?

Was it this? Her gaze traced the lines of the familiar waterways of her home. The Claudius Cache? Maybe a part of him wanted her, but this was his real quest.

Treasure.

He was a pirate, after all.

Veronica stood, startling everyone and obliging all gentlemen to do the same. Everyone, that was, but the Rook. "Now that you have what you came for, may we be released?"

"Absolutely not." Moncrieff's hazel eyes shouted silent warnings at her. "You are now privy to our plans. It wouldn't do to have you contact the authorities and tell them where we are whilst we're pilfering the treasure."

"Released?" Farah echoed, a worried frown deepening her cherubic dimples. "As in . . . from captivity?"

"Yes," Veronica hissed. "We've been the Rook's prisoners for days." She put her hand on Lorelai's shoulder. "We just want to go home."

"Prisoners?" Blackwell turned to Lorelai, whose thoughts and emotions were as unruly as a litter of curious kittens. "I was told you were his wife."

"She *is* my wife." The Rook stood, towering over her.

"Why didn't you mention your captivity before?" Farah pressed.

"Because we weren't certain we hadn't simply changed one captor for another when we were beset upon at the beach by your guards," Veronica answered.

"That was more for your safety than anything else," Dorian said.

"No one is a prisoner here," Farah reassured them. "You are free to leave at your leisure. Though I'd suggest prevailing upon our hospitality until the morning."

"*She* goes nowhere," the Rook stated in a voice hard enough to shatter diamonds. "She is my *wife*."

A new tension sliced through the library, robbing it of air. All the moisture deserted Lorelai's mouth, but she had to wipe freezing, clammy hands on the skirt of her borrowed gown, unable to look up from her lap.

Lord, she hated this. Detested it when people stared. When their voices rose in both pitch and sound. She loathed aggression or conflict of any kind.

Pain always followed.

She could feel their gazes, heavy with expectation. They

were waiting for her to pull the rope on the guillotine. Veronica. The Rook. The Blackwells. Even Moncrieff.

Air. She needed air. Where had it gone? Had the black void in the Rook's chest swallowed it all?

Her lids began to flutter. If she were lucky, she could just leave. Sleep. And wake when the carnage was over.

Escape. Like the coward she'd always been.

Farah Blackwell's abidingly soft voice whispered through the atmosphere thick and hot with suspicion and challenge as she rested a hand on Lorelai's shoulder. "Lorelai, dear. Are you . . ." She paused. "Do you consider yourself married to the Rook?"

His gaze burned a hole into the crown of her head. She didn't have to look up to fathom the possession and demand in his eyes. "I—I don't know. I couldn't say that our ceremony was exactly legitimate."

"It was by the rules of maritime law," the Rook insisted.

"It's true that I've been more of a captive than a wife," she confessed, her cheeks burning with mortification. "And . . . the marriage hasn't been consummated."

"Thank God." Veronica sighed with more relief than Lorelai, herself, felt.

"Do you *want* the Rook for your husband?" Farah urged.

"That is inconsequential." Her would-be husband pushed the table between them aside with one swipe, advancing until his knee boots were planted before her. "She belongs to me, and where I go, she goes. End of fucking discussion."

Fearing the chaos he might have stirred by removing the physical barrier, Lorelai made to stand, but Farah beat her to it.

Lorelai was once again stunned speechless when she reached up to save Farah. Instead of fear, or aggression, or even caution, both the Blackheart of Ben More and his pretty wife shared an odd, secret smile.

"The discussion ends when you answer one question, Captain." Farah stood between her and the Rook, and Lorelai thought her braver even than Joan of Arc.

"What's that?" he asked in the voice of a wolf at the end of his tether.

"Do you love her?"

CHAPTER SIXTEEN

It was one of a million questions the Rook didn't know the answer to. The one word he hadn't a definition for.

Love.

He only understood possession. There were laws about it. Wars fought over it. Countless souls martyred in its name.

But love? How did a man feel what he did not understand?

How did he convey what he'd never been shown?

Was he expected to love when Lorelai didn't? She wouldn't even look at him. He'd not allowed her to answer Lady Northwalk's question because her rejection might have deflated the tiny bloom of humanity he'd begun to sense within himself since he'd claimed her.

And even he couldn't predict his reaction if she'd denied him now.

Blackwell threw him a lifeline. "What is she to you?"

It was as if he knew. As if he understood that love was a fragmented hypothetical to men like them.

A tranquility shimmered inside of him. Were she not there, an arm's length away, he'd have done monstrous things already. She kept his beast at bay. It was for her that he spoke instead of struck. And because of it, he'd discovered a piece of the puzzle from his past. Before her, he'd have taken the offensive. He'd have destroyed any possible enemies, before he'd the chance to find an ally.

What *was* Lorelai to him? What had she been since the first time she'd bade him to live? "She is my wife. She . . . is my . . . peace."

Gasping, she struggled to her feet. He reached out to help her, but she slapped his hands away with shockingly uncharacteristic temper.

"I am *not* your piece, you—you . . . mercenary . . . scalawag!"

He tried not to find it endearing that she had to search her infinitely gentle mind for an insult, and had possibly come up with the most benign one in existence.

"I've begged you again and again to let poor Veronica go!" Her eyes sparked with an azure flame he'd never before witnessed, and it roused something inside of him that didn't even resemble ire. "Hasn't she been through enough? You murdered her husband!"

He shrugged and swatted her accusation away like a troublesome gnat. "I did her a favor and both of you know it."

Neither of the Weatherstoke women argued the point, but they glowered at him with identical, mutinous expressions. One glare emerald, the other sapphire.

The Weatherstoke Jewels, indeed.

Blackwell made a pithy sound of consternation. "We find ourselves in a rather complicated predicament."

"How's that?" Moncrieff stepped to his captain's side, his hand in his jacket, presumably on a weapon.

Blackwell's eye speared the first mate, glittering with

reservation, his own hand reaching behind him. "I cannot, in good conscience, allow innocent women to be held at Ben More against their will."

Farah snorted. "Since when?"

It was a line in the sand, drawn by a man who claimed to be his brother. A line the Rook would gladly leap across and spill blood to keep Lorelai at his side.

Whether she wanted to be or not.

His hand found his own weapon, secure in the knowledge that he and Moncrieff could gut Blackwell and his valet before they could call for reinforcements.

But would he do such a thing? In front of the man's wife? In front of Lorelai?

"Try and take her from me." His warning was a mercy, he hoped Blackwell understood that. "And I'll send your black soul to hell, you son of a—"

The Blackheart of Ben More held two empty hands up in a gesture of capitulation. "Dorian."

"Don't call me that," he barked. It was his name. And yet . . . it wasn't. He didn't know the Blackheart of Ben More. He hadn't seen any documentation to validate anyone's claim to the name Dorian Blackwell.

But the emotion in the man's eye was hard to ignore, and the story he told not only possible, but plausible.

Probable even.

He had the Scythian Dragon.

"Very well." Blackwell glanced speculatively at the women gathered to the Rook's left. "Permit my wife to show the ladies and your first mate to their chambers. I wish to speak with you, alone."

"How do I know you won't spirit them away?" More than anything, the Rook wanted the offer to be genuine. But very few men in this world could be believed, and none could be trusted.

"I offer myself as surety. A hostage, even. I'll go to your ship, if you like."

"No," Farah contended with one word.

He gazed over at his wife, and a silent communiqué passed between them. It wasn't as though he commanded her compliance, but he requested it.

And she gave it. She trusted him.

The lucky bastard.

"This could be a trap," Moncrieff cautioned.

Blackwell didn't bother to hide his dislike as he measured Moncrieff, but he addressed the Rook. "There are questions I can answer. About the Cache. About the past. I know you. Maybe better than you know yourself. All I want to do is talk."

Finally, the Rook nodded, then commanded Moncrieff. "You keep watch on the women. No one leaves until I say."

"Yes, Captain." Moncrieff followed the colorful procession of skirts out the library door. Murdoch kept a watchful eye on the pirate, sticking close to Farah Blackwell's side.

Lorelai didn't look back at him.

What cause had he given her to do so? *I'm sorry,* he thought. *But I can't let you go . . .*

Her absence left the room colder, and without thinking, he pulled his collar tighter to him, as though protecting himself from a northern wind.

"Before I answer any of your questions, may I ask you one?" The clink of a crystal stopper harmonized with Blackwell's voice, drawing the Rook to turn around. Blackwell held up a second glass in silent query. He could use a drink. But did he trust it? Could he surrender his wits in a place like this?

He shook his head.

So, Blackwell made his own drink a double. "How did

you survive?" The amber liquid in his glass caught the firelight as he lifted it to his lips and drank away an unpleasant memory. "I'll never erase the sight of your broken body from my nightmares. You were dead. You were basically just . . . meat when they dragged you out of my cell."

"I woke in a mass grave, a pile of meat, as you say. With no name. No past. No idea where I was or who'd tried to kill me. I'd five broken bones, and lye burns over a third of my body." He held the ruined tattoo on his forearm out for another inspection. "That's what happened to this . . . and to my neck and jaw."

Blackwell inspected the scars crawling up his jaw and into his hairline with neither pity nor disgust. "Only *you* could have resurrected yourself," he recalled. "Murdoch always used to say, 'where there is a will, there is a way.' When we were together, I was the way, and you were the will. I've never met anyone more driven than you. If you decided to live, no amount of broken bones or blood lost could have taken you."

"I had no will." His quiet admission surprised them both, he gathered. "Not until I heard *her* voice."

"Lady Lorelai? She had a hand in rescuing you?" Blackwell speculated.

The Rook nodded. "She was a child. All of fourteen. But she became my world as she nursed me back to health. I spent the better part of a year watching her play doctor to a slew of other broken, wounded animals. I went from not being able to walk, to romping about the Black Water bogs with her. And never once did she leave my side." He remembered a question that no one else had ever been able to answer. "How old was I, when I . . . when you thought I died?"

"Eighteen." He spoke the age with the warmth a good whisky lends the throat.

"So, I'm eight-and-thirty." Somehow, having an age felt . . . better.

"How disconcerting it must have been not to know that," Blackwell mused. "So, you've known your Miss Weatherstoke for twenty years . . ." Blackwell's unspoken question was lost in the burn of whisky.

"Yes . . . And, no."

"What parted you?"

"Her brother, the countess's husband." A familiar rage, white and absolute, rose within him. "He shanghaied me. I was a slave in the East for . . . for so long. With only my hatred to keep me company. With only her memory to keep me alive."

Blackwell summarized the rest of his story. "And so, you became the Rook. You cut a path back to her door. A road cobbled from corpses and mortared with blood. Then, you murdered the man who parted you, right in front of her, and claimed her as yours, heedless of her protestations."

It was refreshing not to hear that part spoken with censure, but respect. "How did you know?"

"It's what I would have done." Blackwell's lips twitched with the threat of a smile. "Hell, it's almost verbatim what I did do in Farah's case, just under different circumstances. And, I might add, with a great deal more finesse."

The Rook looked at him sharply, but any ire died when he noted Blackwell's threatening mouth tilted in an earnest smirk.

No one *dared* tease him. Moncrieff sometimes attempted humor, but even *he* was careful not to approach certain boundaries.

The Rook found he didn't mind. This seemed . . . both

foreign and familiar, to share with this stranger. This stranger who called him *brother.*

"Finesse isn't a skill I've had to acquire." Carefully, he lowered himself to the edge of one of the monstrous chairs, letting the fire warm the chill established by Lorelai's absence. It would be folly to allow himself to be comfortable. To let down his guard.

"Of that I have no doubt." Blackwell claimed the chair beside him, crossing an ankle over his knee. "But with a woman like yours . . . it may be in your best interest to obtain some. If not finesse, at least a bit of diplomacy."

His eyes narrowed. "What do you mean, *a woman like mine*?"

"Bit shy, isn't she? Tenderhearted." Blackwell swirled the contents of his glass, inspecting the caramel liquid with unnecessary absorption. "It's difficult not to notice her damaged leg . . . her brother's doing?"

"Part of why I killed him."

"Just so."

Blackwell didn't ask another question, and antithetical to his nature, the Rook felt a need to fill the silence. "I spent twenty years thinking of nothing but getting back to her, and now that I have . . ."

"You realize you are no longer the boy who loved her. You're . . ."

"Someone else," he finished, pleased to have found a sympathetic soul. A heart as black as his own. "All I know is the sea. How can I navigate *these* waters when the sky is opaque? When the stars do not shine to light my way? How do I behave? How do I make her care for me? How do I stop her from fearing me?"

"She may yet fear you," Blackwell conceded. "But it is undeniable that she cares for you."

"Is it?" He searched his memory of their interaction for

just which part of the last few hours made her feelings for him undeniable. He came up frustratingly empty.

Blackwell regarded him over the top of his glass. "When I went to meet you in the valley, she begged me not to kill you. She wept, and pleaded for you, and would not be consoled until I promised to do what I could to defuse the situation."

A tiny spark lit in his chest, before sputtering out. "She knows nothing of who I am. She cares for who she wants me to be. Who I once was to her."

Blackwell slid him a look. "And you cannot be that man?"

Dejected, he shook his head. "Even as a boy, a part of me knew I was not good enough for her. That I was a killer."

Dorian examined him over the rim of his cup, as though crafting a plan before he spoke. "Then, perhaps, the kindest thing would be to set her free."

The Rook's eyes snapped up. "I am not equipped with that sort of kindness. How many times do I have to say it? She. Is. *Mine*."

"I know. There's nothing to be done for it, I'm afraid." Dorian smiled that secret smile. "If she is yours, and you have her, then why the aggression?"

"I am an aggressive person," he said blandly.

"The frustration, then. Is it of a . . . sexual nature?"

He looked away before nodding. "It seems that if I am to have her, I must *take* her. She will not submit to me. She . . . doesn't want me. I'd erroneously thought that wouldn't matter . . ."

"What stops you?"

He thought on this for a spell. He'd intended on taking her. He'd vowed that after everything he'd been through, he deserved her. He'd thought he'd lost enough humanity to be inured to her tears. To her needs. He'd show her that his attentions wouldn't hurt her and eventually she'd submit to him. And yet . . . "For so many years, I've taken anything I want through brutality and force. But with her . . . I want her to give herself to me."

Blackwell idly toyed with the corner of his eyepatch, adjusting the strap. "I'm reminded of a crocodile that my friend the Duke of Trenwyth told of upon returning from holiday to Egypt," he said. "These are the most vicious creatures you'll ever meet. Solitary monsters. They'll eat each other. Feast upon their own young. They are the descendants of dragons, some say." His gaze flicked to the Scythian Dragon on the seal in front of them.

"Their bite is so lethal, so strong, that even the largest of land predators give them a wide berth. However, there is a tiny bird, a plover, the most unimpressive-looking thing, who will perch in the monster's open mouth without fear, and is never harmed. Never eaten. Because these fragile little creatures floss the carrion out of the crocodile's teeth. And so, they have struck an almost ridiculous but mutually beneficial relationship for any hundreds of years."

The Rook squinted at the man who had claimed his name. Was he drunk already? "I don't gather your meaning."

"My point is, some tiny plover, somewhere, had to gather enough bravery to land in a crocodile's mouth. And that crocodile had to show enough trust, enough patience, to see what happened next without snapping his jaw shut and devouring the poor creature."

Scowling, he tried to draw the comparison to him and Lorelai.

A sound of wry amusement drifted through the space between them. "You never were fond of metaphors," Blackwell muttered.

"Wasn't I?" He'd always yearned to meet someone who could answer questions about his past. Though he'd never considered how disconcerting it would be to share a room with someone who knew more about him than he did about himself.

"I taught you how to read, you know," Blackwell revealed. "During those long nights in prison."

He *didn't* know. He could read, rather well, in fact. But just where he'd acquired the skill had been one mystery in a lifetime of a thousand.

Blackwell sighed. "The little bird is your wife, obviously. You, yourself, said she was fond of wounded animals, did you not?"

"Yes."

"Show her your wounds, then. Bare your scars. Be the crocodile with the sore tooth. The wounded lion. Let her pluck the thorn from your paw and smooth away the pain of it. Perhaps then, she will no longer fear you. Perhaps *then*, she will accept her desire for you."

Assuming she *had* desire for him.

Blackwell continued. "We monstrous men, we think we must be invincible all the time. But I've learned women like them . . . they need to know that we are human. They will do what they can to discover that humanity. Because, eventually, they will require you to love them, and you'll find you cannot help yourself." This was said with a droll sort of amusement.

"That's just it." The Rook stared down at the palms of his hands, traced the nautical star tattoo on his wrist and the snake coiled above it. "I don't know that I *am* human anymore," he admitted to his arm. "Even if she loved me, we would be doomed, wouldn't we?"

"Why is that?"

"Because you can't love the teeth out of a shark."

"Is that what you are? A shark?"

His open hands became fists. "I don't *know* what I am. I've barely learned *who* I am—who I was—and that's if I take you at your word. I've been in chains all my *life*, it seems. And some of those chains I deserved. I'm little more than a beast of burden. When I became the Rook, I thought I knew what freedom was, but . . . even leadership has its own cages."

When Blackwell spoke, he wanted to strangle the pity from the man's voice. Or maybe the truth from his words. "There is more than one prison, brother. I sense you carry yours wherever you go."

"I will never be free of it."

"Then why not grant *her* freedom?" he pressed. "Would you inflict your chains upon her?"

The Rook surged to his feet, driven by a desperate gloom, and stalked to the window. "Yes, dammit. Because without her my confinement is solitary, and in that void, where I am alone, I'm locked up with my worst enemy." He found golden tassels on the drapes that precisely matched the hue of her hair. He twisted one with his finger. "But she . . . she's the only one who could share my cage. The only one whom I'm certain I wouldn't eventually tear to shreds."

"You do love her," Blackwell asserted.

"No," he insisted. "Love is soft. Love is kind. I know nothing of that. What I feel for her is . . . well, it's neither of those things. It's too obsessive. It's marvelous and terrifying. It is the cruelest affliction for a merciless man. Because it leaves me at *her* mercy. So unprotected. So easily damaged. It is a bizarre thing to accept, that when entire armies have failed to destroy me, one word from her lips could dismantle me."

Dorian returned to the sideboard for a second drink. "You were always a romantic, even back then. Even before her."

"Do not tell me I've always been this pathetic," he lamented.

"You were the best of us, Dorian." Something about the barely leashed emotion in the man's voice chipped at the ice in his chest.

He couldn't face it, so he studied the ruined dragon tattoo. The web of scars he carried over so much of his body, no amount of ink could hide it all. "How monstrous I am. I can kill a man faster than he can take a breath. I can wage war with the sea. But the stratagems of *this* battle remain unknown to me. The rules of society. The needs of a woman. When do I smile at her? When do I stand? And sit? I don't remember how to laugh . . . And, how do I kiss her? And for how long? How do I make her want to kiss me back? The last time I thought she did . . . she fainted. For *hours*."

At least this time the Blackheart of Ben More had the sense to try and hide his mirth. "Take it from me, brother. Twenty years of unrequited desire can be overwhelming to you both." A clap on the shoulder was warm. Welcome. And so the Rook didn't shove it off. "Believe it or not, we've led similar lives. I kidnapped my bride, as well. How apropos, that we should have found analogous women. Fair-haired and kind and tender."

"Your wife loves *you*."

"Yes, but she had to learn to trust me first."

"What did you do?" It was the most humbling question he'd ever asked, right before the next one. "What . . . do I do?"

"Open your heart to her, Captain. It's the only way. A

woman of true worth needn't be wooed. Not with poetry and flowers. But with honesty and gestures of your devotion. Farah loved me as Dougan Mackenzie as a child. And when I . . . coerced her into marriage with Dorian, she had to learn to fall in love with him all over again. Perhaps your Lady Lorelai works in reverse. She will not give herself to the Rook, just as Farah did not give herself to the Blackheart of Ben More. But perhaps she could love you for who you used to be . . . as Dorian?"

Something about that felt wrong. His body, his brain, rejected the name. "If I became Dorian again, who would you be?"

The hand slid off his shoulder as his Blackheart brother leaned against the casement and scrubbed at his face. "That . . . is an excellent question."

They stared into the night together. He sensed night hadn't always been their ally. That they'd done this before, stood sentinel against the moon.

The Rook studied the man next to him in profile, coming to a conclusion. "You have given my name back to me, my past, but . . . you have lived longer as Dorian Blackwell than I ever did. He is what you have created. His legacy is yours, I don't want it back."

Despite his lack of memory, the Rook read the man in front of him. Knew him. Understood the wordless communication glinting in a dark eye more deep set than his own.

"If I am Dorian, what do I call *you* now?" Blackwell asked the night. "The Rook?"

Keeping his gaze firmly fixed on the moon casting the Isle of Ben More in a mystic silver glow, he answered from that place he'd thought empty. "I—I find I like that you call me brother."

Dorian didn't look at him, either, but the glass in his

hand trembled a little. "And who will you be for your Lady Lorelai?"

"For her, I must learn to be someone else . . . Or no one at all."

CHAPTER SEVENTEEN

How was one to focus on anything when locked in an actual tower like some fairy-tale princess? Lorelai huffed out a frustrated breath and let the book she'd been attempting to read fall to her lap. Reaching down, she fluffed the pillow beneath her throbbing ankle. The storm outside and the adjustment from being at sea to coming ashore had angered the ancient injury.

Who'd have ever thought that she'd need to find her land legs?

She studied the door with a pensive frown. Another thing the Rook and the Blackheart of Ben More had in common. Certain rooms with doors that locked from the outside.

Close thunder shook the stones and rattled the glass of the oil lantern at the bedside table of yet another luxurious prison. The bed was comfortable, at least, and the room spacious, done in dark wood and autumn tones.

Still, the storm stirred a restlessness inside of her she

couldn't appease. Something wild. Something indefinable and inescapable. Like time or fate.

But didn't she exist outside those constructs? It certainly seemed thus. Was she a married woman, or a captive? Her physical desires and her emotional ones were ever at odds when it came to the dark and damaged man who could in the span of a breath be both threatening and tender. It seemed if she were to search for Ash, she'd have to live with the Rook.

As much as the prospect terrified her, it thrilled her, as well.

And the question remained. Did she have a choice?

Did she want one?

A chill lanced up her spine, spreading bumps down her arms, and Lorelai knew *he* was on the other side of her bedroom door. All six-plus feet of him.

He hadn't made a sound. He didn't cast a shadow.

But he was there.

The electric presence of him radiated from just beyond the thick oak as extant and intense as the lightning outside. She was acquainted with his unparalleled strength. The barrier wouldn't protect her if he decided to pit his body against it.

She didn't breathe until the bolt slid open, the latch released, and he let himself into her room.

The sight of him freed the band from around her lungs and created a new pressure. One she'd felt awaken inside of her more fervently with each moment they passed in each other's company.

A lower pressure. A moist desire.

She'd not felt it since their kiss all those years ago. But it was different now. Less innocent. More insistent.

Lanternlight had a way of softening people, but not

him. His eyes were too black, too fiendishly clever. His features—dark as a heathen's—were too hard. His expression, intemperate.

He was a living, breathing sin.

In her bedroom.

Lightning blanketed the sky in blinding brilliance, shifting the deep hollows and broad planes of his features into a queer white light. For a ghostly moment, she caught sight of the boy she'd once known.

Ash. Her Ash. All tender yearning and impetuous youth. Only Ash had gazed at her like that, once upon a time.

By the time the percussion of the thunder broke their stillness, his expression had again smoothed to that eerie tranquility she'd come to despise.

Instead of many, regular beats, her heart gave one great thump. Had he come to finish what he'd started in his quarters this morning?

She'd not known men were such creatures as he until he revealed his unparalleled body to her. Now that she thought of it, most men weren't.

There was no one like him.

Not that she'd chanced upon many naked men, but she doubted any resembled him in the flesh, a smooth and fearsome canvas poured over hard, iron power.

He approached the bed, and her hand fluttered up to the high neck of her nightgown, clutching it closed against skin gone suddenly flush.

Was he angry? She couldn't tell. Had he come to punish her for leaving?

Unabashedly, he stared down at her lap. Between her legs. "What do you think of Captain Nemo?"

What? She squinted at him for several silent seconds.

Oh, right. Her book. "I find him conflicted," she answered carefully. "He is a man both riddled by remorse and driven by vengeance."

"Indeed." He took the book from her lap, causing her thighs to tense, and inspected the gold-leaf pages. "Did you know the Egyptians believe your *ka* is in your name?"

"*Ka*?" she echoed. What a strange conversation to be having at a time like this. When there was so much else to say.

"Orientals call it variations of *chi,* Christians call it your soul. So many believe there is power in a name. That it is what makes you immortal. Demons are expelled at the revelation of it. God's name is so sacred it cannot be spoken. It cannot be known." He spoke to her in a voice every bit as rich and opaque as Turkish coffee. "For so long I have felt such an affinity with Captain Nemo. Nemo literally translates to *no name*. Did you know that?"

"I didn't," she whispered.

"It has served me well to be no one. A shadow. A faceless shade. The terror of the high seas, the architect of my own mythology."

She scrutinized him closely, noting a new vulnerability beneath his indifference that hadn't been there before. "Are you not glad you've found your name? That you know who you are?"

"I thought I would be." He waited for another clash of thunder to abate. "I do not share a kinship with the name Dorian. Nor any memories. But it's haunted me, and now I know why," he admitted, returning the book to her lap. "It doesn't matter. The name Dorian Blackwell remains with the man who's earned it. I don't want it."

Lorelai sat up from her pillows aching to reach for him,

but afraid of where such an intimacy would lead. "He seems glad to have found you," she postulated. "He truly feels you are his brother."

He made a derisive sound. "I met his brothers. I'm not certain that's a compliment."

"Do you believe him? Do you remember anything about him?"

"Maybe. Somehow. I believe he is someone I trust. *Trusted*. I don't know." He gritted his teeth and threaded his fingers through his sable hair, pulling it in frustration. "All of these fucking revelations, and I still don't know who I am. I don't *remember*."

"I know who you could be," she ventured. "I gave you a name."

He looked at her sharply. "We've been over this."

"I still don't understand," she pressed. "You say it is impossible, that Ash is dead. But here you are. Not Dorian. Not the Rook. Doesn't that mean there is still hope?"

His hard glare softened. "Hope is for fools. I am not Ash anymore."

"Tell me one good reason you couldn't be again," she challenged.

"I kill people. *A lot* of people."

There was that. She chewed on the inside of her cheek. "Could you . . . ever try . . . not to kill people?"

Something tender toyed with the edges of his mouth. "You know how it is in the world. It is kill or be killed. It has always been thus."

"Maybe in your world . . ." Lorelai scooted even closer, encouraging him with a cheeky smile. "My experience is that if you don't try to kill people, they usually won't try to kill you back."

Instead of amusing him, she seemed to make it all worse. A bleakness radiated from him as he sank to the side of her bed. "You're fortunate, Lorelai, that this is your experience."

His words sliced a leaking wound into her heart. "Are you angry with me?" she asked.

"Why would I be?" His puzzlement seemed genuine.

"Because I—I fainted when we . . ." She couldn't finish that sentence without possibly repeating the humiliation. "And then I—Veronica and I—escaped." She softened the word. "We left."

She flinched when he reached for her, but relaxed as he traced the soft underside of her jaw with gentle, callused fingertips. "Veronica mentioned you do that when you are afraid. That you sleep as though you'd left your body. And nothing can wake you. Where do you go?"

"I—I'm not sure." His touch was doing something twitchy to the muscles of her neck. "It's like my mind is no longer in my body, as my body has never particularly been a comfortable place to live. Somehow, I've created in my sleep a quiet place. A safe place." *A place where Ash has always lived*, she didn't say.

"A quiet sleep. How would that be?" He caught one of the loose curls at the nape of her neck and ran it through his fingers, testing its consistency. They seemed to hold a certain fascination for him, the wild, willful strands that refused to be tamed. "How long have you done this?"

"Since childhood. Since my leg . . ."

He frowned. "I never noticed it in the time I spent at Southbourne Grove."

"I never left when you were there. I felt safe when awake, I suppose. Mortimer never hurt me again until you were gone."

Suddenly the air was charged like the moment between lightning and thunder. Dangerous. Anticipatory. "I would kill him again if I could," he vowed. "Slower this time."

"I never knew you hated him so much."

"Didn't you hate him?"

"No," she answered honestly. "I admit I strongly resented him. I feared him, mostly. But over time I learned to be indifferent. And, with his death, I think I will easily forget him."

He gestured to the ankle she had propped up on a pillow. "*How* do you forget something like this? He broke you. Terrorized you. He—"

"You only have to forget once, and then it's all over," she said. "To hate you must remember, you must dwell. You must hold it in your heart all the time and feed it. Nurture it. I found that too exhausting. Hatred for Mortimer made me physically ill. And that didn't hurt him, it only made me suffer."

He dropped her ringlet, his hands tight fists by the time they lowered to his sides. "I have become my hate, Lorelai. I *am* loss and wrath and loathing."

"You are more than that," she contended, her hand hovering like a butterfly over his broad back.

"It is all I am." The butterfly never landed, because he surged to his feet and stalked a safe distance away, taking refuge by the fire. "You can't take my hatred from me, Lorelai. Or . . ."

"Or what?" she prompted.

"You'll take the last thing away that I know." The fire gleamed an eerie shade off his midnight hair. "I'll truly be nothing . . . No one."

Lorelai helplessly watched an inner battle rage across features usually so implacable. He'd been so cold since his return. So very frighteningly unyielding. His scars now bunched and twitched with the movements of his jaw beneath. His restless soul called to her with a volcanic sense of pressure.

Perhaps he just needed to let it out.

"I had so much reason to hate Mortimer," she professed. "But you say that you do, as well. What reason had you to kill him?"

"You," he clipped.

She blinked at him. "What?"

"*He's* the reason we've lived apart these twenty years. *He* killed Ash. Over. And. Over. And. Over." It was the lack of inflection in his voice, the unhurried repetition of the syllables that made his declaration that much more dreadful. What horrors must it have taken for enough of Ash to disappear, to create the Rook?

"W-what did he do?" she whispered, all the while terrified of the answer.

He gave her his back, taking the iron tool from its stand and stabbing at the glowing coals. "Have you ever heard of being shanghaied?"

His voice was so low, she had to strain to hear it. "I haven't."

"It's a widespread practice these days. The maritime shipping industry is booming, you see, but it's also dangerous, tedious, and backbreaking work. Most working men are better suited to the fields and factories than the sea. This has created a shortage of willing sailors. And so, in some places, a brawny man with a body built for labor will go to a pub or a brothel, to eat and drink his fill. He won't know that some enterprising flesh peddler drugged his ale until he wakes up on a ship halfway to Shanghai. The captain of that ship is now his world, his king, and the only hope he has of getting home is to work on a crew and save the money for passage from some foreign port."

"Oh my God," she whispered. "You're saying Mortimer drugged you and gave you to a ship captain?"

When the coals glowed red enough for him, he stooped to

add another log to the fire. "It's worse than that. Mortimer sold me, and it was up to me to work off the money the captain had paid him."

Lorelai gaped, her fingers curling into fists around the hem of the bedclothes. For all her talk of forgiveness, his story stoked a rage to match that of the flames now licking up the chimney. "How long did that take?"

"I was a special case," he continued. "Mortimer had made a singular deal for me. I was sold again and again. My life was to be one of continuous indentured servitude, until I became too broken, old, or ill. Then I'd be discarded to the sea once I was of no use to anyone. I witnessed that happen more than once. An old or injured man pushed from a deck. Calling out for salvation. It used to be my greatest fear."

Lorelai didn't realize she'd been crying until a hot tear dropped from her chin onto the cold hands clenched in her lap. "I didn't know," she marveled. He'd mentioned that Mortimer deserved to die seven thousand deaths. Seven thousand. The number of days stolen from them.

"I always wondered what he'd told you, about why I didn't come back."

"He said you'd remembered," Lorelai managed, though her emotions threatened to strangle her. "That you didn't want to return to Southbourne Grove only to break my heart. He said you had someone else and you went to her." Even that heartbreak hadn't come close to touching this one. She'd cried for months, but a part of her had understood. She'd done her best to comprehend, at any rate.

"All this time . . ." he murmured to the fire. "You thought I'd abandoned you."

"To think I was *happy* for you!" she railed. "I assumed you were living your life, your true life, and that offered a modicum of comfort. When I missed you, I'd tell myself I had a hand in healing you enough to send you home to the family and loved ones you'd lost."

"Did you not believe the words I spoke to you when we parted?" he asked in a low, dangerous voice.

The sun will set in the west, and I'll come for you.

Shame lowered her gaze to the counterpane, to the silhouettes of her feet beneath the covers. "If you loved someone as Mortimer claimed. Someone who already meant so much to you. Why keep your promise to a sheltered cripple?"

His hand tightened on the poker. "Even then, you assumed I was without honor?"

"That's not what I—"

"You were right, it seems. As Dorian Blackwell I was a thief and a murderer." He stabbed the instrument back into its place and whirled on her. Backlit by the fire, his features took on a demonic cast. "You think I'm a monster?" he rumbled. "You don't know the *half* of it. But there are creatures out there far more horrendous than I. They do things, horrific things. *Unspeakable* things. To girls. To boys. To men. To women . . . to *me.*"

She wanted to call his name . . . to make him stop. But what name did she use? He didn't know who he was, and she knew even less. "How long did you suffer? How long were you a slave?" She didn't want the answer. But she needed it.

"Fifteen years." He stalked to the foot of her bed, a tower of shadow and wrath and revelation. "When my crew and I were able to free ourselves, we were little better than animals. But at least we'd learned to be predators. We hunted down these men. Slavers, mostly, from every country you could fathom. I've done atrocious things, Lorelai, I've torn whole crews apart with my bare hands. These hands." He showed her his open palms, as though to demonstrate the stains of blood. "It was them or me . . . and it's *always* them. It will always *be* them."

A darker emotion underscored the pain and pity she felt. Pride.

These slavers *should* have suffered. Deserved it. She hoped they died screaming. She'd never felt wrath like this before. "And so, you only took from these men? You kept plunder from their fleets?"

"And why shouldn't I?" he challenged. "I've had *so much* taken from me. My freedom. My dignity. My humanity. My name. My memory. *Myself.* But *your* brother took from me the one thing I couldn't get back. The only thing I truly wanted. *Time.*"

Lorelai deflated a little, berating herself for expecting him to say something else. "I—I wish I could take it all back." She sniffed. "I wish I could have spared you pain."

"I'm not after your pity." He sneered. "I'm trying to make you understand. This body, this shell some-fucking-how survived everything. The beatings, the torture, the labor, the other . . . molestations . . . but *Ash* didn't. Something, *someone* dark and terrible took his place. And that is the man who came for you."

Lorelai tried to respond, but the agony was too heavy in her throat, the storm of her tears was beginning to gather the strength of the one raging outside.

He walked around the bed frame toward her, but reached out and grasped at the post, as though desperate to hold the rest of him back. "I tried to get to you sooner. And in doing so, I lost what was left of me. I told you, I've been watching you for a long time . . . Initially, the plan was to rescue you, to protect you from Mortimer. But once I did find you, I realized it was more imperative I protect you from myself. From the things I want to—" His lips slammed shut and he looked away.

Her head snapped up. "That makes no sense. You said you don't want to hurt me." She hated how plaintive her voice became when laced with tears.

His eyes became two tortured orbs of onyx. "I—I can't promise I won't. As evidenced by what's been done already. And the chances are great that you'll be harmed because of me. I've more enemies than the queen. Enemies who would revel in tearing you apart to get to me. I've only been fearless because I'd nothing to lose. If I have you . . . they have a way to hurt me. It is the reason I stayed away from you as long as I did. Ash's promise put you in danger."

"Then why come for me at all?" she snapped tartly.

His grip tightened on the post, producing a loud, splintering sound. "To go through what I went through, to survive, a man needs a purpose. Something to live for. You were that for me. And for a while, knowing that you were just as I left you, romping about the estuaries with your animals, was enough. You were a memory I could visit. Something pure I hadn't tainted. And for the past several years, Mortimer was always away in London. He'd largely left you alone since he'd taken a wife."

It was true. Mortimer had all but ignored her since he married Veronica. He'd taken what her father had left for her dowry and bought a place in town. Southbourne Grove was a sanctuary in his absence. She'd loved the sprawling manor. It was her home.

"I knew if I killed Mortimer before he produced an heir, you'd lose your precious Southbourne Grove to some distant male relative. So, I installed Barnaby and went on a quest of my own. To find . . ." He trailed off, distracted by an extra close flash of lightning out the casement window.

"The Claudius Cache?" she finished for him.

"That, too," he said cryptically. "But when Barnaby told me your brother had betrothed you to a cruel bastard like

Sylvester Gooch. That did something to me that all the slavers in all the world could not." Finally, he approached her. Looming over her bedside, he reached down and wiped a tear from her cheek, his touch agonizingly tender. "I've known pain. I've known pain you've never . . ." He didn't finish the sentence, but grappled with a few harsh breaths. "But agony. True agony. Was knowing you were so far away for so long. That I might not again feel your touch. Hear your voice. Bask in your smile. There is pain and sometimes it's excruciating. But then there is suffering . . ."

She caught his hand in hers, turned it palm up, and buried her cheek against it.

He remained absolutely still, staring at the seam of their flesh. "Nothing mattered but getting to you before your betrothed touched you. My instinct overcame my reason, I can see that now. And that day, I saw Mortimer at the church and I . . . I snapped. I regret that you witnessed what I am capable of. That you watched your brother die in such a brutal manner."

"I'm *not*," she sobbed, making a pool of grief and rage in his palm. "I'm not anymore. You're right. He deserved it. They all did!"

His other hand stroked her hair, infinitely gentle, like the caress of silk against velvet. "Don't cry," he admonished her. "Don't you understand what I'm telling you? I am not worth all of this. I am not worth your tears."

"Yes you are!" she insisted. He was worth his weight in gold, her pirate king. He had wounds deeper than the trenches of the Pacific. He wasn't a monster, he was a *man*. A man who'd survived the unfathomable and emerged as a mountain of strength. "I thought you were the devil. I thought you selfish and brutal and cruel, but now . . ."

He pulled his hand from hers, gently, but firmly. "I *am*

the devil, Lorelai. That's what I'm trying to tell you. I *am* selfish and brutal and cruel. All I've considered is what was best for me. What I wanted to do to you. What I wanted you to do to me. To *feel* for me. I thought I could live with you as my captive. That I was cold enough to ignore your protestations. But I'm not."

"I know you're not," she encouraged him. "And that's good. This is what we can build on." She reached for his other hand, but he backed away. The rift in her heart widened, pouring hurt through her veins.

"No." He shook his head in perpetuity, as though convincing his own body as well as her. "In taking you, I always knew I would corrupt you. Break you. Destroy you. That's what I've been telling you. It's why I waited so long. Perhaps it was better if I never came at all."

"Don't say that." She threw the covers off her, struggling with her long nightgown to free her legs and stand. To follow him as he retreated.

"What kind of life would you have with me?" he demanded. "With Nemo, a man obsessed with and possessed of power and infamy? You were right, Lorelai. I have everything in the world, but nothing to offer you."

"But . . ." Finally, her feet touched the floor and she struggled to put weight on them as he reached the door. She hobbled around the bed, too unsteady to let go of the bedpost.

Sorrow touched his gaze as he watched her, but he made no move to help. "You are an angel in a world full of devils. And I have made myself king of them all."

He opened the door and turned away.

"Wait!" she cried. "Stay! Please stay with me. We can discuss this."

He violently shook his head, gripping the door handle as one would a lifeline. "I thought I deserved you . . . that

I'd earned you through suffering somehow." His throat worked over a wretched swallow. "I find that I cannot take your purity from you, Lorelai. That I cannot claim the years you have left, shackling you to my side. I will *not*. I've come to realize it's the one sin I cannot commit."

"But what if I—"

"I used to love you because I thought you were weak, but I understand now, your goodness makes you stronger than us all."

She froze. His words like daggers slicing through her heart until it bled into her extremities, turning them numb.

Used to love you.

"You may leave in the morning when it is safe. Take poor Veronica with you. I will make certain both of you are cared for but . . . I will no longer be your jailor. I will not keep you in chains."

Lorelai slid to the floor in a puddle of tears to the sound of the bolt securing her door.

CHAPTER EIGHTEEN

Lorelai woke with a jolt, even though the hand on her shoulder was gentle.

Farah Blackwell's gray eyes and silvery hair shone like a Fae creature's in the sputtering lanternlight. "I'm sorry to wake you, but there's something—"

A primal sound rent the night, full of both terror and warning. It was the sound a wounded lion might make when cornered by a tribe of hunters.

Lorelai had heard the sound before. On a stormy night much like this one some twenty years ago.

Ash.

Farah had a silk wrapper at the ready as Lorelai flung off the covers and slid from the tall bed. She belted the robe and limped after the Countess Northwalk, cursing the storm's effect on her leg.

Sensing her distress, Farah offered her arm and they hurried as fast as they were able into a lavishly decorated, dark wood hallway. The plush burgundy carpets cushioned her bare feet as she made her way two doors down from her own, where the Blackheart of Ben More stood with a lone candle dancing gold over his bleak features.

Lorelai found the sight of him without his eyepatch disconcerting. A gash dissected his left brow down to the cheekbone, and the wound had left his right eye a milky blue instead of deep brown. The effect was stunning, on many levels.

He speared her with a desolate gaze upon her approach, and Farah left her side to go to her husband.

They all had scars, Lorelai realized. The pain they wore on their skin warning of deeper, more dangerous wounds within.

They stood for a moment as a crack of departing thunder overshadowed the roar of a man held prisoner by desperate nightmares. It chilled her to the bone and tore at her heart. It strained credulity to think that such a piteous, tormented sound could come from such a sinister and self-possessed man.

Blackwell put his hand on the wood of the door, as though testing it for the heat of a fire on the other side. "We all have them," he said through a voice made husky with sleep. Or maybe with the lack thereof. "All of us who came of age in Newgate. It is hard to find rest, when sleep makes you vulnerable to the cruelty of others."

The connotations of that sentence tore at Lorelai's insides every bit as much as the raw, low cries of agony on the other side of that door. She truly couldn't comprehend the depths of suffering a man must have borne in his waking hours to battle such demons in his dreams.

"We used to take shifts sleeping. He, Argent, and I. One of us would stay awake, take watch against the older men who would . . ." Blackwell's hand slid to the latch. "He always fought them off the best. But we none of us won the battles all the time. Not until we were older. Stronger."

Lorelai's gaze collided with Farah's, and the confirmation she read there finished turning her heart into a puddle of pain. She'd not have been able to conceive of such things as a girl. She'd not known the real demons he fought in the night when she'd woken him all those years ago.

It made sense now. His aversion to the doctor's touch as a boy, his distrust of other men.

The chaos in his room reached an agonizing crescendo, like a ghost being dragged through hellfire. A soul bereft of hope. A helpless child screaming through the chest of the man who'd forgotten him.

Blackwell turned to her. "Before I go in there, I wanted to ask if you were aware if your husband sleeps with weapons." He quirked a sad smile at her. "Most of us do, and I'm not after being shot by a brother returned from the dead. Even *I* don't enjoy irony that much."

"I'll go," Lorelai breathed before she was truly aware that she'd made the decision.

"Darling, do you think that's wise?" Farah worried. "He's in such a state."

"I've done it before, when we were young," Lorelai said. "He had these same nightmares. I used to think it better he not remember the past, if those are the demons he has to fight in the dark."

"You're not wrong about that, my lady." Blackwell's mismatched gaze was warm on her. Approving. "But my wife is right to worry. It may not be safe for you in there."

Lorelai put her hand on Blackwell's arm, nudging it away from the latch. "I fear it is not safe for anyone *but* me in there."

He considered her with the thoroughness of a chemist, as though mentally dissecting all her parts and then putting them back together. "Very well," he finally said. "But

I will stand guard should you need help, until I'm certain you're out of any danger."

"Thank you." She took the candle he offered, filled her lungs with air and her heart with courage, and opened the door.

Her candle flickered and danced as she entered. He'd left his window open to let in the storm, and heavy drapes flapped in the wind like unsecured sails.

As she drifted closer to the bed, the low light revealed his distress in heartbreaking increments. The bedclothes tangled about his long legs as he thrashed against them like a prisoner would against his chains. The heavy muscles of his bare torso arched and strained as though some invisible force pinned him.

Lorelai couldn't imagine a man alive who could pit his strength against all the raw, sinewy power stretched taut over his heavy bones.

But when he was a boy, he'd been leaner. Smaller.

She set her candle on the edge of the nightstand, out of his reach, the sounds of his hissing breaths and grinding teeth wore down her resolve.

He was so dazzlingly large. He tore whole crews apart with his bare hands, he'd only just said so.

What could he do to her, here in the dark? What if he mistook her for one of his demons?

He whimpered, and suddenly none of that mattered.

Bracing herself, she slowly lowered to perch on the edge of the cavernous, canopied bed.

That was all it took.

His shoulders sprang from the mattress, and his fingers wrapped around her neck before she had the chance to make a sound. He stared at her with fathomless, unfocused eyes long enough for panic to set in as she fought to draw air through her throat. Unable to use her voice, Lorelai did the only thing she could think of. The only thing that had worked before.

She reached out her left hand, and pressed it over his heart.

His gaze cleared in an instant, and he released his grasp with a low groan that might have been her name.

Both his hands flew from her neck to cover the one she held against his chest, as though to trap it there.

Each of them breathed too violently to form words, and so they sat like that for several moments, focused on the feel of his heartbeat. It threw itself at her palm, looking for a way to escape the prison of bone and blood if only to be held in her hand.

He was a colorful kaleidoscope of muscle, bathed in golden light. His body a profusion of swells and divots, of brawn and bone. They were both of the same species, but how could they possibly be? His chest expanded in hard disks, while her breasts were softer and more teardropped with every passing year. His ribs scaled down a broad, flat torso, narrowing to obdurate mounds of stomach muscles disappearing beneath the bedclothes. Hers. Well . . . her ribs could sometimes be seen, but not in a way anyone would consider remarkable.

He shook his head, his raven eyes both accusing and appealing to her. The silent messages hurled at her in the wan light of the lone candle were both as loud and undeniable as if he screamed them.

You shouldn't have come.

Don't leave me.

Her replies were equally as tangible and unmistakable.

I know.

And I won't.

His skin blanched pale beneath his tan. Sweat gathered at his temples, cooling in the stormy breeze let in through the window.

A hesitant knock sounded on the door, and Farah's voice called softly, "Is everything all right?"

He tensed, but looked to her.

Lorelai had to clear her throat before replying, "All is well."

"Good night, then." Lorelai was certain his ears also pricked to the sound of *two* sets of footsteps retreating from the door.

She went to move her hand, and he hesitated in letting her go, as though reluctant for her to see what was beneath her palm.

The action befuddled her. One cannot see another's heart through the chest, only through the eyes. Everyone knew that. So, why did he seem disinclined to show her his chest?

She blinked down at the hands covering hers, scarred and rough and square. They trembled slightly, or did they only mirror her own quivers?

Instead of tugging away again, she slid her hand down over the iron mound of his pectoral, gasping at what she uncovered.

His nostrils flared, as did a spark of something wild and dangerous in his eyes, but he sat unnaturally still as she stared for what seemed like hours at her discovery.

She'd not noticed it until now, even when he'd stood naked before her. She'd been so focused on *not* looking at him, that she'd missed the very confirmation she'd been waiting for all along.

There. On his chest. Protected by a fierce tiger above, and a serpentine dragon beneath, was inked the ruby silhouette of small, perfect lips.

Her lips.

The lips she'd used twenty years ago to kiss the nightmare of darkness away from his heart.

She'd once again stopped breathing as she gaped.

I knew it, she thought, both humbled and elated at once. He'd lied to her, but her discovery of the truth wasn't at all unpleasant. Nor was she angry.

I knew Ash was alive. That he loved me.

Here was the proof.

She quirked her eyebrow at him.

His lips thinned and his eyes narrowed. The air darkened with a threat. Then a warning. Followed by a promise.

Everything spoken and unspoken hung suspended between them, and for the first time since she could remember, Lorelai didn't question her place. She was meant to be here. Now. In this bed, with this man.

"Go," he forced through a labored breath. "If you don't leave, Lorelai, I'll forget—"

Lorelai lunged before she could change her mind, driving her body against his and stopping his words with a desperate, artless kiss. He said he'd not take her, but this time, she'd come to him.

He'd crossed oceans, and she'd only crossed a hallway. But it seemed as though some greater divide had been forged in doing so.

This time, *she'd* come for *him*.

Though, if she'd thought to be the one to do the taking, she immediately learned her folly.

With a powerful, effortless grace, he enfolded her in his arms and rolled them until he'd pinned her beneath the animal heat of his body.

Only when he seemed to have secured her, did he soften the kiss from desperate to reverent. His mouth didn't just take hers, he worshiped it. Every bit of him was so much harder than her. So much bigger, stronger, but for his lips, which were unexpectedly soft.

He kissed like a man unused to kissing. He applied no artful, seductive skill nor patient, practiced moves. He simply drank pleasure from her mouth, and returned it in generous, overwhelming increments.

Lorelai had forgotten this. That a kiss was so much more than warm, wet sensation.

A kiss had a taste. A singular flavor. Something bold and yet subtle.

A kiss had a scent. Mint, hers, and whisky, his, expelled on the breaths they shared.

A kiss was a rare and strange perspective. The other so close, the sight of him blurred into flesh and flashes of eyes.

A wild jolt speared through her, an animal reaction of her own, at the possession she spied in those eyes.

Her womb clenched on an aching emptiness and, as though he sensed her need, his knee split her thighs and he settled, once again, between her legs. Only the barrier of her nightgown separated the smooth, long barrel of his arousal from touching her aching flesh.

From slipping inside.

Her chilly fingers grazed the warmth of his neck before threading through raven strands as sultry as silk.

This was real, and this was right.

This was Ash. *Her* Ash. Despite his protestations to the contrary. She'd found him, here. She'd found him in the nightmares she wished he didn't suffer. She found him in the darkness he ruled. In the storms he summoned.

She found him, and was determined not to lose him again.

The pressure of his mouth became more urgent, his tongue sweeping into hers with voluptuous strokes, doing things to her she never knew could be done. His kiss became many. A stanza of kisses. His tongue working the syllables of poetry into her mouth, his lips creating the meter and rhyme, the ebb and flow.

And his body. Oh, his body. Long and lithe and lethal, it rocked against her in a percussion so ancient, so achingly necessary, it called to the very soul of her. To that place woven together from the whispers of her ancestors into the finely spun tapestry of her own arrangement. The one that was born to dance beneath him.

Her hands smoothed away from his hair, down the cords of his neck, and over his muscled back. She feathered soft caresses over his scars, soothing him to relax deeper into her. To press himself down against her.

But he didn't, not entirely. He held himself with the strength of one arm, his other hand trailing over her nightgown, heating the quivering skin beneath until he covered her breast.

A muffled groan passed between them. His. Hers. She couldn't be sure. It was low. And it was raw. And it was followed by a violent reaction on his part.

He reared back, breaking the kiss, and grasped the lace collar of her nightgown in both hands, rending it in half from her body with one smooth, powerful jerk.

It was in her shy nature to cover herself, and she moved to do so, but her arms were still trapped in the sleeves, which he tucked down next to her body, rendering her immobile.

He stared down at her silently. Like a pilgrim would a relic, his eyes bright and savage. So opposite from what they'd been that first night when all she'd read within was a selfish, unsympathetic hunger.

She worried now that he considered her something

other than she was. Not a skinny cripple on the wrong side of thirty. But a woman. A provocateur. Someone who enticed and aroused him.

Would he always see her thus?

He gave her no words, no platitudes. He didn't call her beautiful. He didn't have to. She caught the image of herself reflected in the hunger tightening his brutal features. In the awe glowing from his gaze. In the hitch of his breath, and the heat of his sex.

Tonight, words served them not at all. There was so much to say. And so little language to properly convey what was lost and found between them.

First. There must be this. This merging of selves. This meeting of the inevitability of their past and the indefinite future.

He'd not take her. Not this time. He'd promised not to.

This time, she would give.

Lifting herself, she blindly sought his mouth, unable to reach for him as her arms were still trapped.

He responded immediately, descending on her, ravishing her mouth as his hands explored her body where his eyes no longer could. She had one blurry glimpse of dark lust on his features before he did, indeed, press her down. Down. Engulfing her with the yielding mattress below, and his hard body above in a cocoon of warmth and need.

Where her calm had surprised her before, now she fought another sensation. The urge to move. To squirm against him as he took his time shaping his hands to her body. He'd claimed to want this for twenty years, dammit, so why did he insist on touching her in places that mattered not at all?

His mouth moved to nibble delicately at her jaw, her ear, the hollow of her throat as his hands spanned her ribs, followed the curve of her waist to the flare of her hips, charted over the smooth expanse of her belly. None of those places were even remotely sensual, were they? Just various innocuous parts of her, and yet he seemed to delight in finding them. In stroking them. In exploring them as though he'd never before touched a woman.

After so long, she made an impatient noise, flexing her quivering knees and wriggling impatient hips.

Lord, what a heathen she was turning into all of a sudden . . . But she couldn't help it.

She'd not been the only one waiting for twenty years, and since Ash was here in the room with her, she was good and ready to make up for missed time.

An appreciative sound purred from his throat, and he gave her what she wanted, and then some.

His hot mouth closed over her chilly nipple at the same time his hand slid over the soft nest between her legs.

She didn't know upon which incredible sensation to focus. The dance of his tongue on her breast, or the stroke of his hand over her sex. He petted her downy curls before parting them. His fingers were cool against her hot, intimate flesh.

They gasped together as she saturated his questing hand with moisture. For a moment, she surrendered to it all. Both the sweetness, and the shame.

The heat of his breath against her breast distracted her for a moment, before his clever, careful fingers began to dip and toy with the slick desire her body had released, drawing it up to the tiny place that swelled and ached for him.

She dared to look down at him, to gauge his expression. She found it intent with lust, his color high and fevered. His gaze desperate.

But his hands, his infuriatingly stable hands belied what she read on his face. They made sly and circular motions around that place where her sensation culminated, unhurried even as she writhed beneath him, clutched at him. Gasping wordless pleas for something she didn't understand. Couldn't express.

She. Just. Knew. Knew he was taking her body on a taut, excruciating journey with a devastating end.

He seemed to draw pleasure from her agitation. To savor it. So, unable to stand it anymore, she pressed her head back into the mattress and squeezed her eyes shut. Surrendering to the moment.

To him.

A finger found its way inside of her, and she jerked, but he crawled up her body, soothing her with a gentle, probing kiss. His strokes became wicked, then torturous. Quickening in pace and rhythm until she surged in trembling, taut thrusts. Riding his fingers as she imagined one rode a horse, hips moving in time with the animal, urging it onward.

He slid another finger inside her, and she sobbed at the pressure of it. The pleasure of it. It threatened to annihilate her. To rush toward her with the speed and inevitability of a rogue wave, and there was nothing to be done but brace for the onslaught.

Which she did. She clutched him, her true source of strength, as it crashed down upon her and threatened to sweep her away. He held her. Soothed her. Encouraged her. All the while continuing his ministrations, his fingers slipping easily into her wetness. Pulled deeper by grasping, pulsing muscles.

He never let her go, not even when he brought her down slowly. Dragging his lips over hers as she twitched and shuddered long after his hands withdrew from her swollen flesh, leaving it not only empty, but oddly unfulfilled.

She blinked up at him with dazed fascination. His

sweat-misted brow. His unconcealed tenderness. But, where his hands were steady before, now they shook when they touched her.

A dark intent lurked beneath his tenderness. A hunger too long denied.

He'd reached the edge of his legendary self-control.

And now, he meant to claim her.

He'd meant to wait. To draw this out. To wring every last moment of pleasure he could from her body.

This was what he'd come back for. Wasn't it? To take her. To fuck her. To claim what he'd been denied all these years.

And he was about to. God help him. Because he was a man no longer used to denying himself.

Except . . . He'd forgotten various and sundry things in his life, but never anything so important as what her gentleness did to him.

That was what he'd come back for. He understood now. He admitted it to himself.

It wasn't this raging inferno of desire. This rutting instinct. Not entirely.

It was the small hand delicately exploring the surface of his chest. The softness of her beneath him. The sweet, feminine fragrance of her. The heavy-lidded satisfaction bedazzling her sapphire gaze. The trusting, lazy half-smile she offered him.

The absolution she offered so freely.

He knew he'd lose himself in her body, but he'd never expected to become so thoroughly absorbed in her pleasure.

Gods, was it exquisite.

He held himself levered over her for a tense moment. Paralyzed by a radiant, infuriating arousal. It battered at him with all the frenzy of madness, pulling his muscles taut.

He could do it now. Surge inside of her, take her virginity in one quick thrust. She'd be his then. He could pound into her all of his pain, his past, and his passion.

But . . . Some astounding part of him refused to move. Choosing, instead, to luxuriate in her insanely tentative exploration of him. Her hands smoothed down his arms, tracing engorged veins pressed against his skin by flexed muscle. Dainty fingers tickled along his ribs, and it took all of his hard-won stoicism not to flinch or twitch.

Or smile.

Her hands paused at his hips and they both ceased to breathe. Indecision blinked into her eyes, warring with curiosity.

He had to stop this. If she touched him now, he'd lose himself. One way or the other, and neither option was desirable.

A primitive fear became a surge of satisfaction as her thighs parted wider for him, making that infinitely sweet cradle for his hips.

Neither of them needed to use hands to guide him. Their bodies found exactly the right position. His cock slid into place, parting her soft folds. He bent to her, surrounding her with his strength, hoping to lend it to her. Sorry for her pain. Wishing he could kiss it away somehow. Or take it upon himself.

He placed his hands on either side of her head, kissing her as he pushed into her gently resisting flesh with infinite slowness.

She gasped and he froze. Their kiss became two people sharing panting, openmouthed wonder.

"More." It was the only word she'd spoken since they'd

begun. It would be the only word spoken until they finished.

He fed her inch by agonizing inch. Her hot, wet flesh closing around him, drawing him inside, inviting him to take his pleasure there. It was beyond even the bliss he'd spent a lifetime imagining.

He dimly wondered, as he watched her eyes widen in direct proportion to his penetration, if only someone who'd experienced the depths of suffering he had, could truly appreciate an ecstasy like this.

He was glad, in a way, that he'd not known it would be this good. This sweet. That he'd feel this much.

Because maybe he'd not have waited until this moment. This perfect moment.

The moment Lorelai Weatherstoke became his.

For the first time in his life he felt both freedom and power. Both surrender and strength.

She moved with him, then, practicing shy little thrusts upward. Twitches and rolls of her lithe body sent him spiraling out of control as she reacted to every sensation and his every movement with raw, almost giddy amazement.

Her little gasps of discovery stroked not just his body, but his ego, as well.

She was enjoying this. Enjoying him. On top of her. Inside of her.

That thought unleashed something within him he'd not expected. A patience he'd never known. An overwhelming tenderness he wanted to both embrace and escape. It held his monster in check as he initiated her untried flesh in long, slow, deep strokes. It allowed him to shore up his threatening release until her head pressed back into the mattress, then began to strain from side to side, her eyes squeezed closed.

Maybe he'd be able to coax two orgasms from her body before he gave in to his own.

Once the hoarse cry escaped her, and her feminine muscles began to tighten in rhythmic pulses, he was forced to admit his folly.

She pulled him with her into a transcendent place. One made of harsh breaths and incoherent moans. Time coalesced with the storm, as a flash of lightning lanced the night, blinding them as its equal speared through their joined bodies. The pleasure just as hot and searing. The bliss just as blinding. And the emotions as binding as a contract one signs with fate.

He'd been lost so many times. For so many years. But, he realized, when he lost himself inside of her, he found something few men ever would.

CHAPTER NINETEEN

Lorelai assumed she'd feel more like a woman after her first time. More grown-up, or something, which was a ridiculous expectation to have for a woman her age.

Instead, she'd regressed into a much younger, more naïve version of herself. One who could pretend again. One with an imagination still hued with optimism and hope.

It felt as if the candle not only swathed them in its sonorous light, but glowed through her veins, as well. Soft and golden and intimately warm.

She'd been happy to let him treat her like a rag doll, allowing him to fetch a cloth by the basin and wash them both before he lifted and draped her over his magnificent reclining body.

She listened to the storm for a long silent while, waiting for their breathing to return to normal. His arms encircling her felt like the most natural thing in the world.

For the first time in twenty years, she was safe.

Drowsily, she traced the edges of a few of his tattoos,

admiring their work. The tiger on his chest stood beneath an Asian waterfall, the dragon stood in flames. Unburned.

On his other pectoral, jungle cats leaped from rushes, a tribal bear roared at a majestic stag. Other creatures littered his torso. A strange mammal with a ringed tail. A shark so realistic, it could have leaped off his skin. Serpents, fish, wolves, foxes, glass-eyed raptor birds, Indian elephants with exotic markings.

How much pain it must have caused him, to capture these renderings beneath his skin.

She touched her finger to the tiny lips, the ghost of *her* lips, covering the oblong they made. One of the only designs on his body not an animal.

When the silence finally felt as though it'd stretched too tightly, she asked, "Penny for your thoughts?"

His torso rippled with an amused breath. "You'd not be getting a bargain, they're barely worth that much."

"They are to me."

His big hand settled against her hair, idly undoing her loose braid with careful motions and dragging her long curls over his skin as though the sensation pleased him. "You drained me of thoughts," he rumbled in a silken tone. "Gifted me a quiet mind."

She smiled against his chest, thinking she didn't do much more than lie there and enjoy his body. His incredible, colorful body. "Would it interrupt your quietude too much if I asked you a question?"

That flex again, low across his abdomen. A tightening of impossibly defined muscle and sinew denoting his pleased hitch of breath. "You could ask me to invade China right now, and I'd find a way to do it."

Most men would be jesting, but with him . . . one could never tell.

"Why so many tattoos?" She traced the detailed horns of the elk. "Why all the animals?"

The hand stroking her hair stilled. "I've been just about everywhere. When I saw these creatures, in captivity or in the wild, I thought of you. I thought of showing them to you, and so I put them on my body."

She lifted her head to look over his shoulder at him. "Are you in earnest?"

He nodded down at her.

Incredulous, she regarded his artwork with new eyes. "You've seen all of these creatures? And then you brought them back to me?"

"All but the dragon, obviously."

"Obviously," she echoed, pushing herself up to sit and wrapping the sheet around her. She'd have told him it was because the storm chilled her, but the truth was she didn't yet feel comfortable with her state of nudity.

She splayed her hand over his skin, leaving his more . . . masculine parts modestly covered. "Where did you see a bear?"

"Mongolia." He rested his hands behind his head, examining his own topography as though mildly interested. The movement did interesting things to his muscles.

Lord, if she had her druthers, he'd never put his clothing back on.

"And wolves?"

"America."

"This snake?"

He checked. "That's a black mamba, the deadliest snake known to man."

She covered her open mouth with her fingers. "Did you catch one?"

"One almost caught me." The ghost of a smile whispered at the corners of his mouth. "In sub-Saharan Africa."

She liked him like this. A lion at rest, the ever-present tension leached from his muscles. The vigilant void of his gaze warmed to something almost . . . human. Alive.

Part of her wanted to ask him about his nightmares tonight, another about his dreams for the future. She wanted to know what had happened during the last twenty years. She wanted to know what happened next.

But no force on this earth could convince her to say a thing that would ruin the first interaction they'd had that wasn't fraught with danger, passion, or pain.

This was what she'd wanted. To be in bed with Ash, sharing small, inconsequential intimacies. This was how she'd fallen in love with him the first time.

Now, instead of a bleak-eyed boy with an empty past, he was an experienced man who'd seen the whole world. And still he brought little parts of that world back to her.

The very thought of it melted her heart.

"What manner of creature is this?" She pointed to the strange, big-eyed mammal that didn't seem to fit with the theme of hunters painted on the body of the most alpha predator.

"It's a ring-tailed lemur." He smoothed his hand over hers. "I met her in Madagascar. She followed me through a market and leaped on my shoulder, tried to share a plantain with me."

"She didn't!"

"By share, I mean she peeled it daintily and shoved it in my eye."

She let out a surprised giggle. "Tell me you didn't hurt her!" she said.

"I ate her plantain, that's for certain." A smile didn't sit easily on his hard mouth, but it seemed like it wanted to. "But we parted as friends."

"I thought you said you didn't have friends," she taunted.

"Not of the human variety."

She petted the lemur, somewhere left of his navel, a frown tugging at her brows. "I wish I could see these exotic creatures, but I know I never shall."

His fingers lifted her chin with a gentleness she'd not thought him capable of. "A lot can happen between now and never."

The words she'd spoken to him as a child glowed in her chest and spiked her lashes with threatening tears. "True," she said haltingly, "but with my leg, there's no traipsing around jungles or climbing mountains for me. I'm essentially useless."

"Nonsense," he soothed. "I'll hire elephants to take you through the jungle, and sedans carried by ten bronzed men to conduct you through foreign cities. Arabian horses will convey you through the deserts, and we can take trains or my ship everywhere else."

She sniffed, wishing she weren't such a ninny. "And what about all the places elephants, and bronzed men, and Arabians and trains and ships can't go?"

His playful gaze sobered, and warmed. "I'll carry you."

Driven by a desperate hope, she collapsed back to his chest. "Can we leave tomorrow? Just leave pirates and treasure and our names behind? We could start our lives anew."

His hands toyed at the tendrils beside her face, as a gentle regret settled on his expression. "I have to find the Claudius Cache," he murmured. "I've promised my men."

"Couldn't you just give the map to your men? Let them find it?"

"I have to see this through," he insisted.

"But why? You have more money than you could spend in five lifetimes. Do you really need more treasure? Hasn't this search taken enough from you?" She traced her fingers over his ruined tattoo. "It almost killed you once, already."

He watched her with glittering black eyes. "I've been searching for this treasure since before I was Dorian Blackwell. When I think about it, I feel like my past is hurling itself at the iron door separating me from my memories. I feel like if I find the Claudius Cache . . . I'll find myself."

At this, she nodded reluctantly. "I understand." And she did. "What then?" She was almost afraid to ask. "What will drive you once you've found what you seek?"

"Drive me?"

"You've been everywhere, seen everything. You have nothing left to conquer. What will you live for then?"

His eyes swung to the window as he contemplated the storm that had calmed to a light, pattering rain. "I have seen everything," he said tightly. "I've met every kind of man. There are those who would risk their lives to climb the highest mountain or find the source of the most treacherous fjord. They crawl over themselves to build the highest building. Or to mine the deepest cave. They crave power. Glory. Danger. Excitement. They seek to taunt death. To defy God. To dominate nature . . . And only that thing, that obsession, makes them feel alive."

She contemplated him with as much intensity as he did the storm. "Do . . . any of those things make you feel alive?"

"Not even close."

"Then . . . what does? What will?"

He looked at her then, almost as though she'd disappointed him. "How can you not know?"

The air between them crackled with the promise of something cataclysmic. The promise of a shift in their cosmos, a rotation of their fates.

"Did you love me?" The moment the words escaped her, she regretted them.

His eyes shifted away from her. "I was young. I hadn't yet learned to fear the folly of a fool in love."

The emotion that had threatened the entire night spilled over her lashes, and his thumb smoothed it away. "It's too late for love, Lorelai. To me, love is no more than the construct of poets. As easily bought and discarded as trust or loyalty. But I understand possession." He rose up to bring his face close to hers, so they were once again breathing the same air. "You are mine. That is what I know."

"So . . . you don't love me."

He pressed his forehead to hers. "I should have said it," he lamented. "Back when I still had the ability to feel it. Back when I knew what fear was. What love was. I should have said I loved you before I rode away with Mortimer that day. It was there on the tip of my tongue. Right then, it was *there* in my heart when I was young enough to have one."

Hope permeated the pain of his words as he brushed his mouth against hers. If love had been there once before . . . maybe she could put it back.

"It doesn't matter," she soothed. "I love you." She wrapped her arms around him, letting the covers fall away. She didn't want to look at him. Didn't want to see fear or guilt or rejection in his eyes. She pressed her heart to his heart, her lips to his lips, and this time, when he moved above her, she had the sense he'd be much more wicked.

CHAPTER TWENTY

Lorelai made space for Veronica as her sister-in-law joined her on the upper deck of the forecastle to watch the bustling below as they steamed toward the pier.

"I never thought I'd be so happy to see Southbourne Grove." Veronica shielded her eyes with her hand and gazed over the branching tendrils of the estuary toward their home.

"I never thought I wouldn't." Lorelai shared none of Veronica's enthusiasm, which surprised her. Since they'd left Ben More Castle earlier that morning, she'd fought a strange sense of impending doom.

It unsettled her even more that she seemed to be the only one.

The general morale on the ship could only be called jolly, if one ignored the furtive and untrusting feeling toward the new small contingent of Dorian Blackwell's men. Still, the prospect of imminent treasure was to a pirate ship what the prospect of a ducal marriage was to an equally mercenary crew of matriarchs at Almack's in its day.

Indeed, Lorelai had diverted herself greatly by watching the antics of eight little kittens roaming freely about the main deck, befriending a band of rough-and-tumble pirates. It caused her no end of amusement to observe a rather gigantic chap by the name of Cutthroat Bill set the little fluff ball on his shoulder for the entire afternoon and refer to his new companion as "Little Bill."

Shifty Rodriguez, on the other hand, almost lost an eye when he'd been unaware that a tiny orange tabby had fallen asleep in his hat. He'd lifted it to put it on, and was rewarded with a jack-in-the-box pounce to his face that caused more apoplexy then actual damage.

He and the orange fellow seemed to have made peace, though, and he even put his hat back on the table where it had been should the *gatito* be in need of another *siesta*.

Barnaby had taken to dragging a red tassel the size of a mouse at the end of a fishing twine from his belt as he paced the deck about his work. Any number of hunting kittens could be found stalking him, swiping at the lure with murderous enthusiasm.

By the time they reached the estuary, all the kittens had names and, it seemed, had been unofficially claimed by one pirate or another. If Lorelai had it correctly, there was Little Bill, Gatito, Katjie, Neko, Ikati, Bast, White Bastard, and Jim.

Lorelai initially thought each name had a story, but was disavowed of that notion when Barnaby mentioned that the more exotic names were simply variances of the word *cat* in different languages.

Of course they were, she'd sighed to herself.

Men.

As they steamed closer to shore, Lorelai was struck again by the beauty of her home. A teeming flock of a thousand starlings ascended in the distance, using the same wind to paint a dancing portrait in the rare blue sky.

The sea air was mild and sweet, and it tossed the strands that had come loose from Veronica's braid across Lorelai's shoulder.

They were returning to the past, she realized, as she found her handsome husband standing below her at the bow of the ship, watching the same spectacle of birds.

For better or for worse.

She thought of what was beneath that expensive black suit. The gigantic raven wings spanning over muscle built upon muscle. The sinew and scars. The passion and pain. The courage and cleverness. All the things that made this man. That made *her* man.

"Do you love him?" Veronica murmured.

"I do," she answered, perhaps even surprising herself. It was the answer to the question she hadn't been asked on her wedding day. "I—I think I always have."

"Have you told him?"

"I have."

Veronica hesitated. Bit her lip. "Has he told you?"

Lorelai tried not to let her shoulders slump. "He's shown me his devotion, and that's different than mere words. Better, surely."

"Surely . . ." Veronica didn't sound quite as convinced. "Who'd have thought that you and I would be embroiled in a search for treasure? That we'd be whisked away on a pirate adventure?"

"I'm glad you're choosing to see it as an adventure and not an ordeal."

Veronica gestured toward where Blackwell had joined the Rook, striking up a discussion. The briny sea breeze carried the masculine voices, if not their words, up to the ladies. "Your Rook was right about one thing, he's done me a favor, I suppose. I know it's savage of me to say, but I fear had he not killed Mortimer, I'd have ended up doing it myself, one day. Or trying to. The blood is on his hands . . . I suppose I should be thankful for that."

Lorelai hooked her arm through her beloved friend's. "If ever there was someone who deserved what he got . . ."

"Indeed." Veronica seemed surprised to hear Lorelai say it, but she didn't comment. "I suppose I'll go back to my family and pretend to mourn, when all of this is done. Though, Lord knows, I'd rather do anything else."

"I hope you still consider me family." Lorelai squeezed her tighter.

"Of course I do, darling." Veronica dropped a fond kiss on her temple.

"You could stay here," she offered.

Veronica glanced over to where Moncrieff coiled threads of chain that must have weighed as much as he did. "I don't think that's for the best, at least until the fervor over Mortimer's death dies down. Besides, who knows who will next inherit Southbourne Grove?"

Lorelai frowned. "I hadn't thought of that. Some distant relative of Mr. Gooch's, I suppose."

Veronica made a wry sound. "A dowager at my age, can you imagine?"

"No more than I can a pirate at mine."

They shared a laugh until Lorelai sobered and turned to her sister. "You don't have to return to your family, you know. You'll have a dowager stipend settled on you and, of course, whatever money is granted me by my unconventional marriage to the Rook will be offered as recompense for this entire . . . adventure. Though I know nothing comes close to remuneration for the past couple of years. When I think of how you suffered . . ." She had to swallow past a lump of guilt.

"Let's not mention it again," Veronica offered with a false brightness that didn't reach her haunted eyes. "Upon second thought, I don't think I shall return to my family." She put her head on Lorelai's shoulder. "But I'll make my own way in this world. A widow has far more social freedoms than wives or maidens."

"Where will you go?" Lorelai asked.

"I've always wanted to lose myself in the fashion salons of Paris," she replied dreamily.

"Then you should."

"I believe I will."

Lorelai clung to her for a desperate moment. "Each of us starting a new life . . . why does it feel ominous? Like an ending?"

Veronica thought on it for a while. "Not all happy endings are without a modicum of sadness."

"I suppose not." Lorelai gazed out toward the two similar men at the ship's bow, their dark heads now bent over their map. From this vantage, they could be twins. It would be difficult to tell them apart but for Blackwell's eyepatch.

"I wonder which of us are truly more jealous creatures," Veronica mused. "Men, or women?"

Speculating as to what prompted the question, Lorelai followed Veronica's gaze out over the deck to see Moncrieff, Barnaby, and several others posturing and scowling at a few of the Blackheart of Ben More's men.

The effect was somewhat ruined by romping kittens.

Lorelai laughed merrily, drawing the attention of a pair of dark eyes, which heated her skin with the memory of the previous night. "I hazard that women would answer men, and men would answer women."

"I expect they'd both be right."

Off the starboard bow, the little port town of Easton-on-Sea clustered beneath the gray stone grandeur of Southbourne Grove. Three islands, Mersea, Osea, and Tersea, hunkered like sentries in the tidal causeways. Mersea and Osea were flat islands with miles of tame sandy beaches. She supposed, if one squinted, Tersea could appear like the back of a sleeping dragon, half submerged, curled around its treasure. Waves breached the rocks, sending a white spray of warning to those who would dare approach.

What would they discover there on the morrow? she wondered. *An ancient Roman cache? A tortured man's past? Or something infinitely more dangerous?*

The Rook finally understood why people begged for their lives.

Even the most coldhearted villains, the ones who turned a blind eye to the suffering of the weak, still pleaded with desperation before he ended them.

He'd distantly wondered why over the years. They had to have known, hadn't they? That if God or the devil didn't find them, *he* would. And when he did, they'd be praying for hell by the time he finished with them.

But still they tried. They cried. They bargained. They supplicated.

He'd thought them pathetic.

Until now.

He didn't need to puzzle over it anymore. Everyone, he learned, feared death when they had something to lose. Their hearts had attached themselves to life, to something that mattered, and the thought of separation became untenable.

For his part, he'd taken it all from those men—power, money, land, titles, revenge—and had truly desired none of it for himself. That was his genuine tragedy. He'd started as a thief, became a slave, then a conqueror, a lord, and finally a pirate king. All the while, he'd been plagued by ambivalence. By a lack of fear. A part of him always assumed should a blade, a bayonet, or a bullet find purchase in his chest, it would do no damage.

Because he didn't have a heart. Just a body built around a fathomless black void that no amount of endless acquisition could fill.

God help him, he'd tried.

He'd been so wrong. He could see that now. It wasn't that his heart didn't exist. It was that it had resided elsewhere all this time . . .

He'd left it here. At Southbourne Grove.

Little by little, Lorelai was returning it to him, shard by shattered shard.

Did he want it back? Not especially. But he wanted her enough to suffer whatever she asked of him.

He'd ached for her for twenty years. Now that he'd tasted her, claimed her, made love to her . . . his vocabulary didn't extend far enough to form the word for what a separation would do to him.

He stood in his old room at Southbourne Grove and pondered the gloaming as it darkened the Black Water Estuary and the sea beyond. He understood the name now.

Nigrae Aquae. The Black Water.

Facing east, the branching rivers of the estuary became inky, labyrinthine ribbons of chaos beneath a sky quickly draining of all color. Stars already began to prick the dark canvas of the firmament on this side of the manor, though a line of gray still clung to the horizon in the west.

He wanted her again, cad that he was, he desired her splayed across things, bent over other things, on her knees, on her back, over him, under him, beside him. Against that wall . . .

Christ. He scrubbed a hand over his face, and then through his hair, tugging in frustration.

He yearned to claim every inch of her. With his mouth. With his cock. He could keep her naked for the next decade, fucking away the last twenty years. Listening to her voice, the only sound in the world with the power to soothe his restless rage, or to stir his listless soul.

Her fragile innocence reminded him of just what a devil he was. An insatiable beast. A terrific villain.

He'd done his level best to focus on the quest. To pay attention to Dorian, Moncrieff, and his crew as they planned their approach and excavation of Tersea Island with painstaking care. But dammit if Lorelai hadn't wandered his ship with her distracting loveliness. She'd stood on the forecastle deck for an eternity, posing with her attractive sister. It was a marvel anyone had accomplished anything.

When she'd tugged her earlobe, he'd remembered biting it as he came inside her from behind. When she rested a hand on her dramatically tilted hip, he could see it through the folds of her borrowed gown. His hand would burn at the memory of the pale shape of it in his hand as he'd guided their rhythm. When she'd bent over to scratch at one of the infernal kittens, he'd nearly fallen over the railing at the sight of her backside.

Here he was, near forty, and his body was acting like a besotted teenager's. His cock had been at half-mast nearly all day, as just the sight of her was enough to create a lack of available space in his trousers.

And he could do fuck all about it with so many of his crew around at all times. He'd half a mind to just toss them all in the sea and have her on whatever part of his ship he fancied.

What stopped him was a comment she'd made this morning upon peeling herself out of bed. His little wife reminded him none-too-gently that she'd never been particularly fond of mornings, and she'd admitted to an intimate tenderness after he'd demanded an explanation for a wince she'd not hidden fast enough while beset by early sluggishness.

So, instead of whisking her into the room with the first available bed upon their arrival at Southbourne Grove, he acquiesced to the plan of allowing her to explain away his presence here.

The story she and Dorian had concocted was a simple and effective one, he had to admit. He was to be her long-lost cousin of some considerable distance, Ash Weatherstoke, a continental duke who had purchased Southbourne Grove back to the family from the Gooch estate. He was supposed to have rescued her from the Rook's dastardly clutches and conveyed her back to inspect his new British holdings. This story would be corroborated by only a handful of staff left who might recall a relation by the name of Ash Weatherstoke staying at Southbourne Grove a few decades ago. A distant cousin, if their memory served, convalesced here after a tragic accident.

The staff had been so relieved at Lorelai and Veronica's safe return, along with a visit from the infamous Blackheart of Ben More, that they'd barely paid their supposed new master any mind, other than a few polite courtesies and skeptical glances.

He'd immediately retreated, allowing Lorelai to receive the adoration that was her due. First, he'd double-checked preparations for tomorrow's excursion, and then he'd drifted here. To the room where he'd first heard her voice.

This place, for all intents and purposes, was where he'd been born. The residence of his earliest memory.

Her voice.

Did you love me?

Love was too tame a word. Obsession too plain a concept.

Worship might cover it. Might come close to—

A quickening in his body and a thrill in his blood alerted him to her approach long before his ear pricked to the swish of her skirts or her uneven gait.

His every muscle tensed, every hair on his body prickled with awareness of her. It always had. It was as though she had an electromagnetic pull on him, her nearness charging the air between them, calling him closer. To touch. To hold.

He had no choice but to obey.

"I thought I might find you here," she murmured.

He shoved his fists in his pockets.

She stopped next to him, to gaze out the same window.

Close. She was too close. He could smell the sea in her hair and the fragrance of the lilac soap she'd bathed with this morning warmed by her skin.

His jaw cracked.

"I come in here all the time," she admitted. "I look over to the horizon, and understand why people used to assume that the distant sea was the edge of the world. I think a part of me knew you were out there. That this ocean separated us. You *felt* that far away from my heart."

The suppressed longing in her voice pricked a hole in his lungs, but he continued to stare at the dark water, the threads and branches not unlike the pitch-black ice he boasted for blood.

Her shoulder brushed his arm. "The sea calls to a man, or so they say. I wonder if he has no choice but to answer."

"I had no choice." His lips barely moved, but still the bitter words cut through the air like a blade of rime.

"I know." She put her head against his arm, and

something in his middle melted. "I always questioned why something so incomprehensibly large, so deadly, so inhospitable to man, could take us away from who we are. From what we love. From the land upon which we rely." She tilted her golden head up to regard him, and her gaze felt like the first warmth of dawn. "How brave you men are, who make your lives on the sea."

Bravery had nothing to do with it. "I met a holy man in Tanzania, a few years ago. His people believe that we were all creatures of the sea. That one day we left, searching for survival on land, but that was not so very long ago. His claim is that when the sea calls to us, it's not calling us away, it's calling us home. A home to which we can never return."

"I like that," she murmured. "The call home is the most powerful."

He couldn't disagree.

Reaching out, Lorelai pressed her hand to the window over where Tersea Island was a mere blotch in the distance. "Do you think you'll find the Claudius Cache before you are discovered?"

He lifted a shoulder in a halfhearted shrug. "Dorian's an earl. He has a great deal of influence, and I've always outsmarted, outrun, or overcome anyone who would try to contain or control me. With Moncrieff and my crew, and Dorian and his men, we should be able to find and plunder the treasure with little difficulty."

A shadow flickered over her delicate features, as though she fought to grab hold of her own memories. Turning to him, she asked, "This Moncrieff . . . do you trust him?"

"Trust is for fools," he clipped. "Not much to build a partnership on. But mutual self-interest, now that is something to rely upon. The greed of others, it's never let me down."

He yearned to smooth the wrinkle of worry from her

forehead as she blinked up at him. "Your assessment of others is rather grim."

"It's not grim, it's reality. It's how things are." He touched with his gaze everywhere his hands burned to go. "It's how *I* am." He was warning her. Cautioning her that he was close to the end of a tether. That he was trying to be good. He could not—*would* not—touch her. Or the tether might snap.

"People can change," she ventured.

The hope in her blueberry gaze threatened to be his undoing.

Not a subtle woman, his wife. "People don't change, Lorelai, only circumstances do."

"You have changed," she insisted. "Because circumstances forced change upon you. Doesn't that mean you could reclaim who you once were?"

"Do you really believe that?"

"Time is a great healer, or so I'm told." She smiled wryly. "I believe in you. Don't you believe in me?"

He didn't know how to answer her question. Couldn't bring himself to tell her that she shouldn't believe in him, and that he couldn't allow himself to have faith in, or even hope for, anything.

"I've been asked to believe in a lot of things," he began. "In a man's word. His promise. His God. In heaven and in hell." He retreated from the window a step, away from her alluring scent and siren's lips. "I don't know about heaven, but I know hell exists. I've spent most of my life there." He ignored her soft sound of distress. "But through all that. Through everything that's been done to me, I've only ever believed in one thing."

"What's that?" she whispered.

"That the sun would set in the west, and that I would come for you."

Her face melted into an expression so achingly lovely, he had to look away or be overcome.

She reached for him, and he backed away further, putting up a staying hand against her.

"Be mine." His voice sounded hoarse and rough, even to his own ears, but the need to hear her say the words drove him past the point of rationality. "Give yourself to me."

She regarded him as though he'd lost his mind. "I already did. Thrice, to be exact. I'm trying to do it again, but you won't hold still."

"Not your body, dammit." He was muddling this. Maybe if she wasn't standing so near. Or looking so desirable. Maybe if they were in a different room. One bereft of the only happy memories he'd been allowed in his merciless life. "Be my wife, Lorelai," he blurted. "That is . . . without any coercion. Or force. Or fear. Just . . . consent to be mine." Christ, it was the most ridiculous thing he'd ever said out loud. His skin felt hot and waxen at the same time. His breath was held in both desperation and despair.

"If I can call you Ash, then you can call me wife," she bargained with a triumphant smile.

"This isn't a negotiation," he barked.

Her eyebrows lifted. "Is it not?"

He stared down at her for a long time before he could summon a reply. He wanted to call his armor back. Could he not be made of steel and stone instead of this flesh-and-blood man who hungered for her so vehemently?

"Very well," he finally acquiesced. Did he ever have a choice? Could he deny her anything? "Now that I know who I am . . . I also know who I am not. I am not Dorian Blackwell. And I . . . no longer wish to be the monster created by a lifetime apart from you. Maybe, in time, I can be who you want me to be. You'll . . . you'll have to show me how."

She rushed to him, ignoring the hand he held against her. Flinging her small, warm body against his with a dangerously contagious exuberance. "We could finally start our life together, once you find your treasure."

He'd already found it.

Swept away by the tide of her emotion and his need, he crushed his lips against her offered mouth and secured her lush body to his.

Desire slammed into him with all the violence of a war hammer, lancing the breath from his chest. Years of forgotten needs roared to the surface, overwhelming his senses. Everything that made him lethal and ferocious snarled to claim her. To be tamed by her.

But he couldn't do that. Not to this soft creature in his arms. She was the antithesis to the endless battle of pain he'd only surmounted by the force of his will and the strength of his back. His Lorelai was lush and warm where he was unyielding and hard. Instead of seeking revenge, she survived by means of endurance. Despite her own difficult battles, she healed her little broken creatures with all the care she had left to give.

Her lips parted beneath his. Inviting. Pliant.

God, what he could do to her mouth.

With a raw moan of protest, he thrust her from him. "Not now," he gasped. "Not tonight."

Hurt shimmered over her features as she stood where he abandoned her. Lips swollen and slick. Eyes clouded with what he wanted to believe was desire.

"You . . . don't want me?"

"Christ, Lorelai," he growled, wiping the sweet taste of her from his lips. "You can't be that naïve!"

Her eyes went positively owlish, little reserves of tears gathering in her lashes. "Wha— I . . . You just said—"

He grasped her hand and shoved it between his legs where his cock strained against his trousers, desperate to be thrusting into any part of her. Her lips, her hands, her ass, her sex. He'd claim it all before their lives were through.

"Does this feel like a lack of fucking desire to you?" he gritted out.

Her eyes became as dark as the sea tossed about by Calypso's wrath. Color tinted her cheeks and lips, as blood rushed through her. "No," she breathed, her fingers twitching against him. "But . . . then . . . why?"

"I am not myself," he warned. "And you still need to recover from last night. You said it earlier."

To his utter astonishment, she grinned. "It's happening already," she marveled, sidling closer.

He squinted at her, trying to make out her meaning. His move, meant to shock her, had backfired somewhat, and he was having a devil of a time stringing thoughts together with her shy fingers now cupping his shaft through the fabric.

"Not so long ago, you claimed my discomfort wouldn't have mattered," she said with a sense of triumph.

He closed his eyes against the onslaught of guilt at the thought of terrifying her. He'd been such a barbarian with her only days ago . . . and that barbarian was now screaming to be let out.

"That's what I'm saying." He tossed her wrist away. "It *won't* in a matter of minutes. If I were you, I'd find a sturdy door, get behind it, and lock it. Now that I've had a taste of you, I want everything, selfish bastard that I am."

His nostrils flared. His chest couldn't seem to hold enough air as he watched her throat work over a swallow.

"You think I feel less need than you?" she challenged. "Less frenzy or wildness? That after last night, I want you any less than you want me?"

"I *know* you do." Nothing she could conceive of could match the hunger he now battled.

She stepped to him, sliding her hand down his front until it gently, but instantly, clutched his cock. "I can take it, Ash," she whispered in a low, needful octave he hadn't thought her sweet voice capable of attaining. "I can take you. *All* of you."

"Lorelai." His last warning was underscored with a plea. Who was this woman before him? This temptress?

This goddess.

"You don't know what hurting you would do to me," he rasped, held prisoner by her lithe little fingers.

Her other hand reached around his neck, tugging his head down to hers for a scorching kiss. A feral beauty licked her innocence away, leaving him utterly speechless. "Veronica told me of a way to pleasure you that would cause me no pain."

When she lowered to her knees, he lost his ability to move.

There was power in this, Lorelai realized. Veronica had neglected to mention that.

This beast in a black suit. This primal, ferocious male was hers to command. It was her hand that absorbed him. Her lips that would claim him.

He mouthed her name, but no sound escaped. His nostrils flared, but he remained motionless, his eyes swirling with unmitigated lust and something else that broke her heart.

The gasp that fled his throat as she freed him from his trousers was laced with pain.

She'd almost forgotten how intimidating his sex could seem, every bit as immense as the rest of him.

His body went splendidly rigid as she wrapped her hand around the thick base of him. Moisture suffused her mouth as she breathed over the length of him.

"Lorelai," he groaned. "You don't—"

The words were ripped from his throat by a harsh cry as her lips closed over the blunt tip in a vulgar parody of an openmouthed kiss.

She found she enjoyed the flavor of his flesh. Salt and musk and something so intoxicating she felt a bit light-headed.

Another desperate sound ripped through him. This one an overt plea.

Slowly, she slid her moist lips over the plush, velvet head of him and let her tongue ease down the ridge beneath until he met the back of her throat.

She felt his knees tremble, and was rocked by a wave of victorious feminine lust. She widened her jaw to its capacity and secured her lips over her teeth before dragging those lips as far as she could, leaving trails of moisture in her wicked wake.

Despite his desperate growls and incoherent curses, she refused to hurry. She rhythmically explored his shaft with her fingers as she sucked him deeper. Her tongue found the absorbing ridges of veins beneath the thin skin and swirled and darted about them.

His hand clamped behind her head. Strong, demanding fingers ruined her coiffure as they threaded through her hair and tightened to a fist.

Something slick and succulent welled from his sex, easing the glide of her lips.

Lorelai greedily enjoyed his broken breaths. The black inferno she found when she looked up into his eyes. He bared his teeth like a wolf, and his grip on her hair became more dominant than demanding.

Did he want to play with power? The thought both excited and frightened her.

She braced a hand against his hips, which had begun slight, instinctive thrusts in time to her own rhythm. So, she changed her pace, drawing back so completely, he popped out of the seal of her mouth with a lewd sound.

"It would behoove you to behave." She echoed his words from their wedding night against his sex, giving it a playful lick.

He let loose a string of blistering curses, not all of them in English as he, one by one, uncurled his fingers from her hair.

Satisfied, she latched onto him again, taking him as deep as she could, using her tongue to swirl around his engorged head as she let her hand resume its previous rhythm.

He said things. Lusty things. Demanding and degrading things. And they meant nothing, or everything. She couldn't tell. She didn't care. She'd become a glutton for this, for the illicitness of it. The transformative intimacy of it.

This was something she could give a man from whom everything had been taken.

He grew impossibly larger inside her mouth. Hotter. The vein at the underside of his sex began to pulse.

"Stop," he gasped. The involuntary jerks and twitches of his hips became more frantic. Desperate. "If you don't stop . . . I . . ."

She knew what he would do. He'd release the same substance he'd coated her womb with last night.

She was ready. She wanted it. Wanted him.

"No." This time, when he clutched at her hair, he arched

her neck back slightly, releasing his sex from her mouth once again.

"Wait," she panted. "It's all right. It's—"

"I'll tell you what it is," he said darkly, as he dragged her off her knees and toward the bed. "It is my turn."

The force of his raw passion unleashed upon her with the unrivaled strength of a sea gale, as he tossed her on the bed and yanked her skirts above her knees.

He growled his approval when he found her without undergarments.

Lorelai had no compunctions about borrowing a dress from the Countess Northwalk, but she drew the line at sharing intimates.

He spread her legs with rough hands, and she braced herself for the pleasure his fingers would surely impart.

"You're so fucking beautiful." His voice had become deeper, more savage. "I need to taste you."

"What?" He couldn't mean—

Without warning a strong, wet lick split her sex, strangling all protestations along with her breath. The pleasure elicited by the wicked deed rocked her so incredibly, her knees instinctively closed.

Ash's strong arms anchored her thighs apart, his mouth burrowing into her core, lips exploring the pliant ridges of flesh and the throbbing apex above.

Unlike his callused, clever fingers, his tongue was warm against her sensitive sex, smooth, and delectably wet. It slipped and slid among her increasingly slick topography, leaving trails of pulsating pleasure behind.

Now *this* was something Veronica had never prepared her for. This shocking, scandalous act. Something so selfless and sacrosanct, she wasn't certain God allowed for it.

Because nothing so heavenly should be allowed in the human experience.

She blinked down at the dark head playing between her thighs, her insides both quivering and aching. If the depths of physical pain and suffering could be so acute, so terrifyingly exquisite, shouldn't moments of pleasure be, as well?

Had they not both earned this?

He thrummed at the sensitive bud that was the center of her need. His tongue rolled, and his lips nipped at it, playfully teasing her with apparent delight before he gently ground against it with the flat of his tongue. A thrill of bliss shot through her with such force, her fingers sought and clutched at his hair, tugging insistently in no particular direction.

His sound of appreciation vibrated against her core, unleashing a tide of need from deep in her belly. She couldn't call back an insistent mewl, then a hoarse cry as her need bloomed beneath his expert mouth. Her toes curled in their boots as her soul began to sing. A rhythm so ancient and primal melding with the dance of his tongue until ecstasy pulsed from her womb, to her bones, and sang through her blood.

Her body strained against the strength of his hold, her limbs thrashed, and her hips bucked beneath him. Later she'd be mortified that she'd become this uninhibited creature of wanton, voluptuous lust. That she'd abandoned all sense of modesty or dignity in favor of craven desire and this all-consuming rapture. The pleasure melted her into a miasma of shuddering wet pulsations. She'd become weightless with it, a being both created and dismantled by its relentless, agonizing waves.

A few helpless sobs escaped her as the sensations flowing from his mouth to her core reached a peak so indescribable, she wasn't certain her body could contain it.

As though he sensed he'd overwhelmed her, he lifted

his head, allowing her hips to float back to the bed. She'd been unaware they'd ever thrust away from it.

He crawled up her body, licking his glossy lips like a satisfied cat, his eyes glittering like volcanic shards of dark intent.

Her muscles, replete and heavy, melted beneath him.

"Did you mean it?" he asked tightly. "Can you take all of me?"

Sighing, she wrapped her arms around his wide torso with more urgency than even she had expected, her heart contracting with a thousand different forms of love. "Every part of you."

He sank inside her, stretching her untried muscles in warm, luscious increments. Her still-pulsing core gave way reluctantly at first, but his second slide was faster, wetter, and he didn't stop until he was buried to the hilt.

"Yes," she hissed into his ear as he buried his face into her hair. "Please." It wasn't the insistent plea that caused him to set a deep, stroking rhythm that quickly catapulted them both to the stars. It was what she whispered next. What she'd cried before her intimate muscles clenched around him in yet another release.

"Ash."

CHAPTER TWENTY-ONE

"Lord and Lady Southbourne."

Ash didn't recognize the designation as belonging to him until Lorelai said, "What is it, Jenkins?"

He glanced up from where he, Lorelai, Moncrieff, and Blackwell were bent over the map, listening intently to her observations on how to safely approach Tersea Island.

"I've installed a Scotland Yard inspector in the parlor. He insists on speaking with you both." His repugnant message delivered, Jenkins clicked his heels like a Hessian, and marched away.

They'd been expecting a police inquiry of some sort, of course. Mortimer Weatherstoke, a peer of the realm, had been recently murdered rather publicly, after all. His wife and sister kidnapped by the infamous Rook, only to be returned some three days later none the worse for wear by an unknown cousin of dubious Continental origin.

Ash Weatherstoke.

Gods, after all the time he'd spent insisting the boy was dead, he had to resurrect him. Here. At Southbourne Grove. Yet again.

Because of his cowl, no one had seen the Rook up close when he'd murdered Mortimer, and very few other souls over the years had borne account of his visage and lived to tell about it.

Dorian Blackwell had accompanied them in part to assist with just such a situation. He had unprecedented influence with Scotland Yard, Parliament, in all the right social circles, and—more importantly—all the wrong ones. To have such a man call him brother was a boon in more ways than Ash could begin to define at this juncture.

"Scotland Yard?" An apprehensive frown tilted Lorelai's lips as she echoed his thoughts. "I assumed we'd only have to endure the local magistrate."

"We never should have left the ship," Moncrieff grumbled, already doctoring his tea with spirits from a nearby decanter. "Why would someone call all the way from Scotland Yard unless they already found the holes poked into our criminally thin fiction?"

"Is he always like this?" Blackwell nudged a thumb at the scowling first mate.

"No." Ash smirked. "He's usually much more opinionated."

"God help you."

"If only she would."

"She?" Blackwell queried.

"I've always been of the opinion that storms, ships, and God are a strictly female trifecta."

"It would explain a great deal—"

"Now hardly seems like the time for jest." Lorelai interrupted their smile of collusion, stepping in front of a red-faced Moncrieff, her own features pinched with anxious disapproval. "You could be in profound danger from the law."

Ash traced the line of her jaw, yearning to kiss those lips back into a smile. "Darling, men like us are perpetually in profound danger from the law . . . or so the law likes to imagine."

"Do you think they mean to threaten us with Newgate?" Dorian casually speculated, picking at an invisible piece of dust from his cuff.

"Perish the thought," Ash volleyed with equal dispassion. "Maybe it's the gallows for us this time."

"Or the firing squad."

"I suppose they could resurrect the practice of drawing and quartering." Ash cocked an unrepentant brow at Lorelai. "I should hazard that my nether quarters are the most desirable."

"Our heads would look altogether sinister next to each other on the vacant pikes at London Bridge," Blackwell suggested.

"You make an excellent point. Do you suppose they'd leave the eyepatch on?"

"It'll be my final request."

"As it should be. It's rather iconic, if you ask me."

With a startlingly animalian sound, Lorelai seized his lapels. "Do you not understand what this means?" She tugged at him frantically. "They could take you from here in chains! I could lose you again. Forever, this time. How can you act as if your execution would be nothing more than a lark?"

Sufficiently chastised by the threat of hysterics, Ash sobered immediately. "I jest because the idea of anyone taking me from your side is laughable." He covered her hands with his own, touched and feeling guilt because of the tremors of panic he sensed in her elegant fingers.

"An entire contingent of Scotland Yard bruisers couldn't overwhelm us," Dorian soothed from over his shoulder. "They'd have to bring an army."

"And we'd see the army coming and make our getaway," Ash amended, pressing a kiss to the wrinkles of worry on her forehead. "Come now, all is well. Let us rid ourselves of this nuisance and be about our day, shall we? We've treasure to hunt."

"Count me out," Moncrieff growled, swiping the entire decanter from the sideboard. "I'd rather lick bog mud from the devil's twat than share a room with a member of the London Metropolitan Police."

"Can't say as I blame you," Blackwell told his retreating back before turning to Ash. "I don't think he's over-fond of me."

"He loves none so much as himself." Ash stared after Moncrieff until he disappeared up the back stairs. "Though I suppose I should remind him of his place."

"Perhaps you should, instead, assure him that his *place* at your side isn't threatened," Lorelai suggested, casting a surreptitious glance at his new coconspirator.

"A wise woman, your wife," Blackwell approved.

Ash glanced down at her, enjoying the way her small hand felt in his as he tucked her against him and sojourned the long marble hall from the library to the front parlor.

A part of him had expected an army. Or the fall of an executioner's ax upon entering. Maybe even the devil come to call him home. Because today he'd awoken with an angel in his arms. Her soft curls draped over his torso in a waterfall of spun gold. Her breath warming him and her lashes fluttering against his chest as she slumbered.

For the first time in twenty years, he'd felt settled. No, more than that.

He'd felt as if he'd come home.

Even when her head had rolled to his shoulder, and eventually blocked the feeling in his arm, he found he'd rather chew off the limb than disturb her.

Instead, he navigated the downy curve of her cheek, and the slope of her patrician nose, the peachy fullness of her generous mouth.

Generous, in every possible sense of the word.

He'd found grace in that moment. True enjoyment.

Dare he say . . . happiness?

So, he'd approached the rest of the day with a sense of caution. Contentment led to complacency, and that was a condition of which to be wary.

Which was why he advanced on the parlor expecting the absolute worst.

Only one man awaited him, however, surrounded by arabesque wallpaper and anachronistic *objets d'art* acquired by generations of deceased Weatherstokes.

One lean, elegant male with golden hair and eyes the color of the Adriatic Sea. He wore his affability like armor. His handsomeness was approachable, his strength politely contained within a lean-cut jacket patently crafted to make him appear less threatening.

Ash's heartbeat erupted into hundreds, imprisoning both his boots to the ground. His chest filled with rocks and his mouth with sand, weighing him down with an almost bone-crushing sense of impending doom.

An abrupt and absurd image transposed upon the man . . . Nordic features smeared with grime. Sharp incisors bared in a snarl as sharper fists flew. Hidden blades. Lock picks. Patchwork clothing. He was a . . . cutter? Strange word . . . A dead eye.

Had they met before?

He flinched as the sound of shattering glass echoed in

his head. Shattering glass, and the crunch of bone. And . . . blood?

So much blood.

That infernal ax came back to pick at the nerves behind his own eye as he swung his gaze to look at Blackwell, who regarded the man with a friendly sort of recognition.

"Chief Inspector Morley." Blackwell strode forward and exchanged a familiar but wary handshake with the man. "May I introduce my longtime friends Their Graces, Ash and Lorelai Weatherstoke, Duke and Duchess of Castel Domenico. The Comte and Comtesse de Lyon et de Verdun. Though, on English soil, I suppose they're most lately the Earl and Countess of Southbourne." He swung his arm expansively at them. "Your Graces, this is Sir Carlton Morley, chief inspector of the London Metropolitan Police."

Ash fought the overwhelming urge to press his fingers to his throbbing temples, keenly aware of Lorelai's reassuring squeeze on his arm.

He almost missed the way the inspector's hand went loose in Blackwell's grip. Virtually as slack as his angular jaw as he stared at Ash as though he'd been cuffed in the mouth by a ghost.

"Dorian . . ."

"Are we finally on unofficial terms, Inspector Morley?" Blackwell smirked. "I'm not certain I'm comfortable sharing the intimacy of first names with you just yet."

Ash's brows drew together as he studied the pair. They'd an obvious past, one not unoccupied by enmity.

Without warning, the inspector's composure completely splintered, and he struck Blackwell in the nose with one lightning-fast jab, causing the Blackheart of Ben More to stumble back several steps. "All this time!" Morley bellowed. "All this time you lived as him. You let the world think he was dead!"

The pain in Ash's head intensified. His missing seventeen years pounded on the inside of his skull with a sledgehammer. The world beneath his feet became as unsteady as his ship when tossed about in a storm, and he fought the urge to grasp onto the high back of a chair to acquire stability.

"Gentlemen, please contain yourselves." Lorelai tucked tighter against him, and he miraculously drew strength from her nearness.

But why did he need it? What was happening?

Blackwell regained his equilibrium with impressive speed, lunging for the inspector with murder etched into his features and blood dripping from his nose.

Ash barely reached them in time, placing his body between the two men who'd apparently lost control of their faculties. "Someone kindly explain just what the fuck is going on here," he ordered.

"I'd like to know, as well!" Blackwell snarled. "I've never in my life confessed a death to you, Morley." He surged against the shoulder Ash employed to hold him back. "This lack-wit has been trying to see my neck stretched by a rope since the day he became a lowly constable."

"And why do you think that is?" The carefully composed London accent slipped a bit in the inspector's homicidal state, hinting at a dose of Cockney.

"Any number of reasons. I made you and your bobbies look like fools. I have noble blood and you couldn't be more ordinary. I pulled myself out of the gutter where you're convinced I belong. Or . . . perhaps because you loved Farah, my wife, to distraction, and the moment I kissed her she forgot you even existed." A dark triumph laced through Blackwell's cultured voice. "You never had a chance, Morley, she was always mine. The better man won. Admit it and begone!"

To everyone's utter astonishment, the inspector merely laughed, though the sound was laced with enough hostile bitterness to sour the air. "You sanctimonious, arrogant bastard. I'll grant that you took the most important person from me. You appropriated the last hope I had for family years ago . . . but Farah didn't have a goddamned thing to do with it."

"Horseshit!"

"Dorian Blackwell was *my* best mate!" Morley roared. "Furthermore, he was engaged to my twin sister."

Lorelai made the choked sound they all were too astounded to echo.

"I was there the day they released *Dorian Blackwell* from prison, did you know that?" the inspector boomed. "I stood at the gate, waiting to take my friend, my brother, *home*. I'm the one who buried his mother when influenza took her not a year after his incarceration. We'd never had the chance to properly grieve for Caroline, the woman who meant more to us both than life. And *you*!" He shoved a finger in Blackwell's face. "You sauntered out of Newgate like you owned the name, and you've been throwing it in my fucking path for the better part of two decades. *That*. That is why I've hated you all this time."

It was a good thing that Blackwell had ceased to struggle against Ash, because the pronouncement stunned the strength right out of him. He turned and gaped at the man whom he'd somehow known wasn't a stranger.

But a brother? Another one?

"You *knew* I wasn't Dorian Blackwell?" The Blackheart of Ben More gaped. "Why didn't you ever let on?"

Morley's features tightened with a mélange of wrath and agony. "Because I had secrets of my own. Ones that died with Dorian . . . Or I thought they did." He speared Ash with an accusatory glare, one underscored by ancient wounds. "Where in the ninth level of hell have you been for two bloody decades?" he demanded.

The ninth level of hell . . . about covered the whole of it.

"How cruel of you, after what we were to each other, almost brothers-in-law, that you would let me believe—God!" Morley plunged his fingers in his hair, interrupting the perfect sheen created by his pomade. "And to think that both of you black-hearted bastards were in on this poxy farce."

"He didn't remember." Lorelai rushed to Ash's aid, as though sensing he'd lost the ability to form coherent sentences. "There was a terrible incident in prison," she explained. "When my family found him, he'd no memory of his past."

"I don't believe that for a blessed moment."

Ash didn't like the way Morley stared at his wife. Hard. As though she invoked a memory he'd rather not suffer again.

"Why not?" Her eyes darted around nervously. "I can attest to it. I was there."

Whirling on Ash, the inspector's lips curled in a sneer of disgust. "You claim your memory is damaged?"

"It is," Ash managed.

"Then why did you select a wife who resembles my twin sister, Caroline, in almost every respect?"

All sense of time and place fell away into some auditory void as Ash's gaze collided with Lorelai's.

Blue. Blue like the Baltic Sea.

Like the inspector's.

Like . . . Caroline.

The wall in his mind began to crumble, along with his sanity and the strength in his knees.

On Lorelai's beloved face, a gaunt ghost began to superimpose herself.

Young. Pale. Gold . . .

Gold hair glinting in the gas lamps. Sometimes short, other times waist length.

Caroline . . . she'd sold it. For him. To pay his bail when he'd been nabbed for stealing a loaf of bread and cash from a local baker.

"You shouldn't've done that, Caro." His own young voice filtered through the past. "I deserve to rot for a dirty thief."

She'd pushed him into a grimy alley behind crates full of skinny Spitalfields chickens. Her fingers had been cold on his chest. "You owe me now," she'd whispered.

"Any'fing," he'd vowed, fighting for breath against a young lad's lust. "I'll give you whatever you ask."

"A kiss." It hadn't been a request, but a command.

The kiss had been his first, but not hers. Not Caroline. She'd been kissed too early and too often. They'd been sixteen in that alley, and she'd been charging money for her favors for two years.

Cutter hadn't liked that. There had been a new frenzy to their theft after she'd taken to the streets. A sense of urgency. If they could make enough to pay for a regimental commission, their lives could drastically improve. They could send their wages home.

Cutter. Cutter "Dead Eye" Morley. Caroline's twin brother. The stickiest fingers in Spitalfields. Maybe in all of London. He could throw a pebble in a pail at fifty paces and break a window with his slingshot from down the row. He'd been light and fleet-footed, scaling buildings and scanning the city from rooftops while Ash—then called Dorian—had been the brute on the ground. Lifting, beating, or breaking what he had to.

"You could marry Caroline," Cutter's young self suggested earnestly as he balanced on a dock rail while they'd dawdled through the markets smelling worse than the wares of dead fish. "Then we'd be brothers. If you died, she'd get a widow's pension."

"Could do," Ash had agreed. He could marry the pretty Caroline. He could save her from the streets. If he excelled, she'd be an officer's wife. "Could do," he'd repeated, liking this idea more and more. "But if I was supporting your sister, who'd get *your* pension if you were killed?"

"Easy." Cutter's slim shoulders shrugged as he slid his friend a sly look. "Your mother. She's still got her charms, hasn't she? Think she'd marry me?"

"Buggar off!" Ash had snagged at Cutter and he'd jumped away, laughing.

"Don't be sore at me. I won't make you call me Papa."

They'd chased through the markets, upsetting both crates and fishmongers in their mad dash. Ash had been fast, but no one could catch Cutter. If he had, he'd have done the boy no true damage. They'd have grappled and brawled, as brothers are wont to do, before one of them cried peace.

Theirs had been a merry threesome. Cutter, Caroline, and Dorian. He couldn't remember all their years together. He couldn't recall their meager meals or their magical moments. But an innocent, boyish love speared his chest with a point so exquisitely sharp, it robbed him of breath.

They'd been family.

Until there had been blood.

Blood and water. Always blood and water.

And gold.

Gold hair waving like reeds in the soot and soil of the Thames.

Caroline.

With a raw sound, Ash's knees gave out. He pressed

both his palms to his temples as he groaned her name with the same anguish he'd felt the morning they'd lost her.

Word spread that a body had been pulled out of the river by Hangman's Dock, so he and Cutter had drifted to that part of Wapping to catch the spectacle and maybe pick a few pockets.

Once they'd lazily made their way to the front of the crowd, he'd amassed nearly two shillings' worth.

Then Cutter had screamed. A pitch of agony which he couldn't believe he'd ever forgotten. A sound like that left scars on one's soul.

Caroline. Saucy, seductive, resourceful Caroline. Her wit and smile had both been quick as her brother's feet.

Quick enough to draw the attention of a killer.

Cutter had gone mad. He'd knocked out two bobbies and had to be restrained by seven more to keep away from his beloved sister's body.

A part of him had died that day.

As inconsolable as Cutter was, that was Ash's first taste of cold, calculating fury. He didn't want to grieve. He didn't want to talk to the coppers. He wasn't interested in justice.

He wanted vengeance. Blood for blood.

He'd dragged the disconsolate Cutter around the city, asking the right questions, sussing out the exact customer who'd enticed her home that night.

They'd found him at the docks not two days later.

And Ash had held the fucker down while Cutter . . . well, he did the cutting.

It had been a first kill. For both of them. And the screams had drawn the constable from his watch. To protect Cutter, Ash had broken a window and nabbed something valuable in plain view of the police. He'd taken off, leading the patrolman away from the site of their revenge.

He'd even allowed himself to be caught.

For Cutter.

For Caroline.

They'd thrown him in Newgate for a handful of years. He hadn't cared. Justice had been served with a blade in the dark. As it would ever be for the subsequent two decades.

"Caroline," he groaned, wiping at his face, startled that his hand came away wet, though whether from sweat or tears he couldn't tell.

His first love. His first blood.

The memories began to flood him like a dam breaking. The cold overwhelming his veins as year after year returned in fragmented images and broken emotions. Faces. Names. Scents. Sounds.

With a raw breath, he reached out for his anchor. For the one soul he needed to ground him back to this time. To this place.

Lorelai.

He reached, almost to the point of flailing, and it was Cutter . . . Carlton? Who took his hand and hauled him to his feet before he and Blackwell settled him into a chair.

Because Lorelai had disappeared.

Lorelai blindly stumbled out to the back garden, gulping in breaths of sea air that were exhaled as broken sobs.

She'd never forget the way Ash had said another woman's name. His eyes had been glossy, his voice reverent. His ever-placid, forbidding features had crumpled with a sentimentality she'd never before witnessed. She'd thought, until now, Ash was incapable of experiencing the depths of such emotion. It was all right, she'd reasoned. She could love enough for the two of them.

What a fool she'd been. Because it wasn't that he *couldn't* feel. It was that he didn't feel those things for *her*.

He felt them for Caroline.

If the girl had been half as handsome a woman as Inspector Morley was a man, Lorelai could certainly understand Ash's love for her.

Catching her reflection in a window renewed the torrent of Lorelai's tears. What had she to offer a man like him now that her youth had faded, and her hope had waned? Was she only the stonewashed specter of his first love? Had his eyes caught the sight of a familiar girl some twenty years ago, and evoked the forgotten passions he'd cultivated for another?

Did he seek to return for her, to claim her, so intensely because he thought he'd regained some semblance of a love long dead?

The tragedy of it was a thousandfold, for them both.

"Do not weep, lovely," a deep voice soothed from the shadows. "It will all be over soon."

She was drawn against a hard, muscled body from behind. A sweet scent cloyed through her senses, and then the earth became sand beneath her feet as she gratefully sank into the beckoning darkness.

CHAPTER TWENTY-TWO

Two brothers. Ash stared at the men who'd once been the boys upon whom he relied. Two brothers not of his lineage. What a tangled connection they all made.

He'd remembered nearly everything, and what little he could not, Morley and Blackwell had spent the better part of a morning piecing together for him.

It was exhausting, to say the least, reliving two entire decades in one day.

How incredibly strange that Cutter Morley, the boldest thief in the empire, had, because of the death of his sister, become one of the most powerful men in London. The chief inspector at Scotland Yard.

Ash still couldn't fathom it.

"Why the name Carlton?" he queried, making a face. "I wouldn't have pegged you for such a toff moniker."

Morley shrugged, adopting a rather sheepish smile. "I knew I had to reinvent myself, but as a grief-stricken lad, I hadn't exactly thought it through. When I showed up looking to enlist in a regiment, I knew that if I were to attain anything in life, I couldn't be Cutter anymore. When they asked me my name, I panicked, and read Carlton off an advertisement for the Carlton football club."

"Did you ever see war?" Ash tried to picture the lanky lad he'd known in regimental reds.

"I did," he answered. "I served in Egypt and Afghanistan. I never lost the designation Dead Eye" He mimed looking down the barrel of a rifle. "I've more confirmed kills than any rifleman in the Queen's Army."

Blackwell never seemed to cease shaking his head, staring at Morley with one wide, disbelieving eye. "I still can't seem to think past the part where you were a thief."

Ash surveyed the reclining assemblage in the parlor. Perhaps three of the most intimidating, powerful, and somber men in the empire, natural enemies in every way, drinking identical snifters of Scotch whisky as they laughed and reminisced about the skills acquired by means of their misspent youths.

"I—suppose this means we have to make peace." Blackwell extended his hand to Morley, who regarded it like one might a proffered soiled linen. "Oh, come now, Morley. We've made a tenuous connection over the years, haven't we? Dare I say, an armistice of sorts? You have poached my favorite assassin for your own employee."

"I've always maintained criminals make the best coppers." Morley clapped his hand into Blackwell's and shook it, firmly. "I suppose since we share a past with this one, we'll be sharing a future, as well." He shoved a thumb toward Ash. "Though befriending the notorious Rook would most certainly cost me my job." The chief inspector glanced toward the door through which Lorelai had disappeared. "There is the trivial matter of the late earl . . ." A new anger narrowed his eyes to slits of wrath. "Though, after hearing your tale, I can't say I'm sorry he's dead."

It had taken some time, but after Morley and Blackwell had untangled Ash's memories of his first two decades, he had then filled them in on the subsequent twenty years. Waking up in the grave, being healed by Lorelai, then shanghaied by Mortimer, becoming the Rook. The Claudius Cache. All of it.

Blackwell's eyes brightened, as though struck by an ingenious idea. "I don't suppose you can claim your wife's brother was killed by the Rook and, in turn, you hunted the pirate down and took your revenge . . ."

A twinge of displeasure twisted inside of him. "You mean . . . Ash Weatherstoke should kill the Rook?"

Morley gave a rather Gallic shrug. "You'd be a national hero. People would be less likely to consider your past, or investigate the origins of your dukedom."

Ash considered the idea for the space of a drink.

The parlor door burst open, and Veronica rushed in brandishing a hastily scrawled letter.

The pallor of her skin and the panic with which she flung herself at them drove Ash to his feet.

"She's gone!" the former countess cried as she shoved the paper into his hands.

"Lorelai?" Ash seized Veronica, shaking her slightly. "What do you mean, she's gone?"

He'd known Lorelai had been upset by the revelation of Caroline, and his first inclination had been to go to her. However, Blackwell had reasoned it was best for him to unravel his emotions about the past for himself before attempting to present the future to his wife.

It had seemed like wise advice at the time.

"Did she leave?" he demanded as the fraught woman blanched at the sight of his provocation. "Was she angry? Where would she go?"

"This is your fault!" Veronica spat, a righteous verdant

fire blazing in her wide eyes. "You never should have brought *him* into our home!"

Him? A pit of dread opened beneath Ash's stomach as he glanced down at the letter. He had to force his hands not to shake as he scanned the familiar writing. His rage threatened to blind him, but he forced himself to devour every word.

To count every syllable.

For that was the number of times he'd drive his blade into Moncrieff's body until the blighter hadn't a drop of blood left.

"What is it?" Blackwell prompted.

"My first mate is displeased with my taking a bride," he said in a dispassionate voice that belied the rage stoking inside him. "He's sent me an ultimatum of sorts. He's taken a large contingent of my crew and gone after the Claudius Cache. Conversely, he's appropriated Lorelai and placed her on a flesh-smuggling ship full of foreigners bound for Marseilles, from which the cargo will be distributed to places unknown." At the thought of Lorelai, this very moment, sailing farther and farther away from him, the note crumpled in his fist. She was delicate, fragile. He knew the conditions people were forced to endure on just such a shop.

If one of Lorelai's eyelashes were out of place, he'd carve every inch of skin from Moncrieff's body. "He's left me with a choice. I can join him and my crew and plunder the Claudius Cache as was our original plan, or we can chase Lorelai to Marseilles and save her."

"What's it going to be, brother?" Blackwell asked. "Your treasure, your crew, and your kingdom . . . or your wife?"

It took every one of the years he'd spent ruthlessly obtaining a powerful iron will to clutch a sense of calm around his shoulders like a mantle.

If he lost his mind, Lorelai could lose her life.

"The treasure doesn't matter to me," he gritted through his teeth as he glared down into Veronica's colorless features. "The men don't matter to me. Every bolt and fixture on that fucking ship would have been meaningless to me if I didn't need them to reach her."

Veronica's eyes widened as she finally grasped the veracity in his words.

"She. Matters," he gritted out. "She is all that has ever mattered. And I'll kill every man on my crew, I'll circle the globe, hell, I'd set the fucking ocean on *fire* to get her back."

Morley strode to the door, turning to lock gazes with Ash for a protracted moment.

He saw Caroline in those sky-blue eyes.

But all he wanted was Lorelai.

He'd loved Caroline, but he'd loved her for Cutter. Because she was an extension of his very best friend.

She'd always be a tragedy to him, a hole in his young heart. But that heart belonged to Lorelai.

Somehow, Morley read all of this in his gaze. "Come on, then." He wrenched the door open. "What are we waiting for?"

To navigate uneven terrain was difficult for Lorelai with her blasted ankle. She'd never thought to discover how impossible it could be with her hands bound. Every time she looked down the cliff, her stomach took a dive, as her balance threatened to tumble her at any moment into the late-afternoon tide.

By some miracle, her captor seemed able to support

both her weight and his own without slowing down the handful of men who followed them toward a cave set below a treacherous rock face. Her skirts molded themselves to her legs in the tempestuous wind, further impeding her progress.

"Think about what you are doing! What if you don't live to regret this?" she forced through a throat drawn tight by a strong gust. She knew the threat was cliché, but her life had ill prepared her for not just one, but two separate instances of pirate captivity.

Sebastian Moncrieff glanced back from where he pulled her along by a rope secured to the silk bonds at her wrists. The island wind tossed strands of his thick hair from its queue, and he secured it behind his ears.

"I regret this more with every moment I'm forced to listen to you, my lady," he said in an indulgent tone that belied the cruelty of his words. "Take care not to tempt me to gag you, as well."

He helped her over a particularly jagged outcropping of rock across the Tersea Island terrain before consulting a map he'd copied from Ash's original.

Lorelai still couldn't process her astonishment at the sheer boldness of his actions. "Are you not terrified of what the Rook will *do* to you once he comes for me?"

"That's the beauty of all this, you see." His winsome smile might have blinded most women, but Lorelai had long since decided his pulchritude was superfluous. "If the captain 'comes for you,' as you say, he'll end up in Marseilles. I've left him a letter informing him that I've sent you there, and are a damsel in need of rescuing."

"What compels you to have done such a terrible thing?"

"Because if he chases you to Marseilles, that gives me and the lads, here, enough time to plunder the Claudius Cache, and get away."

"Did you allude to the fact that you'd be on the ship with me to Marseilles?" she asked.

"Of course not."

"Then where are you supposed to be?"

His smile widened from mildly amused to wicked delight. "Why, here, of course, plundering the Claudius Cache."

Lorelai gaped. "You can't be that senseless, to let him know where to look for you."

"I can be that ingenious," he corrected. "And, if you think about it, I've done you a great favor."

"And how, pray tell, could you ever claim for that to be the case?"

"Because I gave him a choice." His smile became a sneer, twisting his handsome lips into something sinister. "If he goes after you, you'll know that he was weak enough to give you his heart. If he comes to the caves, as I invited him to do, he'll have proven that he's a pirate at heart and that you mean less to him than his crew and this treasure."

The implications of either choice lanced Lorelai through with fear. What if Ash went to Marseilles and left her to the mercy of this heathen? And yet, what if he found her in the caves?

It seemed, whichever scenario was more likely, she'd be the one to suffer.

"He trusted you," she accused. "It makes no sense that you would so violently and irreparably shatter this legacy you'd built together. This is, for all intents and purposes, a mutiny. Don't most mutinies end in death?"

"They do, indeed." Moncrieff's generally mild features darkened with livid shadows. "The moment your husband decided that love was worth more than treasure, he no longer deserved to call himself a pirate captain. He'd be the first to admit that. It's not like a commission of admiralty in the Queen's Navy. A man becomes captain of a ship like ours out of sheer ruthless force and unwavering capability. If that is no longer the case . . . then a crew will do what it must."

A chorus of hearty agreement met his proclamation, driving Lorelai into silence. Moncrieff had assured her when she'd woken on the longboat halfway to Tersea Island that she'd remain unharmed if she made no trouble.

But the closer they came to the caves, the more palpable the dangerous anticipatory aggression seemed to leach from the men at her back, buffeting her with as much tangible force as the wind.

Even Moncrieff couldn't save her if they decided she wasn't worth the trouble and pitched her over the cliffs.

Or worse.

"There it is, the mouth of the dragon." Moncrieff pointed to the jagged opening only accessible at low tide.

Lorelai decided it was a bit fanciful to have interpreted a dragon into the blunt stones, but she wisely kept her thoughts to herself. At this point, even the wet sand she was forced to stumble through was uncomfortable, and by the time they'd found some even stone within the caves to tread upon, her sore ankle had become less than useless. She'd resorted to dragging it behind her more often than walking upon it.

Moncrieff gave some terse commands for a few of the men to stand watch at the cave's mouth over some crates of excavation tools. The remaining contingent lit lanterns and followed them inside.

Moncrieff's excitement only seemed to intensify as he hauled Lorelai into a cave almost as wide as Buckingham Palace and maybe half as tall.

Despite her discomfort, Lorelai marveled at the immediate change in the wide cavern as opposed to the outside.

Where the island was dank, mossy, and inhospitable, the cave walls sparkled like onyx diamonds shot through with a foreign coral lace colored a vaguely pink hue.

Had she not been terrified, she'd have been awestruck.

However, excitement quickly turned to a frantic disappointment as the mutineers found their treasure cave stark and utterly empty.

"Where is it?" one demanded, running his hands over the gritty walls. "Could it be something that needs mined? A vein of gold or gems, perhaps?"

"You're telling me you've been after a treasure all this time, and you never even knew what it consisted of?" Lorelai marveled.

Moncrieff shoved his hand over her mouth. "Looks like we'll have to do a little digging, lads. The cache might have been lost beneath the sand over a thousand years of tides."

Grumbles of disappointment were laced with hope as several of the men trudged back toward the cave opening to retrieve their tools.

"If the Rook's been lying about the cache all this time," Moncrieff muttered, "I'll be angry enough to kill you, myself, and leave your corpse for him to find."

Lorelai swallowed around a dry tongue. "I didn't ask for any of this," she contended. "There's no need for such aggression."

Moncrieff began to conduct his own examination of the cave. He ran his hand from one side of the walls to the next, holding the lanterns up to the fantastically shimmering wall. A large hole in the ceiling of the cave provided one steady stream of daylight that didn't reach the dark walls.

"I'm not generally an aggressive person," he said conversationally. "I don't often have to be. I merely make the suggestion of violence, and find that's sufficient to get what I want."

"Lord, must you be so arrogant?" Lorelai wrenched the rope out of his hands. Or, rather, he allowed her to.

It wasn't as though she could make any attempt at escape.

"Arrogant is a bit severe, don't you think?" he asked. "I imagine I'm merely confident."

Her decidedly unladylike snort echoed off the stones. "Confidence is quiet. And you, sir, are not."

"I'll grant you that." He dug at the soft cavern floor with his boot and came away with packed sand. Picking up a black rock he'd unearthed, he hurled it at the wall.

A great chunk of it crumbled away and dissolved when it hit the wet sand.

"What's this?" Moncrieff retrieved the rock again and chipped away some of the black substance, which he caught in his palm. He sniffed it, and stuck his tongue out and touched it.

Then spat it out.

"Christ." He wiped his lips with the back of his hand. "It's salt. Pure black salt." Frowning, he gave the entire cavern a second look. "Why would both Emperor Claudius and the Danish king leave treasure in such a place? Surely, they understood the corrosive properties of salt, even back then."

"What if there is no treasure?" Lorelai speculated. "You'll have risked all this for nothing."

"So many men risk so little." He advanced on her, his eyes becoming iridescent in the lanternlight. "I risk it *all* to get what I want."

"And what do you want?" she challenged.

"My desires are simple." He brought his face close to hers. "I only want everything."

A ruckus from outside pierced the darkness of the grotto. Gunshots. Then metallic sounds. Or, rather, the echoes and thuds of metallic objects hitting other softer, fleshier substances created a symphony of gruesome ricochets in the cavern. The grunts and calls of combat, along with wetter sounds. Final cries.

Ash! He'd come for her! No . . . no, he'd come for the treasure.

She just happened to be here.

Moncrieff seized her abruptly, hauling her against him. "It seems our captain has picked logic over love, after all," he said against her ear.

"Then why is there violence?" Her voice shook with equal parts hope and devastation as she listened to the sounds of chaos.

"We are pirates, darling. There is always violence." She wouldn't call the emotion in Moncrieff's voice distress, but neither would she call it calm. He produced a pistol from his belt and trained it on the cave entrance. "I suppose one cannot love the teeth out of a shark."

Nor the avarice out of a pirate.

A body flew through the portal, and Moncrieff pulled the trigger.

Lorelai's ears rang so loudly, she barely heard her own scream. A scream that died when she realized that Moncrieff had inadvertently killed one of his own mutineers. Or perhaps the poor pirate had already been dead. That was a lot of blood on his shirt, more than one bullet could produce.

Another man screeched as he was propelled through the opening, and thrust directly at them.

Moncrieff shot him, as well.

A simultaneous bullet of unknown origin hit the lantern,

which shattered. Flames flared, devoured the fuel, and then sputtered out.

Leaving the only light in the cave from the fissure above.

"Your aim is improving all the time, Captain," Moncrieff taunted as he levered them farther into the shadows, to avoid the spotlight of sun.

"Do you really want those to be your last words, Moncrieff?"

Lorelai's blood quickened at the unholy resonance of Ash's voice slithering through the darkness of the cavern. It surrounded her, enveloping her in hope.

Two twin shadows appeared at the mouth of the cave, and dove in opposite directions as Moncrieff's pistol flashed with another deafening shot.

"Be careful to let your bullets fly at me, I've a pretty shield." Moncrieff lifted her more tightly against his vital organs. "Though I suppose she means less to you than I'd expected, seeing as you came for the treasure and left her to the flesh peddlers."

Lorelai wanted to be more courageous, hated the tiny sound she made as his arm slid from her chest to her throat. She didn't want Ash to remember her last sound being a whimper.

"Let her go, Moncrieff." Blackwell's sinister command echoed from somewhere behind them.

"Give her to me," Ash echoed Blackwell, while adding the caveat, "and I'll let you have whatever else you find in this cave."

"The cave is empty, you capricious bastard." Moncrieff pulled the hammer back with an ominous click. "There's no Claudius Cache here, as you can see. No Roman treasure worth a soldier's weight in wealth."

Lorelai gasped as Moncrieff's words triggered a memory from one of the many books she'd read in the South-bourne library.

Worth a soldier's weight in wealth . . .

Worth a man's weight in . . .

"Salt," she whispered. "It's the *salt*."

A stunned silence met her declaration.

"Don't you see?" She squirmed to get more purchase as she struggled to reveal her findings. "The Romans. They often paid their solders in salt, which is the origin of the word *salary*. Even now, we tell a man he's worth his salt or that he's earning his salt, don't we? Even the Latin word *sal* became the French word *solde*, which means 'pay,' and is the origin of the word *soldier*."

"Your wife's a bloody genius," Dorian marveled.

Moncrieff's chest began to heave behind her. "Salt?" he hissed through a disbelieving breath.

"To the Romans, this cave would have been more valuable than if the walls had been made of pure gold," she revealed. "And it makes sense why, back then, even seafarers with cargo ships could not have taken the trea-sure back with them. They hadn't the wherewithal to mine the mineral from this cave. And Emperor Claudius died before he was able to return for it."

"Fucking . . . *salt*?" Her captor, it seemed, was having a difficult time moving past one point, and she could tell how it affected him by how close his thick arm inched toward her throat.

"It could still be a rather lucrative find," she said, lift-ing an ineffectual hand to pull at the muscle pressing on her windpipe. "Salt isn't worth its weight in gold, granted, but it's still worth a fortune."

"If a pirate is going to mine a mineral, it will be weighed in karats," he said with a sneer. "And it won't have the pro-pensity to dissolve in water."

Lorelai couldn't form an answer through the pressure of his arm on her throat. She clawed at it, still sucking gasps of air.

"Give her to me," Ash demanded, a crack in his voice belying the chill in his tone.

"Did you know about this the entire time?" Moncrieff said, ignoring the order. "Tell me, after all we've been through, were you lying to us about the dragon tattoo just to get to her?"

"I never lied about the Claudius Cache. I thought, as you did, that trunks of gold and gems were contained here." Ash's voice fractured against the ceiling, making it impossible to tell from which direction he spoke. "But *she* is the only treasure I came to find."

A tendril of pleasure thrilled through her at his words. At least she might die knowing he'd cared for her.

"Then why are you not in Marseilles?" Moncrieff snarled.

"Because I saw your boat leave the estuary from the widow's walk, and spied Lorelai upon it." Veronica's lovely lilt sounded from where she took refuge from behind the stone wall of the cave mouth. "I told Lord Southbourne immediately."

At the sound of her voice, Moncrieff's hold on Lorelai's neck slackened. Conversely, his entire body constricted and—she squirmed to find—hardened.

Was the villain keen on Veronica?

"You followed me here, Countess? Bravely done." The deeper, huskier inflection betrayed his desire.

"I assumed, at first, you were helping Lorelai escape, as you did for us on the ship," Veronica said. "I thought that perhaps you had altruistic purposes, but I see now you're nothing but a mercenary cad."

"Sorry to disappoint, Countess." And, for a moment, it truly sounded as though he were in earnest.

"If you let her go, I'll let you leave with your life," Ash bargained once more.

"We both know you better than that. Only one of us leaves this cave alive." Moncrieff stepped into the light. "But if it's you, Captain, you leave this cave alone, just as you deserve." The pistol kissed her temple, and Lorelai squeezed her eyes shut, preparing for the end.

"That's where you're wrong, Moncrieff." Ash stepped into the beam, looking like the very devil he claimed to be swathed in an angelic pillar of light. He appeared as he had that first day in the coach. Cold, ruthless, his sinister aspect unadorned by sentiment as though calculating his next kill. "I've remembered something infinitely important in the past few hours . . ."

"That you are a poxy pretender with a weakness for delicate strumpets?"

"No . . . I learned I had brothers. I've never truly been alone. And that is its own kind of strength."

The sound of a rifle being cocked paralyzed the entire cavern, and Ash glanced up toward the breach in the cave ceiling.

Moncrieff followed suit, and cursed as the pistol left her temple to angle upward.

A shot exploded into the cave at the exact time Lorelai was wrenched from Moncrieff's grip and swept across the entire cavern, only to end up crushed against a smooth salt cave wall by more than two hundred pounds of panicking pirate king.

With a detached sort of wonder, she watched as Chief Inspector Morley, who'd stood above in a strategic placement so as not to cast his shadow upon them, stowed his rife, slid through the opening, and lowered himself until he only held on to the ledge by his fingertips. He then dropped to the soft sand floor below with the sleek grace of a cat.

How he didn't break something, she'd never know.

Dorian and Morley now stood over a felled Moncrieff, who groaned as he applied pressure to his shoulder, all but blown apart by a high-powered rifle.

"You missed," Dorian accused, retrieving the pistol Moncrieff had dropped upon being shot.

"No I didn't," Morley argued.

"You were supposed to shoot him in the head." The Blackheart of Ben More levered the pistol right between the former first mate's eyes.

Morley pressed Blackwell's arm down. "Well, Lady Veronica made an excellent point earlier on the boat across to the island," he said. "Moncrieff *is* technically an earl, and would be an excellent boon for Scotland Yard to have found, and arrested, as a pirate under the notorious Rook."

"Only to have him hanged later?" Dorian protested. "Why not shoot him now and be done with it? Then we don't have to listen to all the horrible sounds he makes what with that hole in his . . ."

"His shoulder?" Morley supplied.

"Well, I was going to say, his face."

"Gentlemen." Veronica drifted forward looking, only as *she* could, as fresh and unflappable as any noble lady in her receiving rooms, even after having hiked to an unmarked dragon cave. "Perhaps we should find somewhere to secure this brigand?" She locked eyes with Lorelai. "I do believe these two could use a moment to themselves."

Morley and Blackwell glanced over to where Ash still held Lorelai a hostage of his prodigious, trembling body.

His face was buried in her windblown hair where he seemed to pull in great, desperate lungsful of breath. His hands clutched at her with bruising strength. She almost worried that she was in more danger of suffocation now than she ever had been with Moncrieff.

Blackwell didn't seem alarmed in the least as he regarded them, and Lorelai wondered if he might be thinking his reaction would be the same were Lady Farah in a comparable situation.

Morley took a step in their direction. "Are you . . . all right?"

Lorelai couldn't be certain if he addressed her, or Ash, but she nodded over her husband's powerful shoulder and waved them away before she began to run soothing fingers over the hairs at his nape. It seemed to help leach some of the agitation from his body, so she fused her arms around his trunk.

It took some doing to haul Moncrieff away, but once he and the bodies had been cleared from the cavern, Lorelai turned her head to press a fond kiss against her husband's temple.

His hot breath against her cheek forewarned her the moment before he turned her soft kiss into something hard and ferocious. He drank from her lips like a stranded man who'd been welcomed into an oasis.

Lorelai felt the unprecedented tension in him. The emotions he had not learned to identify tightening the sinew around his bones until they might just snap.

He needed her. To feel her. To taste her. To be inside of her.

She needed it, as well.

His primal, wordless frenzy touched her in a way she'd never before thought possible. He was a wounded beast, she realized, running her fingers along his jaw and neck, the flesh interrupted by long-ago scars. One in need of her healing touch.

She eased the jacket from the mountains of his powerful shoulders and tugged his shirt from his trousers so she could plunge her hands beneath to find the rest of his unparalleled strength.

His body jerked when her palms made contact with his flesh. His breath caught audibly in his throat, though he never took his lips from hers.

She slid his buttons open with deft fingers, wrenching his shirt over the impressive swells of his arms.

He was a monster. Her monster. A magnificent creature crafted of sinew and scars. Of darkness and shadow.

And lust and yearning.

And loyalty and light.

All the elements that made a man, and then a few most men sorely lacked.

All mine, she thought with a ferocity she'd never attributed to herself, while she explored the inconceivable expanse of his chest, stopping to press her palm to the rough web of wounds forever marring his perfect skin.

She was sorry for all he had suffered. She'd take it from him if she could.

And yet, a swell of something hot and wet clenched deep between her legs. There was nothing her Ash could not overcome. Nothing he'd not endured. He had a resilience and a strength only belonging to men of myth and ancient gods.

He was her own, personal legend.

She clung to him as a wave of lust threatened to buckle her legs.

As if he read her mind, he cupped her bottom with his big hands, and hauled her off her feet, splitting her legs around his lean waist as he bunched her skirts to her hips.

He bit out a harsh noise as she brushed the curious ridge of arousal beneath his trousers before releasing him.

Lorelai didn't feel like herself. Never would she have thought she could enjoy a violent lust such as this. She reveled in the caustic grit of the wall behind her. And in the predatory, almost evil gleam in eyes that had never before seemed so very black.

The strain in his muscles as he held her aloft did more to stoke her desire than any poetry ever could. She released a rush of wet need on a tortured moan, and a tempestuous sound from him told her that he knew exactly what he'd elicited within her.

Lorelai let out an unbidden cry as he impaled her in one sleek thrust, setting her blood on absolute fire. He gave her only a moment to adjust, to dimly wish she were naked against all of his marvelous skin.

Instead she wrapped herself around him as his cock glided through her intimate flesh in slow, strong strokes. Her hands clutched at the wings on his shoulder blades as he fucked her into oblivion. She opened her body, welcoming him deep. She kissed and licked and bit at him as her sex gripped tighter with each of his withdrawals.

He rocked inside of her, stinging her with hard curls of his spine. No word was spoken, no apologies made. Her body hungrily accepted what he pounded into her. All his rage, his pain, his fear and his loss and his longing.

She felt the weight of everything, and wondered how it had not crushed him into the dirt by now.

Her body responded in kind, until she used the wall as leverage to thrust her hips back toward him. To meet him thrust for thrust. Her moans became demands, and then incoherent words.

Their eyes locked. Then their lips. And finally their bodies, every intimate part of them clenched together, pouring secrets and the past through the spaces contained between their molecules.

Pleasure sang behind the inferno that had become her blood, immolating her ability to draw breath. She felt the pulses of their sex synchronize, reveled in the warm jets of release he buried deep against her womb as they rode a simultaneous release so incredibly high, the cave echoed with the song of ecstasy that promised to fuse their very souls.

For the soft moments after, or maybe an eternity, they rested their foreheads against one another, struggling to regain enough breath to say the words that needed to be said.

He used his shirt to clean them, then discarded it to the sand, still unwilling—or unable—to release her from the prison of his arms.

Lorelai collapsed against him, leached of all strength. A willing captive, yet again. "Are you all right, my love?" She smoothed her hands down his heaving back, nuzzling into the muscular cove where his neck met his shoulder.

His gasp landed somewhere between wrath, disbelief, and laughter. "Am *I* all right? Lorelai . . . Jesus seafaring Christ. *You* were just abducted by a mutinying band of pirates, nearly shot, and then ravaged in a way more bestial than human."

"I'm no worse for wear, thanks to you," she said against his fragrant skin. "See for yourself."

He pulled back only enough to look down at her. More like, to devour her with eyes so dramatic, she had the sense he couldn't take everything in at once and it frustrated him. "Ash . . ."

"No, Lorelai, I'm not fucking all right!" he exploded, crushing her to him with even more force, this time. "Goddammit, I saw you slipping through my fingers once again. I was faced with losing you forever. What if you were killed? Taken across an ocean even I wouldn't be able to forge, as surely in the next life we'll be forced in opposite directions."

Lorelai tucked a smile against his chest, as now wasn't the time, and she had to admit to a bit of pleasure in his admission of how much she meant to him. "I could do my level best to be more wicked," she suggested. "After what we've just done, I'd hazard that I'm well on my way. Then, wherever the next life takes us, at least we'll be together."

"No," he said between feathering soft, desperate kisses over the whole of her face. "You are an angel, Lorelai. *My* angel."

"And you are mine."

"Don't tease me," he admonished darkly.

"I'm not. There are many kinds of angels. Fallen ones, for example, avenging ones . . ."

"I *will* avenge you," he vowed against her skin. "Just as soon as I can tear myself from your arms, I'll cut off every finger he touched you with and make him watch as I feed them to the sharks. I'll hang his bleeding corpse out like bait and watch them leap for him, taking great chunks—"

"Just stop, Ash. Stop it." Lorelai ineffectually pushed against his chest, only gaining enough ground to look up into his swirling, fathomless eyes. "I don't care about any of that. It's not what I want."

He gazed down at her in dismay. "What do you want? Anything. Name it. It's yours."

"I want you to love me." She glanced down at his buttons, wishing she'd not admitted it. Wishing she didn't suddenly feel so vulnerable.

He made that devilish sound she'd come to recognize as his amusement. He tucked a finger beneath her chin, dragging her gaze back up to his. What she read there lifted her soul more than words ever could. "Every word I ever said to make you doubt my love is now a blasphemy to me. I meant it when I told you that I should have said it twenty years ago, before I left . . . I should have said it the moment I returned."

A tear slid unbidden down her cheek, and he thumbed it away as he was wont to do. "Why didn't you?" She wasn't reprimanding him. She truly desired the answer.

"As a boy, I was afraid that the sheer, unmitigated power of my love for you was wrong, somehow. You were so young. So innocent. And I . . . I always knew I was this— this monster. Even though I had no memories, there were scars on my soul that were even more ugly and distasteful than those on my body. I couldn't bear to reveal them to you, especially when I couldn't remember what made them."

"And you remember now?" She shaped a hand over his unshaven jaw, her heart welling with a warmth and light she'd not felt since their childhood.

He nodded, swallowing down an emotion that didn't seem to be easily grappled. "When I came for you, I truly thought myself incapable of love. It was a selfish act. I know that. But I couldn't admit that what I felt for you was that exact thing. I thought it merely need. I had a void, not only in my memory, but in my soul. That void was you, Lorelai. I've always known that."

"I missed you, too, Ash. Every day for twenty years, there was a hole in my heart that belonged to you."

"You don't understand." He growled as though angry, though with her or himself, she couldn't be sure. "It's not that I merely missed you . . . You are not a hole *in* my heart, you are the whole *of* my heart. When I think of a life without you, it is like a life without breath. I'm not *me* but for you. I exist, but I'm not *alive*. You said that when you met me, my eyes were dead. They were dead. I was dead. And if I lose you, they will be again. I know I don't deserve you. I know I'm a thief, a killer, a pirate, and worse. There's a darkness in me, Lorelai, one I'm afraid will consume your light. But, God help me, I can't let you go."

Lorelai drew his forehead down to meet hers then turned both of their heads to regard the pillar of late afternoon sun filtering into the cave. "That isn't how light works, is it? Darkness is easily overcome. Not light. The smallest hint of illumination can chase away the heaviest gloom, can slip through the most infinitesimal crack. It is never the other way around." She kissed him softly, and her lips came away salty as a barrage of emotion overwhelmed them both. "There has always been light in you, my love, and no matter how many have tried to smother it with their black deeds and blacker souls, it resides within you, still. I can sense it, even now."

He folded into her, his magnificent body sinking against hers in a gesture of submission. To her, but to fate, to them, to the inevitability of their connection.

He cupped her face between his rough, tender hands and captured her gaze with his own so as to punctuate the fervency of his words. "All that is or ever was good in me begins and ends with you," he breathed. "Every time I said you were mine, I meant that *I* was *yours*. Always. *Always*, Lorelai, I've been yours. I'd go through everything I've suffered in my nearly forty years on this earth if it brought me to this moment. If it meant that I'll *never* spend one more night of the next forty years apart from you."

The capitulations of joy coursing through her were tempered by a dread wrought of too much loss and tragedy. "A lot can happen between now and never." When she'd said it before it had been a declaration of hope, now it was a caution.

"Yes, a lot can happen between now and never." He

kissed away a tear that held no pain or sadness, but joy and hope and the fear that once found, it could be lost. "But time will end before I stop loving you."

"Truly." She sighed. Could this be real? Could the love she bore him actually be returned, not once but a hundred-fold?

"I love you," he whispered, pressing his lips to hers, enchanting her with soft drags of his mouth. "I could be—I have been—sent to the other side of the earth, and it doesn't even matter, because I'll always find my way back to you. I etched the ebony wings on my back years ago because I have always been your raven. Your mate."

She understood now. He'd never truly been *the* Rook.

He'd always been . . .

"Your Rook."

EPILOGUE

Six Months Later

"My, would you look at those handsome men." Lorelai clutched his arm as the gangplank lowered in order for them to disembark the steamship.

Ash scowled. "Don't look too closely. We're still newlyweds, or need I remind you?"

Her merry laugh still invoked a strange tickle low in his chest. "Don't worry, darling," she soothed. "I just find it amusing because from this distance, those men look more like pirates than peerage, what with the eye patch and the other with a metal hand. Perhaps if they give me a peg leg and you a parrot, we'd complete the set."

Ash smiled down at her with infinite indulgence. "Whilst we are guests of the Duke of Trenwyth and his lady wife, I'll thank you to remember that I'm not a pirate anymore," he rejoindered with a bit of haughty melodrama. "I am His Grace, Ashton Weatherstoke. Duke of Castel Domenico, Comte de Lyon et de Verdun, Earl of Southbourne, and so on and so forth."

"I suppose, as your wife, I should be impressed, but all

those flashy titles still seem like such a demotion from the King of the Seas." She flashed him a teasing pout.

"No." He tucked an errant curl back beneath her cobalt traveling hat. "Not if you're at my side."

Ash kept her steady as she leaned on him down the unstable gangplank, silencing anyone who might remark upon her tedious progress with an evil glare.

She was swept into Farah Blackwell's awaiting arms the moment they touched solid ground, and introduced to Lady Imogen, the Duchess of Trenwyth.

"Your Grace," Blackwell greeted him, and Ash had to give his old friend credit because he said the title with much less wry humor each time. "Allow me to introduce His Grace, Collin Talmage, the Duke of Trenwyth."

They exchanged pleasantries as though the entirety of the surrounding society were not gawking at them.

"I'm indebted to you and your wife, Lady Imogen, for agreeing to use your contacts at St. Margaret's Royal Hospital to examine Lorelai's case," Ash said as the men fell in line behind their respective ladies, who all adjusted their speed to match that of Lorelai.

She'd been getting worse lately, slower, and experiencing more pain. There were stormy days, such as this one, where she resorted to using a cane if she could walk at all.

Every time she winced, a part of Ash died a little. If he could lend her strength, or health, or take some of her pain, he would.

Trenwyth, an unusually tall, bronzed Adonis of a man with a paradoxically forbidding expression, regarded the Lady Trenwyth with equal parts adoration and respect. "I'd be just as desperate for a miracle, were Imogen similarly afflicted."

The men strolled behind their wives toward a row of

well-appointed carriages, silently admiring the view of the three uncommonly lovely women.

Farah was dressed in bloodred velvet trimmed in black that sparked silver notes into her riot of curls.

Lorelai, in the middle, favored cobalt blue to match the sapphires in her cane and, of course, her eyes. Ash had watched her pin her spun-gold locks into a fashionable chignon, as she hadn't wanted to bring her lady's maid on this particular trip.

Imogen was a lithe beauty with an open, expressive face and sleek strawberry-blond hair. She had an air of capability about her that set others at ease and, judging by the temperament of her war-hero husband, was likely necessary.

It wasn't any wonder that Ash, Blackwell, and Trenwyth had to hover like morose statuary behind them as they gushed and tittered over each other like long-lost friends, all but oblivious to the attention, both male and female, such a stunning array of ladies attracted.

The appointment at St. Margaret's with a Dr. Longhurst would have gone a great deal faster if Lorelai hadn't had to talk Ash into letting another man take off her stocking and examine her ankle.

"Aren't specialists supposed to be old and blind?" Ash had made what he thought was a very salient point.

Apparently used to protective husbands, the young, serious, and imperturbable doctor agreed to allow him into the examination room with her.

After a painful and rigorous inspection that left Ash more pale and sweaty than his wife, he asked anxiously, "Do you think it can be fixed?"

"Certainly." Dr. Longhurst covered her bare ankle and gently let it rest back on the bed. "All we'd have to do is break it, again."

"Absolutely not."

Lorelai put a staying hand on his arm. "If we do this, I'll be able walk normally again?"

Dr. Longhurst nodded. "It's risky, but if I could find where the initial break happened, then I could break it with a small hammer, realign the bone, and coax it to heal the way it should have years ago."

"Did he say hammer?" Ash boomed.

Both his wife and the doctor infuriatingly ignored him.

"With some time, and some strengthening excercises, you might not only walk again, but run."

Ash swatted the desk with the flat of his hand, garnering him the startled attention of them both. That was more like it. "You said risk." He narrowed his eyes at the doctor. "What kind of risk?"

Longhurst's eyes reminded him of a deer's, or a bunny's. Soft and brown. They were eyes of prey. Shifty, if intelligent. "There's always a risk associated with anesthesia," he stuttered. "But it's less and less frequent the more we learn about it. Then infection is always a worry, but with modern sanitation techniques, it's also becoming—"

"Get your things, Lorelai, we're leaving." Ash gathered his coat and her hat.

She stubbornly stayed where she was. "I'm getting the operation, Ash."

He scowled at her. "Did you conveniently miss the part with the hammer?"

Her gaze was steady and resolute. "I want to do this. I want to go all the places you can take me, and I can't . . ."

"I already told you, I'll carry you, if I have to."

"I want to walk beside you."

Ash had to swallow three times before he could speak. "It's not worth losing you."

She reached up to pull him down next to her, where she

took his clenched jaw in both of her hands. "Let this be, my love. Sometimes, one must be broken, in order to be healed."

Sniffing away vision clouded by emotion, he turned to Longhurst. "Whatever fate befalls her, I'll visit upon your bones threefold, you mark me." That taken care of, he slammed out of the office, but not before hearing Lorelai's sweet apologies.

"Do pardon him, Doctor, he really *is* working on making fewer death threats on my behalf."

"It's all right," Dr. Longhurst replied. "I'm physician to many of Blackwell's associates and their wives and children. That isn't even the worst threat I've received this week. And here I am. Still alive."

A year later, Lorelai was able to cajole Ash to attend Veronica's second wedding, despite her shocking selection of groom.

Lorelai didn't merely walk or hobble down the sunny lane in the South of France to greet her beloved sister.

She ran.

Turn the page for a delicious sneak peek at all the books in the unforgettable

Victorian Rebels series!

THE HIGHWAYMAN

*"In his arms she will never
be the same again…"*

The beats of her heart echoed as loud as cannon blasts in her ears as she entered the private lair of Dorian Blackwell.

Farah tried to imagine a man such as the Blackheart of Ben More in this room, doing something as pedestrian as writing a letter or surveying ledgers. Running the fingers of her free hand along a bronze paperweight of a fleet ship atop his enormous desk, she found the image impossible to produce.

"I see you've already attempted escape."

Snatching her hand back, Farah held it to her heaving chest as she turned to face her captor now standing in the doorway.

He was even taller than she remembered. Darker. Larger.

Colder.

Even standing in the sunlight let in by the windows of the foyer, Farah knew he belonged to the shadows in this room. As if to illustrate her point, he stepped into the room and shut the door behind him, effectively cutting off all sources of natural light.

An eye patch covered his damaged eye, only allowing glimpses of the edge of his scar, but the message illuminated by the fire didn't need both eyes to be conveyed.

I have you now.

How true that was. Her life depended on the mercy of this man who was infamous for his *lack* of mercy.

The black suit coat that barely contained his wide shoulders stretched with his movements, but what arrested Farah's attention was the achingly familiar blue, gold, and black pattern of his kilt. The Mackenzie plaid. She hadn't known that a man's knees could be so muscular, or that beneath the dusting of fine black hair, powerful legs tucked into large black boots could be so arresting.

She backed against his desk as he stepped toward her, evoking once more the image of a prowling jaguar. The firelight danced off the broad angles of his enigmatic face and shadowed a nose broken one too many times to any longer be called aristocratic. Of course, despite his expensive cravat, tailored clothing, and ebony hair cut into short and fashionable layers, nothing at all about Dorian Blackwell bespoke a gentleman. A fading bruise colored his jaw and a cut healed on his lip. She'd missed that last night in the storm, but knew it was Morley's fists that had wounded him. Had that only been days ago?

What had he just said to her? Something about her escape? "I—I don't know what you're talking about."

His good eye fixed on the tarts she'd all but forgotten she clutched in her hand. "My guess is you attempted to leave through the kitchens, and were thwarted by Walters."

Oh, damn. The air in the study was suddenly too close. Too thick and full and rife with—with *him.* Determined not to be cowed, Farah raised her chin and did her best to look him square in the eyes—er—eye.

"On the contrary, Mr. Blackwell, I was hungry. I didn't want to face you without being—fortified."

That earned her a lifted eyebrow. "Fortified?" His callous tonelessness set the hairs on the back of her neck on end. "With . . . pastries?"

"Yes, as a matter of fact," she insisted. "With *pastries*." To make her point, she popped one in her mouth and chewed furiously, though she instantly regretted it as moisture seemed to have deserted her. Swallowing the dry lump, Farah hoped she hid her grimace as it made its slow and unpleasant way into her stomach.

He moved a little closer. If she wasn't mistaken, his cold mask slipped for an unguarded moment and he regarded her with something like tenderness, if a face such as his could shape such an emotion.

Farah had thought it wasn't possible to be more confounded. How wrong she'd been. Though the lapse proved fleeting, and by the time she blinked, the placid calculation had returned, causing her to wonder if what she'd seen had been a trick of firelight.

"Most people need much stronger fortification than a strawberry tart before facing me," he said wryly.

"Yes, well, I've found that a well-made dessert can do anyone a bit of good in a bad situation."

"Indeed?" He circled her to the left, his back to the fire, casting his face into deeper shadows. "I find I want to test your theory."

Of all the conversations she'd expected to have with the Blackheart of Ben More, this had to be the absolute last. "Um, here." She extended the tart toward him, offering him the delicacy with trembling fingers.

Blackwell lifted a big hand. Took a deep breath. Then lowered it again, clenching both fists at his sides. "Put it on the desk," he instructed.

Puzzled by the odd request, she carefully set the tartlet onto the gleaming wood, noting that he waited until her hand had been returned to her side before reaching for it. It disappeared behind his lips, and Farah didn't breathe as she watched his jaw muscles grind at the pastry in a slow, methodical rhythm. "You're right, Mrs. Mackenzie, that *did* sweeten the moment."

A burning in her lungs prompted her to exhale, and she tried to push some of her previous exasperation into the sound. "Let's dispense with pleasantries, Mr. Blackwell, and approach the business at hand." She put every bit of crisp, British professionalism she'd gained over the last ten years into her voice, quieting the tremors of fear with a skill born of painstaking practice.

"Which is?"

"Just what is it you want with me?" she demanded. "I thought I'd dreamed of you last night, but I didn't, did I? And there, in the darkness, you promised to tell me . . . to tell me why you've brought me here."

He leaned down, his eye touching every detail of her face as though memorizing it. "So I did."

THE HUNTER

"There was no one more dangerous for her heart...or soul."

He gazed at her with unparalleled intensity, watching the movements of her fingers with undue interest.

Clearing nerves from her throat, she met his eyes in the mirror and was startled to see that he was the first one to look away.

"Do you enjoy the theater, Mr. Argent?" She ventured a moment of civility.

"I've only attended the once," he replied, seeming to study a wig of long crimson ringlets, going so far as to reach out and test its texture between his thumb and fore-finger.

Millie had to look away. "And . . . did you like it?" she prompted. When she gathered the courage to glimpse at him again, she was surprised to see him seriously consid-ering the question.

"Your performance was without a single flaw," he said with no trace of flattery or farce in his voice. "But I find myself unable to suspend disbelief in the manner that is required to truly enjoy a production. I don't understand why people dress in their in their finest to watch others pretend to be in love. To feign jealousy and cruelty and even death. Why *play* at fighting and killing? There's plenty to be done out in the real world."

And he'd done plenty of his own.

Millie swallowed audibly, trying to decide whether to be pleased at his honest compliment, or to be offended by his dismissal of her entire profession. "Not all of us live a life as exciting and treacherous as yours, Mr. Argent," she said as she added a few more jeweled pins to her intricate coiffure, if only to give her restless hands something to do. "Most of us merely like to be kissed by danger or violence or death. Maybe even let it kiss us, upon occasion. We like to make it a spectacle at which to gasp and laugh, or cry. Though it is only the thrill we want to take home with us, not the reality. We still desire to return to our warm beds, all safe and sound, when the night is over." She considered her words only after she'd said them. She was taking the danger home with her tonight, wasn't she? There was a very good chance her bed would be anything but safe.

And, Lord forgive her, it was more thrilling than she'd like to admit.

"But not everyone makes it home safe and sound," he rumbled.

Not with men like him about.

Millie's heart stalled and her hand froze halfway to her hair. "True . . ." She drew the word out, searching for what to say next. "But we expect to. We hope to, don't we?"

"I know nothing of hope." He leaned forward and placed his elbows on his long, powerful legs. "So people attend the theater to feel afraid and safe at the same time?"

Millie chewed her lip, considering her words carefully. "Sometimes, surely, but mostly they go to play voyeur to the human experience. Drama, I think, does one of two things for a person, it allows us to be a little more grateful for the humdrum of the everyday, or makes us yearn for something above whom and what we are. It can remind us to not let every moment slip into the next without reaching for more. Whether we reach within ourselves or for something we want out in the world. A dream, a home, money, adventure . . . or love."

Feeling impassioned, she turned in her seat to gesture at him. "Drama can make you experience the very extremes of emotion. A good playwright, Shakespeare, for example, can use language to allow an actor to convey an emotion that resonates with the audience. That allows them—sometimes even forces them—to *feel*. Coupled with the performance and the right music and lighting . . . I think that emotion is contagious and complex, and often a person doesn't know which until they experience it under the Bard's very own tutelage. It's quite extraordinary, really, almost magical and—" Millie let her voice die away, noticing that Christopher Argent hadn't blinked for an astonishingly long time.

In the middle of her dressing room, done in all shades of chaos and color, he was a monochromatic study in dove and granite. All but for his eyes and hair, both of which were uncommon in their variegation. His jaw was too wide to be called handsome, his mouth too caustic for its fullness, surrounded by brackets that made him look alternately cruel and somehow inanimate. His eyes made him appear ancient. Not so much in years, but in experience.

What horrors he must have seen in his life, some of them perpetrated by his own hands.

"Forgive me," she breathed, entranced by the moment, as though he were a serpent and she his prey, mesmerized by his menace. "I do tend to get carried away."

He once more brushed aside her words. "You have . . . experienced all these emotions?"

What an odd question. "Most of them, yes."

"Are you—in love—with someone?"

She hadn't realized that someone so still could become even more motionless. It was as though he'd stopped breathing in anticipation of her answer.

"No," she answered honestly, and had the impression that his chest compressed.

"Have you ever been?"

"I can't say that I have truly loved anyone, except Jakub." She glanced at her son, still oblivious to the world around him, and then back to the assassin.

An expression flickered across his features, but was gone before she could identify it. This time when he looked at her, his eyes were gentler, somehow. Still frightfully opaque, but they had lost some of their frost.

"Do you wish to be in love?"

Had any other man asked, she'd have told him that it was no business of his. She'd have lied or misdirected him somehow, to avoid the question. But behind the callousness of Christopher Argent's expression was an earnest curiosity. A lack of judgment or malice.

It was a sincere question that deserved a sincere answer.

"I—I'm never really certain. If there's one thing I've learned from Shakespeare, from most any playwright, it is that love is just as dangerous an emotion as hatred or anger or the lust for power. I think love can make you a stranger, even to yourself. Maybe even a monster. It can be a wild creature just waiting to be unbound. A beast. A feral and selfish thing that will turn you against the world, against nature or reason, against God, Himself. And every time I'm tempted to allow myself to fall, I wonder . . . is it worth the risk?"

His brows drew together. "What if there is no risk? What if God, if He even exists, has turned away from you, and so to turn from Him would be no great sin? There would be nothing in the way of reaching for what you wanted."

Millie blinked, startled by his bleak assessment. "Is that what is going on here? Do you believe God has forsaken you, and so you no longer fear Him? Is that how you're able to . . ." She paused, checking on Jakub to make certain he wasn't listening in. "To *do* what it is that you *do*?"

He lifted his massive shoulders in a dismissive gesture. "Perhaps. I have no fear of God."

"So you do not believe in heaven?"

"This world is all I know."

"What about hell, the devil? Are you not afraid you'll have to answer for your sins, for the blood you've spilled?"

He shook his head, a more adamant gesture than she could remember him making—apart from the times he'd kissed her.

THE HIGHLANDER

*"He moved like a god,
but kissed like a devil."*

"D-did you not receive my references? My letters of recommendation? I assure you, sir, I am beyond qualified to teach your children comportment. Lady Northwalk informed me that after reading the Whitehalls'—"

"Yer references were impeccable. However, the expectations of my children differ greatly from the Whitehalls', ye ken? They were merchants, *I'm* a marquess, if ye'll believe it now."

"A marquess who dresses like a Jacobite rebel," she reminded him. "Forgive me for not believing you earlier, but you *were* covered in mud and ash from the fields, and I'd never met a marquess who assisted in such—physical labor."

Ravencroft stepped forward, and Mena retreated, her hands covering the flutters in her stomach as though holding back a swarm of butterflies. "I only meant—"

"There are some, Miss Lockhart, who would argue 'tis the responsibility of a noble to oversee every aspect of work on the land he owns. And there are others who would find it mighty strange that a proper London governess kens so much about linchpins and carriage wheels."

Mena recalled Miss LeCour's sage advice, that a lie was best told peppered with truth. "My father was a landed gentleman and avid agriculturist, as well as a scholar. I learned quite a few things at his feet as a child which included—"

"And are ye aware of how far behind schedule my men and I are because we spent all bloody afternoon saving yer stubborn hide? If ye'd allowed me to take ye on my horse, we'd not have lost the daylight."

"I do regret my part in that," Mena said, and meant it. "But as I was a woman traveling *alone* you can't expect—"

"Ye'll need to ken more than farm maintenance and how to distract a man with a pretty dress in order to teach my children what they'll need to know to survive in society," he clipped.

"Well, their first lesson will be on how rude and socially unacceptable it is to consistently interrupt people in the middle of their sentences," Mena snapped.

Oh, sweet Lord. She could hardly believe her own behavior. Here she stood, alone and defenseless before perhaps the deadliest warrior in the history of the British Isles, and she'd just called *him* to answer for his bad manners.

Had she escaped the asylum only to go mad outside its walls?

"Go on then," he commanded, his voice intensifying and a dark, frightening storm gathering in his countenance. "I believe ye were about to apologize for wasting my time."

Mena actually felt her nostrils flare and a galling pit form in her belly. What was this? Temper? She'd quite thought she'd been born without one. Affection and tenderness had made up her idyllic childhood, and acrimony and terror had dominated her adult life. She'd never really had the chance to wrestle with a temper.

And wrestle it she must, or risk losing her means of escape into relative anonymity. Closing her eyes, she summoned her innate gentility along with the submissive humility she'd cultivated over half a decade with a cruel and violent husband. Opening her mouth, she prepared to deliver a finely crafted and masterful apology.

"Why aren't ye married?" the marquess demanded, again effectively cutting her off.

"I—I beg your pardon?"

"Wouldna ye rather have a husband and bairns of yer own than school other people's ill-behaved children?" His glittering eyes roamed her once again, leaving trails of quivering awareness in their wake. "Ye're rather young to wield much authority over my daughter, as ye've not more than a decade on her."

"I have exactly a decade on her."

He ignored her reply, as the corners of his mouth whitened with some sort of strain that Mena couldn't fathom. "Were ye a Highland lass, ye'd barely seen Rhianna's age before some lad or other had dragged ye to church to claim ye. Whether ye'd consented or not. In fact, they'd likely just take ye to wife in the biblical sense and toss yer father his thirty coin."

Flummoxed, Mena stared at him, her mouth agape. He still seemed irate, in fact his voice continued to rise in volume and intensity. But it sounded as though he'd paid her a compliment.

"So that causes a man to wonder," he continued. "What is a wee bonny English lass like ye doing all the way up here? Why are ye not warming the bed of a wealthy husband and whiling yer hours away on tea and society and the begetting of heirs?"

Had he just called her "wee"? Was she mistaken or didn't that word mean little?

And bonny? *Her?*

A spear of pain pricked her with such force, it stole her ire and her courage along with it. Was he being deliberately cruel? Had she left one household that delighted in her humiliation and sought refuge in another?

"I don't see how that's any of your concern." She hated the weakness in her voice, the fear she'd never quite learned how to hide.

"Everything that happens within the stones of this keep, nay, on Mackenzie lands, are of concern to me. That now includes ye. Especially since ye'll be influencing my children." He took another step forward, and before Mena could retreat, his hand snaked out and cupped her chin.

The small, frightened sound Mena made startled them both.

Ravencroft's gaze sharpened, but he didn't release her.

Her jaw felt as substantive as glass in his hand. Mena knew it would take nothing at all for him to crush her, a simple tightening of his strong, rough fingers. His dark eyes locked on her lips, and they seemed to part of their own volition, exuding the soft rasps of her panicked breath.

He leaned down toward her, crowding her with the proximity of his forceful presence.

She saw him clearly now, as so many must have at the violent ends of their lives. Inhumanely stark features weathered by decades of discipline and brutality frowned down at her now, as though measuring her coffin.

Suddenly the fire and candles cast more shadows in the grand room than light.

Mena knew men like the laird of Ravencroft Keep rarely existed, and when they did, history made gods of them.

Or demons.

THE DUKE

"There was nothing like fire he could ignite…"

For a moment, it was as though the moonlight had become sunlight. Her hair shone more brilliantly than it ought. A large flower ornament glittering with center gems winked from the coiffure as though held there by magic and a prayer. In the ballroom he'd thought her gown too garish, a silly ocherous flower among precious jewel tones.

But here in the garden she belonged. She . . . bloomed.

Cole hadn't realized that his mouth had dropped open until his pipe clattered to the stones, spilling ashes and cinders at his feet.

She started at the sound, turning to peer into the darkness. "W-who's there?" she asked in a tremulous whisper. "Jeremy, is that you?"

Something vicious twisted inside him. *Jeremy?* Why did that name sound familiar? Who was he to the sainted Lady Anstruther? A lover, perhaps? It surprised him how little he liked that possible development.

Instead of answering, he bent to retrieve his pipe, stamping out the smoldering coal beneath his boot heel.

And instead of fleeing, like many a frightened damsel would, she ventured closer to him, her voluminous skirts swishing softly against the stones and overgrown plants.

"Oh," she said finally when she'd drawn close enough. "It's you."

Cole could decipher little to no affect in her tone, so he remained silent, finding that his heart answered each step she took with alarming acceleration. Damn her, he'd barely calmed the excitable organ down. Though, apparently, it wasn't the only organ that seemed to react to her nearness. Adjusting his position to alleviate a disturbing tightness in his trousers, he slid deeper into the darkness toward the far side of the bench.

The daft woman mistook it as an invitation to sit next to him.

"Worry not, I didn't plan to linger." He lifted his pipe. "This seemed like the place to seek refuge from the insufferable crowd and indulge in a smoke before taking my leave."

"It seems we had similar instincts, Your Grace." She glanced around, and Cole wondered if she used the colorful flora as an excuse not to look at him. "I'm exceedingly fond of this garden. It makes an excellent refuge."

He chose not to reveal that he knew just exactly how often she made use of this sanctuary. That he could spy upon her from his study window and he'd seen more of her than she'd ever intended.

"Though I confess, I didn't expect to find you here." She seemed nervous. In the moonlight, he could make out the intensity with which she clasped her hands together in her lap.

"Obviously." He should have been chagrined to be discovered lingering on her property. "Expecting someone else, were we?" He set his pipe next to him to itch at the straps of his prosthetic. "Some clandestine rendezvous? Tell me, as a merry widow, do your tastes lean toward the gallant lord, or do you keep to the groundskeeper for a more familiar territory?"

"The groundskeeper? Hercules?" She let out a faintly amused sound, leaving the merry-widow comment alone. "Not likely, he's a rather hairy Greek man who's sixty if he's a day."

"He's younger than your first husband," he challenged.

He expected her to slap him, or at least demand an apology for his ghastly behavior. But to his utter astonishment, she tossed her head and laughed, the sound full of moonlight and merriment.

"Touché," she acquiesced, a light glinting in her eyes like she'd absorbed some of the shine from the stars. "Not only does my groundskeeper speak very little English, but the dear man eats nothing but garlic. Also, I'm quite certain he bathes in olive oil, which I'll admit does stir my appetite upon a warm day when he is particularly fragrant, but only for Mediterranean fare. Nothing else, I assure you."

Struck dumb, Cole could only stare at her with agitated bemusement. Why the devil was she being so civil? He'd been a rote bastard to her, shamed and insulted her in front of her guests. And here she was dallying with him in her garden managing to be entertaining.

Christ preserve him, it was both unsettling and alluring. Too intriguing. And bloody hell, were these straps on his prosthetic made of glass shards and wool? He couldn't take his eyes off her brilliant smile as he grappled at it with his one good hand. He wanted to be rid of not only the offending object, but his clothing had begun to likewise chafe. He wished to cast it all off, and hers as well, to be clad in nothing but the night air and moonlight.

"Your Grace." She regarded him with the most absorbed expression, part assessment, and part concern. As though she truly saw him. As though she *knew* him. "Is there anything amiss? Are you . . . all right?"

The breathy quality to her unceasingly feminine voice scratched at a door in his mind that remained stubbornly closed. He'd come across a few of those doors since returning from Constantinople, and knew it best that they remained locked. Most especially when he was like this. Raw, agitated . . .

Aroused.

THE SCOT BEDS HIS WIFE

*"Once in his bed she would
never be the same again…"*

Samantha fished in her frilly purse for some coins she still barely recognized. What was considered generous gratuity in the Scottish Highlands? She hadn't the first idea. "I packed rather quickly, so I only brought the two trunks—"

She froze when he reached out and cupped her elbow. *Shit.* He was touching her again. He really needed to stop doing that.

Was it really necessary to wield a hand so incredibly large? An arm so thick and solid? Samantha fought the ridiculous urge to lean all her weight into the strength she sensed there.

"I occurs to me, Miss Ross, that we havena been properly introduced."

"Oh, right." Introductions were of some significance hereabouts, she'd noted. Annoyed with herself, she wondered how many times she'd break custom. Generally it would mean nothing to her. But this brawny stranger with features the perfect paradox of barbarian and aristocrat seemed to have her thoughts tumbling over each other like a litter of exuberant puppies.

And with her husband only weeks dead by her own fucking hand.

Lord, she really *was* going straight to hell.

"Alison Ross." She stuck out her hand for a shake though the gesture just seemed superfluous now. "Pleased to make your acquaintance, Mr. . . ."

His hand engulfed hers, once again, and he pulled it toward him, looking like a man amused with a joke she was not a part of.

He was someone aware of his effect on women. On her in particular.

Infuriating quality, that.

"When I offered to save ye trouble, I meant the trouble of an arduous ride out to Erradale on such a frigid evening. Ye see, Miss Ross, I am quite sure ye've traveled all the way here on account of the documents of notice I sent ye, as I am Gavin St. James, the Earl of Thorne, and I'm here to take Erradale off yer lovely hands."

She snatched said hand away before he could press those full lips to her glove as he was about to do.

This was Gavin St. James? Alison's adversary. No, her *enemy*?

She couldn't think of a thing to say. She was so incredibly travel-weary, heartsick, seasick, and—if she were honest—more than a bit dazzled by the Earl of Thorne. Alison Ross hadn't exactly given her a physical account of the man. She hadn't expected someone so . . . so . . .

Words failed her, yet again. As did her body, which seemed to be calling for her to surrender her hand back into his so he could place the kiss on her knuckles she'd denied them both.

"If ye'd like, lass, I could conduct ye to Inverthorne Keep, my castle, where we could conclude our business in comfort for a few days . . ." His gaze traveled the length of her burgundy traveling gown. "And a few nights."

"I see," she clipped, crossing her arms over the heart pounding against her ribs. She'd been right when she'd sensed danger. "Well, while your offer is appreciated, it's pointless. If residence at Erradale is necessary to retain the land, as was mentioned in the documents, then Erradale is where I'll be spending my days . . . and also my *nights*."

She turned toward the porter's station, praying to keep her balance on the blasted boots, when his wide shoulders blocked her. Yet again.

"Perhaps ye've not received my generous offer?" His alluring smile became strained, showing too many even, white teeth. "It's nearly twice what the land is worth."

"I received it, all right," she said mildly.

He took a full breath, waiting for her to elucidate.

When she didn't, he was forced to ask the implied question.

"Ye're not saying that ye're refusing the offer, are ye?"

"Well, I wasn't gonna put it like that, but I certainly didn't plan to accept."

"Yer family's had no interest in Erradale for several years. Why now?"

"Why not now?" She shrugged, then picked up her cumbersome skirts and set off for the porter's station, focusing extra hard on avoiding a stumble on the uneven planks of the platform.

She had a feeling he'd not catch her again should she fall.

He waited five entire astonished seconds before easily blocking her path once more, the two rather unobtrusive men taking up their respective posts behind him.

"Did you bring these fellows to intimidate me into compliance?" she quipped, forcing irritation above the unease in her voice. "Because you've obviously never been to Reno."

His haughty brow wrinkled. "I ken nothing about this Reno."

"Well, I do, which is why I'm not impressed." As unimpressed as she was, she still slid her hand into the bag comforting herself with the feel of her pistol.

The earl stepped forward, and Samantha forgot what she'd been taught over the years. *Never* yield ground to the aggressor.

She yielded to *him,* stepping back to maintain their distance, to avoid his touch. His proximity. His earthy, intoxicating scent. Something that reminded her of a loamy forest and cedar soap.

"I brought these men to *pay* ye, lass." He gestured behind him with measured movements. "This is my solicitor, Mr. Roy Mackenzie." He pointed at the kind-faced, rotund man, who nodded and blushed. "And my banker, John Douglass."

The thin man sniffed his disdain.

She sniffed hers right back. "I apologize for your wasted trip, gentlemen."

She would have taken her leave had the Earl of Thorne not gripped her elbow once again. "If my aim was to frighten ye, bonny, ye'd be terrified." He sneered, and then gentled his grip, as though his behavior had shocked himself more than it had her. "I'll do whatever it takes to convince ye to yield. Ye'll be *pleased* to find, Miss Ross, that I do nothing by half measures." The gleam in his eyes was now decidedly more sensual than sinister.

"How nice for you." She flashed him a taut smile. He

might be handsome as the devil, but she'd be damned before she'd let him charm her.

She knew better.

And that knowledge was hard-won.